Garfield ®

HOMECOMING

BY JIM DAVIS

GARFIELD: HOMECOMING, February 2019. Published by KaBOOM!, a division of Boom Entertainment, Inc. Garfield is © 2019 PAWS, INCORPORATED. ALL RIGHTS RESERVED. "GARFIELD" and the GARFIELD characters are registered and unregistered trademarks of Paws, Inc. Originally published in single magazine form as GARFIELD: HOMECOMING No. 1 - 4. ™ & © 2018 PAWS, INCORPORATED. All rights reserved. KaBOOM!™ and the KaBOOM! logo are trademarks of Boom Entertainment, Inc., registered in various countries and categories. All characters, events, and institutions depicted herein are fictional. Any similarity between any of the names, characters, persons, events, and/or institutions in this publication to actual names, characters, and persons, whether living or dead, events, and/or institutions is unintended and purely coincidental. KaBOOM! does not read or accept unsolicited submissions of ideas, stories, or artwork.

BOOM! Studios, 5670 Wilshire Boulevard, Suite 400, Los Angeles, CA 90036-5679. Printed in China. First Printing.

ISBN: 978-1-68415-309-1, eISBN: 978-1-64144-162-9

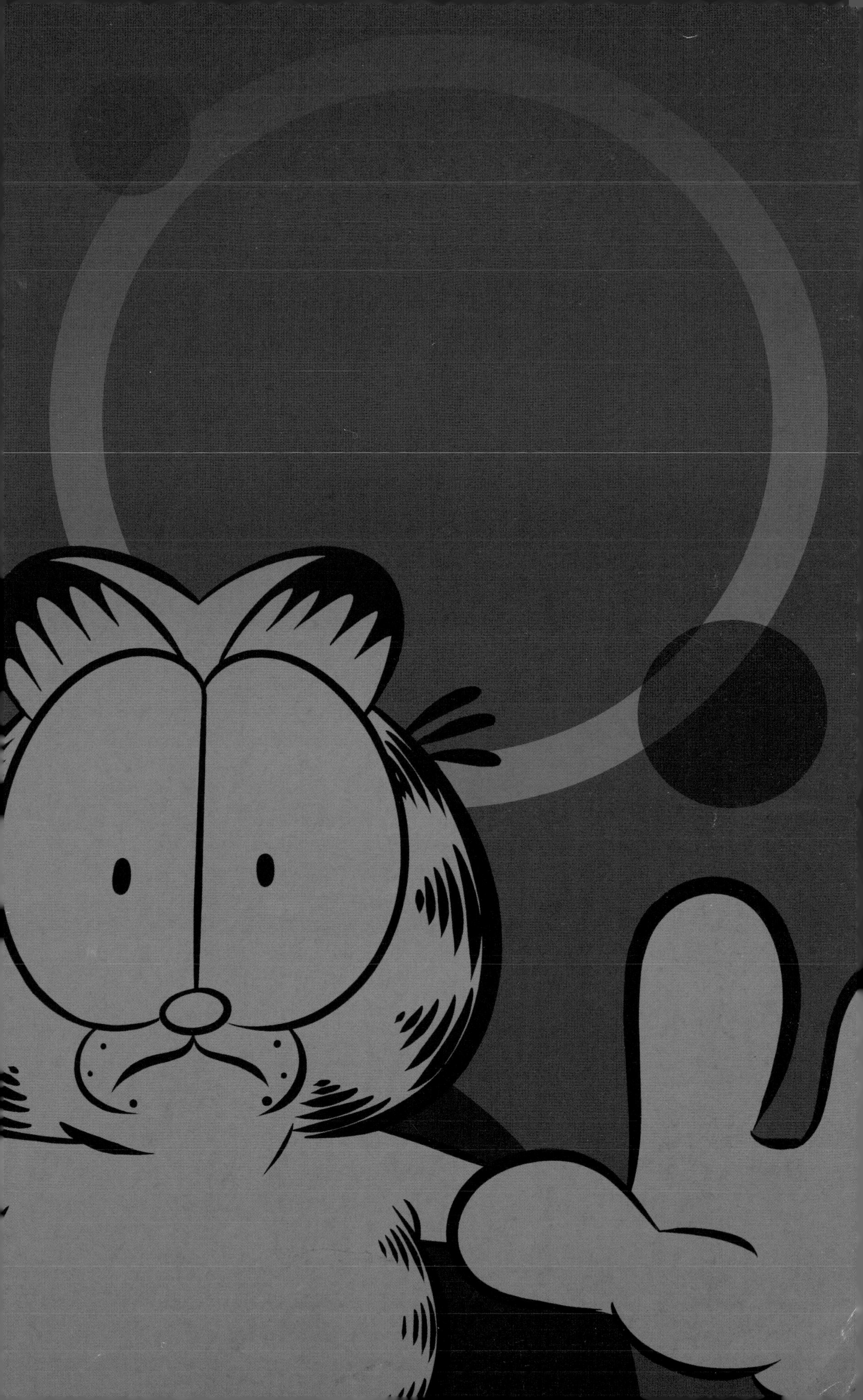

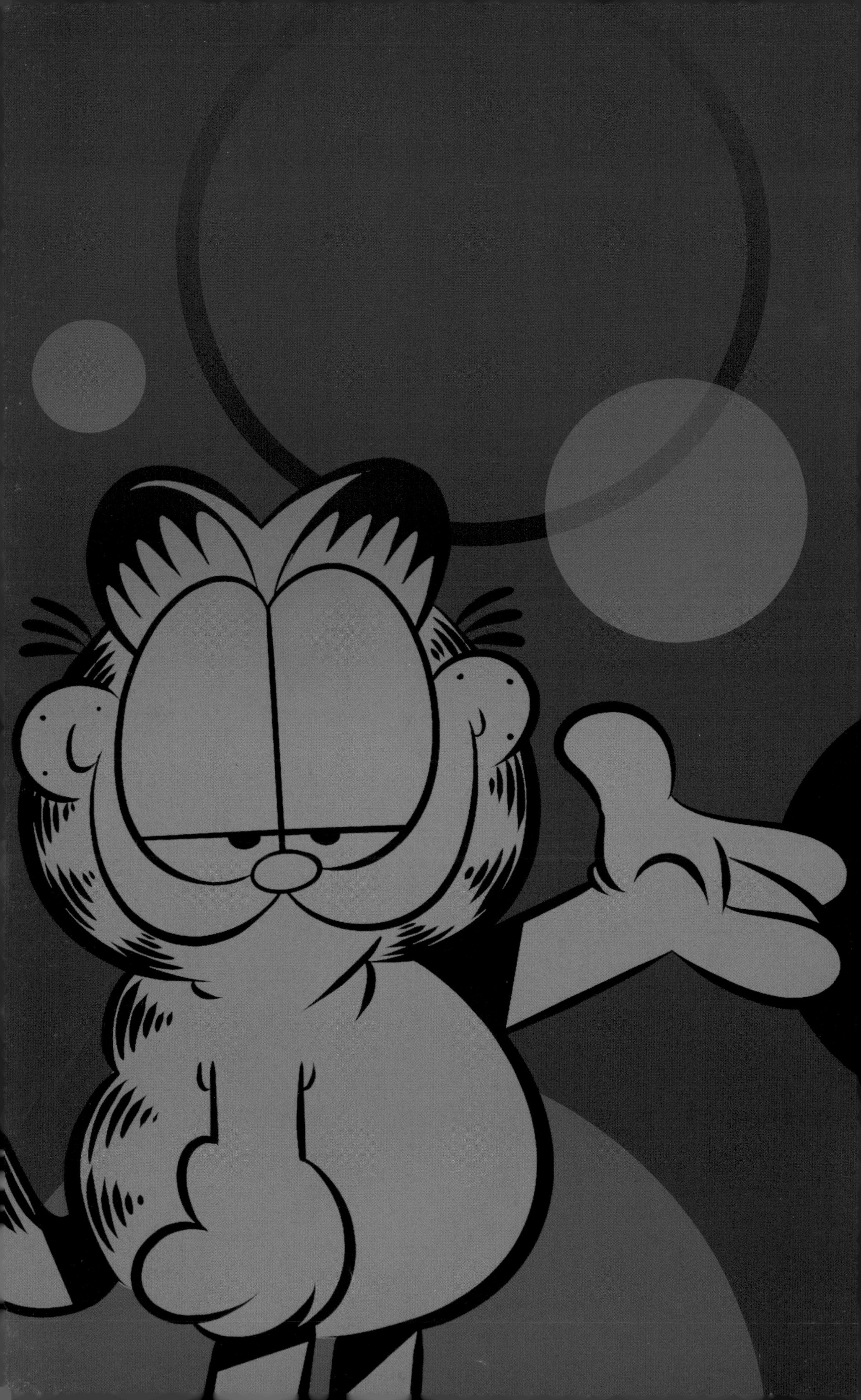

GARFIELD CREATED BY
JIM DAVIS

WRITTEN BY
SCOTT NICKEL

CHAPTER INTRODUCTIONS ILLUSTRATED BY
ANTONIO ALFARO
(COLORED BY LISA MOORE)

CHAPTER ONE ILLUSTRATED BY
SARA TALMADGE
(PAGE 21 ADDITIONAL ILLUSTRATION BY ANTONIO ALFARO)

CHAPTER TWO ILLUSTRATED BY
SHELLI PAROLINE & BRADEN LAMB

CHAPTER THREE ILLUSTRATED BY
BEN SEARS
(COLORED BY LISA MOORE)

CHAPTER FOUR ILLUSTRATED BY
GENEVIEVE FT

LETTERED BY
JIM CAMPBELL

COVER BY
ANDY HIRSCH
WITH SHELLI PAROLINE
& BRADEN LAMB

ORIGINAL SERIES DESIGNER
GRACE PARK
COLLECTED EDITION DESIGNER
CHELSEA ROBERTS
EDITOR
CHRIS ROSA

SPECIAL THANKS TO JIM DAVIS AND
THE ENTIRE PAWS, INC. TEAM.

CHAPTER ONE

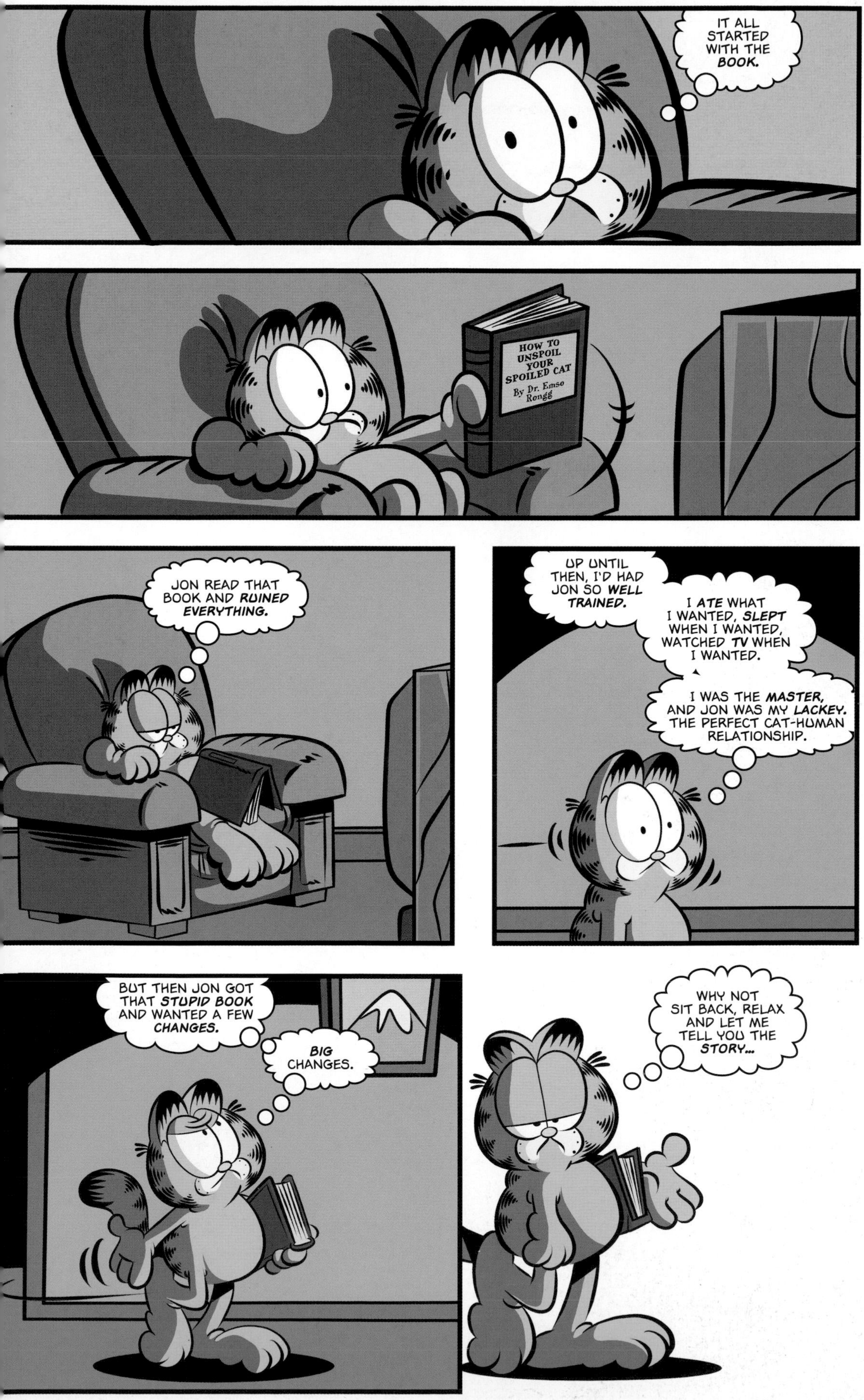

IT ALL STARTED WITH THE BOOK.
HOW TO UNSPOIL YOUR SPOILED CAT By Dr. Emso Rongg
JON READ THAT BOOK AND RUINED EVERYTHING.
UP UNTIL THEN, I'D HAD JON SO WELL TRAINED.
I ATE WHAT I WANTED, SLEPT WHEN I WANTED, WATCHED TV WHEN I WANTED.
I WAS THE MASTER, AND JON WAS MY LACKEY. THE PERFECT CAT-HUMAN RELATIONSHIP.
BUT THEN JON GOT THAT STUPID BOOK AND WANTED A FEW CHANGES.
BIG CHANGES.
WHY NOT SIT BACK, RELAX AND LET ME TELL YOU THE STORY...

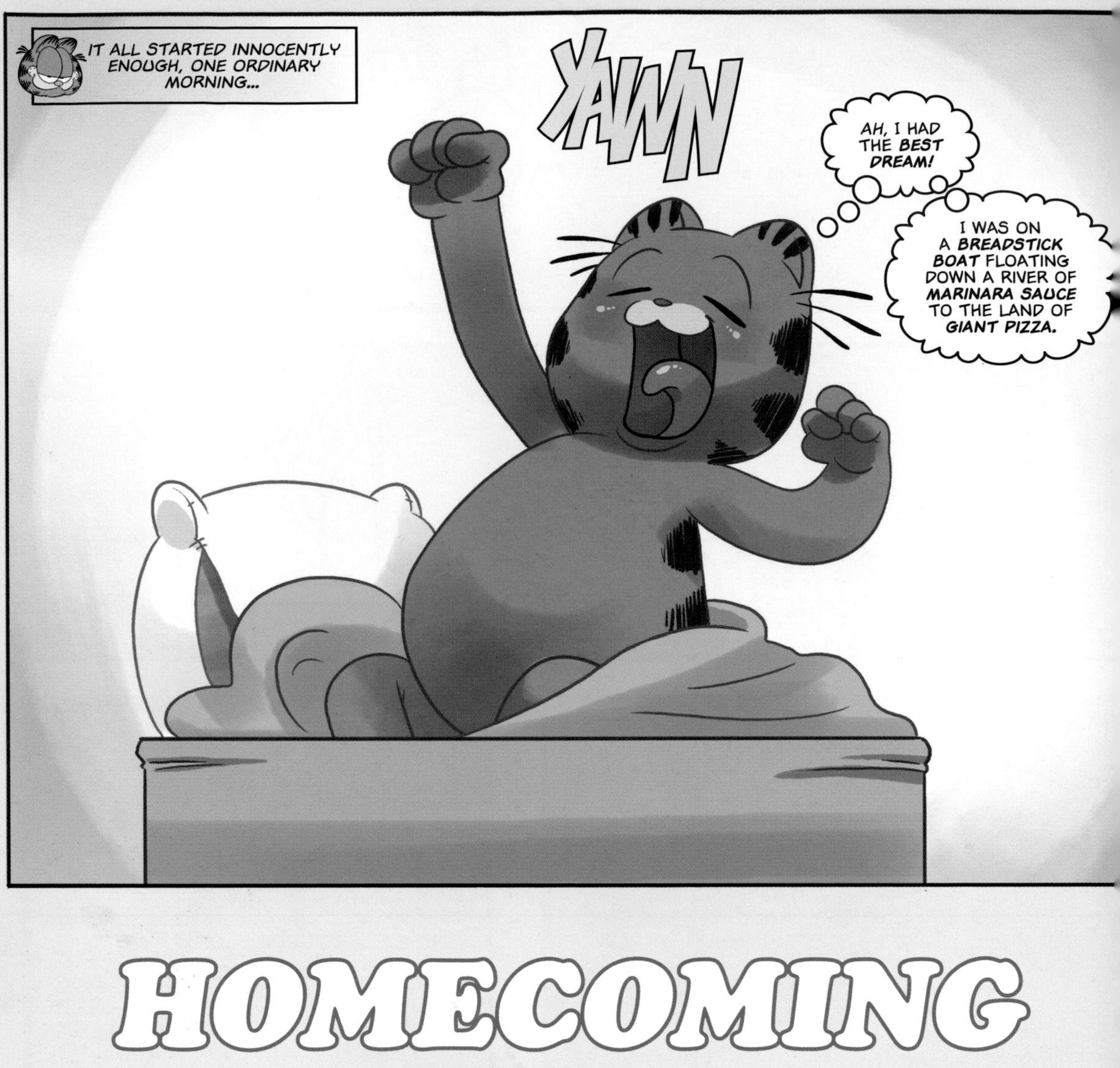
IT ALL STARTED INNOCENTLY ENOUGH, ONE ORDINARY MORNING...
YAWN
AH, I HAD THE BEST DREAM!
I WAS ON A BREADSTICK BOAT FLOATING DOWN A RIVER OF MARINARA SAUCE TO THE LAND OF GIANT PIZZA.

HOMECOMING

Chapter 1:

Big Top Garfield

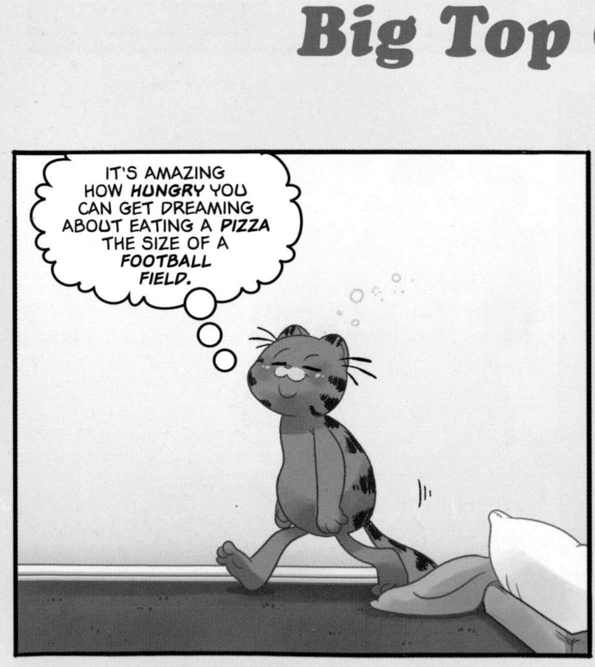
IT'S AMAZING HOW HUNGRY YOU CAN GET DREAMING ABOUT EATING A PIZZA THE SIZE OF A FOOTBALL FIELD.

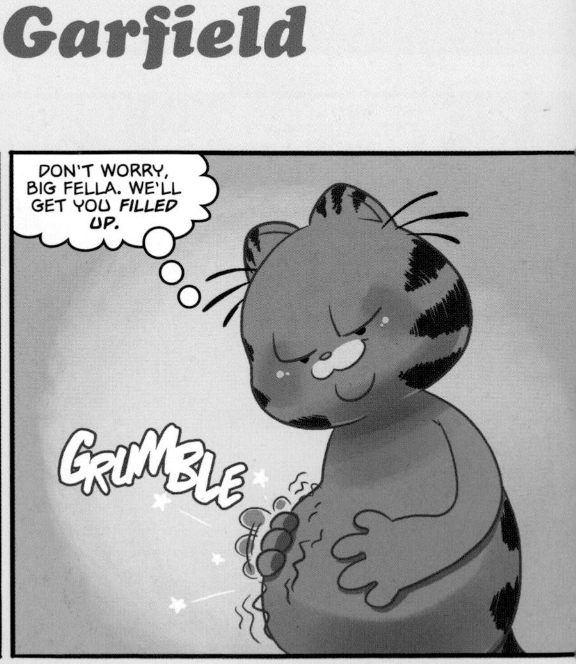
DON'T WORRY, BIG FELLA. WE'LL GET YOU FILLED UP.
GRUMBLE

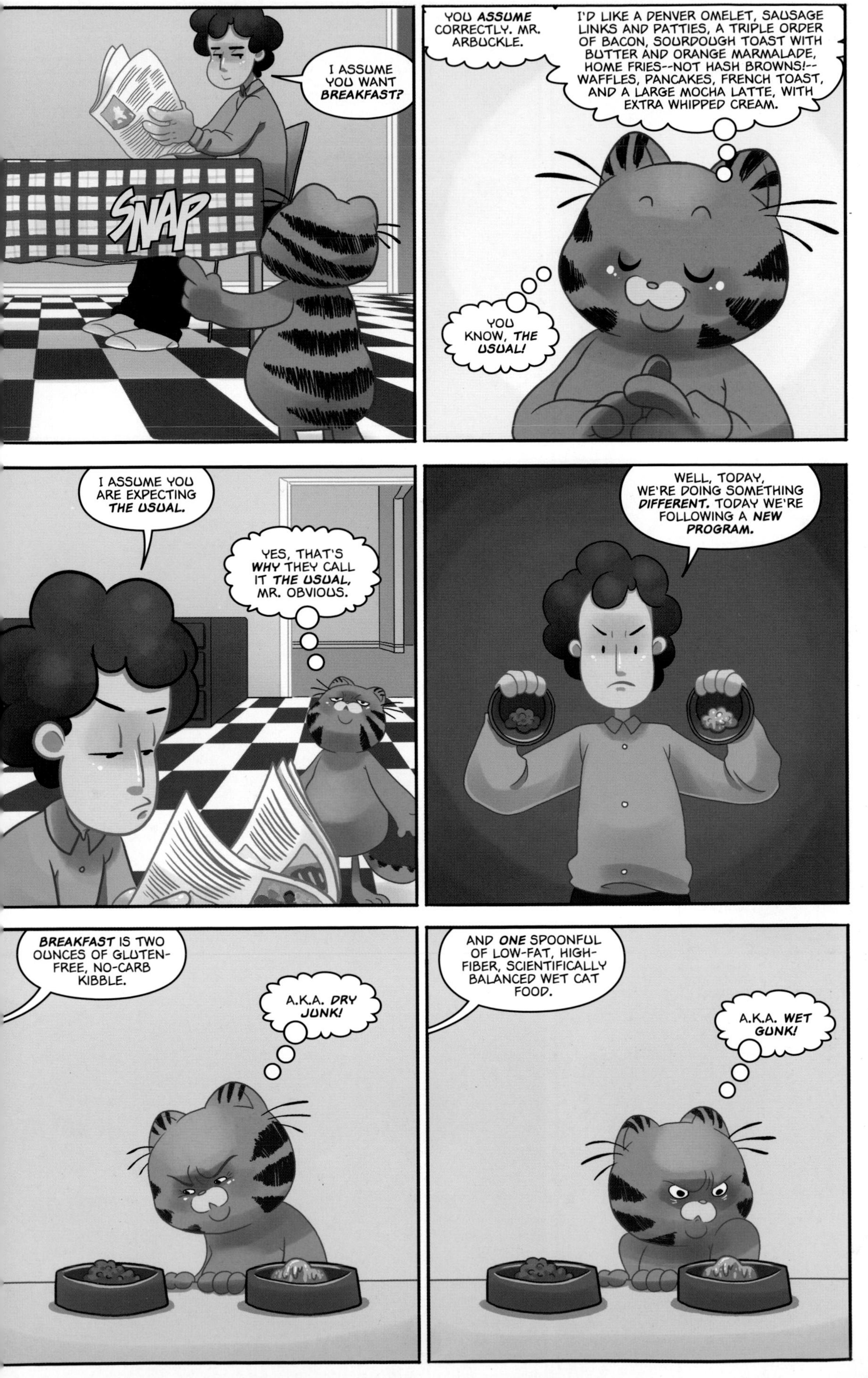
I ASSUME YOU WANT BREAKFAST?
SNAP
YOU ASSUME CORRECTLY. MR. ARBUCKLE.
I'D LIKE A DENVER OMELET, SAUSAGE LINKS AND PATTIES, A TRIPLE ORDER OF BACON, SOURDOUGH TOAST WITH BUTTER AND ORANGE MARMALADE, HOME FRIES--NOT HASH BROWNS!--WAFFLES, PANCAKES, FRENCH TOAST, AND A LARGE MOCHA LATTE, WITH EXTRA WHIPPED CREAM.
YOU KNOW, THE USUAL!
I ASSUME YOU ARE EXPECTING THE USUAL.
YES, THAT'S WHY THEY CALL IT THE USUAL, MR. OBVIOUS.
WELL, TODAY, WE'RE DOING SOMETHING DIFFERENT. TODAY WE'RE FOLLOWING A NEW PROGRAM.
BREAKFAST IS TWO OUNCES OF GLUTEN-FREE, NO-CARB KIBBLE.
A.K.A. DRY JUNK!
AND ONE SPOONFUL OF LOW-FAT, HIGH-FIBER, SCIENTIFICALLY BALANCED WET CAT FOOD.
A.K.A. WET GUNK!

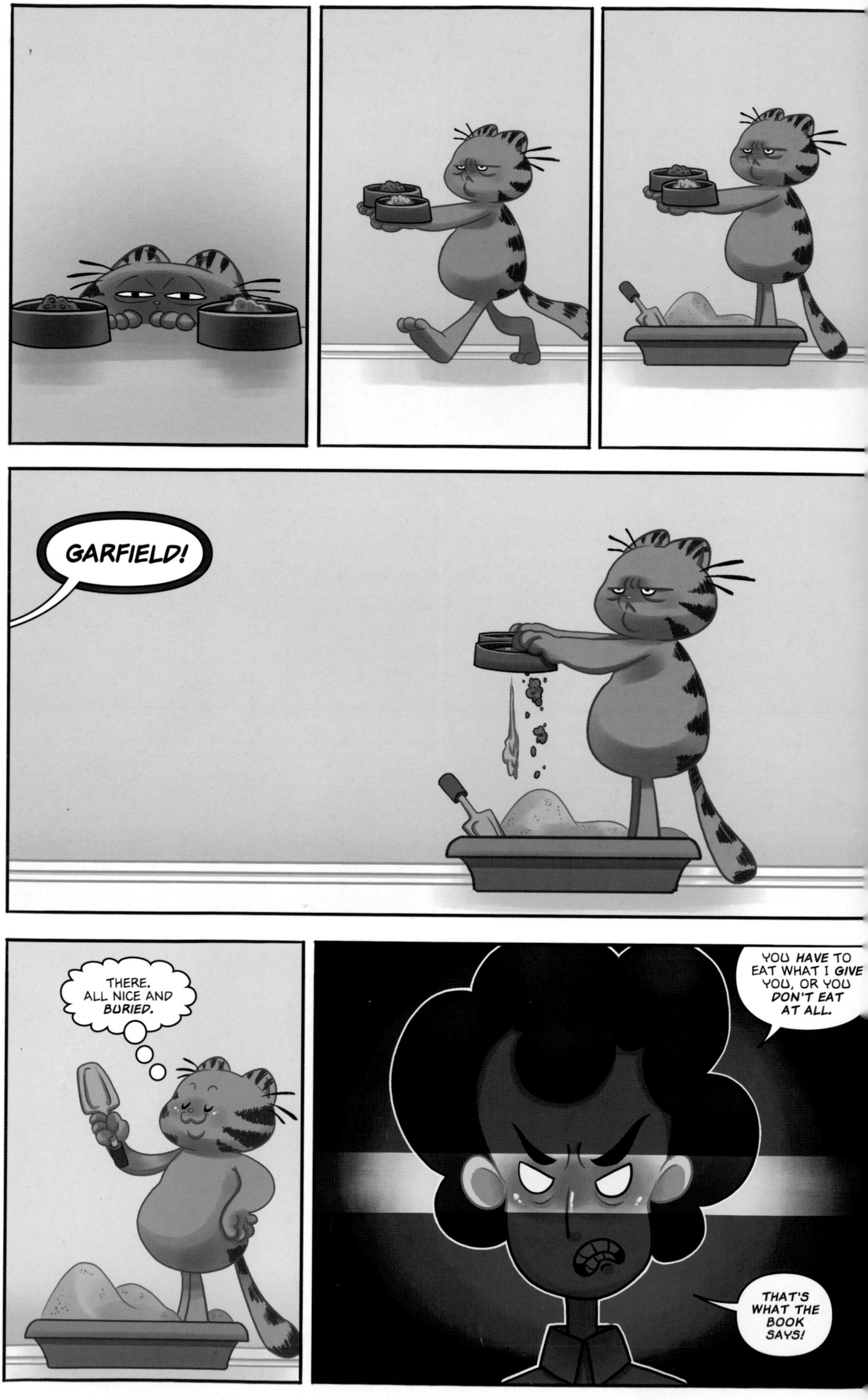
GARFIELD!
THERE. ALL NICE AND BURIED.
YOU HAVE TO EAT WHAT I GIVE YOU, OR YOU DON'T EAT AT ALL.
THAT'S WHAT THE BOOK SAYS!

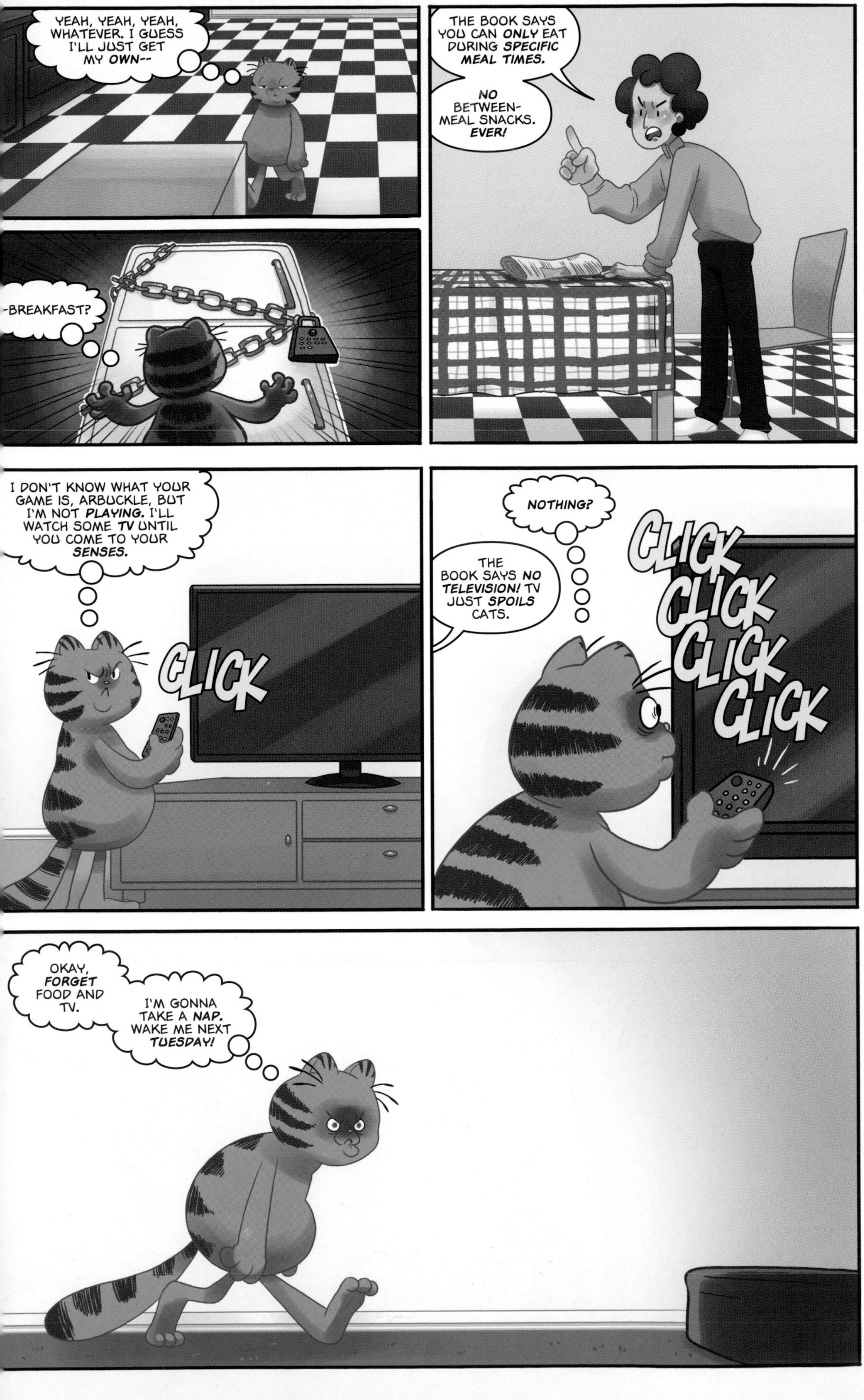

YEAH, YEAH, YEAH, WHATEVER. I GUESS I'LL JUST GET MY OWN--
THE BOOK SAYS YOU CAN ONLY EAT DURING SPECIFIC MEAL TIMES.
NO BETWEEN-MEAL SNACKS. EVER!
-BREAKFAST?
I DON'T KNOW WHAT YOUR GAME IS, ARBUCKLE, BUT I'M NOT PLAYING. I'LL WATCH SOME TV UNTIL YOU COME TO YOUR SENSES.
CLICK
NOTHING?
THE BOOK SAYS NO TELEVISION! TV JUST SPOILS CATS.
CLICK
CLICK
CLICK
CLICK
OKAY, FORGET FOOD AND TV.
I'M GONNA TAKE A NAP. WAKE ME NEXT TUESDAY!

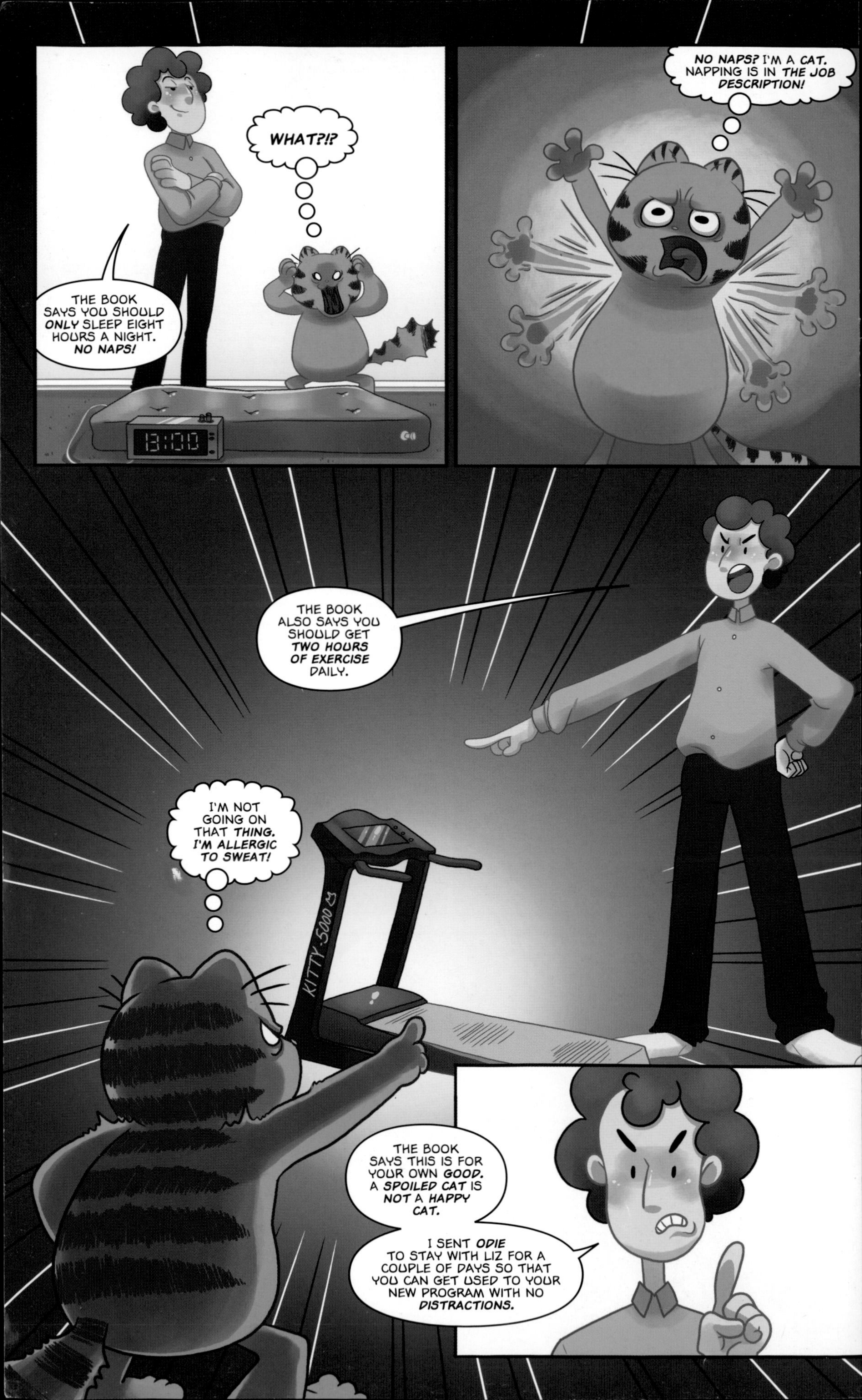
WHAT?!?
THE BOOK SAYS YOU SHOULD ONLY SLEEP EIGHT HOURS A NIGHT. NO NAPS!
NO NAPS? I'M A CAT. NAPPING IS IN THE JOB DESCRIPTION!
THE BOOK ALSO SAYS YOU SHOULD GET TWO HOURS OF EXERCISE DAILY.
I'M NOT GOING ON THAT THING. I'M ALLERGIC TO SWEAT!
KITTY 5000
THE BOOK SAYS THIS IS FOR YOUR OWN GOOD. A SPOILED CAT IS NOT A HAPPY CAT.
I SENT ODIE TO STAY WITH LIZ FOR A COUPLE OF DAYS SO THAT YOU CAN GET USED TO YOUR NEW PROGRAM WITH NO DISTRACTIONS.

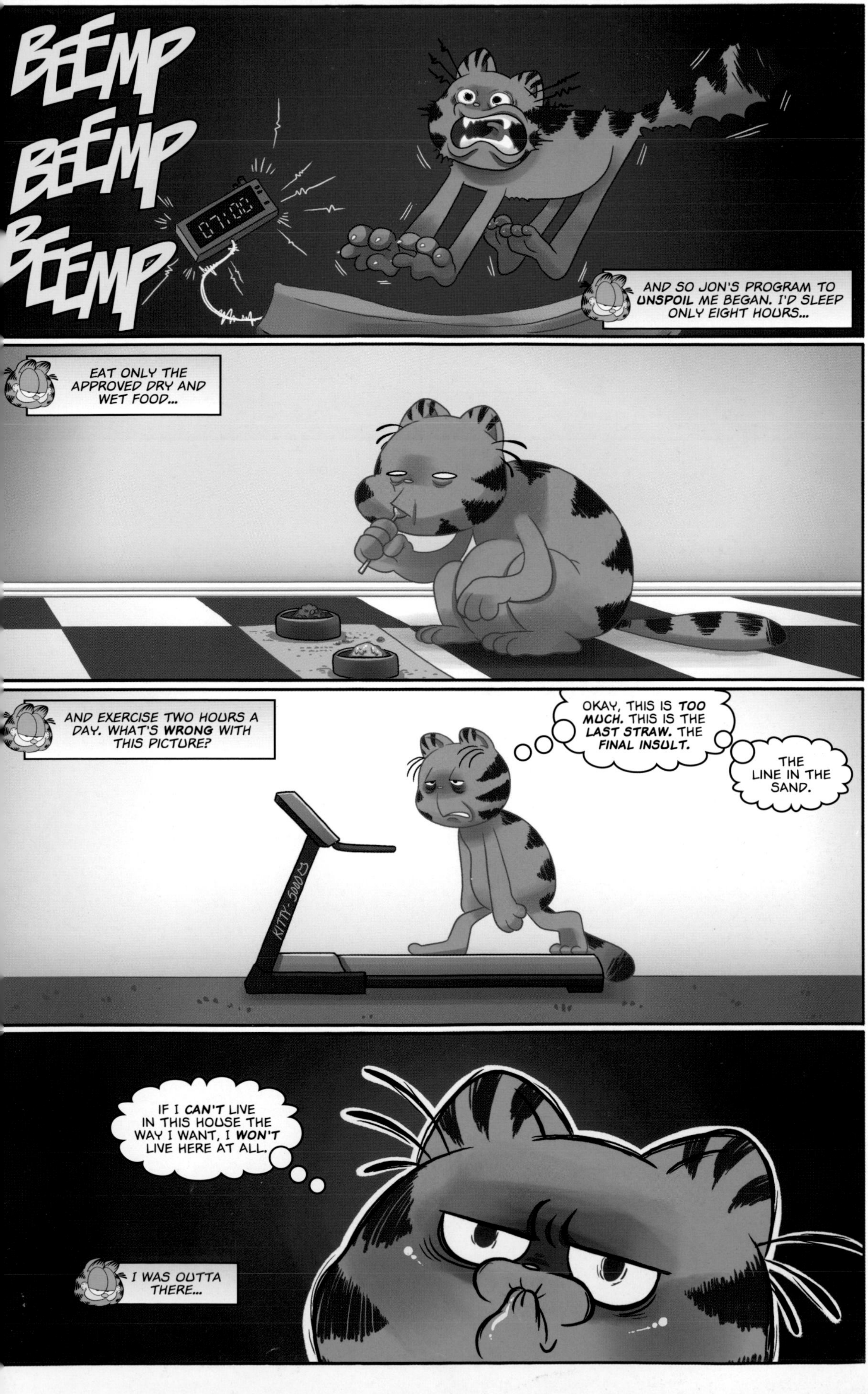
BEEMP BEEMP BEEMP
07:00
AND SO JON'S PROGRAM TO UNSPOIL ME BEGAN. I'D SLEEP ONLY EIGHT HOURS...
EAT ONLY THE APPROVED DRY AND WET FOOD...
AND EXERCISE TWO HOURS A DAY. WHAT'S WRONG WITH THIS PICTURE?
OKAY, THIS IS TOO MUCH. THIS IS THE LAST STRAW. THE FINAL INSULT.
THE LINE IN THE SAND.
KITTY-5000
IF I CAN'T LIVE IN THIS HOUSE THE WAY I WANT, I WON'T LIVE HERE AT ALL.
I WAS OUTTA THERE...

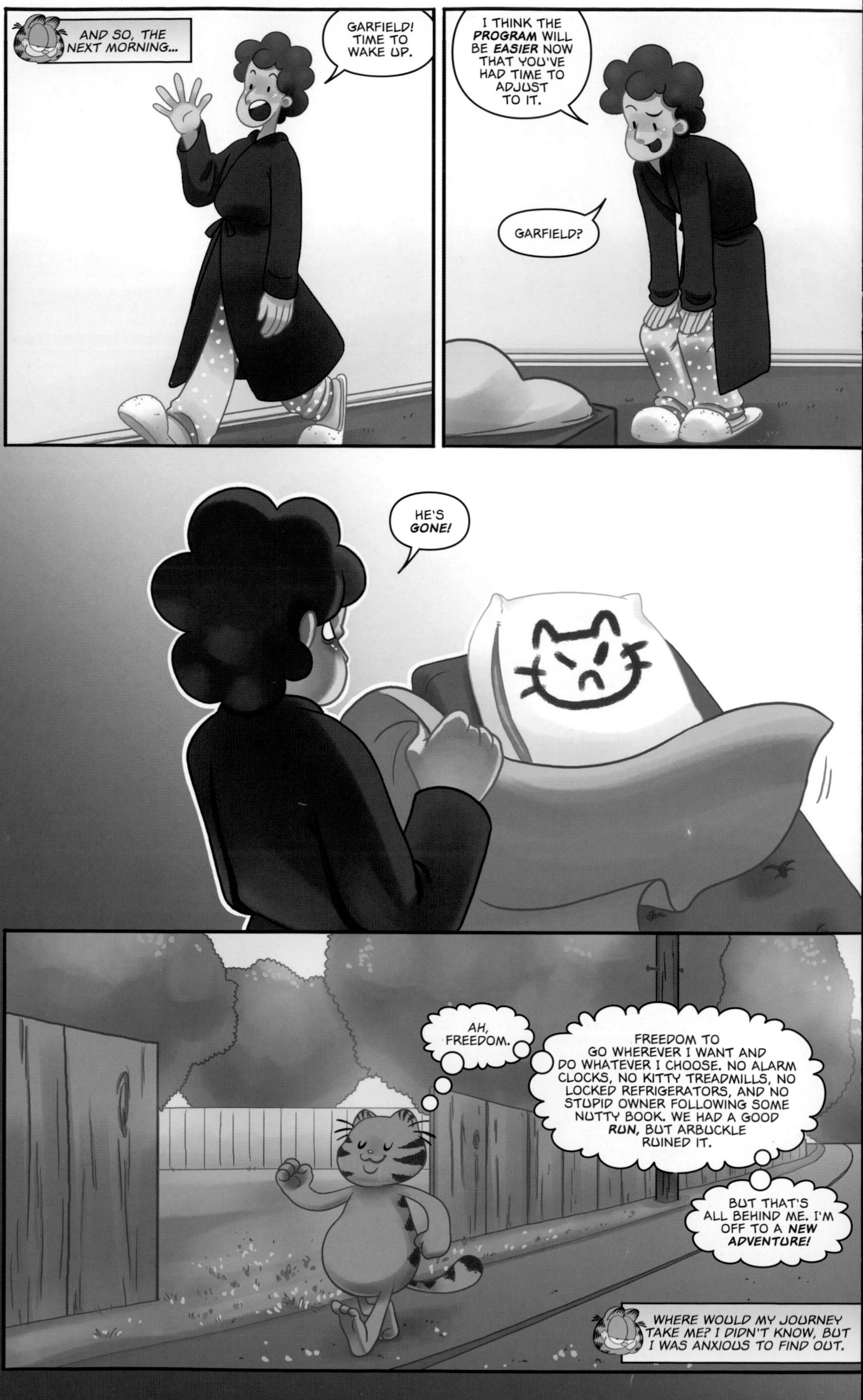
AND SO, THE NEXT MORNING...
GARFIELD! TIME TO WAKE UP.
I THINK THE PROGRAM WILL BE EASIER NOW THAT YOU'VE HAD TIME TO ADJUST TO IT.
GARFIELD?
HE'S GONE!
AH, FREEDOM.
FREEDOM TO GO WHEREVER I WANT AND DO WHATEVER I CHOOSE. NO ALARM CLOCKS, NO KITTY TREADMILLS, NO LOCKED REFRIGERATORS, AND NO STUPID OWNER FOLLOWING SOME NUTTY BOOK. WE HAD A GOOD RUN, BUT ARBUCKLE RUINED IT.
BUT THAT'S ALL BEHIND ME. I'M OFF TO A NEW ADVENTURE!
WHERE WOULD MY JOURNEY TAKE ME? I DIDN'T KNOW, BUT I WAS ANXIOUS TO FIND OUT.

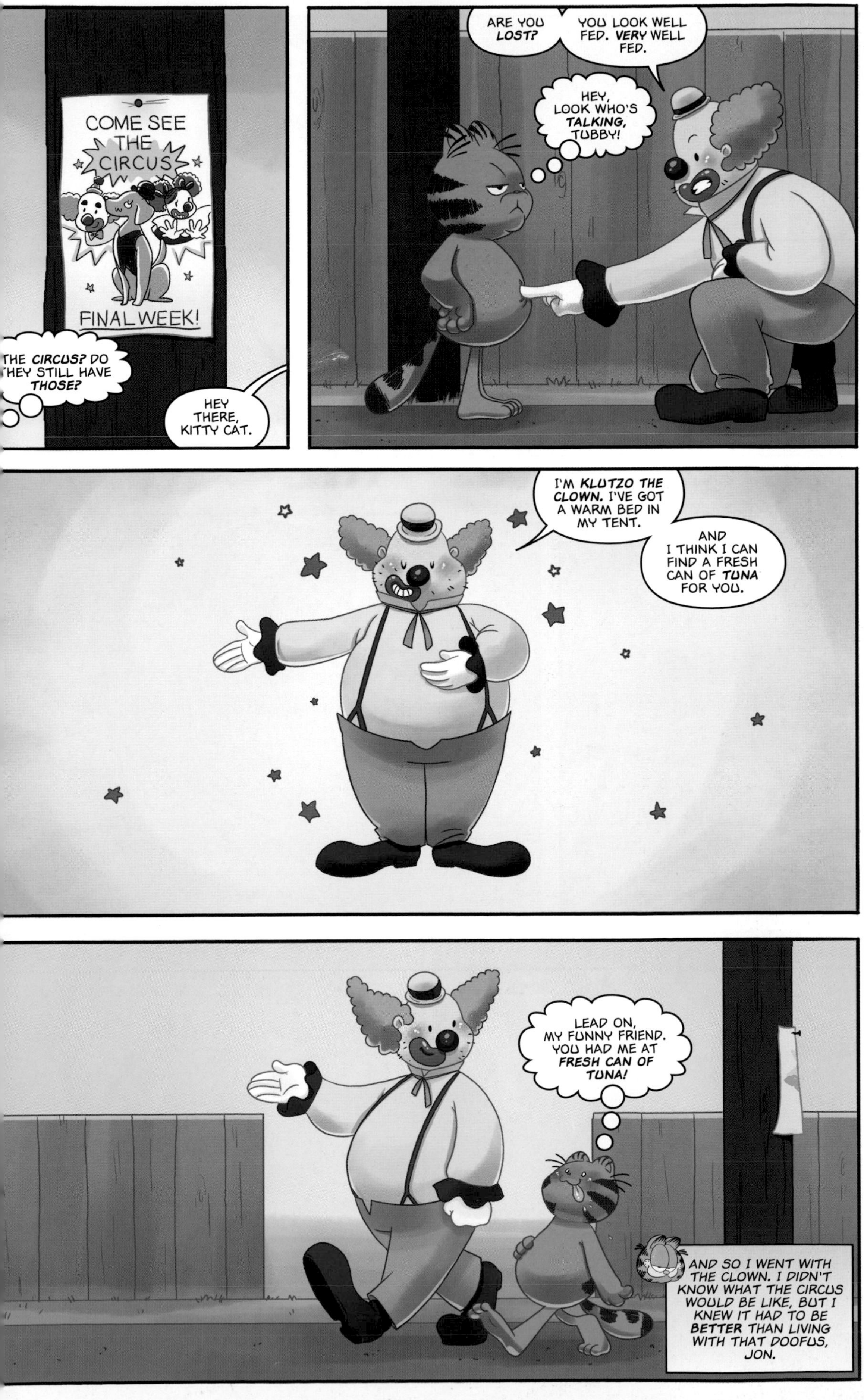
COME SEE THE CIRCUS
FINAL WEEK!
THE CIRCUS? DO THEY STILL HAVE THOSE?
HEY THERE, KITTY CAT.
ARE YOU LOST?
YOU LOOK WELL FED. VERY WELL FED.
HEY, LOOK WHO'S TALKING, TUBBY!
I'M KLUTZO THE CLOWN. I'VE GOT A WARM BED IN MY TENT.
AND I THINK I CAN FIND A FRESH CAN OF TUNA FOR YOU.
LEAD ON, MY FUNNY FRIEND. YOU HAD ME AT FRESH CAN OF TUNA!
AND SO I WENT WITH THE CLOWN. I DIDN'T KNOW WHAT THE CIRCUS WOULD BE LIKE, BUT I KNEW IT HAD TO BE BETTER THAN LIVING WITH THAT DOOFUS, JON.

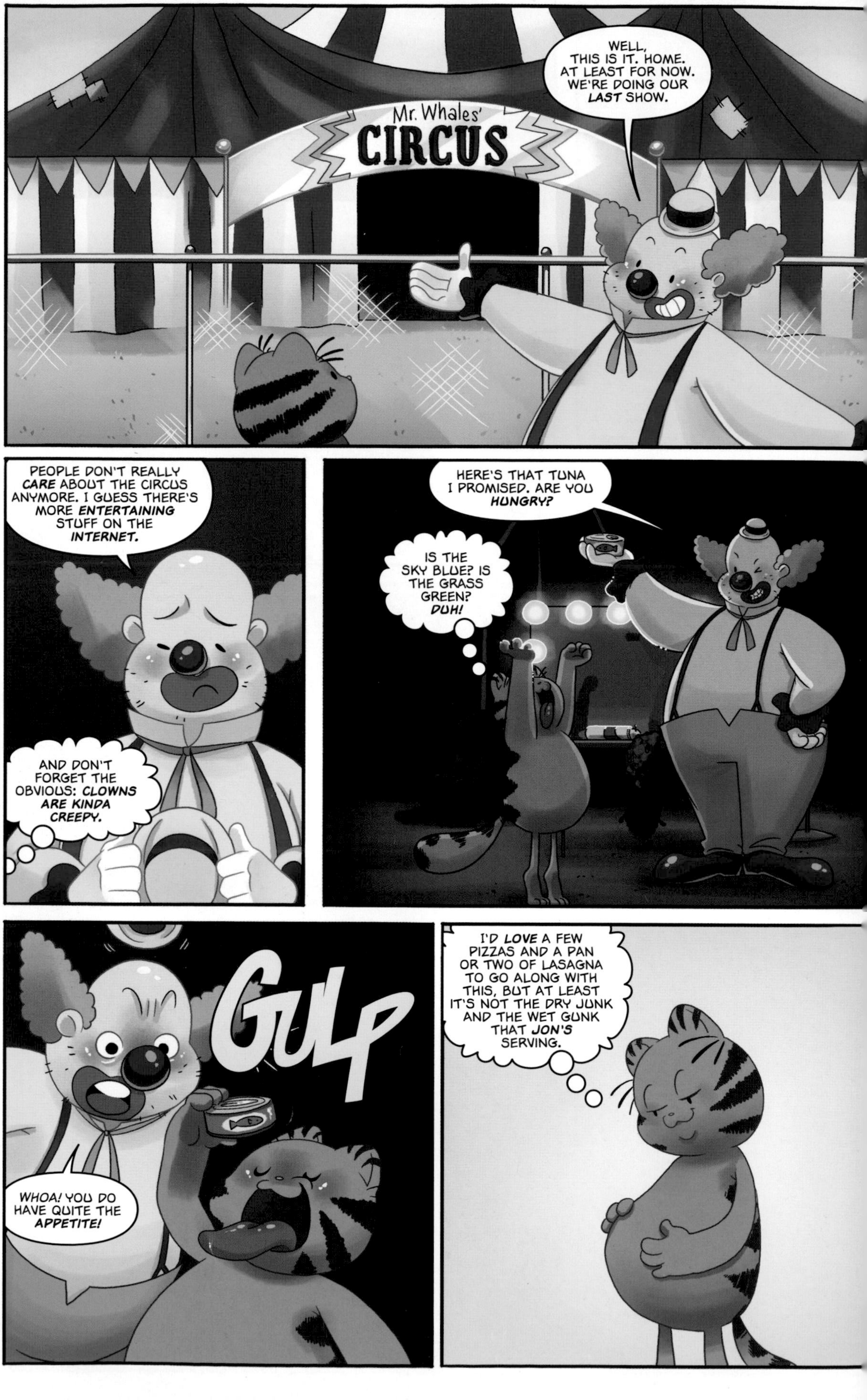
Mr. Whales'
CIRCUS
WELL, THIS IS IT. HOME. AT LEAST FOR NOW. WE'RE DOING OUR LAST SHOW.
PEOPLE DON'T REALLY CARE ABOUT THE CIRCUS ANYMORE. I GUESS THERE'S MORE ENTERTAINING STUFF ON THE INTERNET.
AND DON'T FORGET THE OBVIOUS: CLOWNS ARE KINDA CREEPY.
HERE'S THAT TUNA I PROMISED. ARE YOU HUNGRY?
IS THE SKY BLUE? IS THE GRASS GREEN? DUH!
GULP
WHOA! YOU DO HAVE QUITE THE APPETITE!
I'D LOVE A FEW PIZZAS AND A PAN OR TWO OF LASAGNA TO GO ALONG WITH THIS, BUT AT LEAST IT'S NOT THE DRY JUNK AND THE WET GUNK THAT JON'S SERVING.

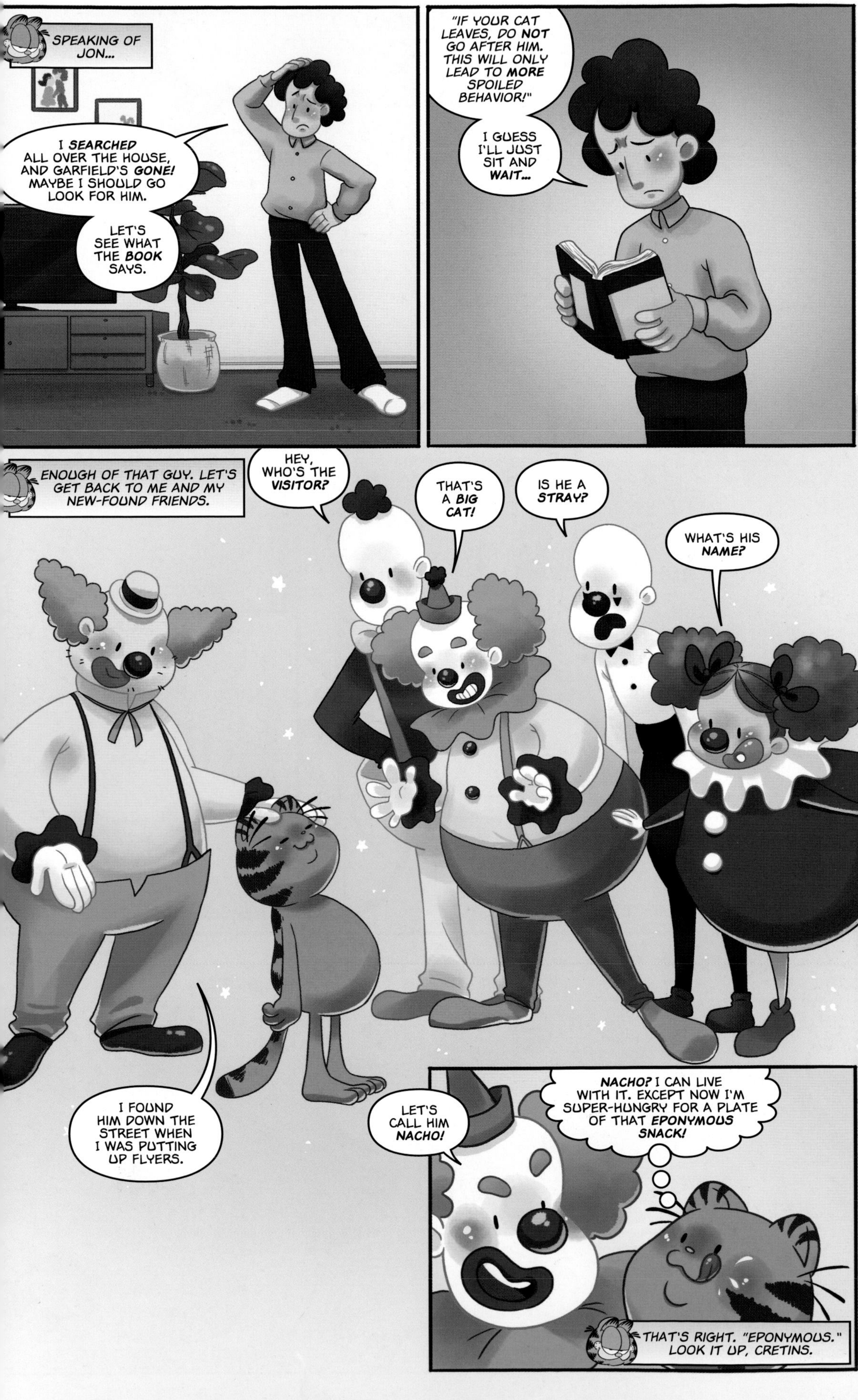
SPEAKING OF JON...
I SEARCHED ALL OVER THE HOUSE, AND GARFIELD'S GONE! MAYBE I SHOULD GO LOOK FOR HIM.
LET'S SEE WHAT THE BOOK SAYS.
"IF YOUR CAT LEAVES, DO NOT GO AFTER HIM. THIS WILL ONLY LEAD TO MORE SPOILED BEHAVIOR!"
I GUESS I'LL JUST SIT AND WAIT...
ENOUGH OF THAT GUY. LET'S GET BACK TO ME AND MY NEW-FOUND FRIENDS.
HEY, WHO'S THE VISITOR?
THAT'S A BIG CAT!
IS HE A STRAY?
WHAT'S HIS NAME?
I FOUND HIM DOWN THE STREET WHEN I WAS PUTTING UP FLYERS.
LET'S CALL HIM NACHO!
NACHO? I CAN LIVE WITH IT. EXCEPT NOW I'M SUPER-HUNGRY FOR A PLATE OF THAT EPONYMOUS SNACK!
THAT'S RIGHT. "EPONYMOUS." LOOK IT UP, CRETINS.

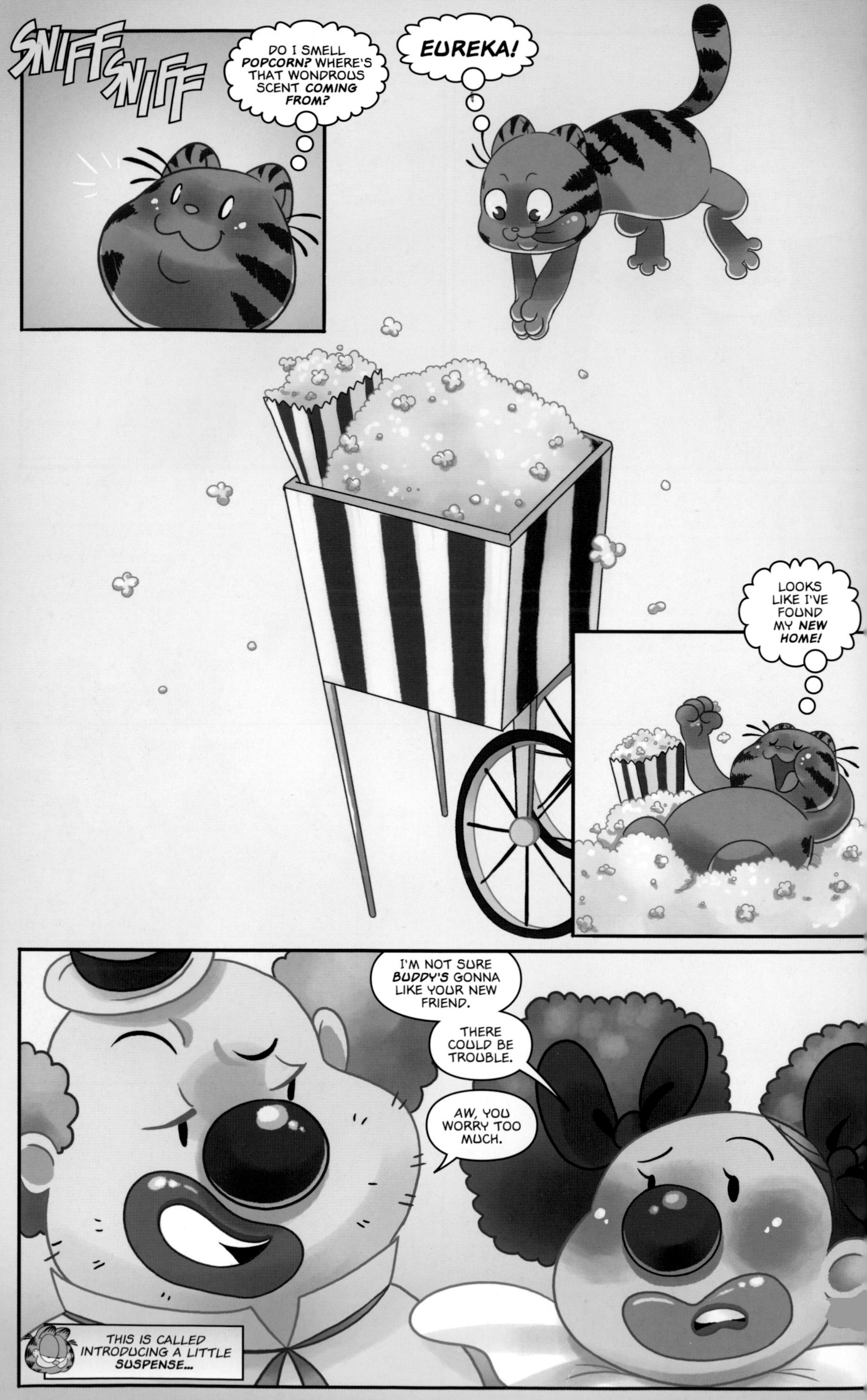

SNIFF SNIFF
DO I SMELL POPCORN? WHERE'S THAT WONDROUS SCENT COMING FROM?
EUREKA!
LOOKS LIKE I'VE FOUND MY NEW HOME!
I'M NOT SURE BUDDY'S GONNA LIKE YOUR NEW FRIEND.
THERE COULD BE TROUBLE.
AW, YOU WORRY TOO MUCH.
THIS IS CALLED INTRODUCING A LITTLE SUSPENSE...

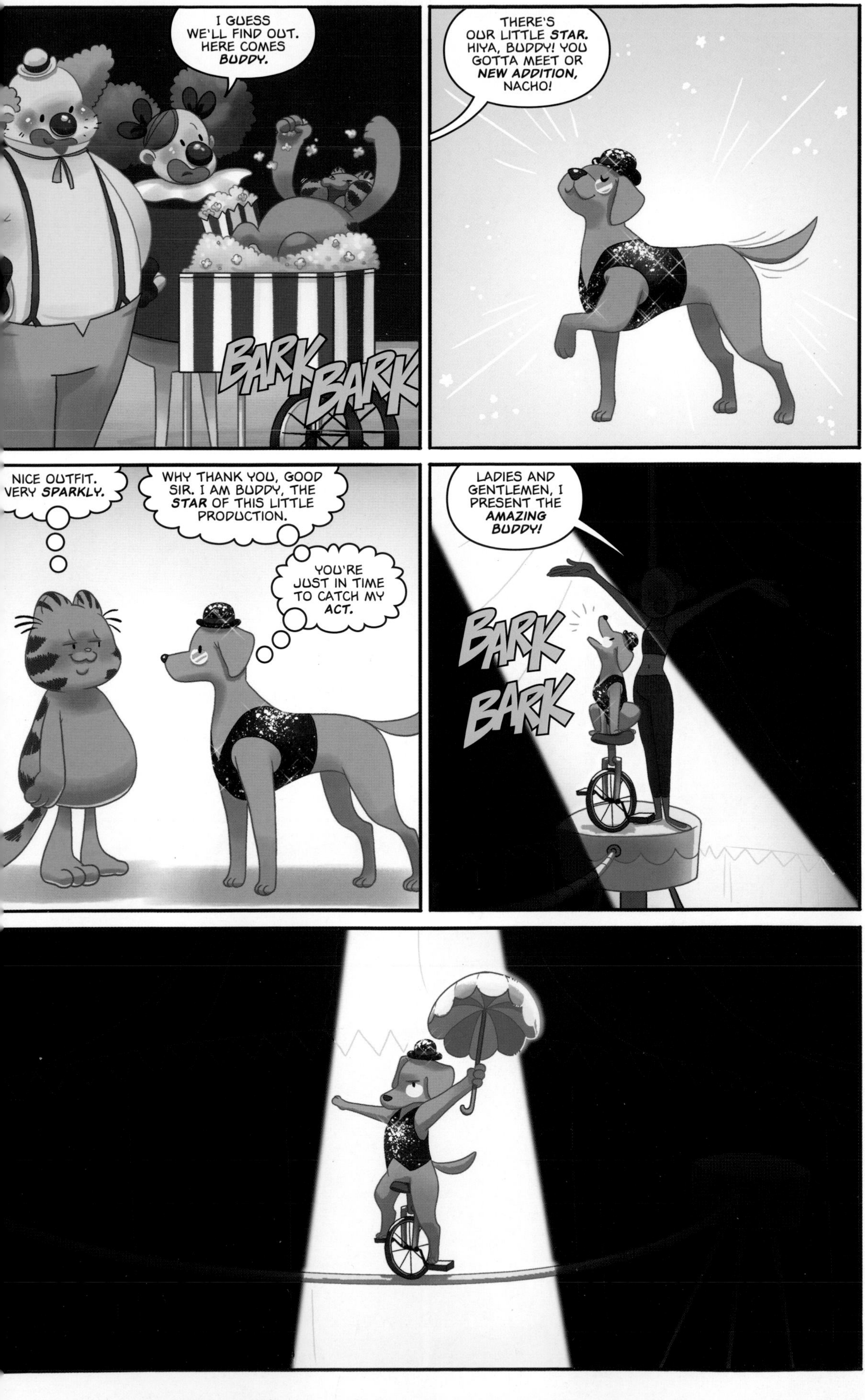
I GUESS WE'LL FIND OUT. HERE COMES BUDDY.
BARK BARK
THERE'S OUR LITTLE STAR. HIYA, BUDDY! YOU GOTTA MEET OR NEW ADDITION, NACHO!
NICE OUTFIT. VERY SPARKLY.
WHY THANK YOU, GOOD SIR. I AM BUDDY, THE STAR OF THIS LITTLE PRODUCTION.
YOU'RE JUST IN TIME TO CATCH MY ACT.
LADIES AND GENTLEMEN, I PRESENT THE AMAZING BUDDY!
BARK
BARK

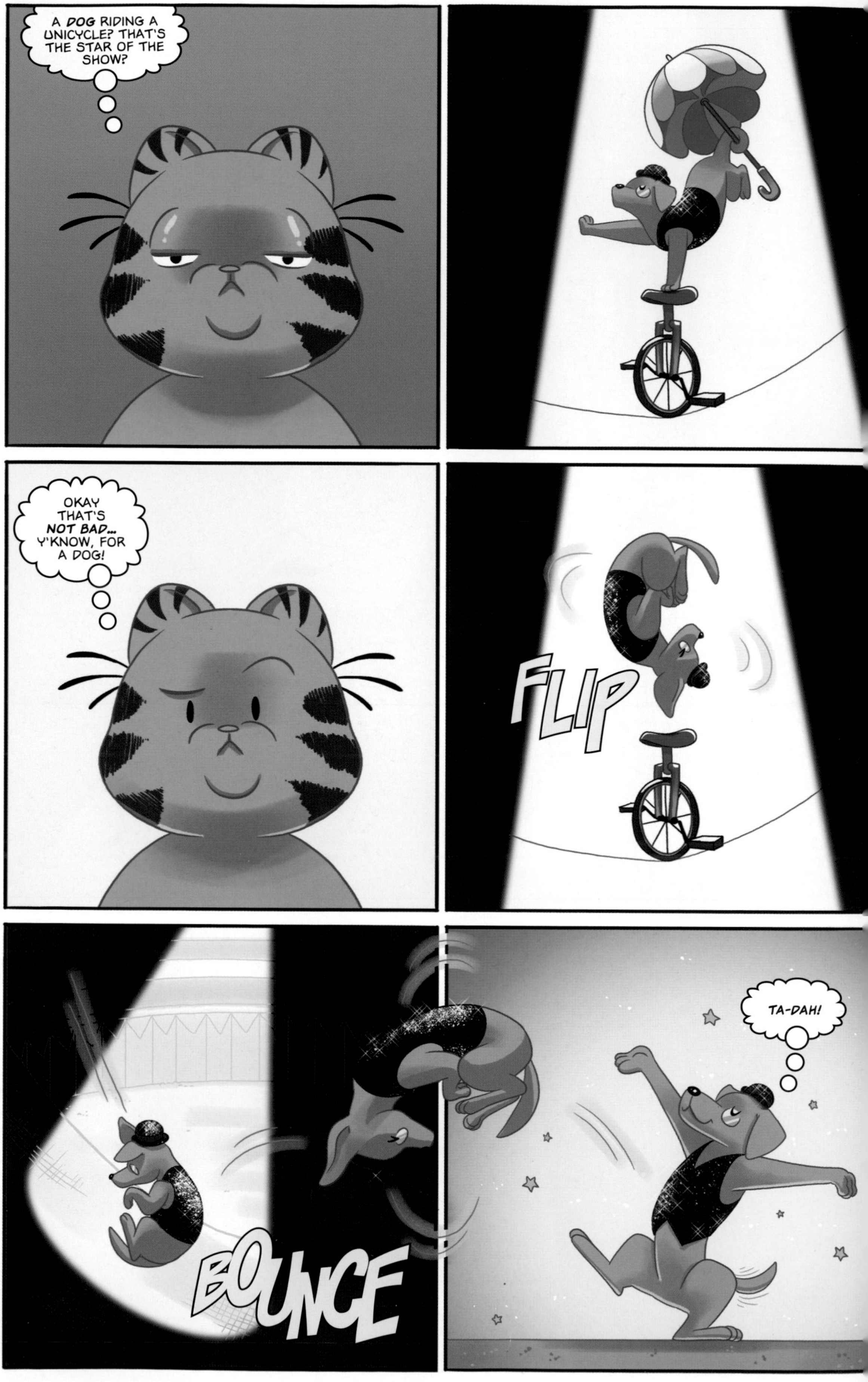
A DOG RIDING A UNICYCLE? THAT'S THE STAR OF THE SHOW?
OKAY THAT'S NOT BAD... Y'KNOW, FOR A DOG!
FLIP
BOUNCE
TA-DAH!

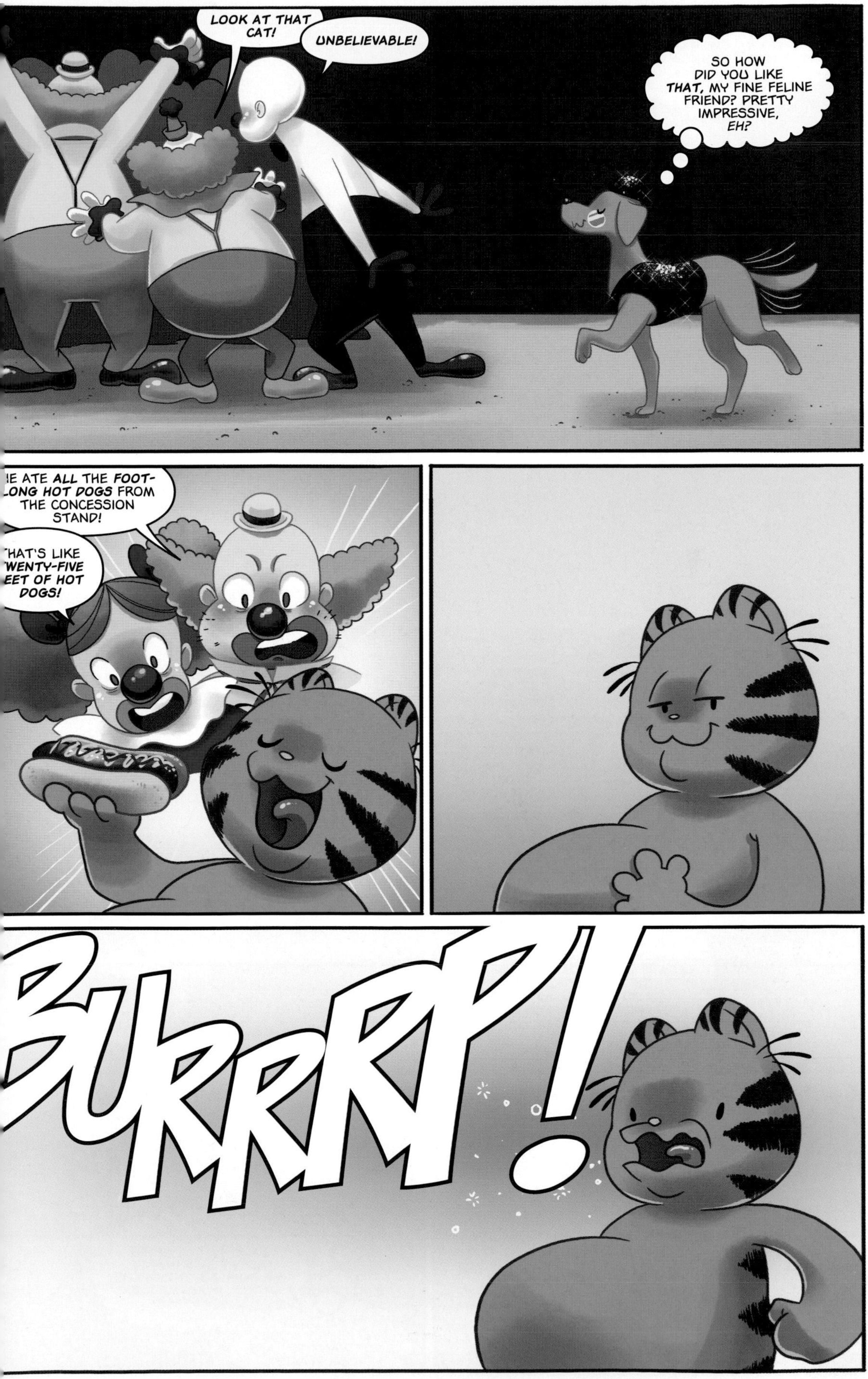
LOOK AT THAT CAT!
UNBELIEVABLE!
SO HOW DID YOU LIKE THAT, MY FINE FELINE FRIEND? PRETTY IMPRESSIVE, EH?
E ATE ALL THE FOOT-LONG HOT DOGS FROM THE CONCESSION STAND!
HAT'S LIKE WENTY-FIVE EET OF HOT DOGS!
BURRRP!

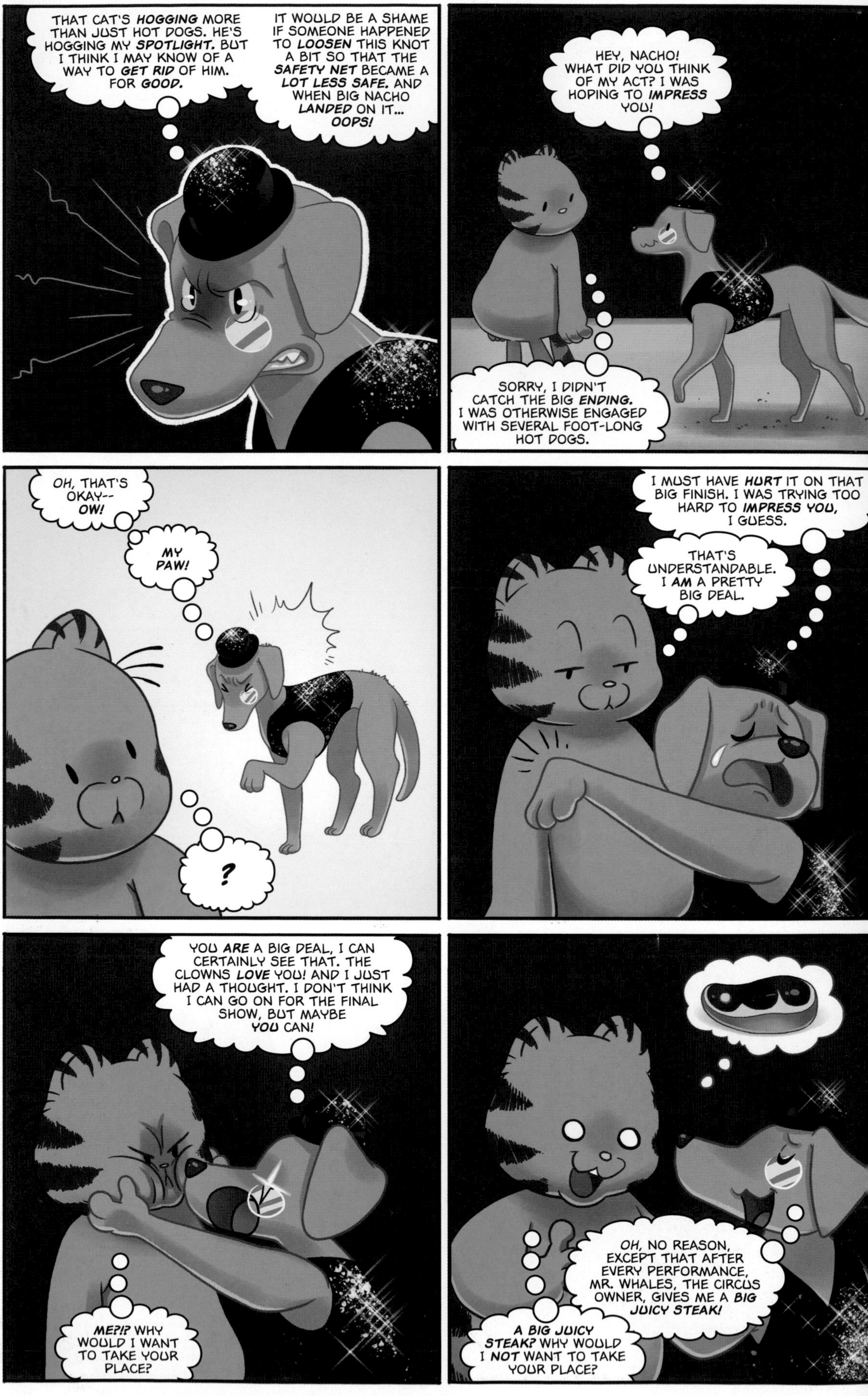
THAT CAT'S HOGGING MORE THAN JUST HOT DOGS. HE'S HOGGING MY SPOTLIGHT. BUT I THINK I MAY KNOW OF A WAY TO GET RID OF HIM. FOR GOOD.
IT WOULD BE A SHAME IF SOMEONE HAPPENED TO LOOSEN THIS KNOT A BIT SO THAT THE SAFETY NET BECAME A LOT LESS SAFE. AND WHEN BIG NACHO LANDED ON IT... OOPS!
HEY, NACHO! WHAT DID YOU THINK OF MY ACT? I WAS HOPING TO IMPRESS YOU!
SORRY, I DIDN'T CATCH THE BIG ENDING. I WAS OTHERWISE ENGAGED WITH SEVERAL FOOT-LONG HOT DOGS.
OH, THAT'S OKAY-- OW!
MY PAW!
?
I MUST HAVE HURT IT ON THAT BIG FINISH. I WAS TRYING TOO HARD TO IMPRESS YOU, I GUESS.
THAT'S UNDERSTANDABLE. I AM A PRETTY BIG DEAL.
YOU ARE A BIG DEAL, I CAN CERTAINLY SEE THAT. THE CLOWNS LOVE YOU! AND I JUST HAD A THOUGHT. I DON'T THINK I CAN GO ON FOR THE FINAL SHOW, BUT MAYBE YOU CAN!
ME?!? WHY WOULD I WANT TO TAKE YOUR PLACE?
OH, NO REASON, EXCEPT THAT AFTER EVERY PERFORMANCE, MR. WHALES, THE CIRCUS OWNER, GIVES ME A BIG JUICY STEAK!
A BIG JUICY STEAK? WHY WOULD I NOT WANT TO TAKE YOUR PLACE?

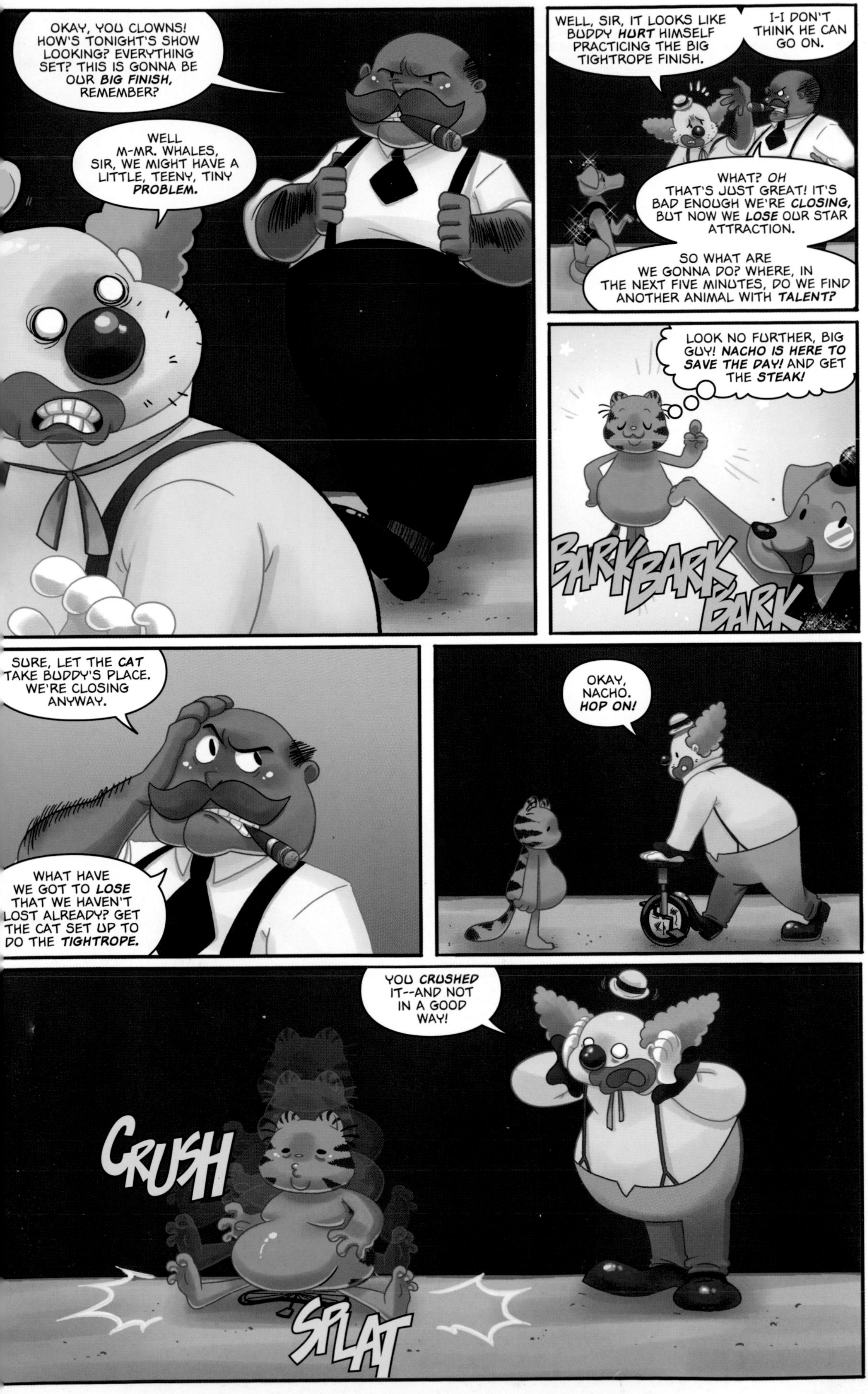

OKAY, YOU CLOWNS! HOW'S TONIGHT'S SHOW LOOKING? EVERYTHING SET? THIS IS GONNA BE OUR BIG FINISH, REMEMBER?
WELL M-MR. WHALES, SIR, WE MIGHT HAVE A LITTLE, TEENY, TINY PROBLEM.
WELL, SIR, IT LOOKS LIKE BUDDY HURT HIMSELF PRACTICING THE BIG TIGHTROPE FINISH.
I-I DON'T THINK HE CAN GO ON.
WHAT? OH THAT'S JUST GREAT! IT'S BAD ENOUGH WE'RE CLOSING, BUT NOW WE LOSE OUR STAR ATTRACTION.
SO WHAT ARE WE GONNA DO? WHERE, IN THE NEXT FIVE MINUTES, DO WE FIND ANOTHER ANIMAL WITH TALENT?
LOOK NO FURTHER, BIG GUY! NACHO IS HERE TO SAVE THE DAY! AND GET THE STEAK!
BARK BARK BARK
SURE, LET THE CAT TAKE BUDDY'S PLACE. WE'RE CLOSING ANYWAY.
WHAT HAVE WE GOT TO LOSE THAT WE HAVEN'T LOST ALREADY? GET THE CAT SET UP TO DO THE TIGHTROPE.
OKAY, NACHO. HOP ON!
YOU CRUSHED IT--AND NOT IN A GOOD WAY!
CRUSH
SPLAT

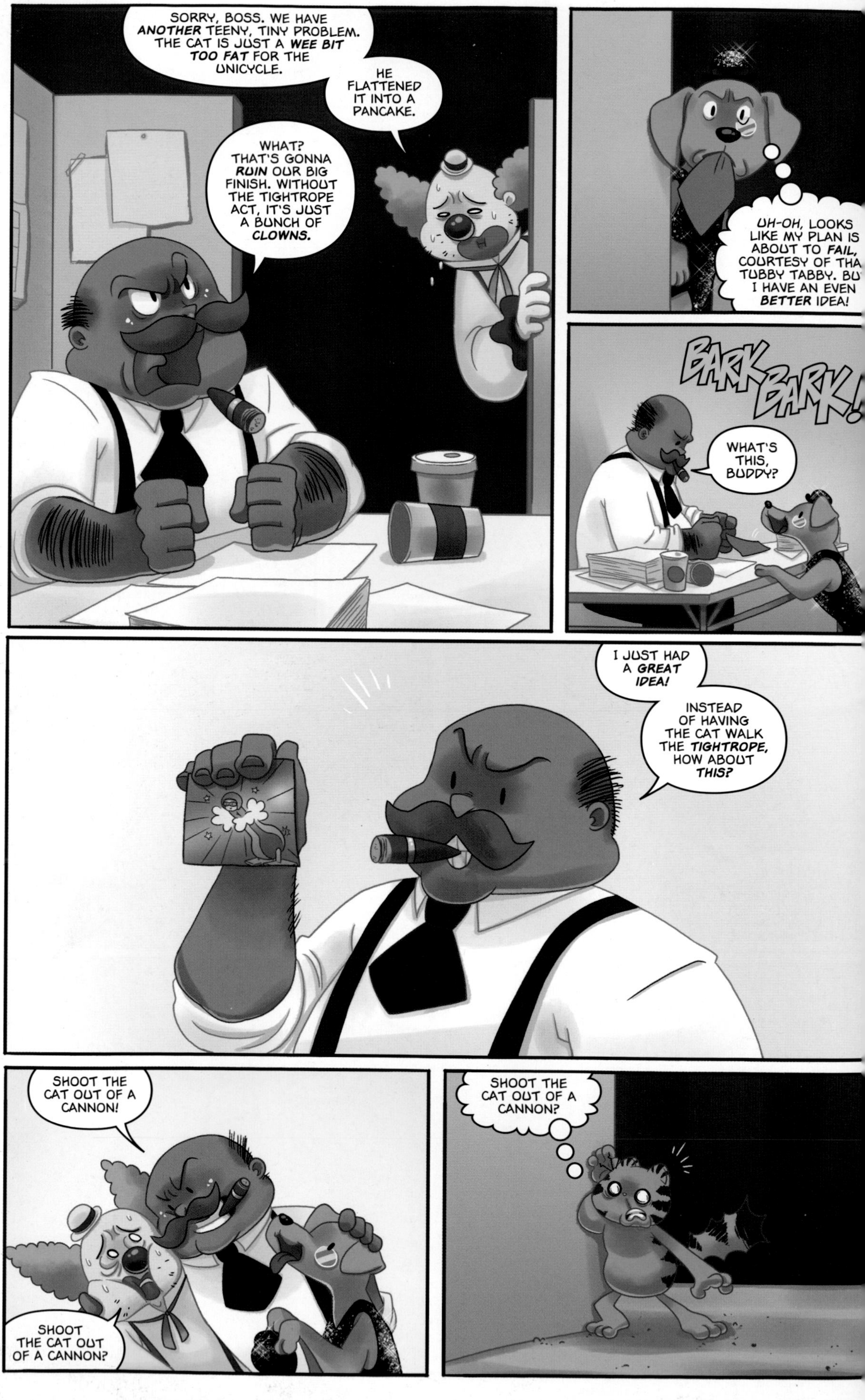
SORRY, BOSS. WE HAVE ANOTHER TEENY, TINY PROBLEM. THE CAT IS JUST A WEE BIT TOO FAT FOR THE UNICYCLE.
HE FLATTENED IT INTO A PANCAKE.
WHAT? THAT'S GONNA RUIN OUR BIG FINISH. WITHOUT THE TIGHTROPE ACT, IT'S JUST A BUNCH OF CLOWNS.
UH-OH, LOOKS LIKE MY PLAN IS ABOUT TO FAIL, COURTESY OF THA TUBBY TABBY. BU I HAVE AN EVEN BETTER IDEA!
BARK BARK!
WHAT'S THIS, BUDDY?
I JUST HAD A GREAT IDEA!
INSTEAD OF HAVING THE CAT WALK THE TIGHTROPE, HOW ABOUT THIS?
SHOOT THE CAT OUT OF A CANNON!
SHOOT THE CAT OUT OF A CANNON?
SHOOT THE CAT OUT OF A CANNON?

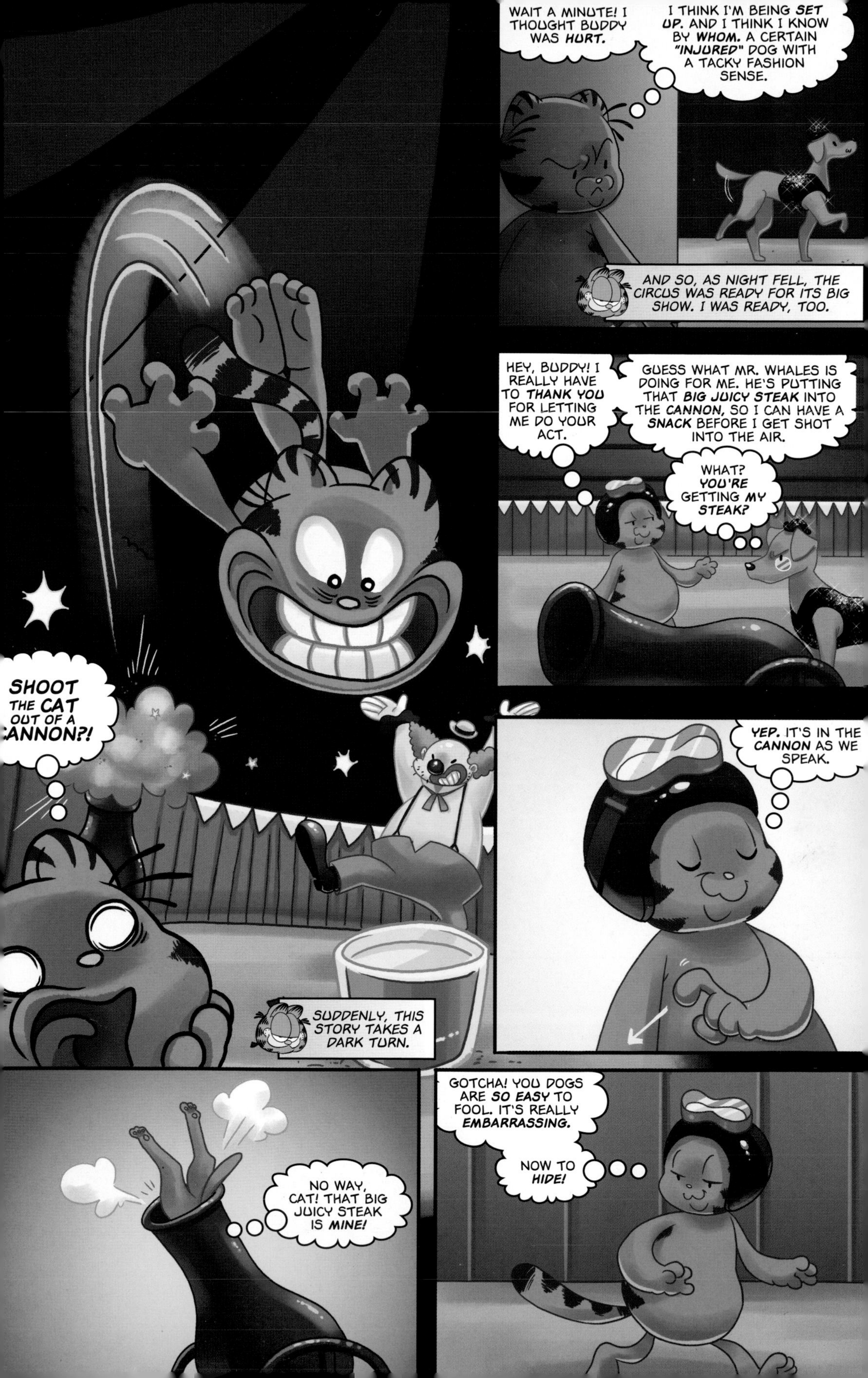
WAIT A MINUTE! I THOUGHT BUDDY WAS HURT.
I THINK I'M BEING SET UP. AND I THINK I KNOW BY WHOM. A CERTAIN "INJURED" DOG WITH A TACKY FASHION SENSE.
AND SO, AS NIGHT FELL, THE CIRCUS WAS READY FOR ITS BIG SHOW. I WAS READY, TOO.
HEY, BUDDY! I REALLY HAVE TO THANK YOU FOR LETTING ME DO YOUR ACT.
GUESS WHAT MR. WHALES IS DOING FOR ME. HE'S PUTTING THAT BIG JUICY STEAK INTO THE CANNON, SO I CAN HAVE A SNACK BEFORE I GET SHOT INTO THE AIR.
WHAT? YOU'RE GETTING MY STEAK?
YEP. IT'S IN THE CANNON AS WE SPEAK.
SHOOT THE CAT OUT OF A CANNON?!
SUDDENLY, THIS STORY TAKES A DARK TURN.
NO WAY, CAT! THAT BIG JUICY STEAK IS MINE!
GOTCHA! YOU DOGS ARE SO EASY TO FOOL. IT'S REALLY EMBARRASSING.
NOW TO HIDE!

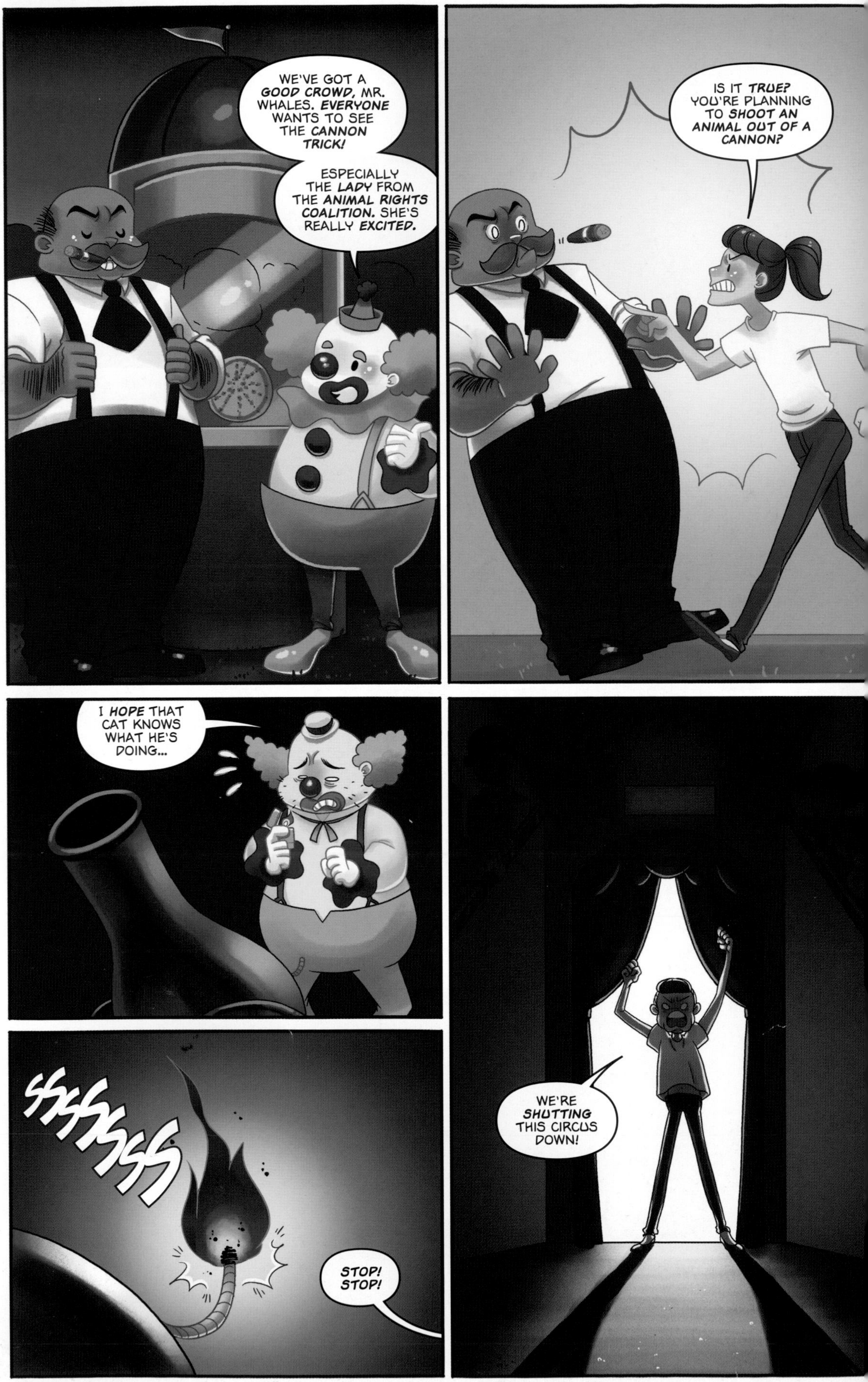
WE'VE GOT A GOOD CROWD, MR. WHALES. EVERYONE WANTS TO SEE THE CANNON TRICK!
ESPECIALLY THE LADY FROM THE ANIMAL RIGHTS COALITION. SHE'S REALLY EXCITED.
IS IT TRUE? YOU'RE PLANNING TO SHOOT AN ANIMAL OUT OF A CANNON?
I HOPE THAT CAT KNOWS WHAT HE'S DOING...
SSSSSSS
STOP! STOP!
WE'RE SHUTTING THIS CIRCUS DOWN!

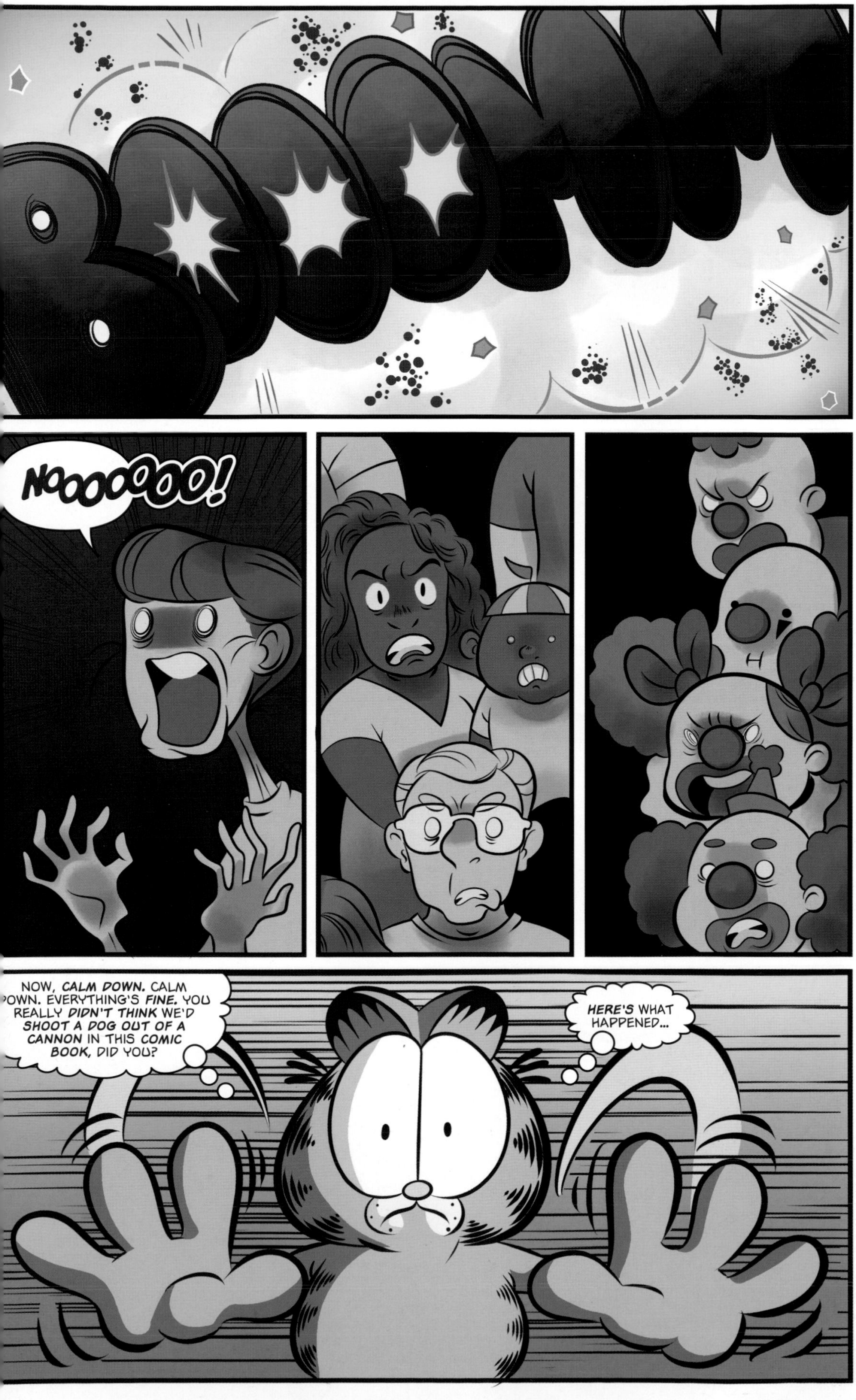

NOOOOOOO!
NOW, CALM DOWN. CALM DOWN. EVERYTHING'S FINE. YOU REALLY DIDN'T THINK WE'D SHOOT A DOG OUT OF A CANNON IN THIS COMIC BOOK, DID YOU?
HERE'S WHAT HAPPENED...

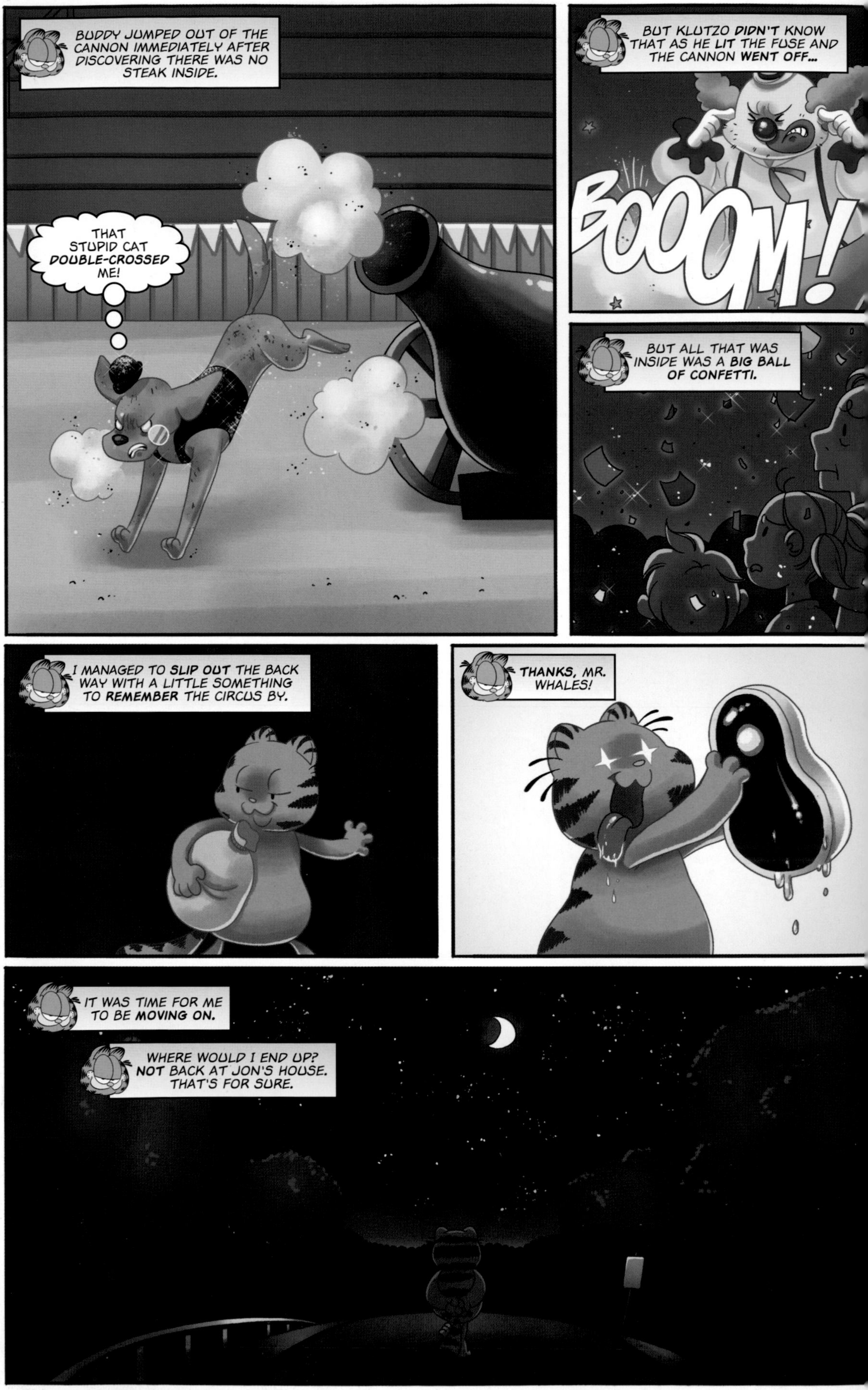
BUDDY JUMPED OUT OF THE CANNON IMMEDIATELY AFTER DISCOVERING THERE WAS NO STEAK INSIDE.
THAT STUPID CAT DOUBLE-CROSSED ME!
BUT KLUTZO DIDN'T KNOW THAT AS HE LIT THE FUSE AND THE CANNON WENT OFF...
BOOOM!
BUT ALL THAT WAS INSIDE WAS A BIG BALL OF CONFETTI.
I MANAGED TO SLIP OUT THE BACK WAY WITH A LITTLE SOMETHING TO REMEMBER THE CIRCUS BY.
THANKS, MR. WHALES!
IT WAS TIME FOR ME TO BE MOVING ON.
WHERE WOULD I END UP? NOT BACK AT JON'S HOUSE. THAT'S FOR SURE.

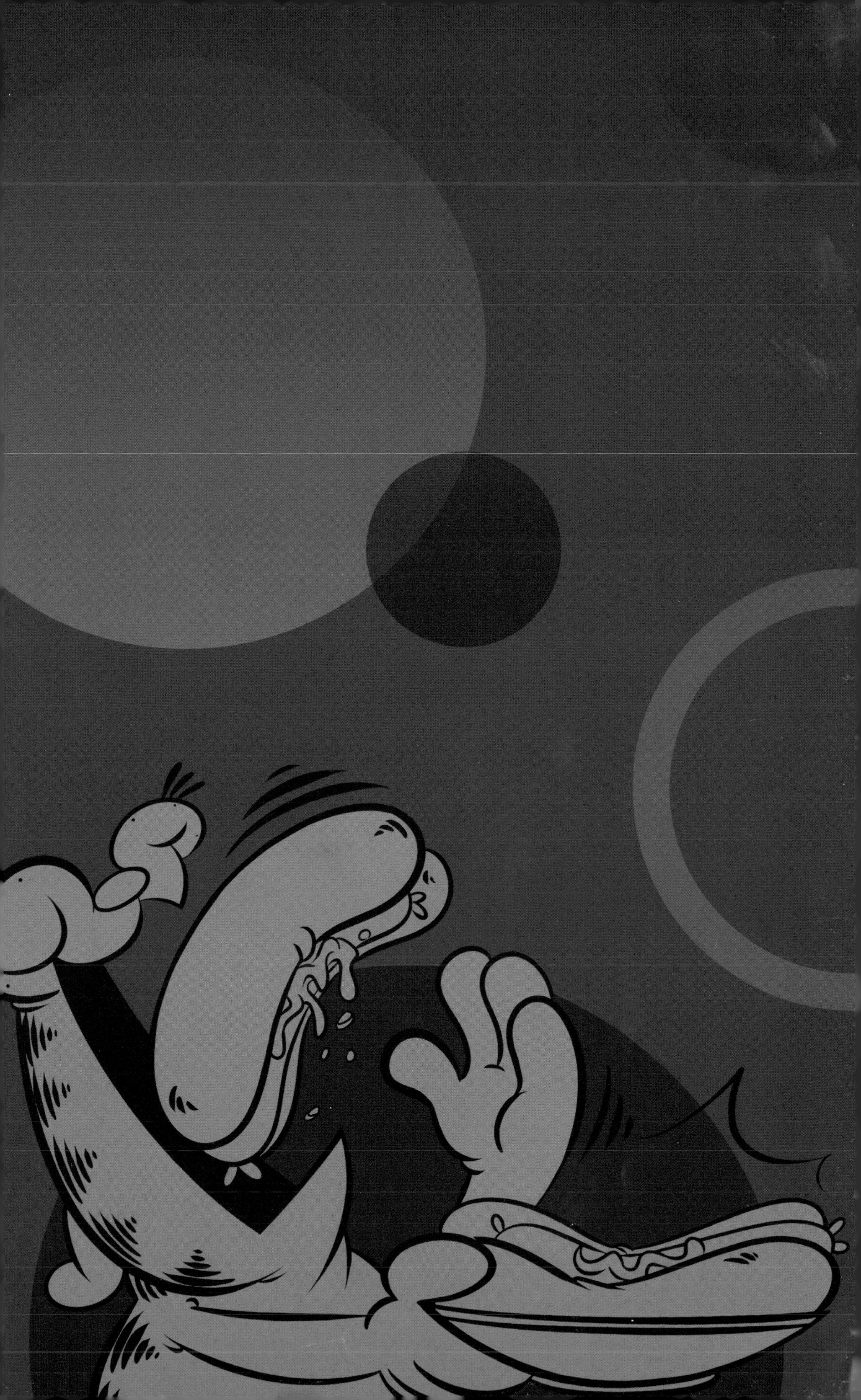

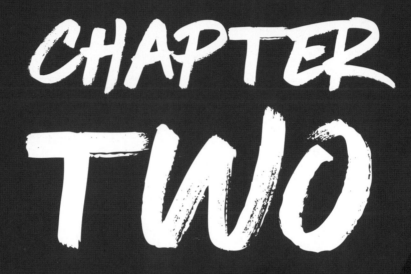

CHAPTER
TWO

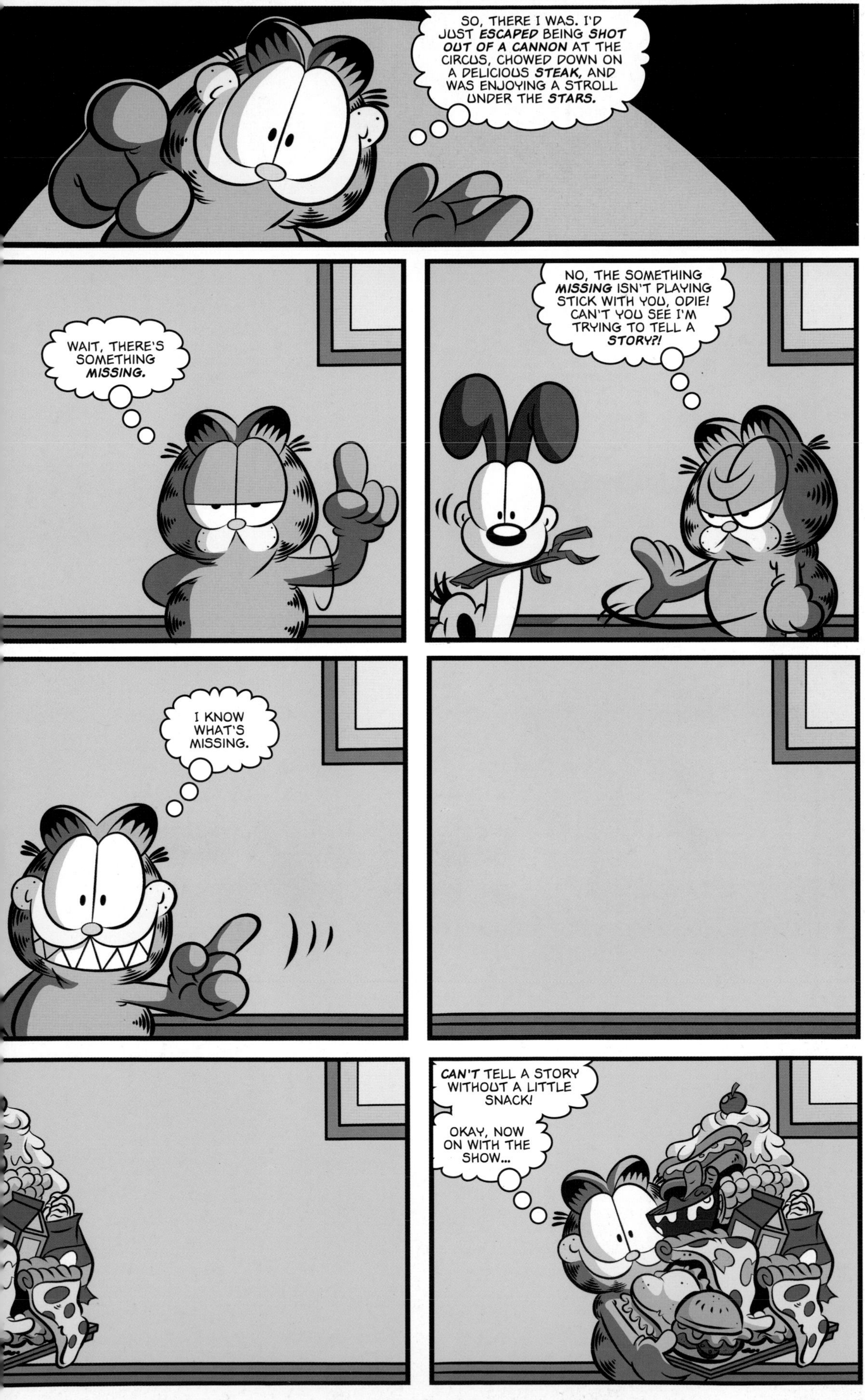
SO, THERE I WAS. I'D JUST ESCAPED BEING SHOT OUT OF A CANNON AT THE CIRCUS, CHOWED DOWN ON A DELICIOUS STEAK, AND WAS ENJOYING A STROLL UNDER THE STARS.
WAIT, THERE'S SOMETHING MISSING.
NO, THE SOMETHING MISSING ISN'T PLAYING STICK WITH YOU, ODIE! CAN'T YOU SEE I'M TRYING TO TELL A STORY?!
I KNOW WHAT'S MISSING.
CAN'T TELL A STORY WITHOUT A LITTLE SNACK!
OKAY, NOW ON WITH THE SHOW...

HOMECOMING

Chapter 2: The Lap of Luxury

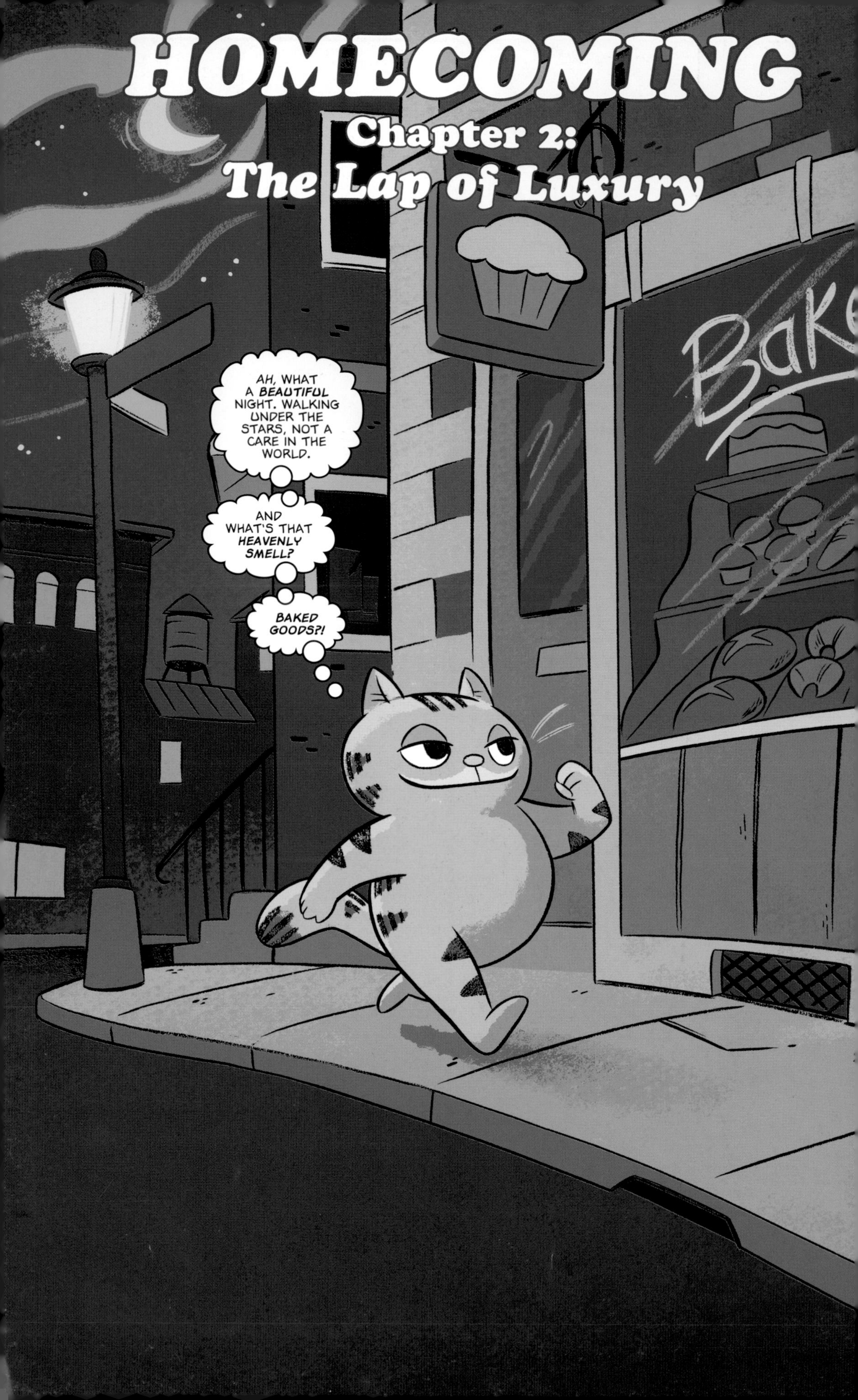

AH, WHAT A BEAUTIFUL NIGHT. WALKING UNDER THE STARS, NOT A CARE IN THE WORLD.
AND WHAT'S THAT HEAVENLY SMELL?
BAKED GOODS?!
Bake

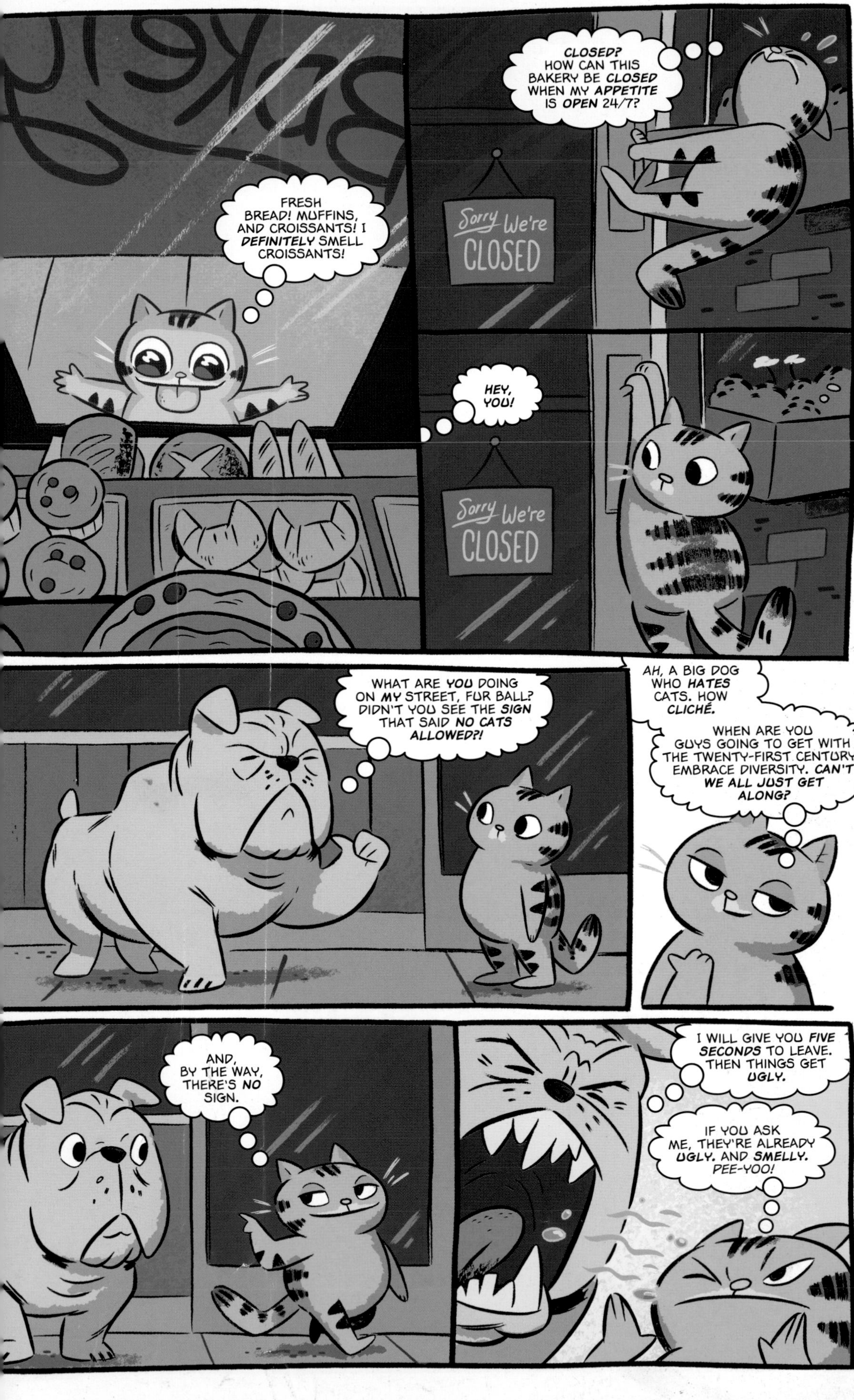
Bakery
FRESH BREAD! MUFFINS, AND CROISSANTS! I DEFINITELY SMELL CROISSANTS!
CLOSED? HOW CAN THIS BAKERY BE CLOSED WHEN MY APPETITE IS OPEN 24/7?
Sorry We're CLOSED
HEY, YOU!
Sorry We're CLOSED
WHAT ARE YOU DOING ON MY STREET, FUR BALL? DIDN'T YOU SEE THE SIGN THAT SAID NO CATS ALLOWED?!
AH, A BIG DOG WHO HATES CATS. HOW CLICHÉ.
WHEN ARE YOU GUYS GOING TO GET WITH THE TWENTY-FIRST CENTURY? EMBRACE DIVERSITY. CAN'T WE ALL JUST GET ALONG?
AND, BY THE WAY, THERE'S NO SIGN.
I WILL GIVE YOU FIVE SECONDS TO LEAVE. THEN THINGS GET UGLY.
IF YOU ASK ME, THEY'RE ALREADY UGLY. AND SMELLY. PEE-YOO!

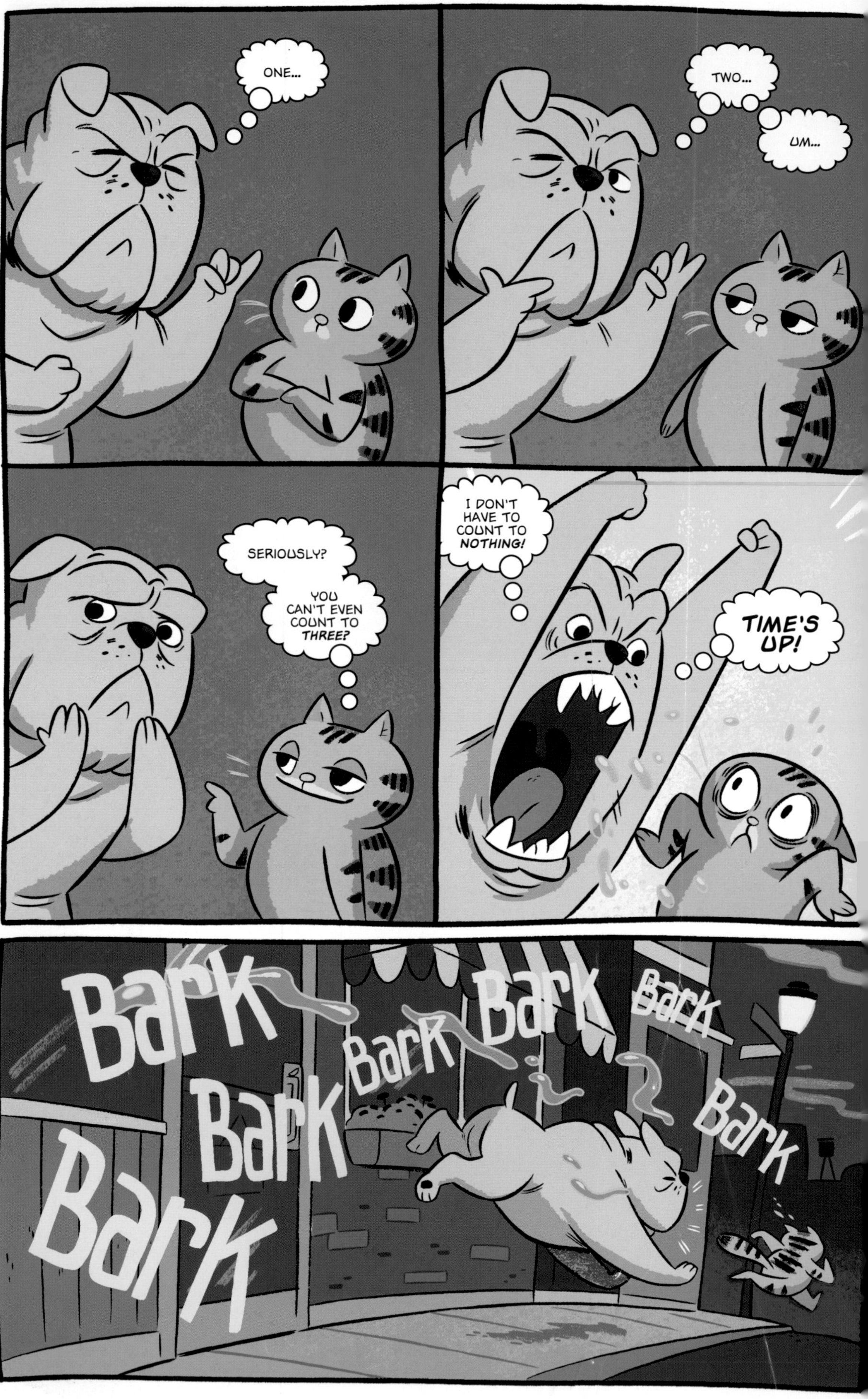

ONE...
TWO...
UM...
SERIOUSLY?
YOU CAN'T EVEN COUNT TO THREE?
I DON'T HAVE TO COUNT TO NOTHING!
TIME'S UP!
Bark
Bark
Bark
Bark
Bark
Bark
Bark

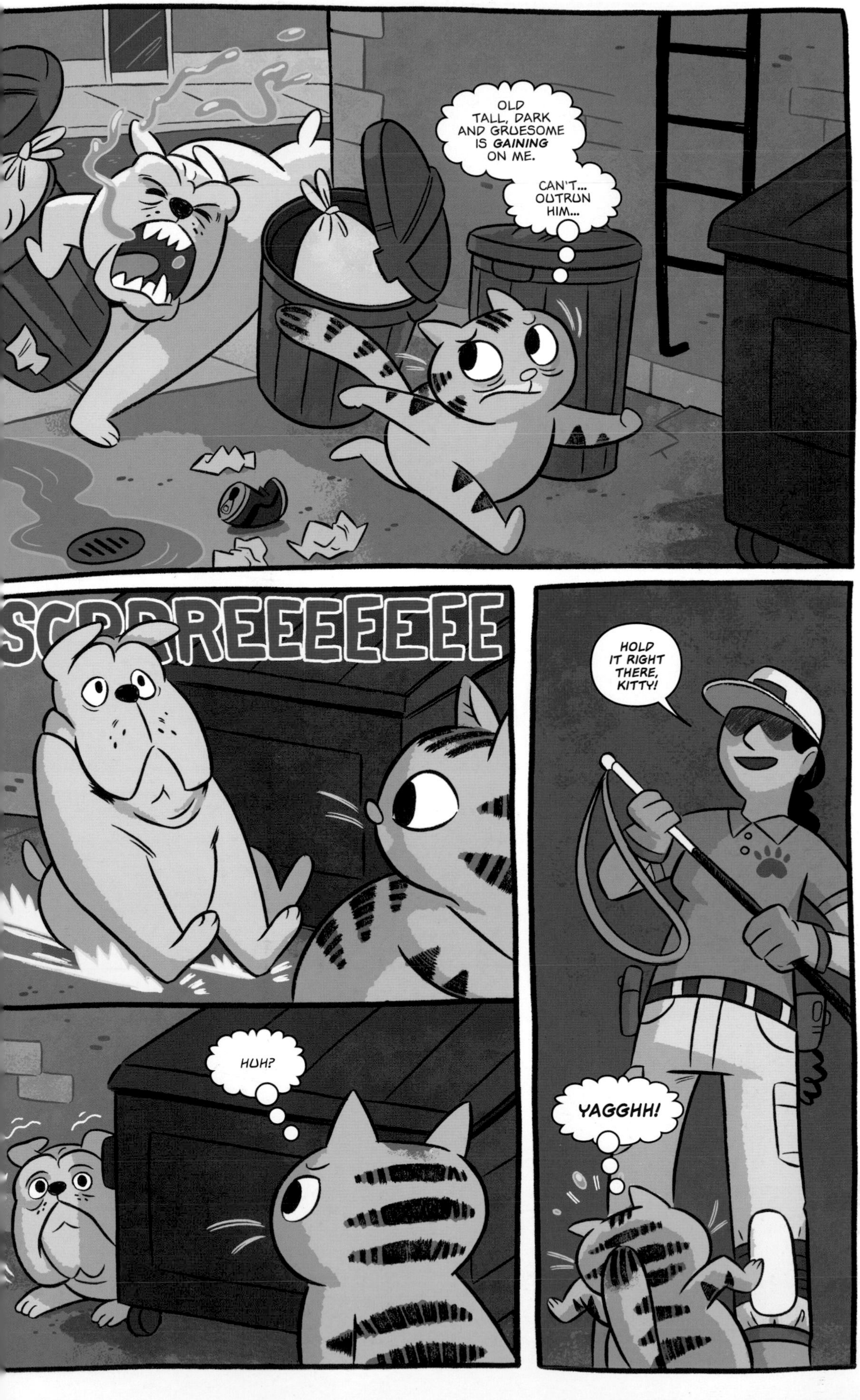
OLD TALL, DARK AND GRUESOME IS GAINING ON ME.
CAN'T... OUTRUN HIM...
SCRRREEEEEEEE
HOLD IT RIGHT THERE, KITTY!
HUH?
YAGGHH!

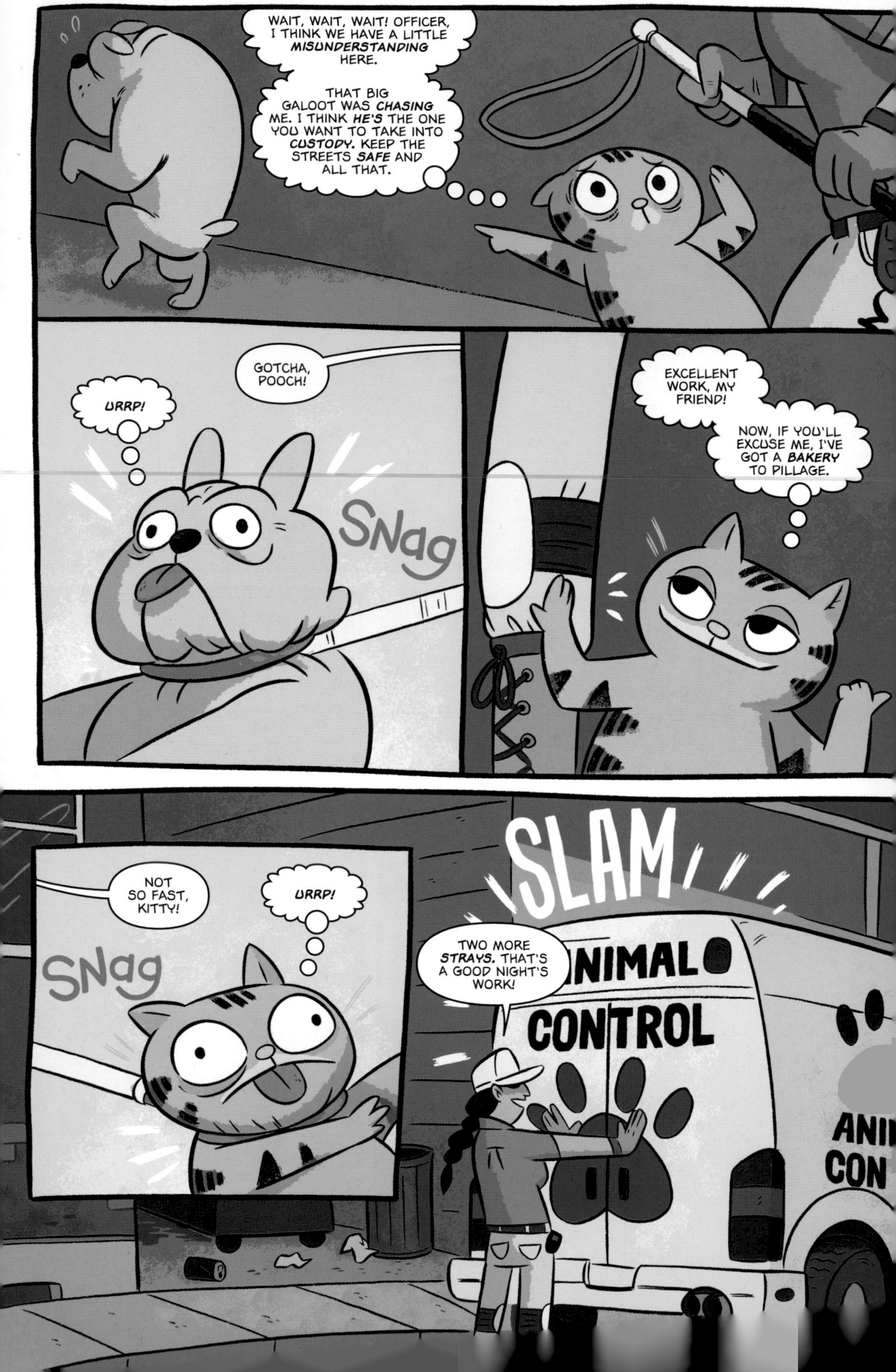
WAIT, WAIT, WAIT! OFFICER, I THINK WE HAVE A LITTLE MISUNDERSTANDING HERE.
THAT BIG GALOOT WAS CHASING ME. I THINK HE'S THE ONE YOU WANT TO TAKE INTO CUSTODY. KEEP THE STREETS SAFE AND ALL THAT.
GOTCHA, POOCH!
URRP!
SNAG
EXCELLENT WORK, MY FRIEND!
NOW, IF YOU'LL EXCUSE ME, I'VE GOT A BAKERY TO PILLAGE.
NOT SO FAST, KITTY!
URRP!
SNAG
SLAM
TWO MORE STRAYS. THAT'S A GOOD NIGHT'S WORK!
ANIMAL CONTROL
ANI
CON

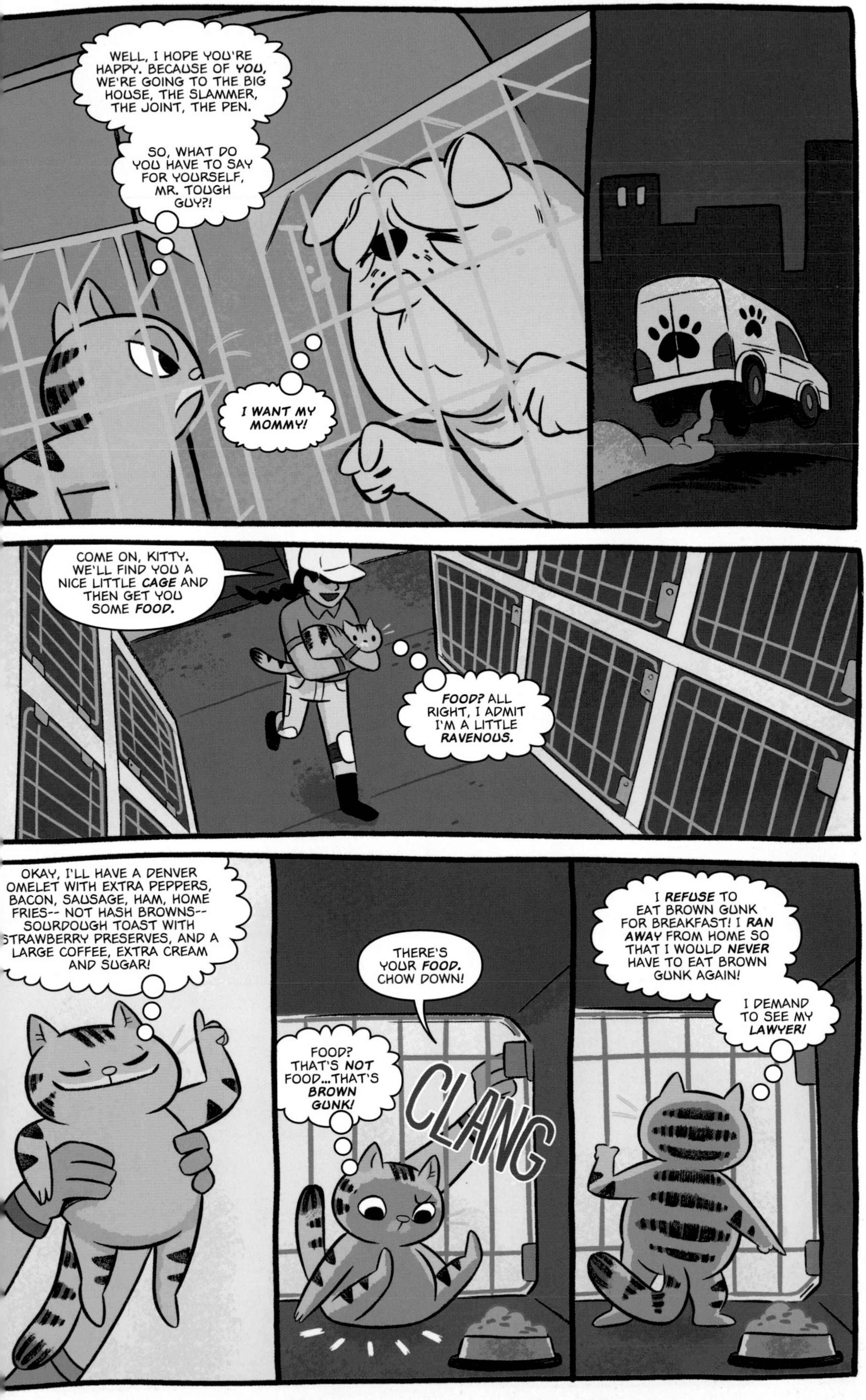
WELL, I HOPE YOU'RE HAPPY. BECAUSE OF YOU, WE'RE GOING TO THE BIG HOUSE, THE SLAMMER, THE JOINT, THE PEN.
SO, WHAT DO YOU HAVE TO SAY FOR YOURSELF, MR. TOUGH GUY?!
I WANT MY MOMMY!
COME ON, KITTY. WE'LL FIND YOU A NICE LITTLE CAGE AND THEN GET YOU SOME FOOD.
FOOD? ALL RIGHT, I ADMIT I'M A LITTLE RAVENOUS.
OKAY, I'LL HAVE A DENVER OMELET WITH EXTRA PEPPERS, BACON, SAUSAGE, HAM, HOME FRIES-- NOT HASH BROWNS-- SOURDOUGH TOAST WITH STRAWBERRY PRESERVES, AND A LARGE COFFEE, EXTRA CREAM AND SUGAR!
THERE'S YOUR FOOD. CHOW DOWN!
CLANG
FOOD? THAT'S NOT FOOD...THAT'S BROWN GUNK!
I REFUSE TO EAT BROWN GUNK FOR BREAKFAST! I RAN AWAY FROM HOME SO THAT I WOULD NEVER HAVE TO EAT BROWN GUNK AGAIN!
I DEMAND TO SEE MY LAWYER!

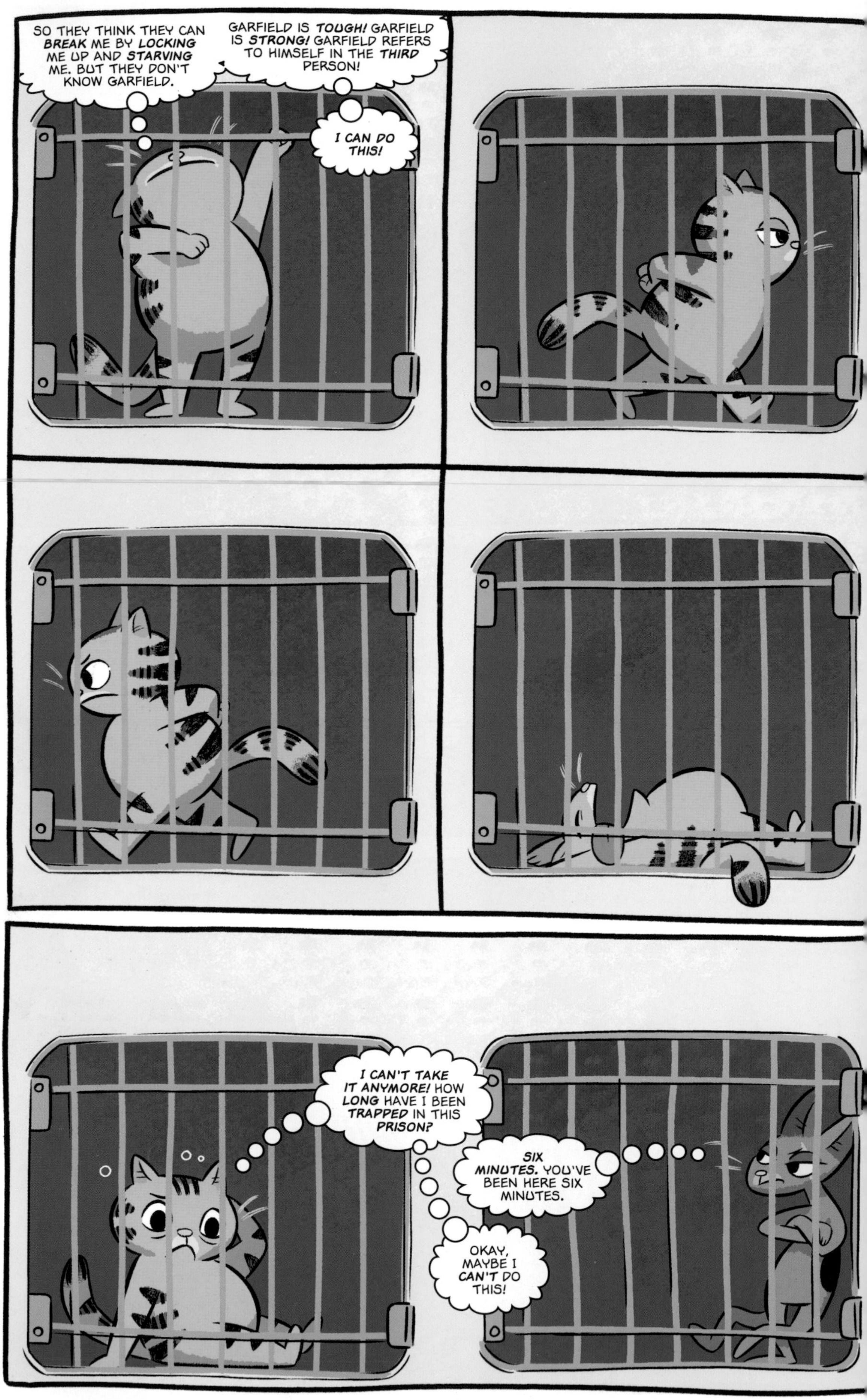
SO THEY THINK THEY CAN BREAK ME BY LOCKING ME UP AND STARVING ME. BUT THEY DON'T KNOW GARFIELD.
GARFIELD IS TOUGH! GARFIELD IS STRONG! GARFIELD REFERS TO HIMSELF IN THE THIRD PERSON!
I CAN DO THIS!
I CAN'T TAKE IT ANYMORE! HOW LONG HAVE I BEEN TRAPPED IN THIS PRISON?
SIX MINUTES. YOU'VE BEEN HERE SIX MINUTES.
OKAY, MAYBE I CAN'T DO THIS!

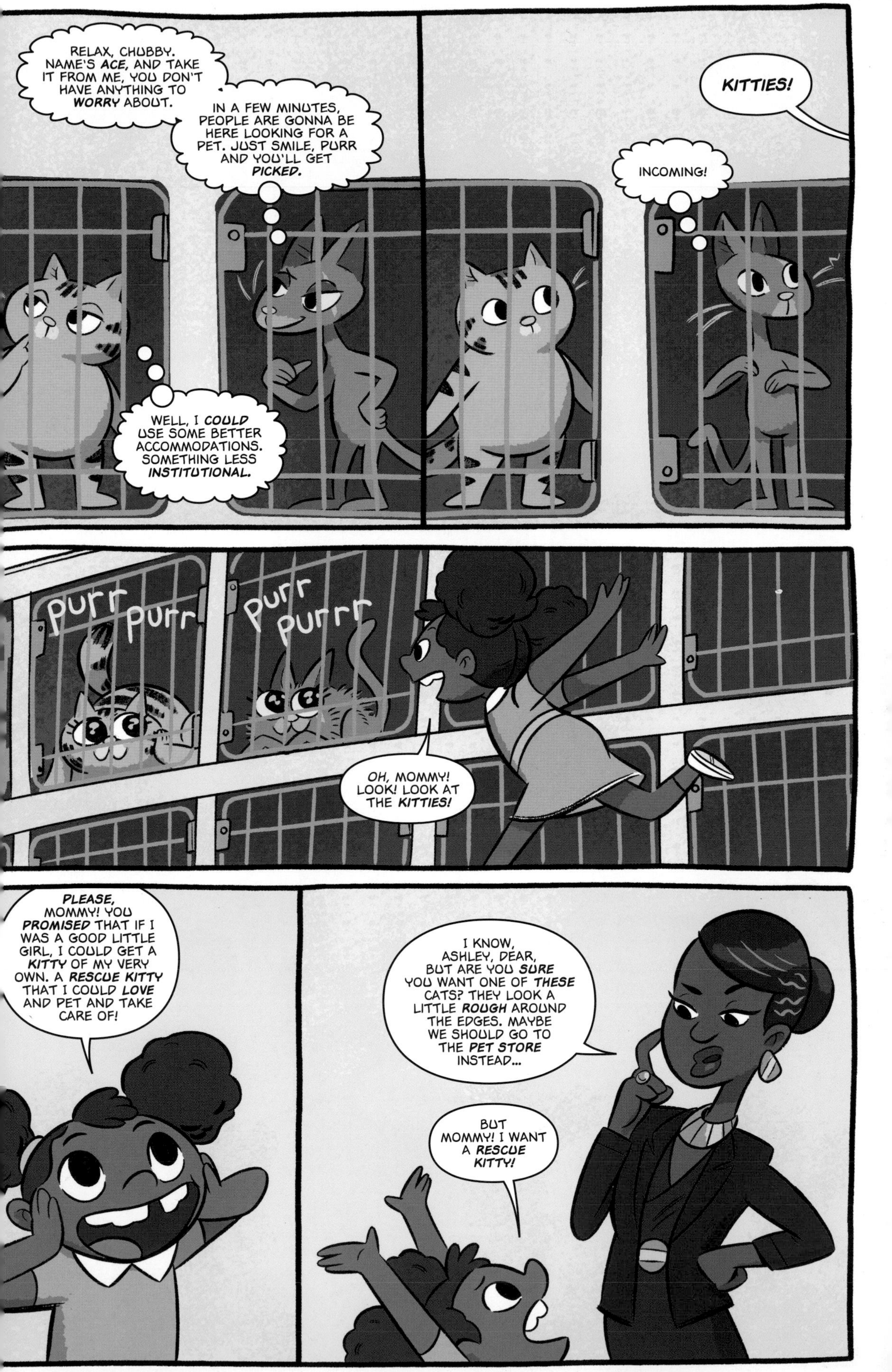
RELAX, CHUBBY. NAME'S ACE, AND TAKE IT FROM ME, YOU DON'T HAVE ANYTHING TO WORRY ABOUT.
IN A FEW MINUTES, PEOPLE ARE GONNA BE HERE LOOKING FOR A PET. JUST SMILE, PURR AND YOU'LL GET PICKED.
WELL, I COULD USE SOME BETTER ACCOMMODATIONS. SOMETHING LESS INSTITUTIONAL.
KITTIES!
INCOMING!
purr purr
purr purrr
OH, MOMMY! LOOK! LOOK AT THE KITTIES!
PLEASE, MOMMY! YOU PROMISED THAT IF I WAS A GOOD LITTLE GIRL, I COULD GET A KITTY OF MY VERY OWN. A RESCUE KITTY THAT I COULD LOVE AND PET AND TAKE CARE OF!
I KNOW, ASHLEY, DEAR, BUT ARE YOU SURE YOU WANT ONE OF THESE CATS? THEY LOOK A LITTLE ROUGH AROUND THE EDGES. MAYBE WE SHOULD GO TO THE PET STORE INSTEAD...
BUT MOMMY! I WANT A RESCUE KITTY!

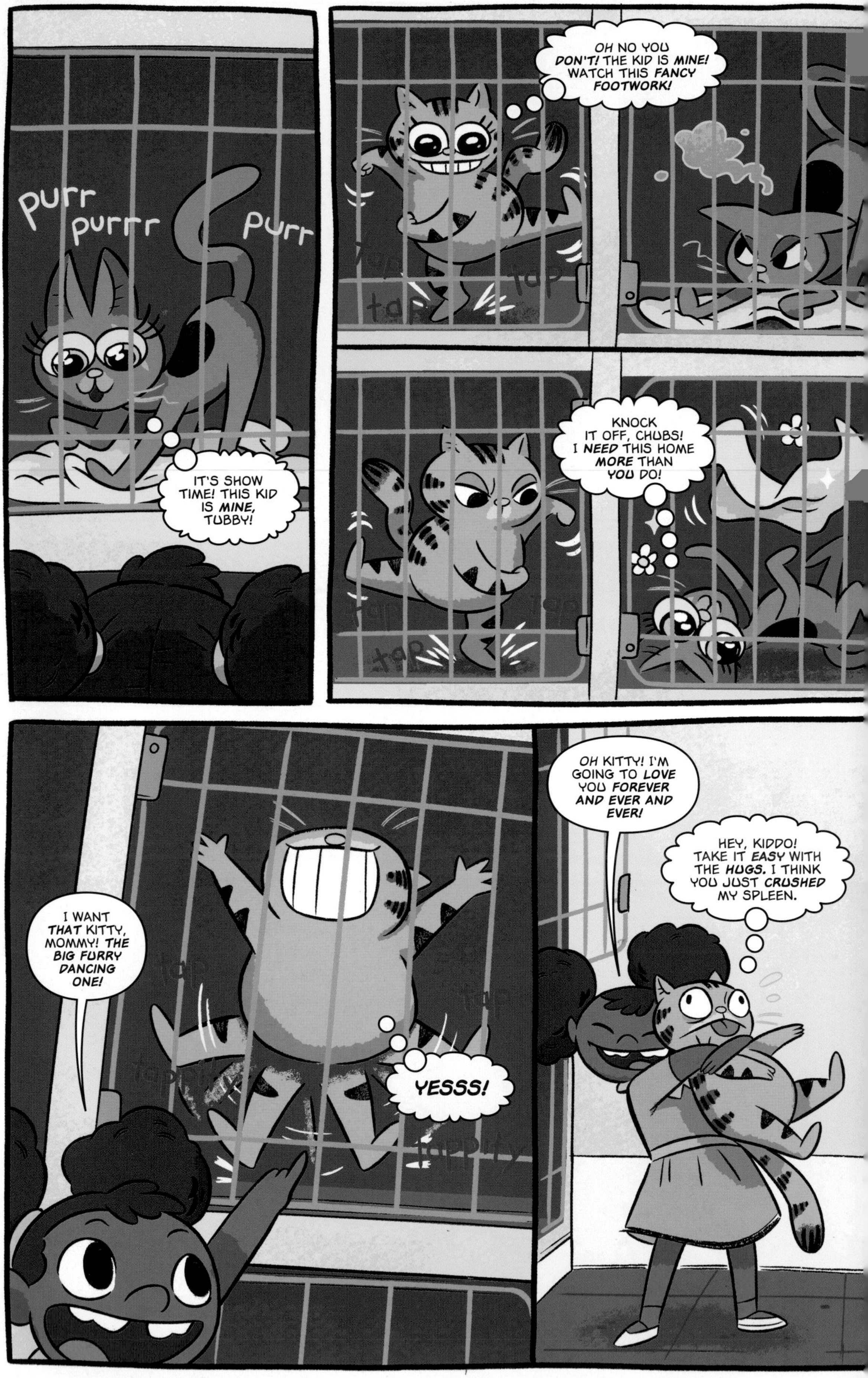
purr
purrr
purr
IT'S SHOW TIME! THIS KID IS MINE, TUBBY!
OH NO YOU DON'T! THE KID IS MINE! WATCH THIS FANCY FOOTWORK!
tap
tap
tap
KNOCK IT OFF, CHUBS! I NEED THIS HOME MORE THAN YOU DO!
tap
tap
tap
I WANT THAT KITTY, MOMMY! THE BIG FURRY DANCING ONE!
tap
tap
tappity
YESSS!
tappity
OH KITTY! I'M GOING TO LOVE YOU FOREVER AND EVER AND EVER!
HEY, KIDDO! TAKE IT EASY WITH THE HUGS. I THINK YOU JUST CRUSHED MY SPLEEN.

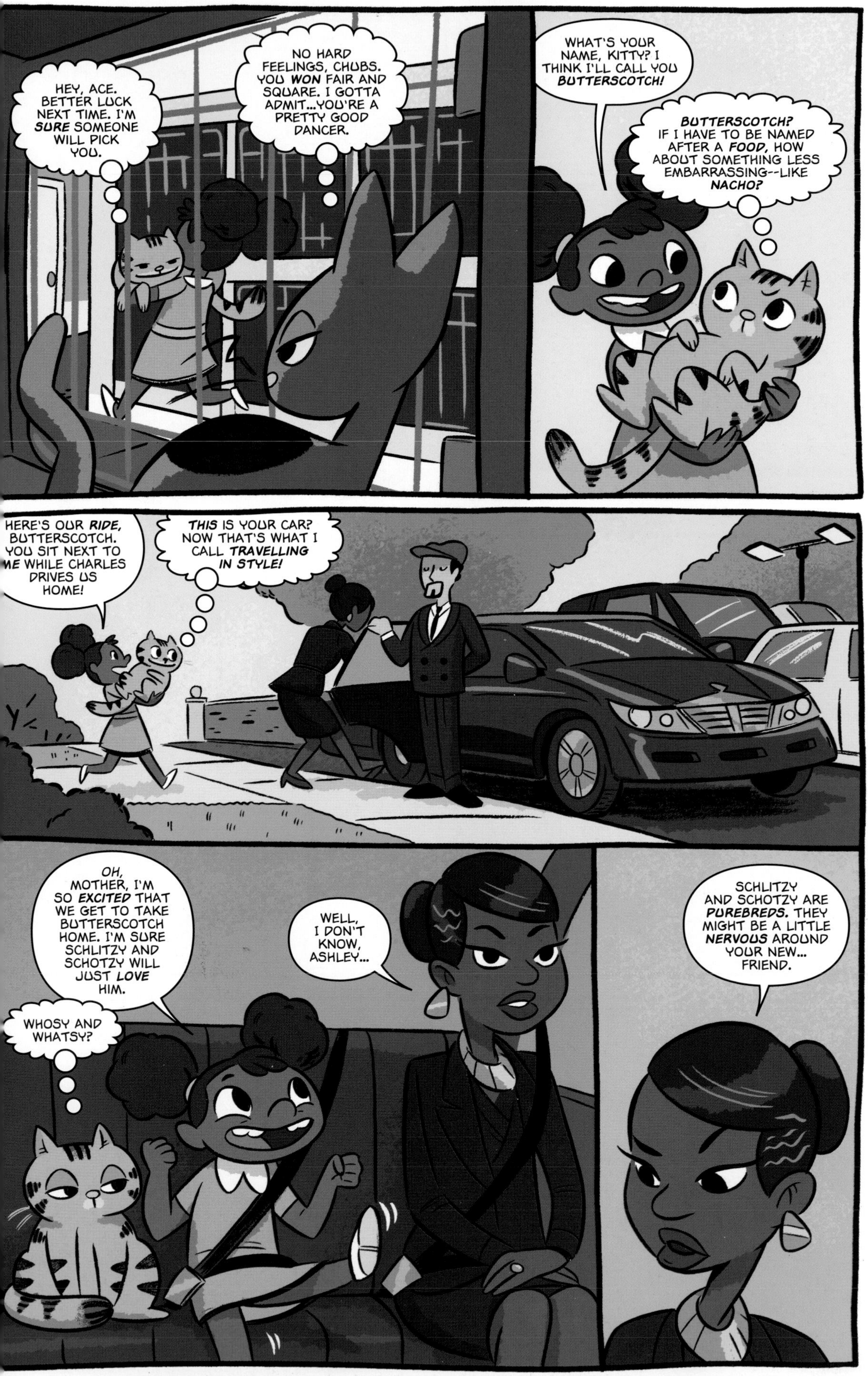
HEY, ACE. BETTER LUCK NEXT TIME. I'M *SURE* SOMEONE WILL PICK YOU.
NO HARD FEELINGS, CHUBS. YOU *WON* FAIR AND SQUARE. I GOTTA ADMIT...YOU'RE A PRETTY GOOD DANCER.
WHAT'S YOUR NAME, KITTY? I THINK I'LL CALL YOU *BUTTERSCOTCH!*
BUTTERSCOTCH? IF I HAVE TO BE NAMED AFTER A *FOOD,* HOW ABOUT SOMETHING LESS EMBARRASSING--LIKE *NACHO?*
HERE'S OUR *RIDE,* BUTTERSCOTCH. YOU SIT NEXT TO *ME* WHILE CHARLES DRIVES US HOME!
THIS IS YOUR CAR? NOW THAT'S WHAT I CALL *TRAVELLING IN STYLE!*
OH, MOTHER, I'M SO *EXCITED* THAT WE GET TO TAKE BUTTERSCOTCH HOME. I'M SURE SCHLITZY AND SCHOTZY WILL JUST *LOVE* HIM.
WHOSY AND WHATSY?
WELL, I DON'T KNOW, ASHLEY...
SCHLITZY AND SCHOTZY ARE *PUREBREDS.* THEY MIGHT BE A LITTLE *NERVOUS* AROUND YOUR NEW... FRIEND.

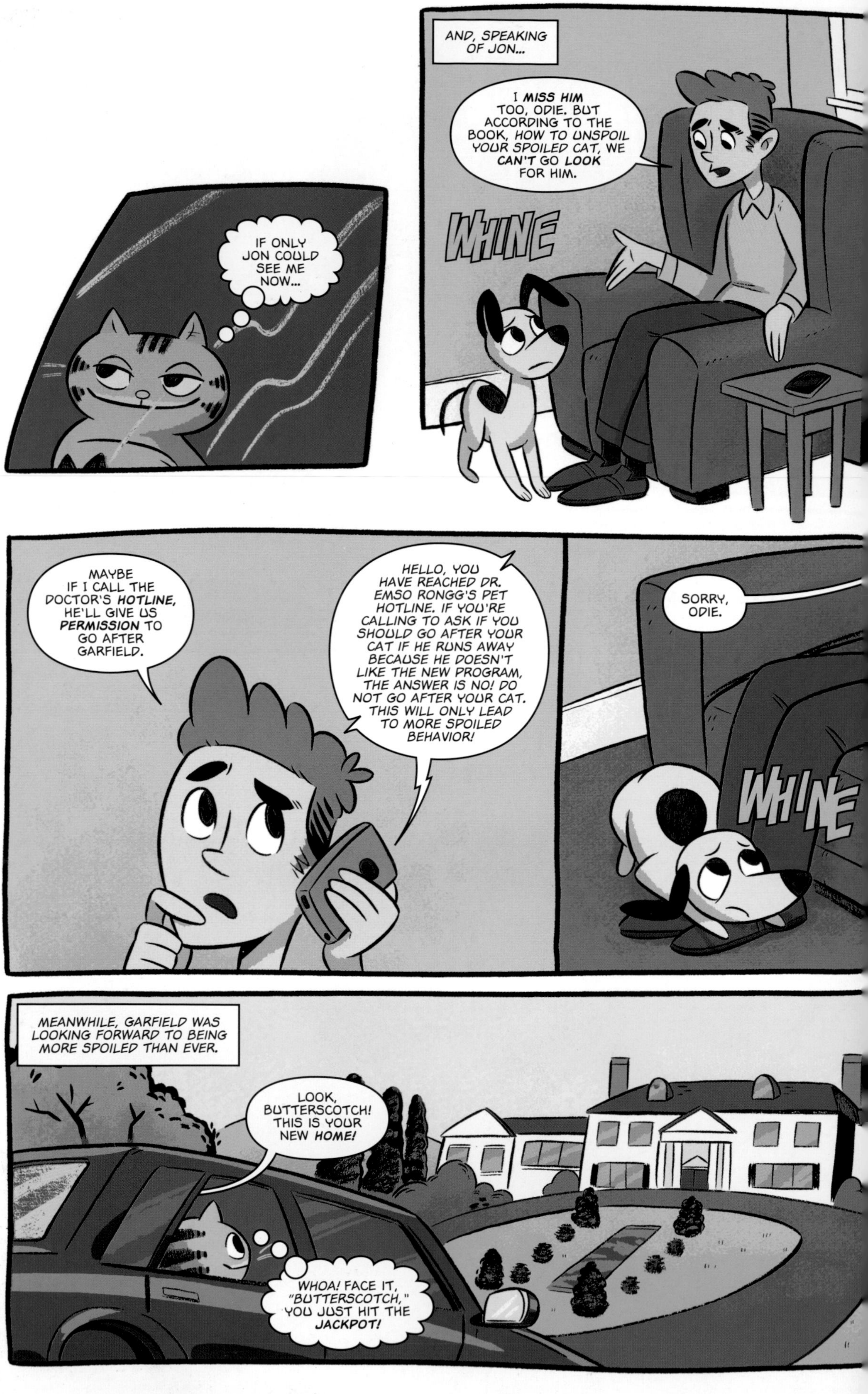

IF ONLY JON COULD SEE ME NOW...
AND, SPEAKING OF JON...
I MISS HIM TOO, ODIE. BUT ACCORDING TO THE BOOK, HOW TO UNSPOIL YOUR SPOILED CAT, WE CAN'T GO LOOK FOR HIM.
WHINE
MAYBE IF I CALL THE DOCTOR'S HOTLINE, HE'LL GIVE US PERMISSION TO GO AFTER GARFIELD.
HELLO, YOU HAVE REACHED DR. EMSO RONGG'S PET HOTLINE. IF YOU'RE CALLING TO ASK IF YOU SHOULD GO AFTER YOUR CAT IF HE RUNS AWAY BECAUSE HE DOESN'T LIKE THE NEW PROGRAM, THE ANSWER IS NO! DO NOT GO AFTER YOUR CAT. THIS WILL ONLY LEAD TO MORE SPOILED BEHAVIOR!
SORRY, ODIE.
WHINE
MEANWHILE, GARFIELD WAS LOOKING FORWARD TO BEING MORE SPOILED THAN EVER.
LOOK, BUTTERSCOTCH! THIS IS YOUR NEW HOME!
WHOA! FACE IT, "BUTTERSCOTCH," YOU JUST HIT THE JACKPOT!

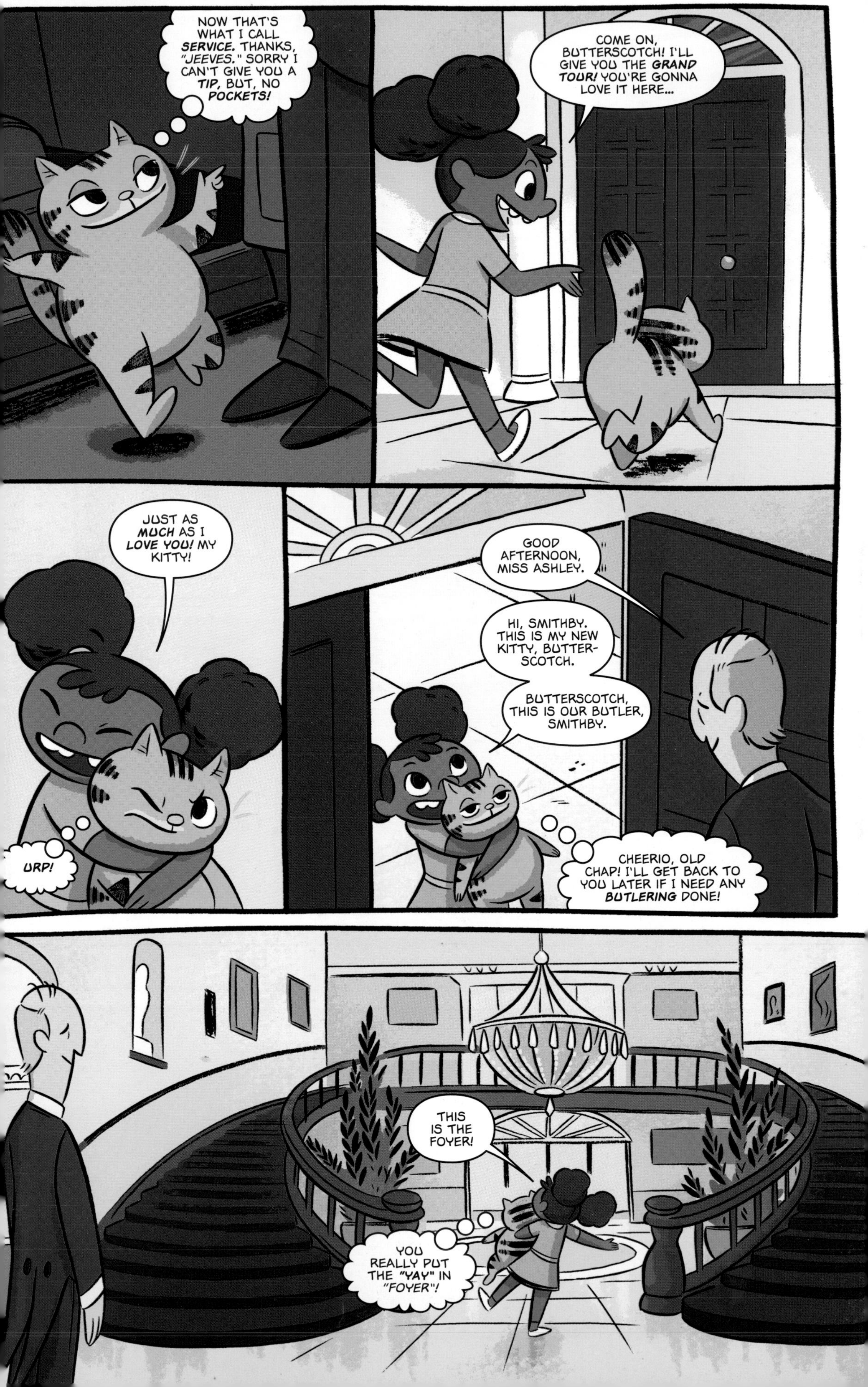
NOW THAT'S WHAT I CALL SERVICE. THANKS, "JEEVES." SORRY I CAN'T GIVE YOU A TIP, BUT, NO POCKETS!
COME ON, BUTTERSCOTCH! I'LL GIVE YOU THE GRAND TOUR! YOU'RE GONNA LOVE IT HERE...
JUST AS MUCH AS I LOVE YOU! MY KITTY!
URP!
GOOD AFTERNOON, MISS ASHLEY.
HI, SMITHBY. THIS IS MY NEW KITTY, BUTTER-SCOTCH.
BUTTERSCOTCH, THIS IS OUR BUTLER, SMITHBY.
CHEERIO, OLD CHAP! I'LL GET BACK TO YOU LATER IF I NEED ANY BUTLERING DONE!
THIS IS THE FOYER!
YOU REALLY PUT THE "YAY" IN "FOYER"!

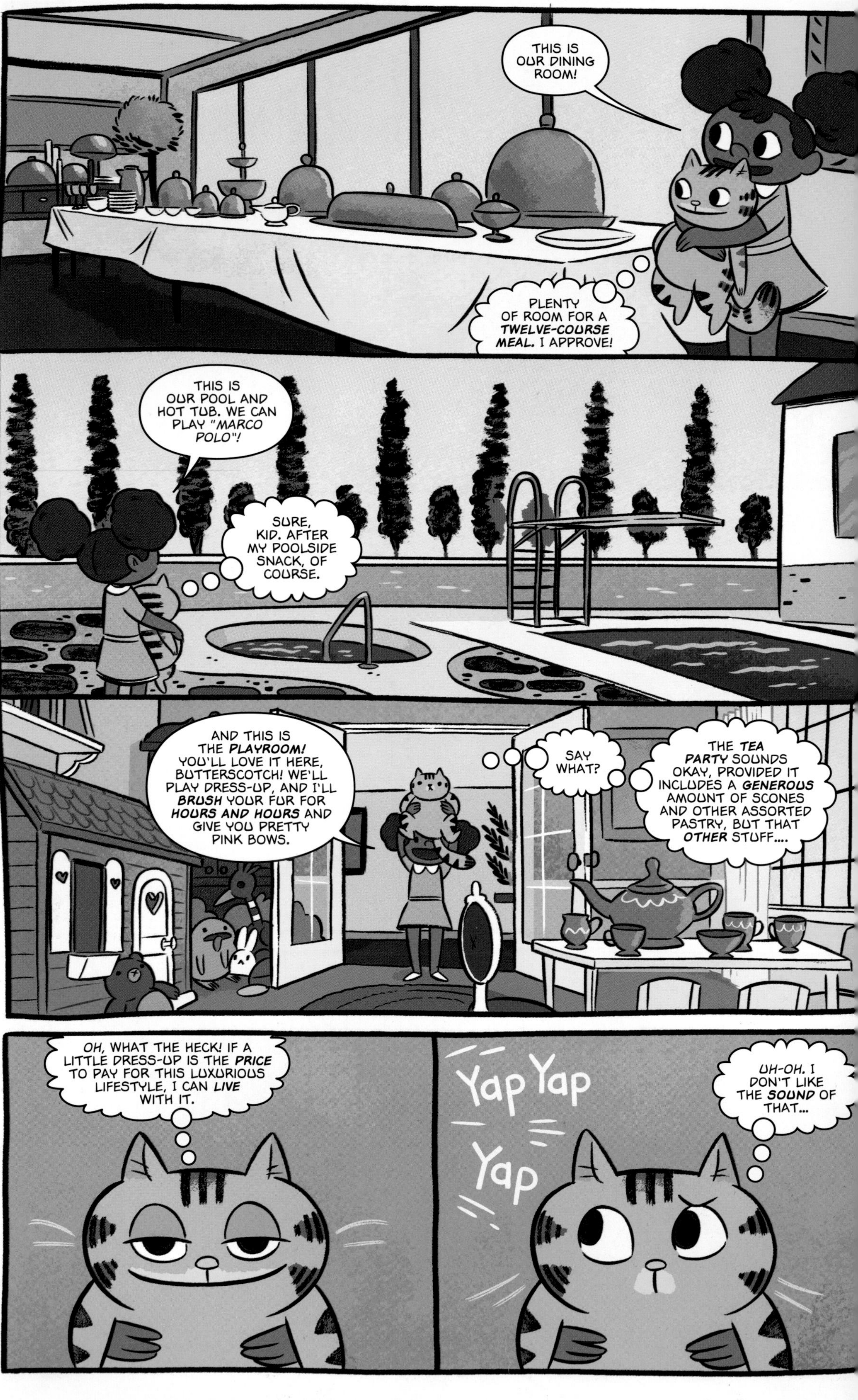
THIS IS OUR DINING ROOM!
PLENTY OF ROOM FOR A TWELVE-COURSE MEAL. I APPROVE!
THIS IS OUR POOL AND HOT TUB. WE CAN PLAY "MARCO POLO"!
SURE, KID. AFTER MY POOLSIDE SNACK, OF COURSE.
AND THIS IS THE PLAYROOM! YOU'LL LOVE IT HERE, BUTTERSCOTCH! WE'LL PLAY DRESS-UP, AND I'LL BRUSH YOUR FUR FOR HOURS AND HOURS AND GIVE YOU PRETTY PINK BOWS.
SAY WHAT?
THE TEA PARTY SOUNDS OKAY, PROVIDED IT INCLUDES A GENEROUS AMOUNT OF SCONES AND OTHER ASSORTED PASTRY, BUT THAT OTHER STUFF....
OH, WHAT THE HECK! IF A LITTLE DRESS-UP IS THE PRICE TO PAY FOR THIS LUXURIOUS LIFESTYLE, I CAN LIVE WITH IT.
Yap Yap
Yap
UH-OH. I DON'T LIKE THE SOUND OF THAT...

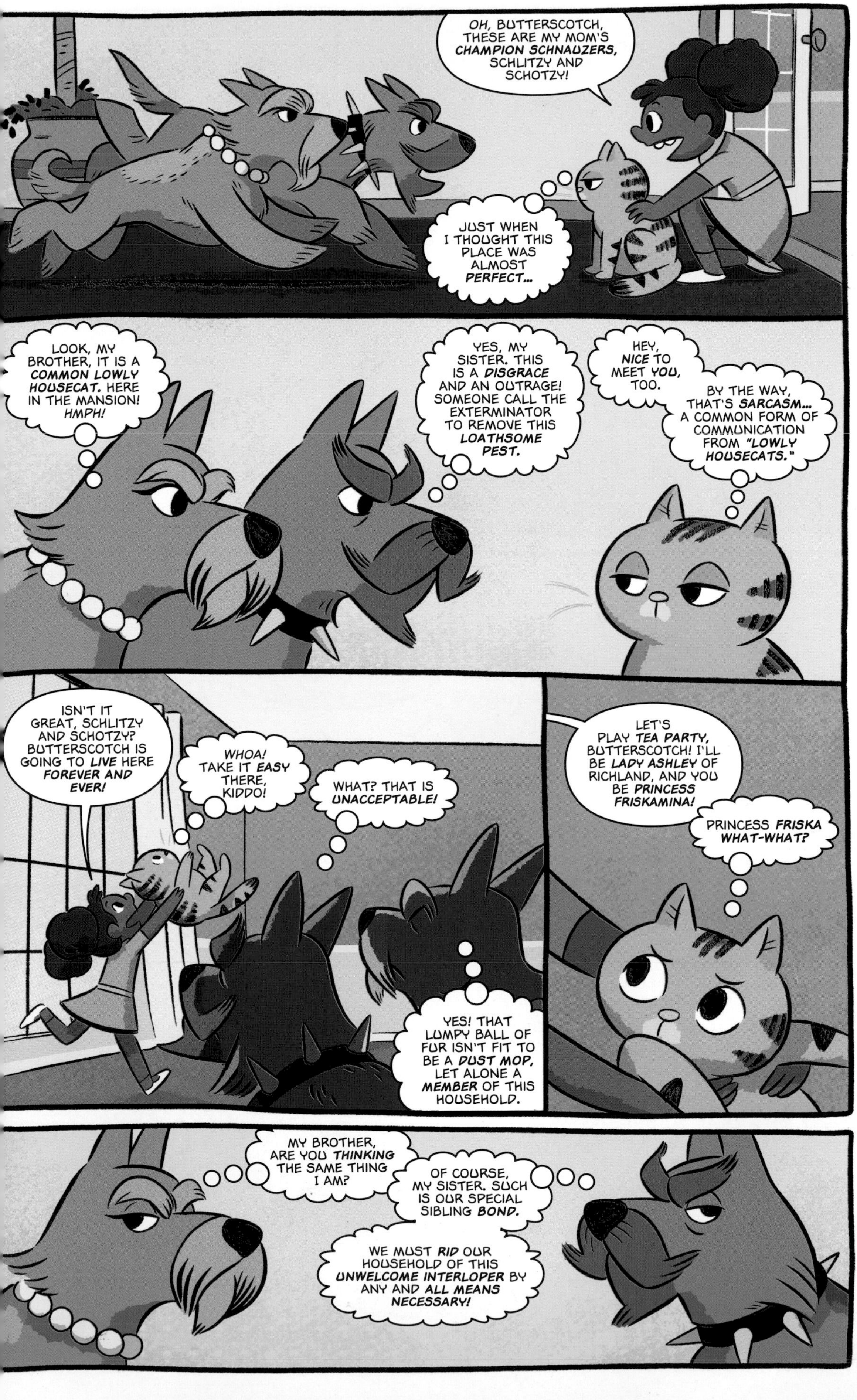

OH, BUTTERSCOTCH, THESE ARE MY MOM'S CHAMPION SCHNAUZERS, SCHLITZY AND SCHOTZY!
JUST WHEN I THOUGHT THIS PLACE WAS ALMOST PERFECT...
LOOK, MY BROTHER, IT IS A COMMON LOWLY HOUSECAT. HERE IN THE MANSION! HMPH!
YES, MY SISTER. THIS IS A DISGRACE AND AN OUTRAGE! SOMEONE CALL THE EXTERMINATOR TO REMOVE THIS LOATHSOME PEST.
HEY, NICE TO MEET YOU, TOO.
BY THE WAY, THAT'S SARCASM... A COMMON FORM OF COMMUNICATION FROM "LOWLY HOUSECATS."
ISN'T IT GREAT, SCHLITZY AND SCHOTZY? BUTTERSCOTCH IS GOING TO LIVE HERE FOREVER AND EVER!
WHOA! TAKE IT EASY THERE, KIDDO!
WHAT? THAT IS UNACCEPTABLE!
YES! THAT LUMPY BALL OF FUR ISN'T FIT TO BE A DUST MOP, LET ALONE A MEMBER OF THIS HOUSEHOLD.
LET'S PLAY TEA PARTY, BUTTERSCOTCH! I'LL BE LADY ASHLEY OF RICHLAND, AND YOU BE PRINCESS FRISKAMINA!
PRINCESS FRISKA WHAT-WHAT?
MY BROTHER, ARE YOU THINKING THE SAME THING I AM?
OF COURSE, MY SISTER. SUCH IS OUR SPECIAL SIBLING BOND.
WE MUST RID OUR HOUSEHOLD OF THIS UNWELCOME INTERLOPER BY ANY AND ALL MEANS NECESSARY!

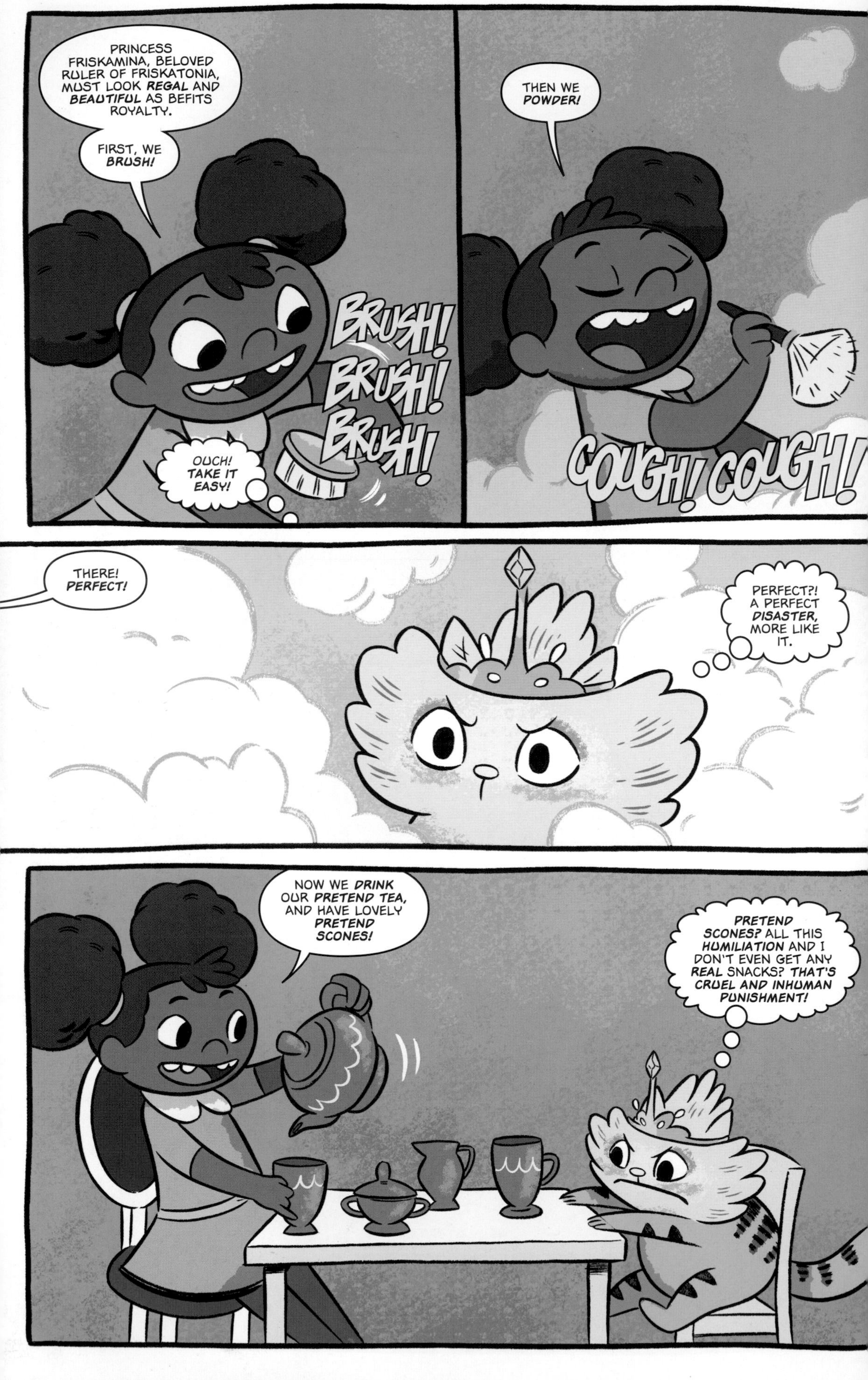

PRINCESS FRISKAMINA, BELOVED RULER OF FRISKATONIA, MUST LOOK **REGAL** AND **BEAUTIFUL** AS BEFITS ROYALTY.
FIRST, WE **BRUSH!**
BRUSH! BRUSH! BRUSH!
OUCH! ***TAKE IT EASY!***
THEN WE **POWDER!**
COUGH! COUGH!
THERE! **PERFECT!**
PERFECT?! A PERFECT **DISASTER,** MORE LIKE IT.
NOW WE **DRINK** OUR **PRETEND TEA,** AND HAVE LOVELY **PRETEND SCONES!**
PRETEND SCONES? ALL THIS **HUMILIATION** AND I DON'T EVEN GET ANY **REAL** SNACKS? **THAT'S CRUEL AND INHUMAN PUNISHMENT!**

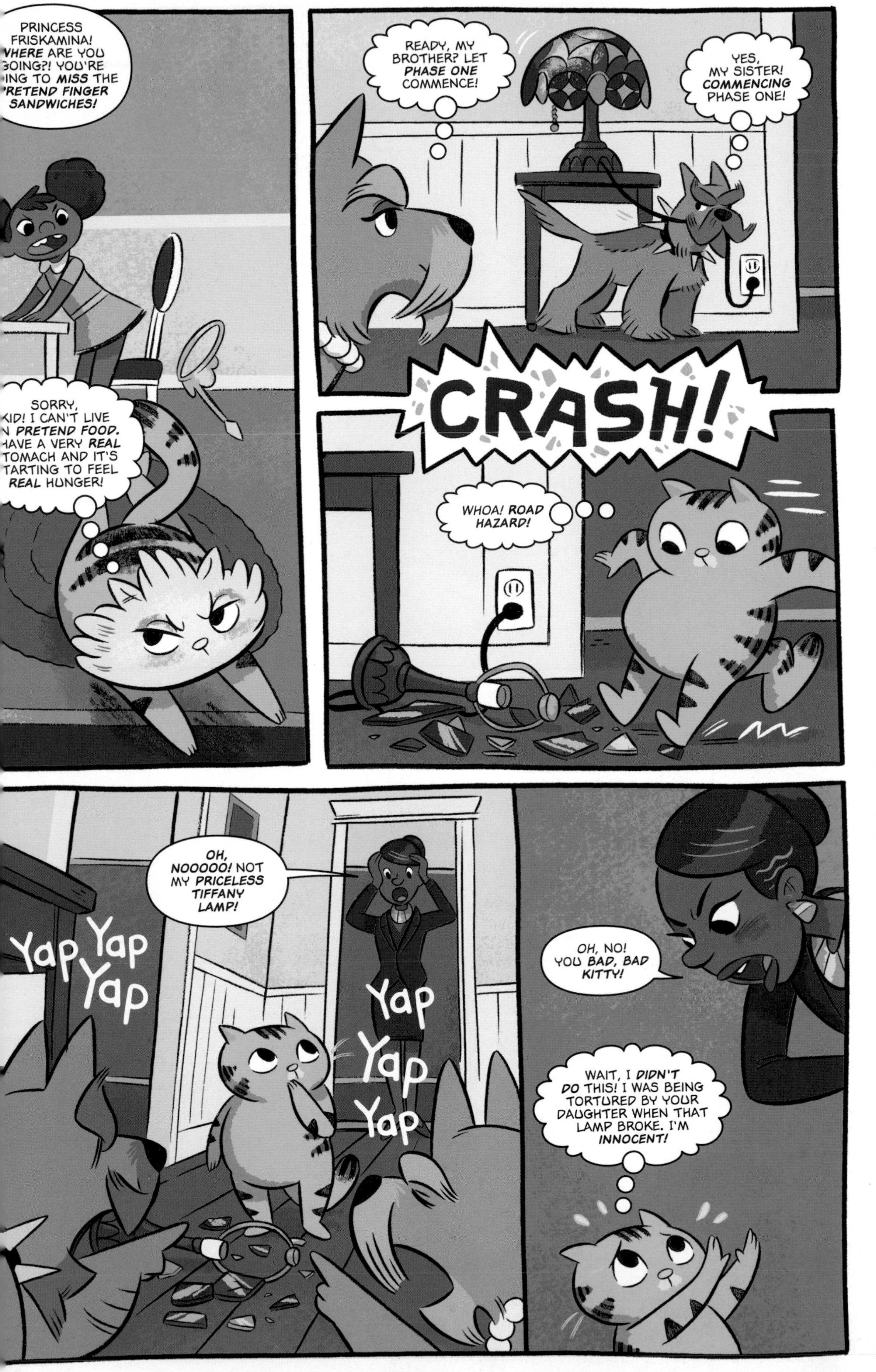
PRINCESS FRISKAMINA! WHERE ARE YOU GOING?! YOU'RE ING TO MISS THE RETEND FINGER SANDWICHES!
READY, MY BROTHER? LET PHASE ONE COMMENCE!
YES, MY SISTER! COMMENCING PHASE ONE!
SORRY, KID! I CAN'T LIVE N PRETEND FOOD. HAVE A VERY REAL TOMACH AND IT'S TARTING TO FEEL REAL HUNGER!
CRASH!
WHOA! ROAD HAZARD!
OH, NOOOOO! NOT MY PRICELESS TIFFANY LAMP!
Yap Yap Yap
Yap Yap Yap
OH, NO! YOU BAD, BAD KITTY!
WAIT, I DIDN'T DO THIS! I WAS BEING TORTURED BY YOUR DAUGHTER WHEN THAT LAMP BROKE. I'M INNOCENT!

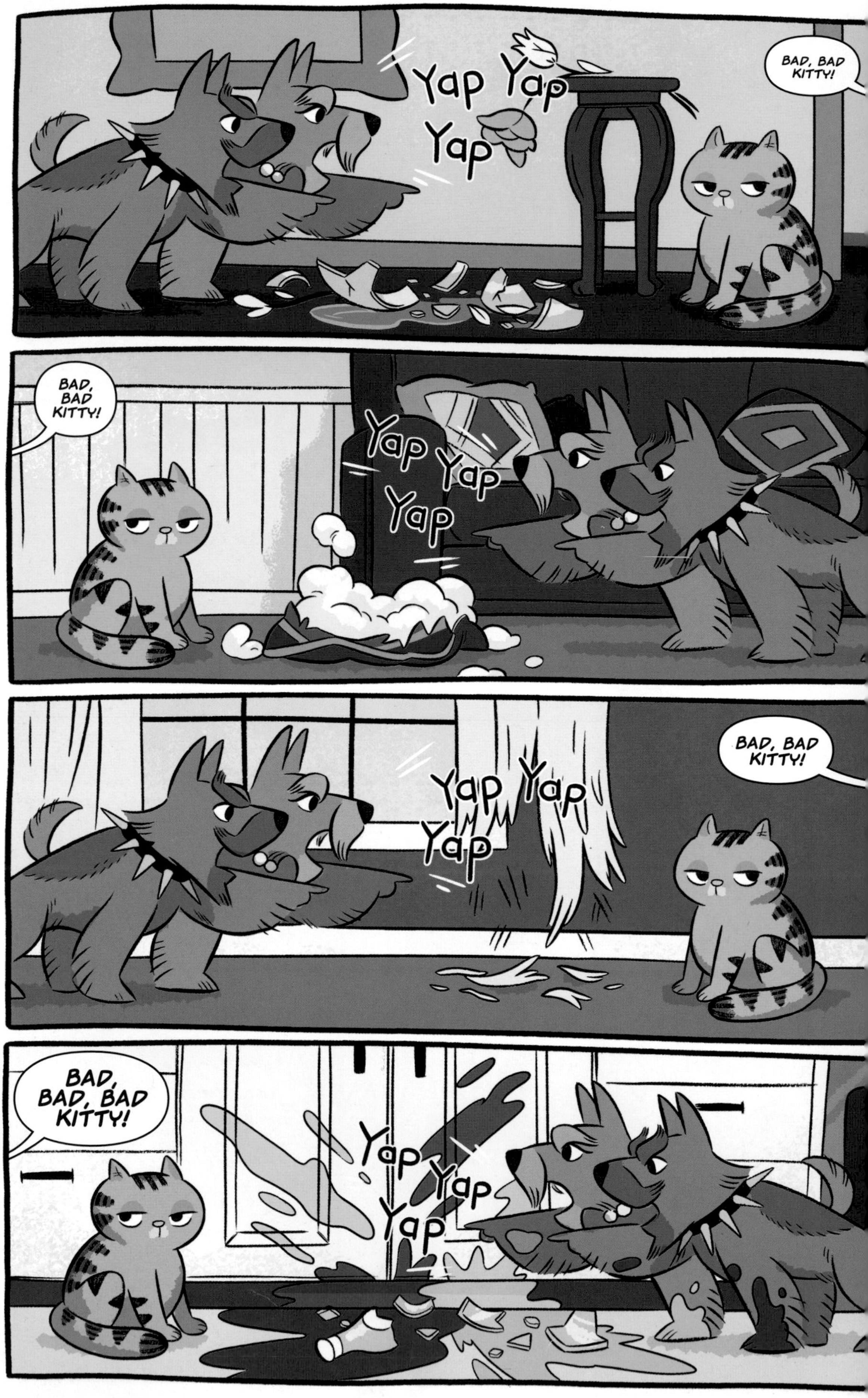
BAD, BAD KITTY!
Yap Yap Yap
BAD, BAD KITTY!
Yap Yap Yap
BAD, BAD KITTY!
Yap Yap Yap
BAD, BAD, BAD KITTY!
Yap Yap Yap

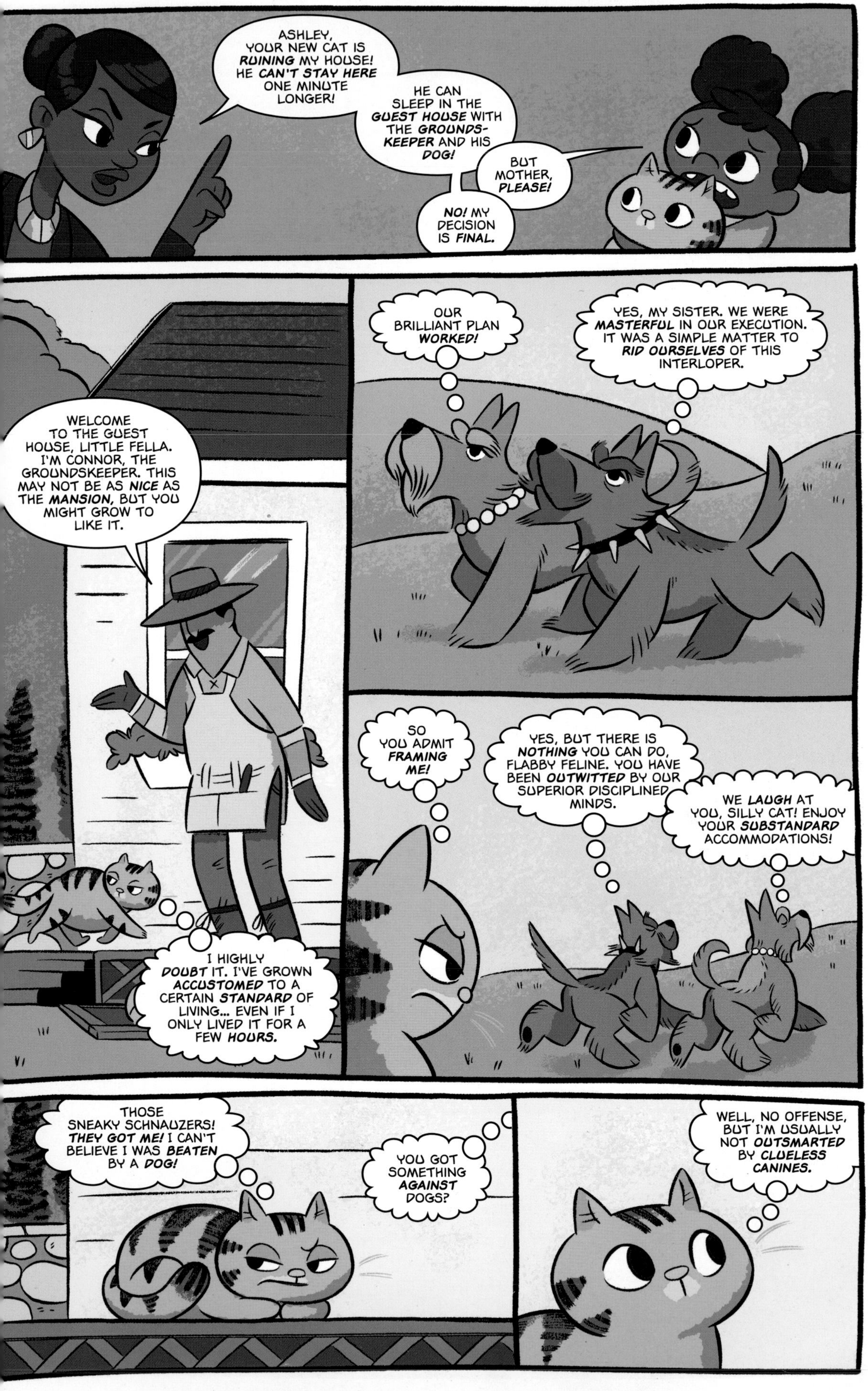
ASHLEY, YOUR NEW CAT IS RUINING MY HOUSE! HE CAN'T STAY HERE ONE MINUTE LONGER!
HE CAN SLEEP IN THE GUEST HOUSE WITH THE GROUNDS-KEEPER AND HIS DOG!
BUT MOTHER, PLEASE!
NO! MY DECISION IS FINAL.
WELCOME TO THE GUEST HOUSE, LITTLE FELLA. I'M CONNOR, THE GROUNDSKEEPER. THIS MAY NOT BE AS NICE AS THE MANSION, BUT YOU MIGHT GROW TO LIKE IT.
I HIGHLY DOUBT IT. I'VE GROWN ACCUSTOMED TO A CERTAIN STANDARD OF LIVING... EVEN IF I ONLY LIVED IT FOR A FEW HOURS.
OUR BRILLIANT PLAN WORKED!
YES, MY SISTER. WE WERE MASTERFUL IN OUR EXECUTION. IT WAS A SIMPLE MATTER TO RID OURSELVES OF THIS INTERLOPER.
SO YOU ADMIT FRAMING ME!
YES, BUT THERE IS NOTHING YOU CAN DO, FLABBY FELINE. YOU HAVE BEEN OUTWITTED BY OUR SUPERIOR DISCIPLINED MINDS.
WE LAUGH AT YOU, SILLY CAT! ENJOY YOUR SUBSTANDARD ACCOMMODATIONS!
THOSE SNEAKY SCHNAUZERS! THEY GOT ME! I CAN'T BELIEVE I WAS BEATEN BY A DOG!
YOU GOT SOMETHING AGAINST DOGS?
WELL, NO OFFENSE, BUT I'M USUALLY NOT OUTSMARTED BY CLUELESS CANINES.

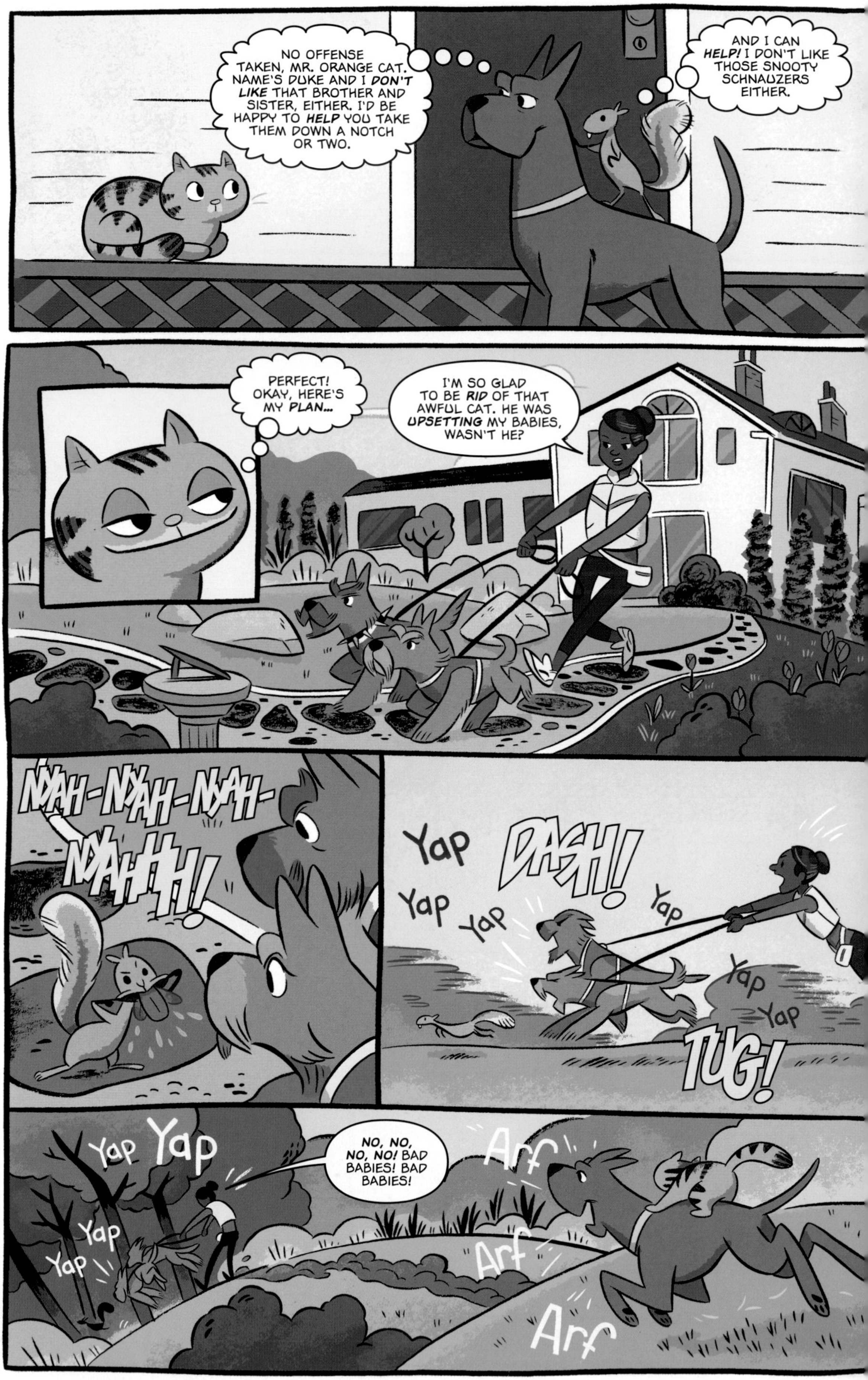
NO OFFENSE TAKEN, MR. ORANGE CAT. NAME'S DUKE AND I DON'T LIKE THAT BROTHER AND SISTER, EITHER. I'D BE HAPPY TO HELP YOU TAKE THEM DOWN A NOTCH OR TWO.
AND I CAN HELP! I DON'T LIKE THOSE SNOOTY SCHNAUZERS EITHER.
PERFECT! OKAY, HERE'S MY PLAN...
I'M SO GLAD TO BE RID OF THAT AWFUL CAT. HE WAS UPSETTING MY BABIES, WASN'T HE?
NYAH-NYAH-NYAH-NYAHHH!
Yap
DASH!
Yap
Yap
Yap
Yap
Yap
TUG!
Yap
Yap
NO, NO, NO, NO! BAD BABIES! BAD BABIES!
Arf
Yap
Yap
Arf
Arf

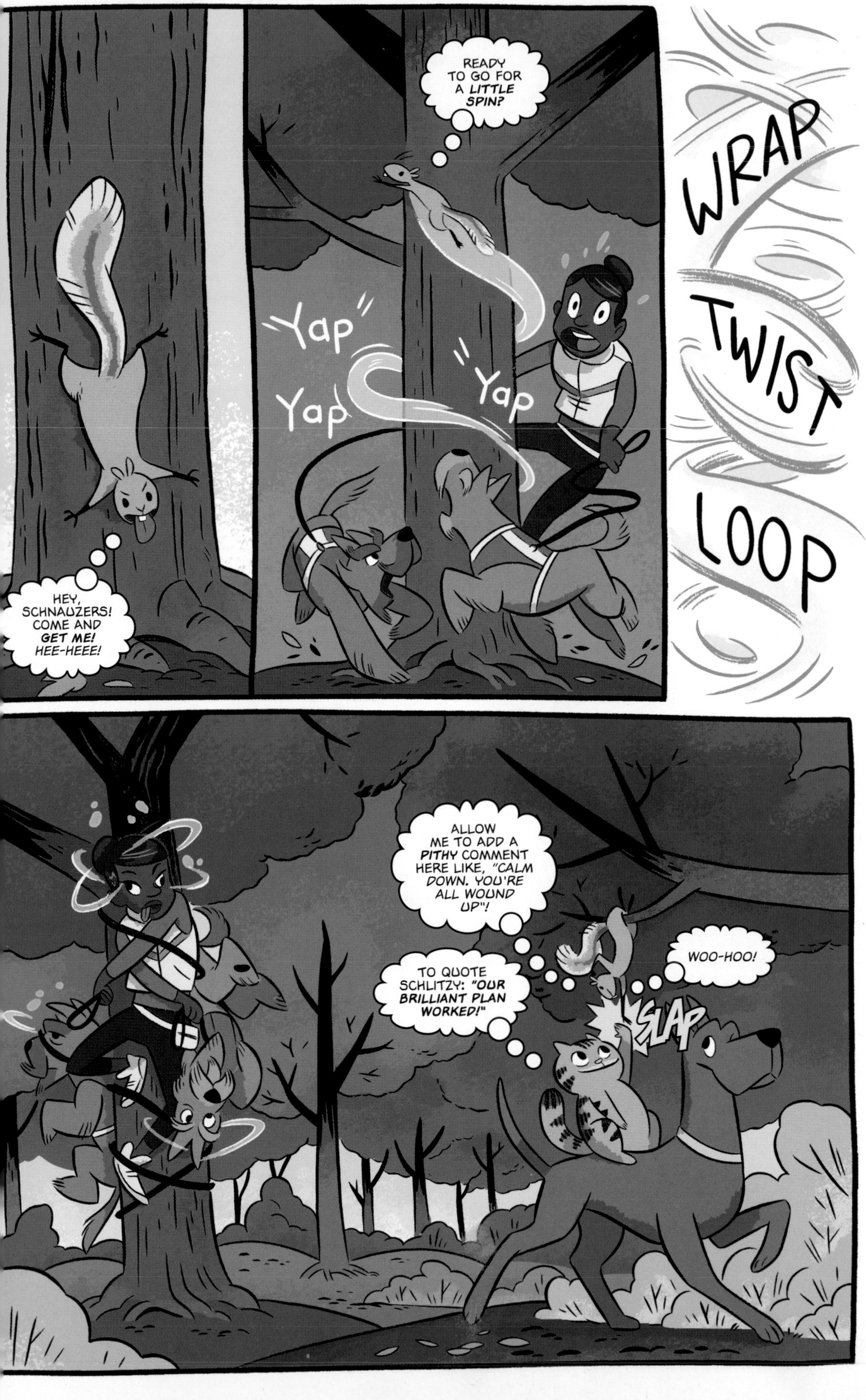

HEY, SCHNAUZERS! COME AND GET ME! HEE-HEEE!
READY TO GO FOR A LITTLE SPIN?
Yap
Yap
Yap
WRAP
TWIST
LOOP
ALLOW ME TO ADD A PITHY COMMENT HERE LIKE, "CALM DOWN. YOU'RE ALL WOUND UP"!
TO QUOTE SCHLITZY: "OUR BRILLIANT PLAN WORKED!"
WOO-HOO!
SLAP

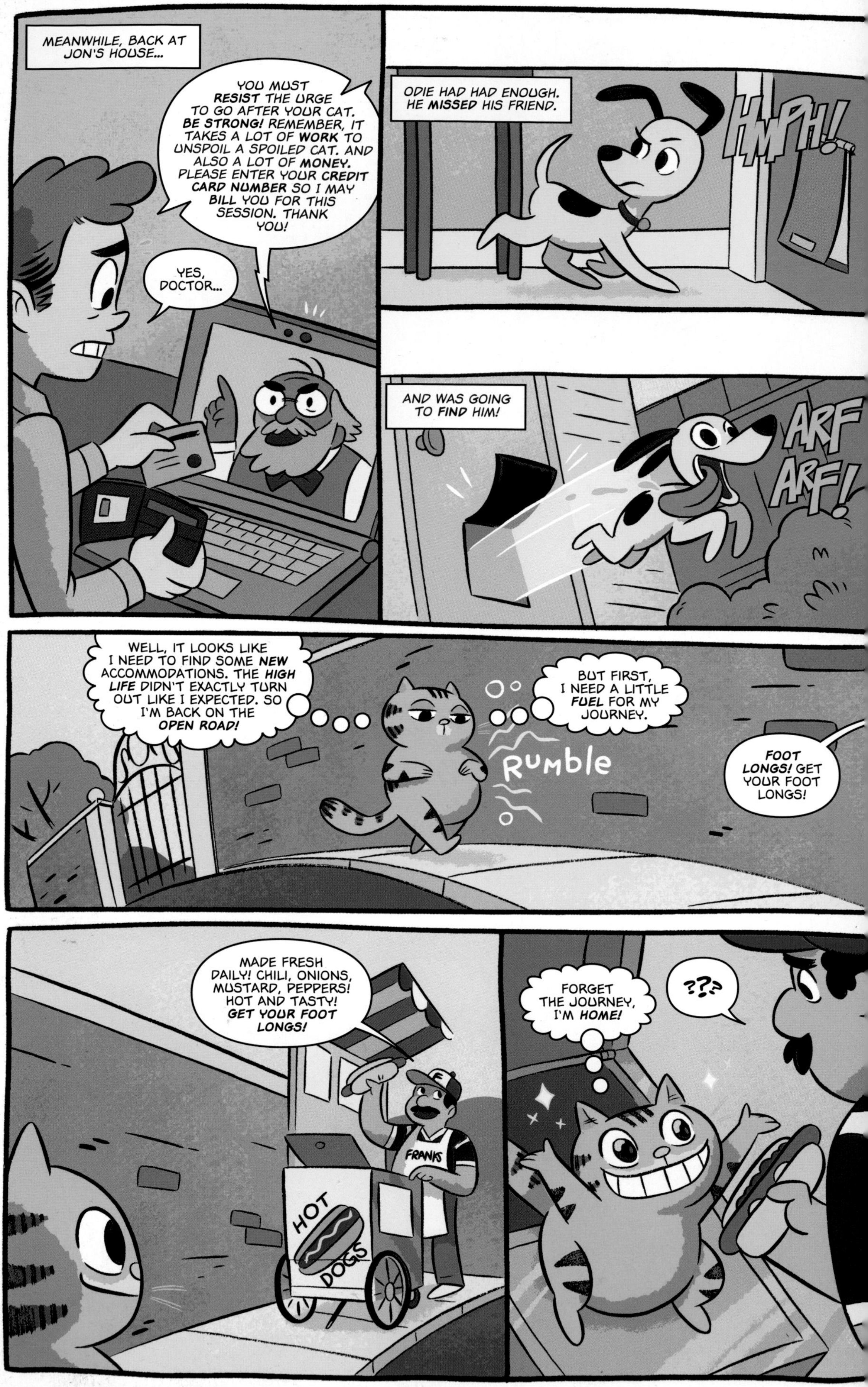
MEANWHILE, BACK AT JON'S HOUSE...
YOU MUST RESIST THE URGE TO GO AFTER YOUR CAT. BE STRONG! REMEMBER, IT TAKES A LOT OF WORK TO UNSPOIL A SPOILED CAT. AND ALSO A LOT OF MONEY. PLEASE ENTER YOUR CREDIT CARD NUMBER SO I MAY BILL YOU FOR THIS SESSION. THANK YOU!
YES, DOCTOR...
ODIE HAD HAD ENOUGH. HE MISSED HIS FRIEND.
HMPH!
AND WAS GOING TO FIND HIM!
ARF ARF!
WELL, IT LOOKS LIKE I NEED TO FIND SOME NEW ACCOMMODATIONS. THE HIGH LIFE DIDN'T EXACTLY TURN OUT LIKE I EXPECTED. SO I'M BACK ON THE OPEN ROAD!
BUT FIRST, I NEED A LITTLE FUEL FOR MY JOURNEY.
RUMBLE
FOOT LONGS! GET YOUR FOOT LONGS!
MADE FRESH DAILY! CHILI, ONIONS, MUSTARD, PEPPERS! HOT AND TASTY! GET YOUR FOOT LONGS!
FRANKS
HOT DOGS
FORGET THE JOURNEY, I'M HOME!
???

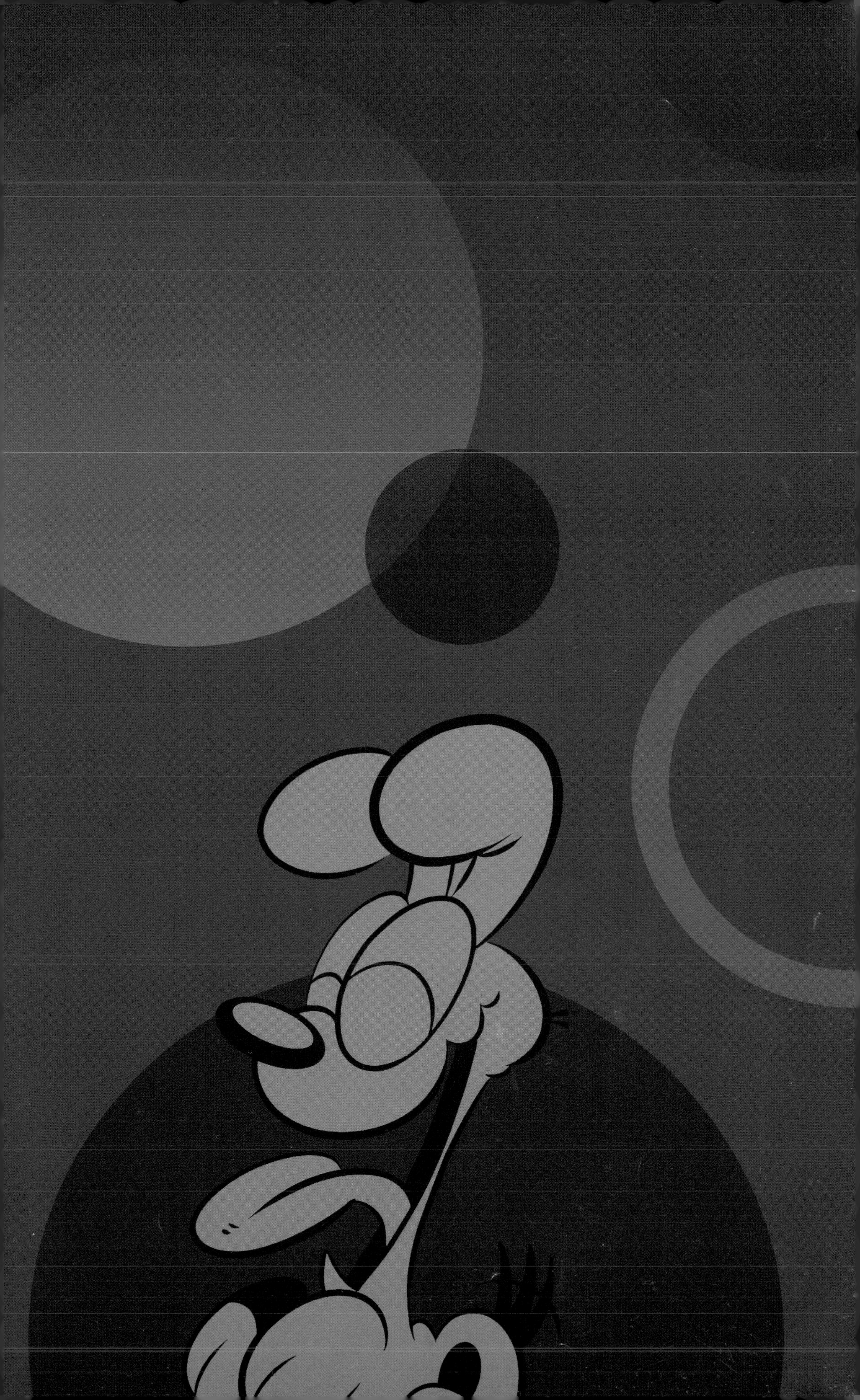

CHAPTER THREE

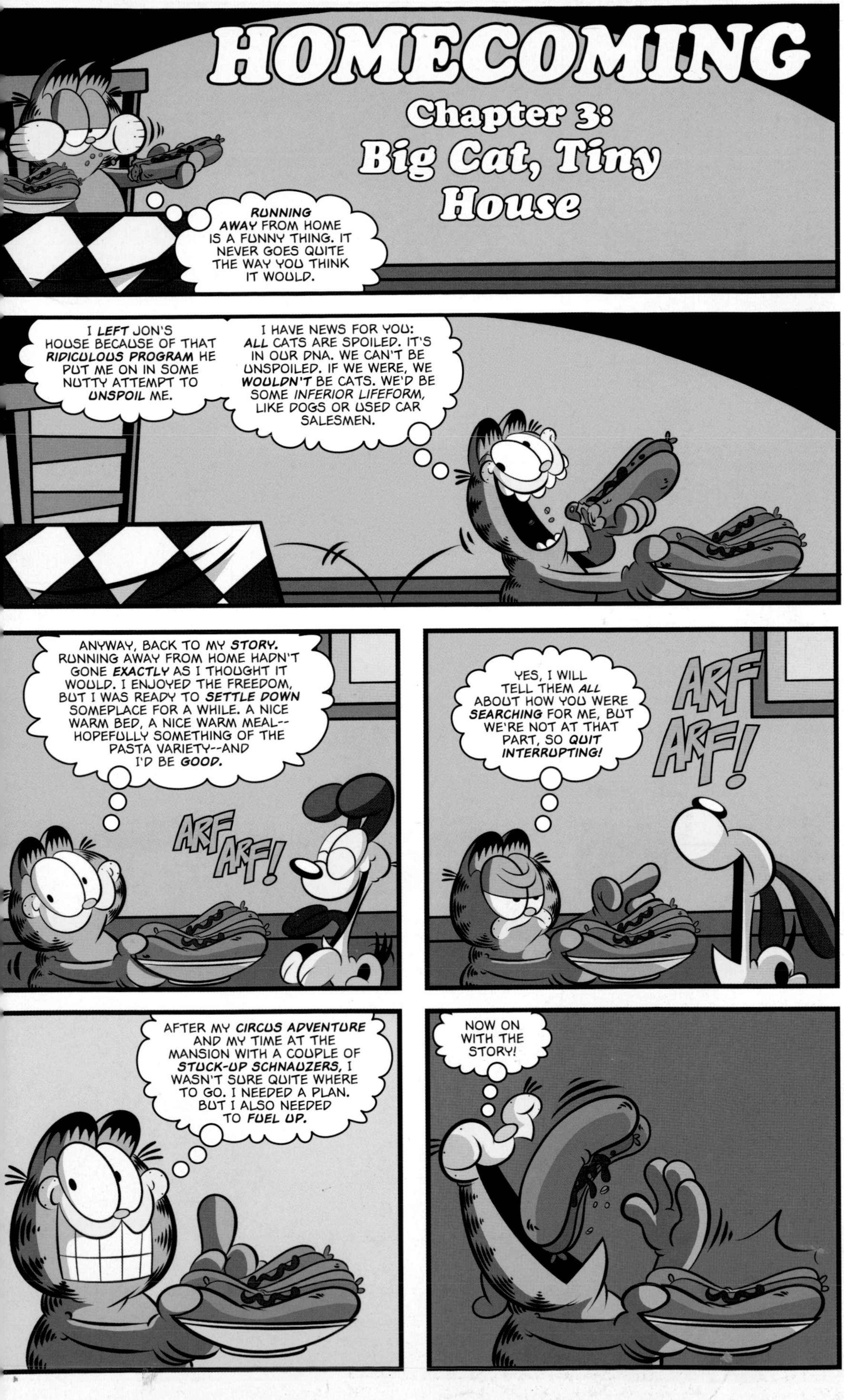
HOMECOMING
Chapter 3: Big Cat, Tiny House
RUNNING AWAY FROM HOME IS A FUNNY THING. IT NEVER GOES QUITE THE WAY YOU THINK IT WOULD.
I LEFT JON'S HOUSE BECAUSE OF THAT RIDICULOUS PROGRAM HE PUT ME ON IN SOME NUTTY ATTEMPT TO UNSPOIL ME.
I HAVE NEWS FOR YOU: ALL CATS ARE SPOILED. IT'S IN OUR DNA. WE CAN'T BE UNSPOILED. IF WE WERE, WE WOULDN'T BE CATS. WE'D BE SOME INFERIOR LIFEFORM, LIKE DOGS OR USED CAR SALESMEN.
ANYWAY, BACK TO MY STORY. RUNNING AWAY FROM HOME HADN'T GONE EXACTLY AS I THOUGHT IT WOULD. I ENJOYED THE FREEDOM, BUT I WAS READY TO SETTLE DOWN SOMEPLACE FOR A WHILE. A NICE WARM BED, A NICE WARM MEAL--HOPEFULLY SOMETHING OF THE PASTA VARIETY--AND I'D BE GOOD.
ARF ARF!
YES, I WILL TELL THEM ALL ABOUT HOW YOU WERE SEARCHING FOR ME, BUT WE'RE NOT AT THAT PART, SO QUIT INTERRUPTING!
ARF ARF!
AFTER MY CIRCUS ADVENTURE AND MY TIME AT THE MANSION WITH A COUPLE OF STUCK-UP SCHNAUZERS, I WASN'T SURE QUITE WHERE TO GO. I NEEDED A PLAN. BUT I ALSO NEEDED TO FUEL UP.
NOW ON WITH THE STORY!

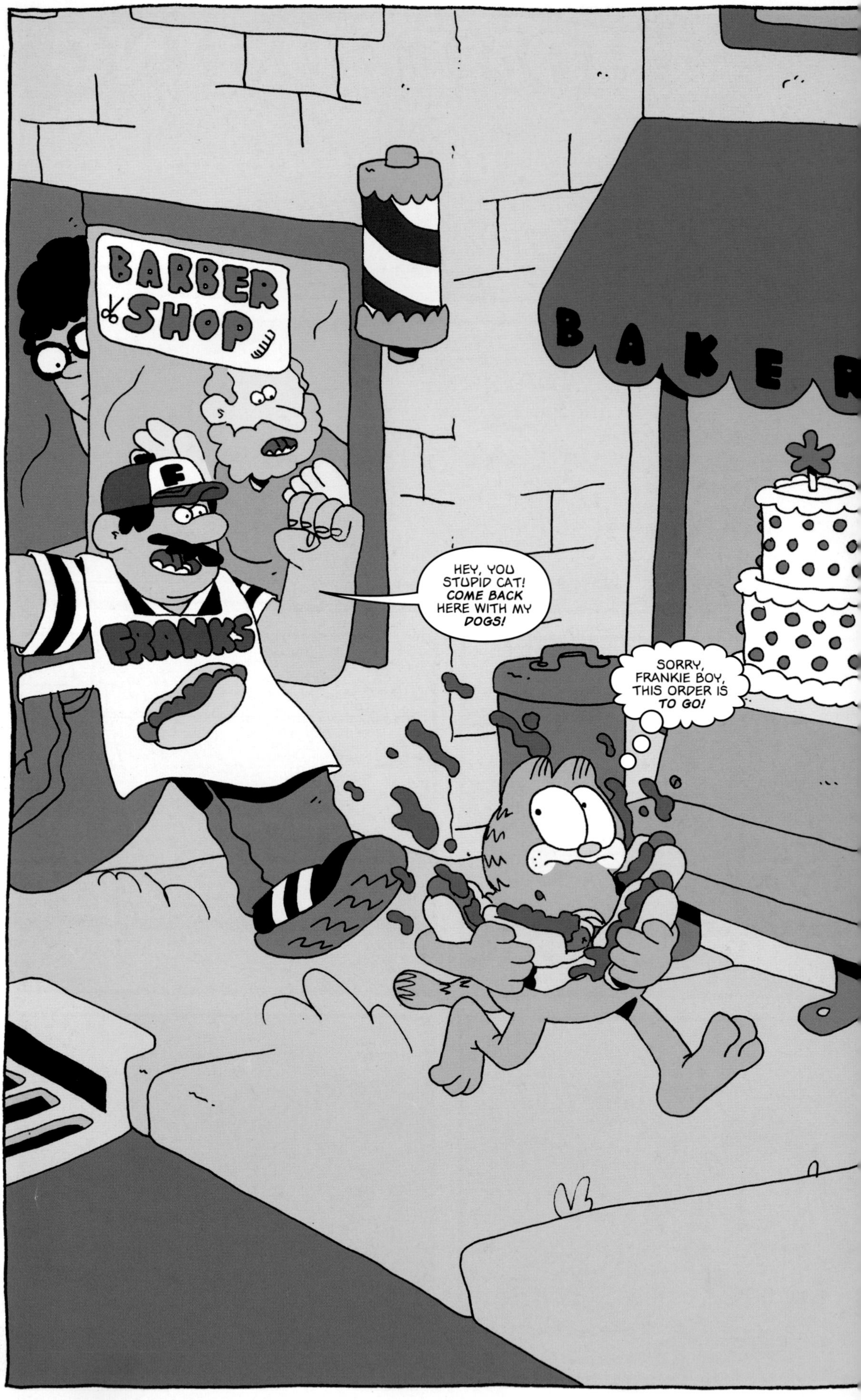
BARBER SHOP
BAKER
FRANKS
HEY, YOU STUPID CAT! COME BACK HERE WITH MY DOGS!
SORRY, FRANKIE BOY, THIS ORDER IS TO GO!

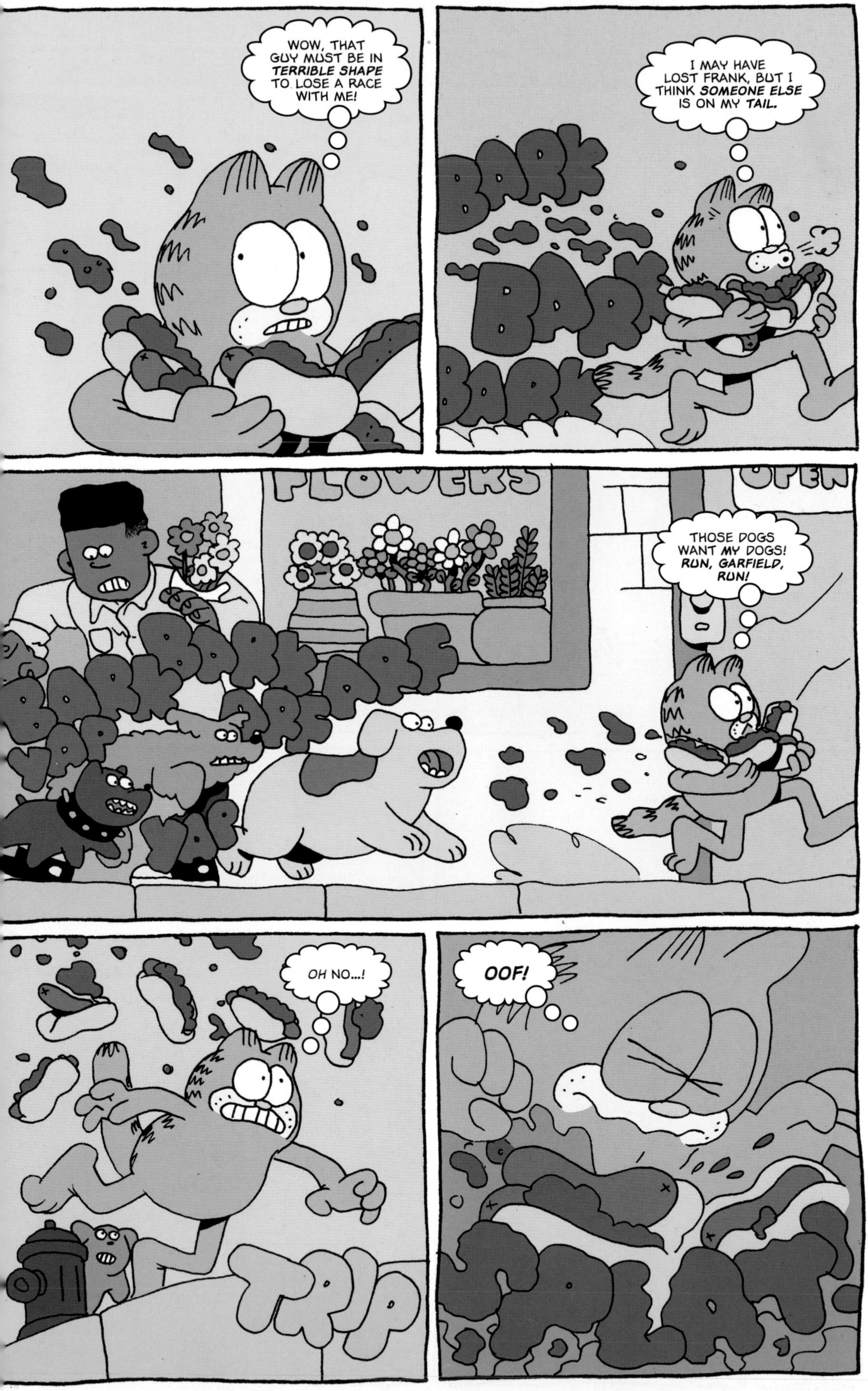

WOW, THAT GUY MUST BE IN *TERRIBLE SHAPE* TO LOSE A RACE WITH ME!
I MAY HAVE LOST FRANK, BUT I THINK *SOMEONE ELSE* IS ON MY *TAIL.*
BARK
BARK
BARK
FLOWERS
OPEN
BARK
BARK
ARF
ARF
YAP
YAP
THOSE DOGS WANT *MY DOGS!* *RUN, GARFIELD, RUN!*
OH NO...!
TRIP
OOF!
SPLAT

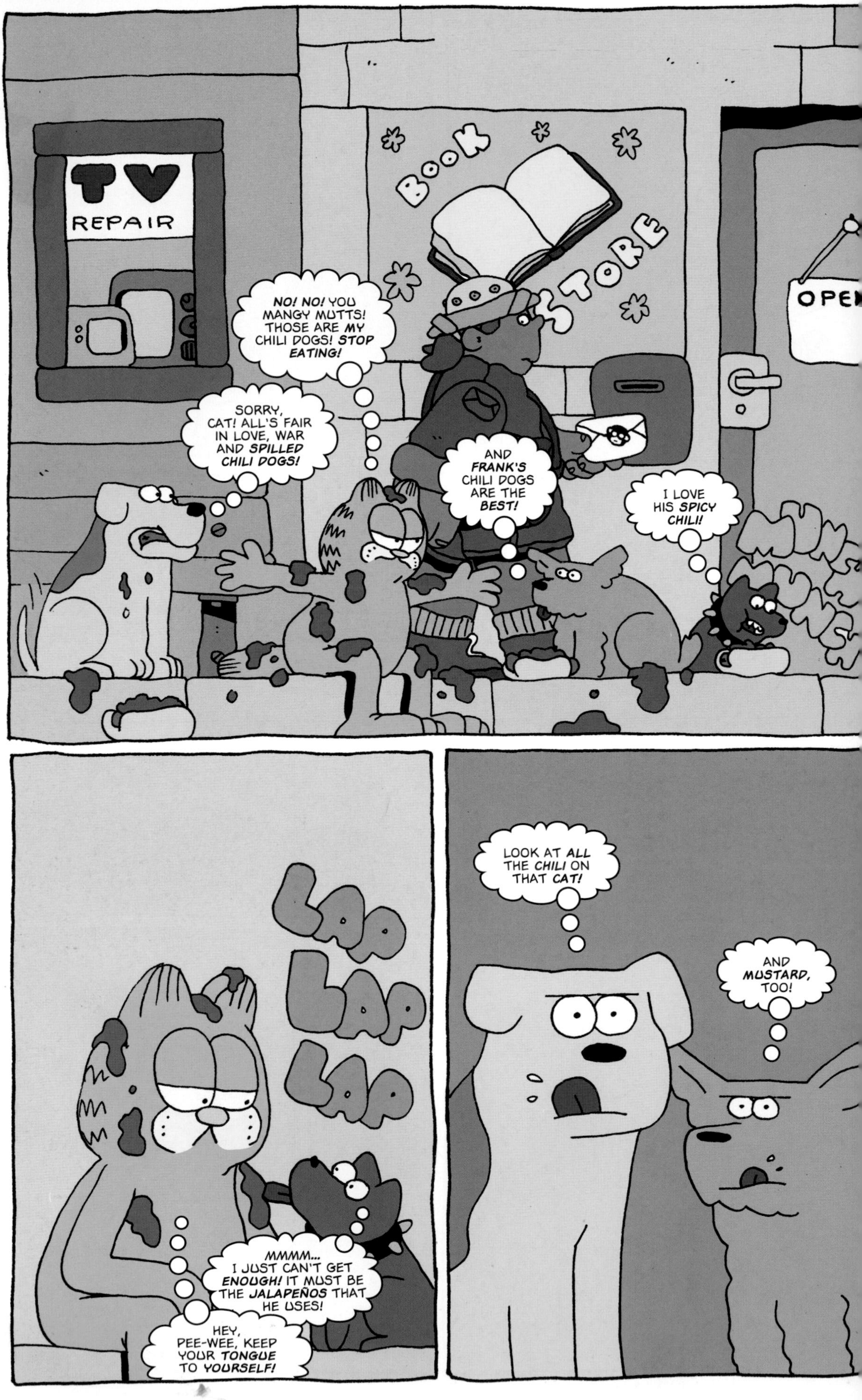
TV REPAIR
BOOK STORE
NO! NO! YOU MANGY MUTTS! THOSE ARE MY CHILI DOGS! STOP EATING!
SORRY, CAT! ALL'S FAIR IN LOVE, WAR AND SPILLED CHILI DOGS!
AND FRANK'S CHILI DOGS ARE THE BEST!
I LOVE HIS SPICY CHILI!
LAP LAP LAP
MMMM... I JUST CAN'T GET ENOUGH! IT MUST BE THE JALAPEÑOS THAT HE USES!
HEY, PEE-WEE, KEEP YOUR TONGUE TO YOURSELF!
LOOK AT ALL THE CHILI ON THAT CAT!
AND MUSTARD, TOO!

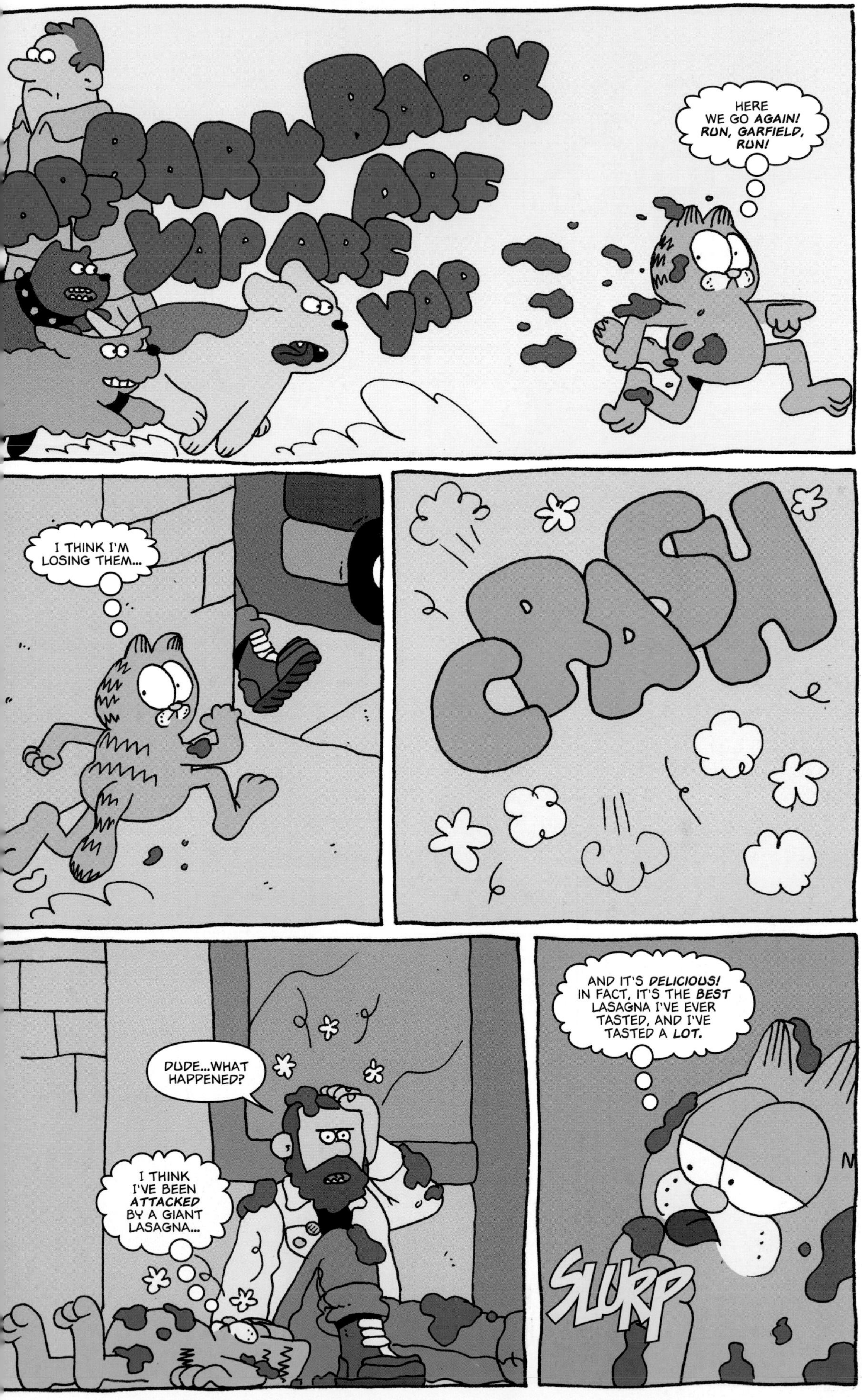

BARK
BARK
ARF
ARF
YAP
ARF
YAP
HERE WE GO AGAIN! RUN, GARFIELD, RUN!
I THINK I'M LOSING THEM...
CRASH
DUDE...WHAT HAPPENED?
I THINK I'VE BEEN ATTACKED BY A GIANT LASAGNA...
AND IT'S DELICIOUS! IN FACT, IT'S THE BEST LASAGNA I'VE EVER TASTED, AND I'VE TASTED A LOT.
SLURP

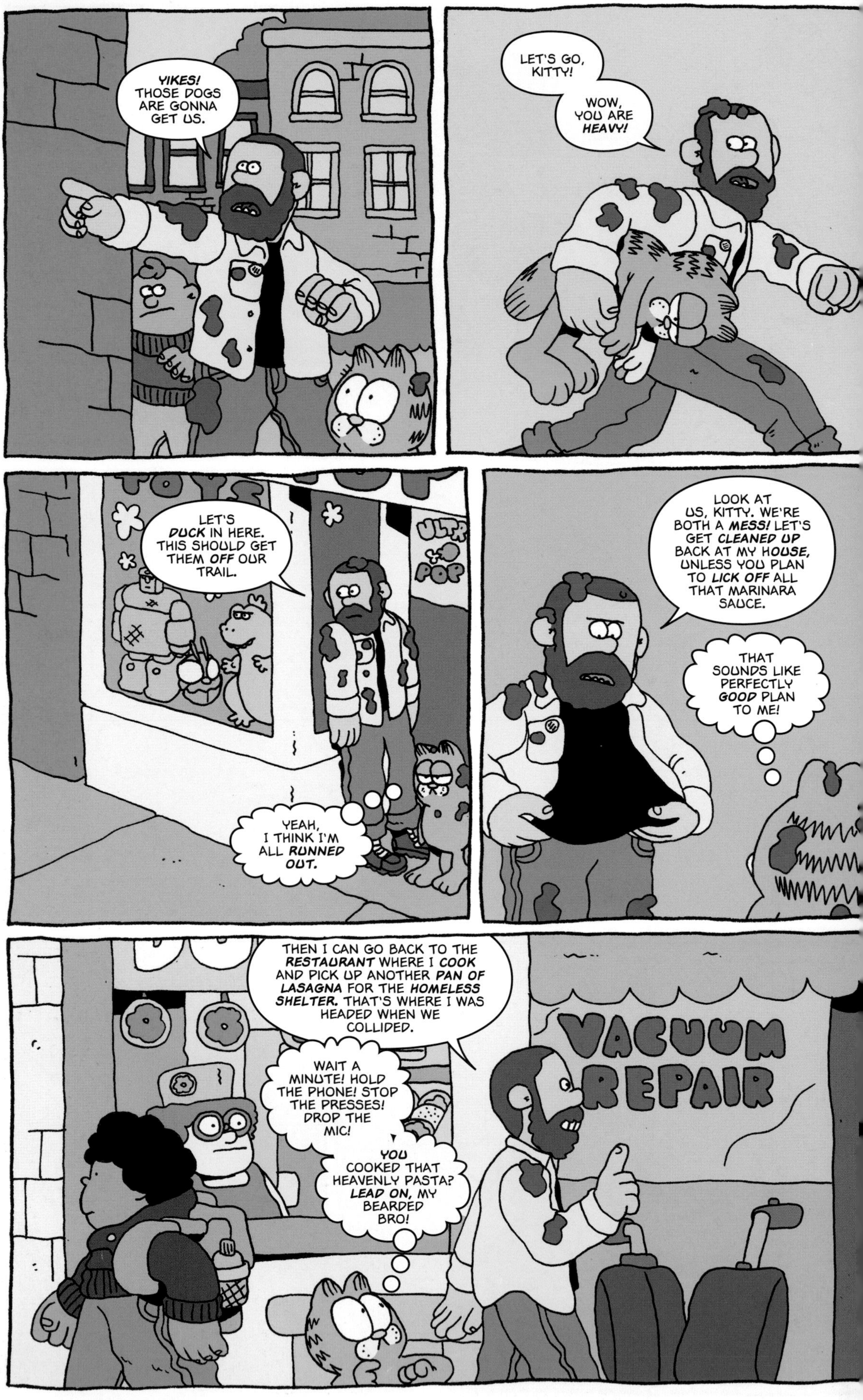
YIKES! THOSE DOGS ARE GONNA GET US.
LET'S GO, KITTY!
WOW, YOU ARE HEAVY!
LET'S DUCK IN HERE. THIS SHOULD GET THEM OFF OUR TRAIL.
YEAH, I THINK I'M ALL RUNNED OUT.
LOOK AT US, KITTY. WE'RE BOTH A MESS! LET'S GET CLEANED UP BACK AT MY HOUSE, UNLESS YOU PLAN TO LICK OFF ALL THAT MARINARA SAUCE.
THAT SOUNDS LIKE PERFECTLY GOOD PLAN TO ME!
THEN I CAN GO BACK TO THE RESTAURANT WHERE I COOK AND PICK UP ANOTHER PAN OF LASAGNA FOR THE HOMELESS SHELTER. THAT'S WHERE I WAS HEADED WHEN WE COLLIDED.
WAIT A MINUTE! HOLD THE PHONE! STOP THE PRESSES! DROP THE MIC!
YOU COOKED THAT HEAVENLY PASTA? LEAD ON, MY BEARDED BRO!
VACUUM REPAIR
ULTRA POP

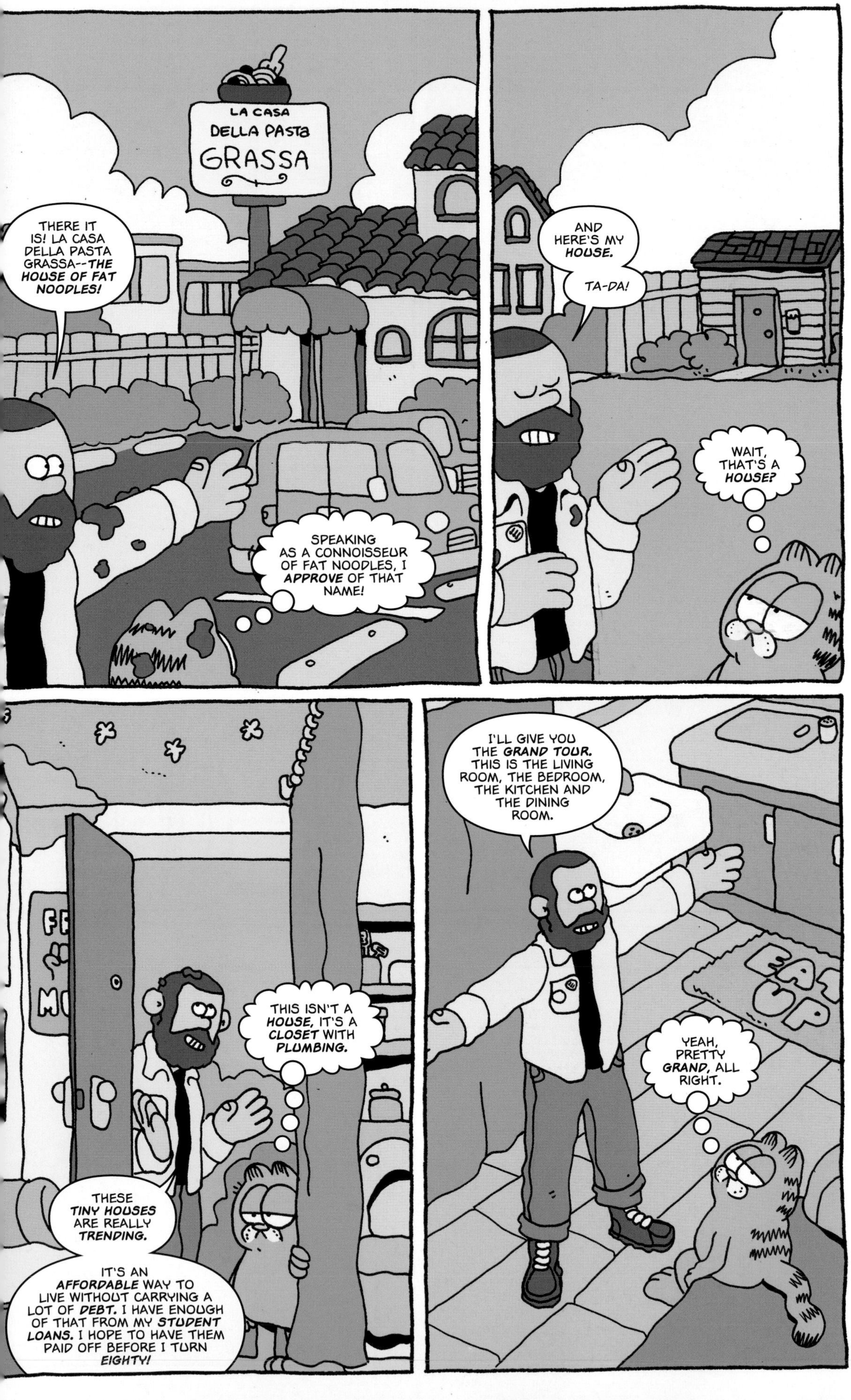
LA CASA DELLA PASTA GRASSA
THERE IT IS! LA CASA DELLA PASTA GRASSA--THE HOUSE OF FAT NOODLES!
SPEAKING AS A CONNOISSEUR OF FAT NOODLES, I APPROVE OF THAT NAME!
AND HERE'S MY HOUSE.
TA-DA!
WAIT, THAT'S A HOUSE?
THIS ISN'T A HOUSE, IT'S A CLOSET WITH PLUMBING.
THESE TINY HOUSES ARE REALLY TRENDING.
IT'S AN AFFORDABLE WAY TO LIVE WITHOUT CARRYING A LOT OF DEBT. I HAVE ENOUGH OF THAT FROM MY STUDENT LOANS. I HOPE TO HAVE THEM PAID OFF BEFORE I TURN EIGHTY!
I'LL GIVE YOU THE GRAND TOUR. THIS IS THE LIVING ROOM, THE BEDROOM, THE KITCHEN AND THE DINING ROOM.
EAT UP
YEAH, PRETTY GRAND, ALL RIGHT.

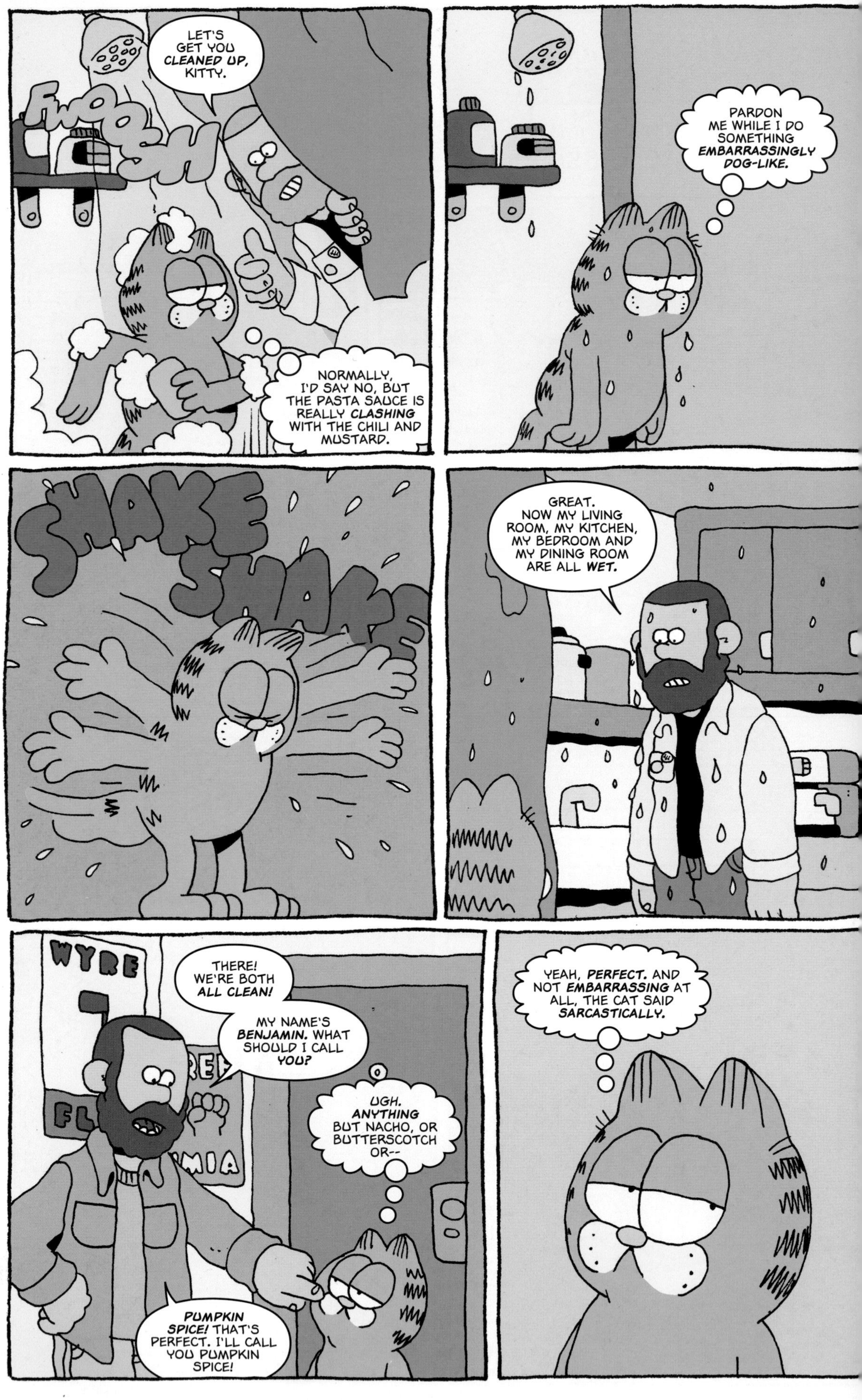
LET'S GET YOU CLEANED UP, KITTY.
FWOOSH
NORMALLY, I'D SAY NO, BUT THE PASTA SAUCE IS REALLY CLASHING WITH THE CHILI AND MUSTARD.
PARDON ME WHILE I DO SOMETHING EMBARRASSINGLY DOG-LIKE.
SHAKE SHAKE
GREAT. NOW MY LIVING ROOM, MY KITCHEN, MY BEDROOM AND MY DINING ROOM ARE ALL WET.
WYRE
THERE! WE'RE BOTH ALL CLEAN!
MY NAME'S BENJAMIN. WHAT SHOULD I CALL YOU?
UGH. ANYTHING BUT NACHO, OR BUTTERSCOTCH OR--
PUMPKIN SPICE! THAT'S PERFECT. I'LL CALL YOU PUMPKIN SPICE!
YEAH, PERFECT. AND NOT EMBARRASSING AT ALL, THE CAT SAID SARCASTICALLY.

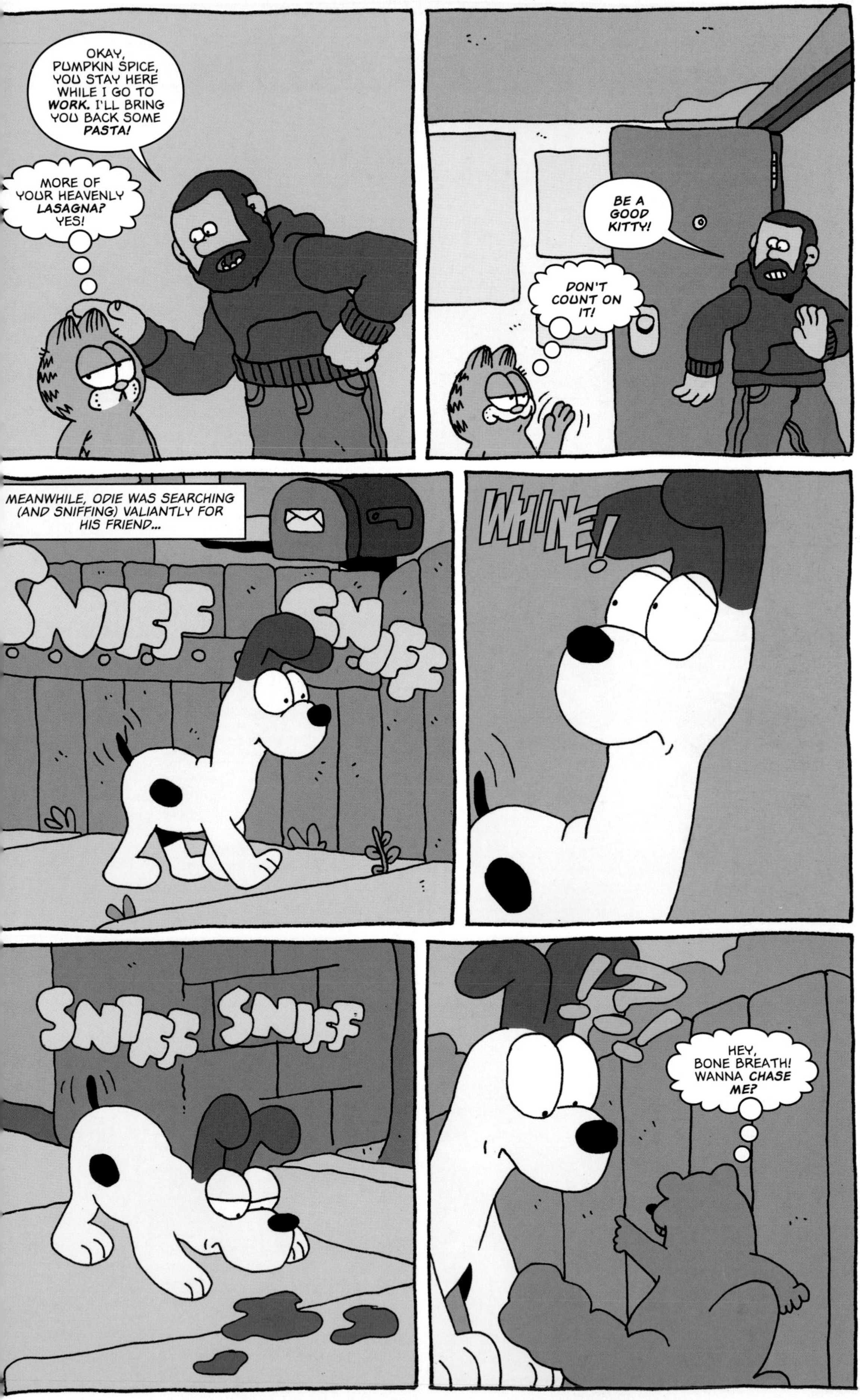
OKAY, PUMPKIN SPICE, YOU STAY HERE WHILE I GO TO WORK. I'LL BRING YOU BACK SOME PASTA!
MORE OF YOUR HEAVENLY LASAGNA? YES!
BE A GOOD KITTY!
DON'T COUNT ON IT!
MEANWHILE, ODIE WAS SEARCHING (AND SNIFFING) VALIANTLY FOR HIS FRIEND...
SNIFF SNIFF
WHINE!
SNIFF SNIFF
HEY, BONE BREATH! WANNA CHASE ME?

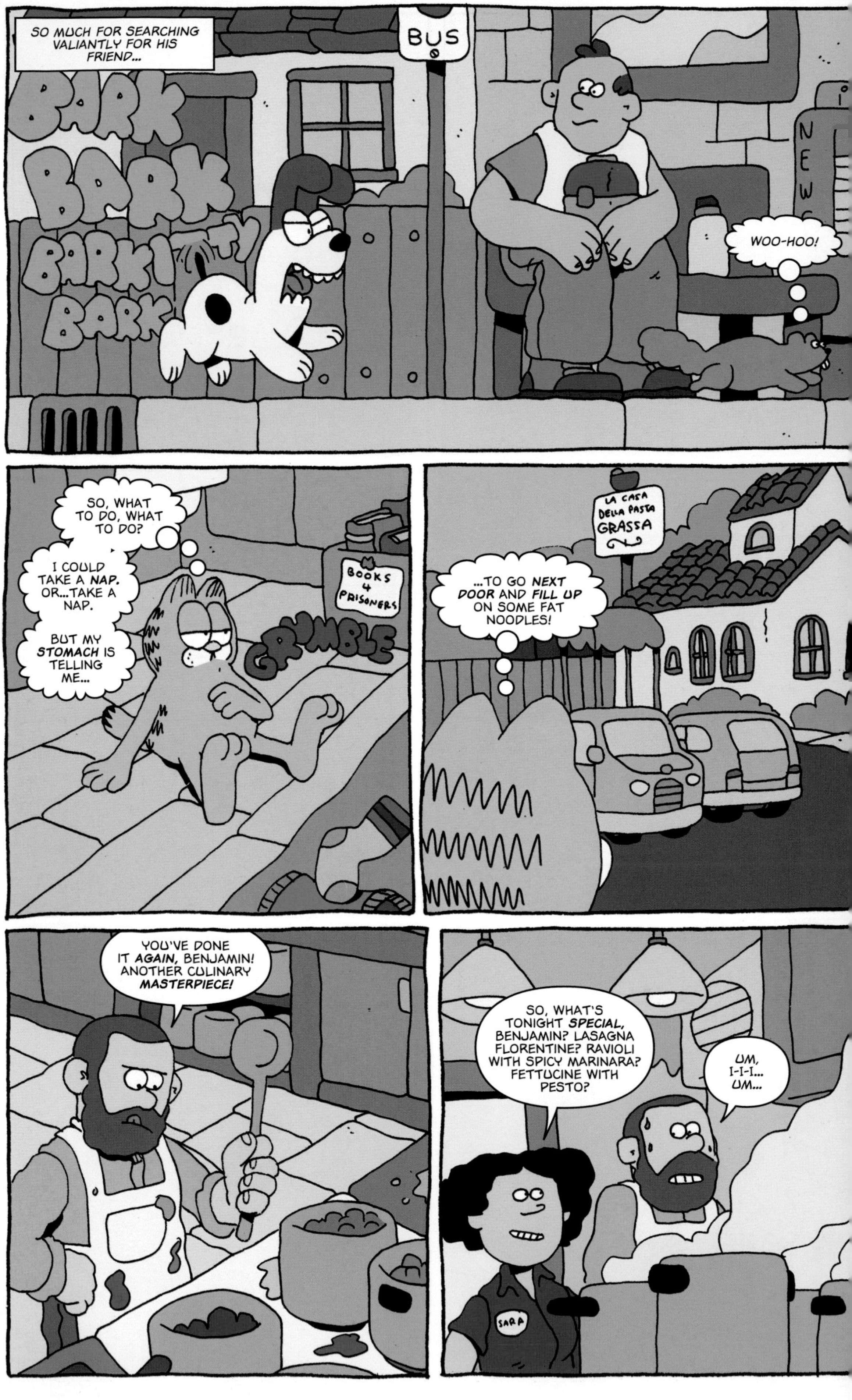
SO MUCH FOR SEARCHING VALIANTLY FOR HIS FRIEND...
BUS
BARK BARK BARKITTY BARK
WOO-HOO!
SO, WHAT TO DO, WHAT TO DO?
I COULD TAKE A NAP. OR...TAKE A NAP.
BUT MY STOMACH IS TELLING ME...
BOOKS 4 PRISONERS
GRUMBLE
LA CASA DELLA PASTA GRASSA
...TO GO NEXT DOOR AND FILL UP ON SOME FAT NOODLES!
YOU'VE DONE IT AGAIN, BENJAMIN! ANOTHER CULINARY MASTERPIECE!
SO, WHAT'S TONIGHT SPECIAL, BENJAMIN? LASAGNA FLORENTINE? RAVIOLI WITH SPICY MARINARA? FETTUCINE WITH PESTO?
UM, I-I-I... UM...
SARA

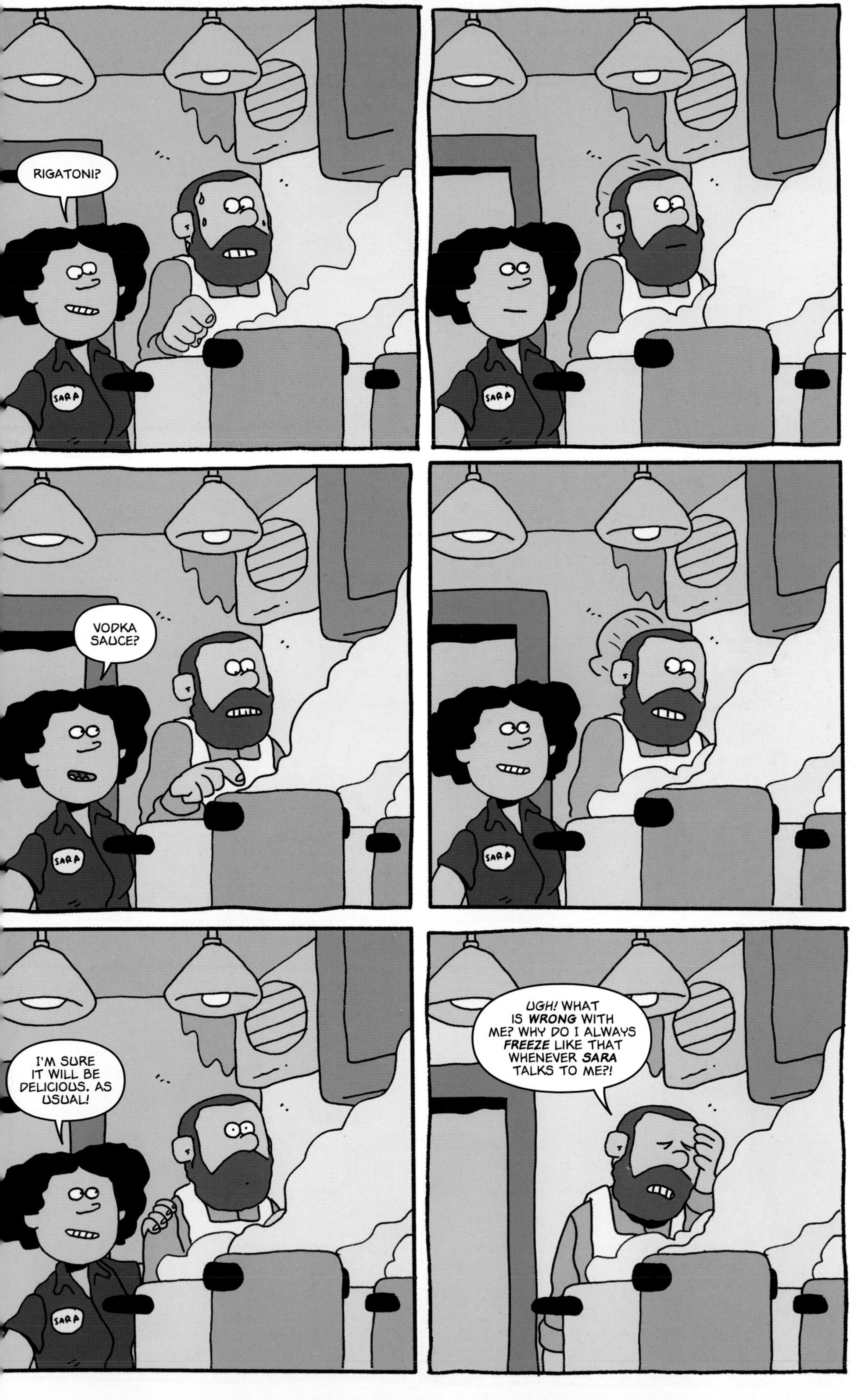
RIGATONI?
VODKA SAUCE?
I'M SURE IT WILL BE DELICIOUS. AS USUAL!
UGH! WHAT IS **WRONG** WITH ME? WHY DO I ALWAYS **FREEZE** LIKE THAT WHENEVER **SARA** TALKS TO ME?!

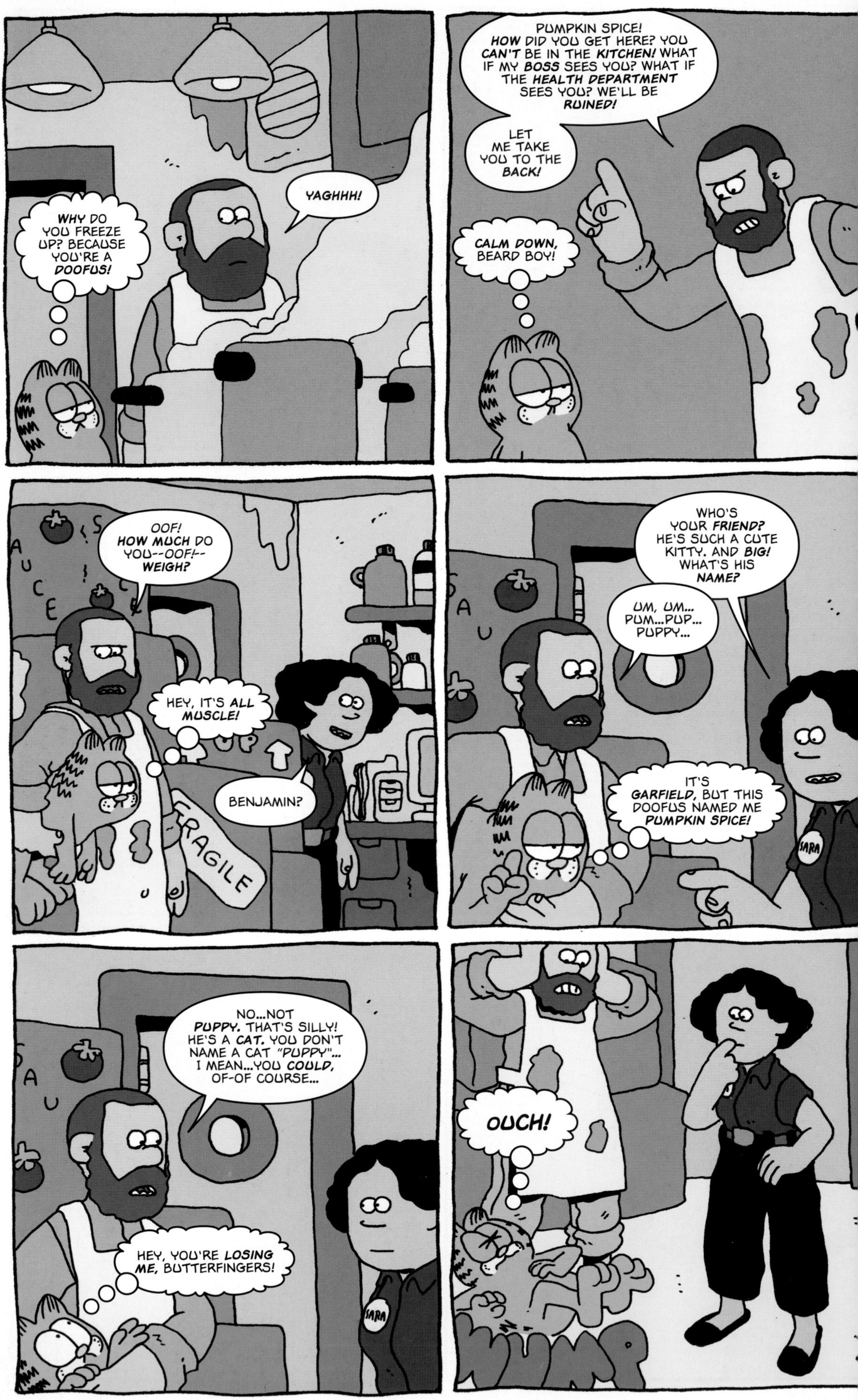
WHY DO YOU FREEZE UP? BECAUSE YOU'RE A DOOFUS!
YAGHHH!
PUMPKIN SPICE! HOW DID YOU GET HERE? YOU CAN'T BE IN THE KITCHEN! WHAT IF MY BOSS SEES YOU? WHAT IF THE HEALTH DEPARTMENT SEES YOU? WE'LL BE RUINED!
LET ME TAKE YOU TO THE BACK!
CALM DOWN, BEARD BOY!
OOF! HOW MUCH DO YOU--OOF!--WEIGH?
HEY, IT'S ALL MUSCLE!
BENJAMIN?
FRAGILE
WHO'S YOUR FRIEND? HE'S SUCH A CUTE KITTY. AND BIG! WHAT'S HIS NAME?
UM, UM... PUM...PUP... PUPPY...
IT'S GARFIELD, BUT THIS DOOFUS NAMED ME PUMPKIN SPICE!
SARA
NO...NOT PUPPY. THAT'S SILLY! HE'S A CAT. YOU DON'T NAME A CAT "PUPPY"... I MEAN...YOU COULD, OF-OF COURSE...
HEY, YOU'RE LOSING ME, BUTTERFINGERS!
SARA
OUCH!

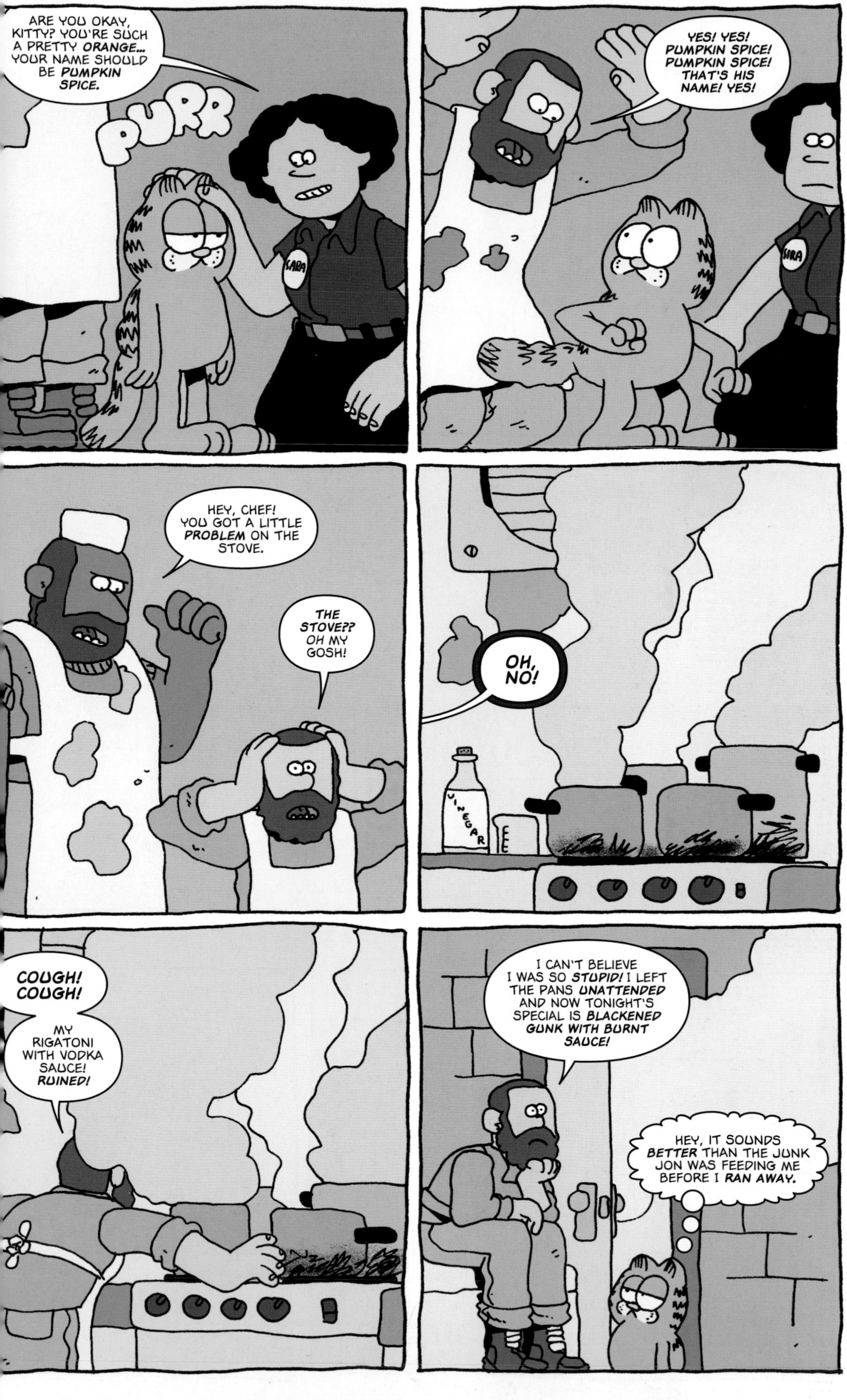
ARE YOU OKAY, KITTY? YOU'RE SUCH A PRETTY ORANGE... YOUR NAME SHOULD BE PUMPKIN SPICE.
PURR
SARA
YES! YES! PUMPKIN SPICE! PUMPKIN SPICE! THAT'S HIS NAME! YES!
HEY, CHEF! YOU GOT A LITTLE PROBLEM ON THE STOVE.
THE STOVE?? OH MY GOSH!
OH, NO!
VINEGAR
COUGH! COUGH!
MY RIGATONI WITH VODKA SAUCE! RUINED!
I CAN'T BELIEVE I WAS SO STUPID! I LEFT THE PANS UNATTENDED AND NOW TONIGHT'S SPECIAL IS BLACKENED GUNK WITH BURNT SAUCE!
HEY, IT SOUNDS BETTER THAN THE JUNK JON WAS FEEDING ME BEFORE I RAN AWAY.

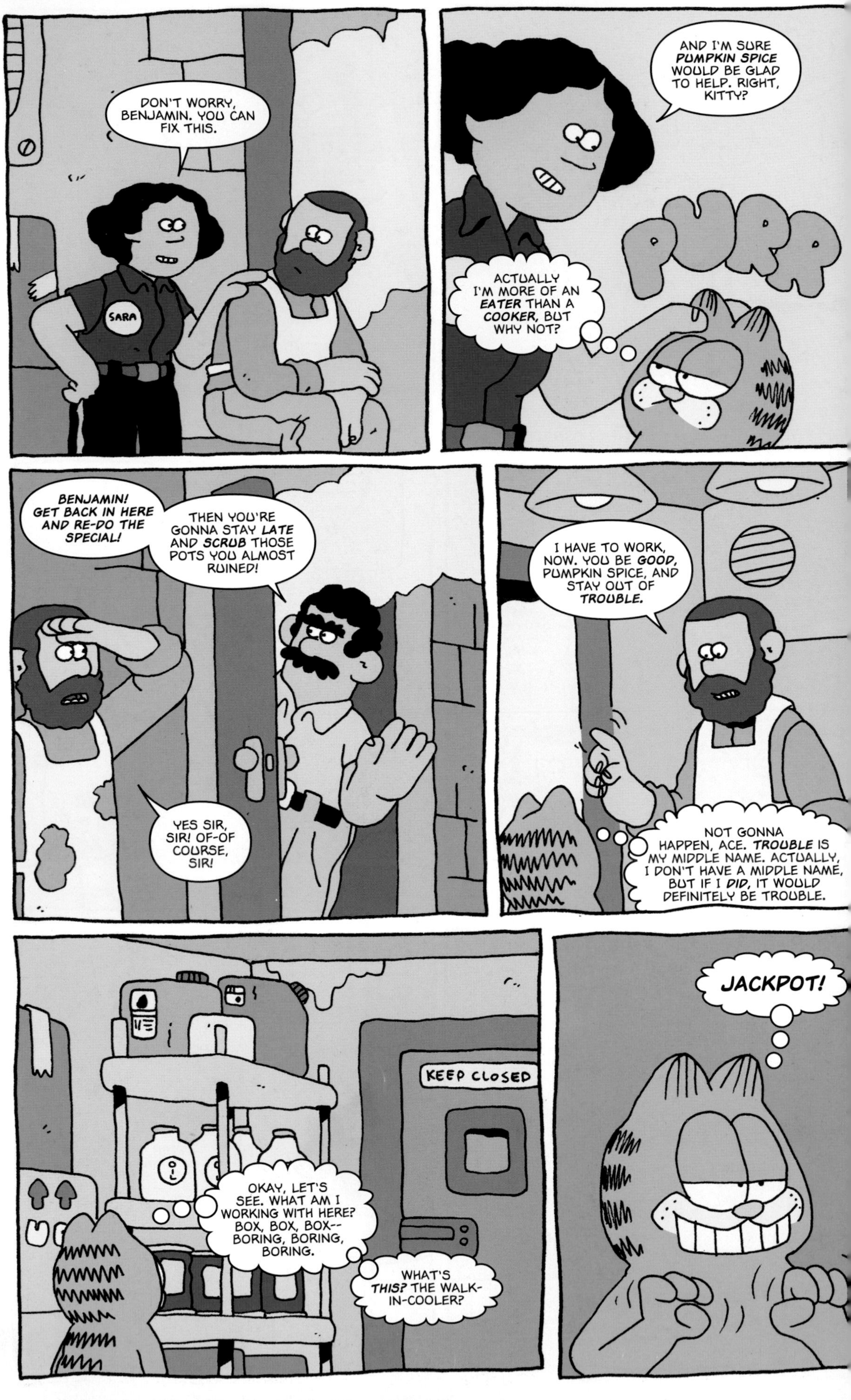
DON'T WORRY, BENJAMIN. YOU CAN FIX THIS.
SARA
AND I'M SURE PUMPKIN SPICE WOULD BE GLAD TO HELP. RIGHT, KITTY?
PURR
ACTUALLY I'M MORE OF AN EATER THAN A COOKER, BUT WHY NOT?
BENJAMIN! GET BACK IN HERE AND RE-DO THE SPECIAL!
THEN YOU'RE GONNA STAY LATE AND SCRUB THOSE POTS YOU ALMOST RUINED!
YES SIR, SIR! OF-OF COURSE, SIR!
I HAVE TO WORK, NOW. YOU BE GOOD, PUMPKIN SPICE, AND STAY OUT OF TROUBLE.
NOT GONNA HAPPEN, ACE. TROUBLE IS MY MIDDLE NAME. ACTUALLY, I DON'T HAVE A MIDDLE NAME, BUT IF I DID, IT WOULD DEFINITELY BE TROUBLE.
KEEP CLOSED
OKAY, LET'S SEE. WHAT AM I WORKING WITH HERE? BOX, BOX, BOX-- BORING, BORING, BORING.
WHAT'S THIS? THE WALK-IN-COOLER?
JACKPOT!

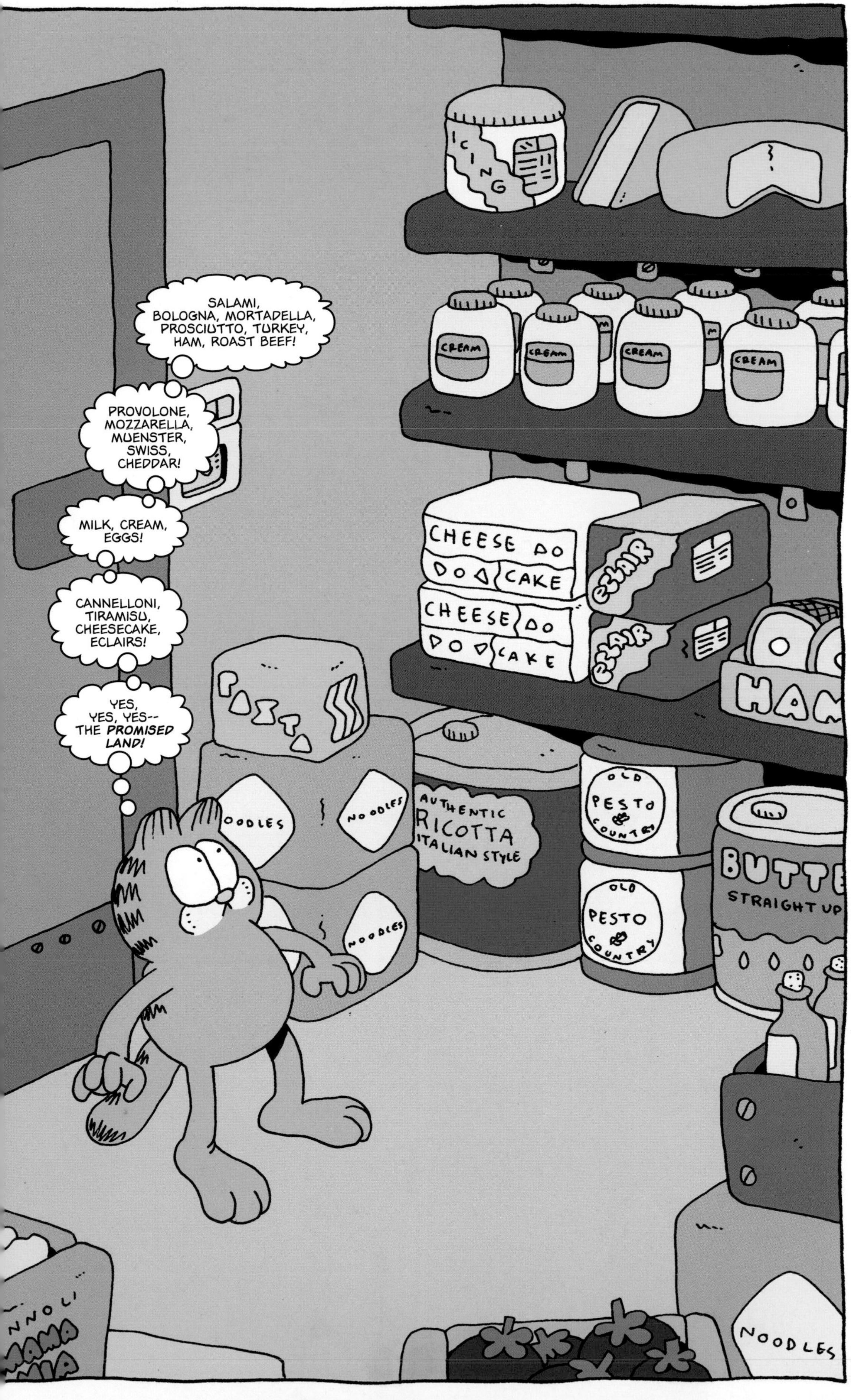
SALAMI, BOLOGNA, MORTADELLA, PROSCIUTTO, TURKEY, HAM, ROAST BEEF!
PROVOLONE, MOZZARELLA, MUENSTER, SWISS, CHEDDAR!
MILK, CREAM, EGGS!
CANNELLONI, TIRAMISU, CHEESECAKE, ECLAIRS!
YES, YES, YES-- THE *PROMISED LAND!*
ICING
CREAM
CHEESE DO DO CAKE
ECLAIR
PASTA
NOODLES
AUTHENTIC RICOTTA ITALIAN STYLE
OLD PESTO COUNTRY
STRAIGHT UP
NOODLES

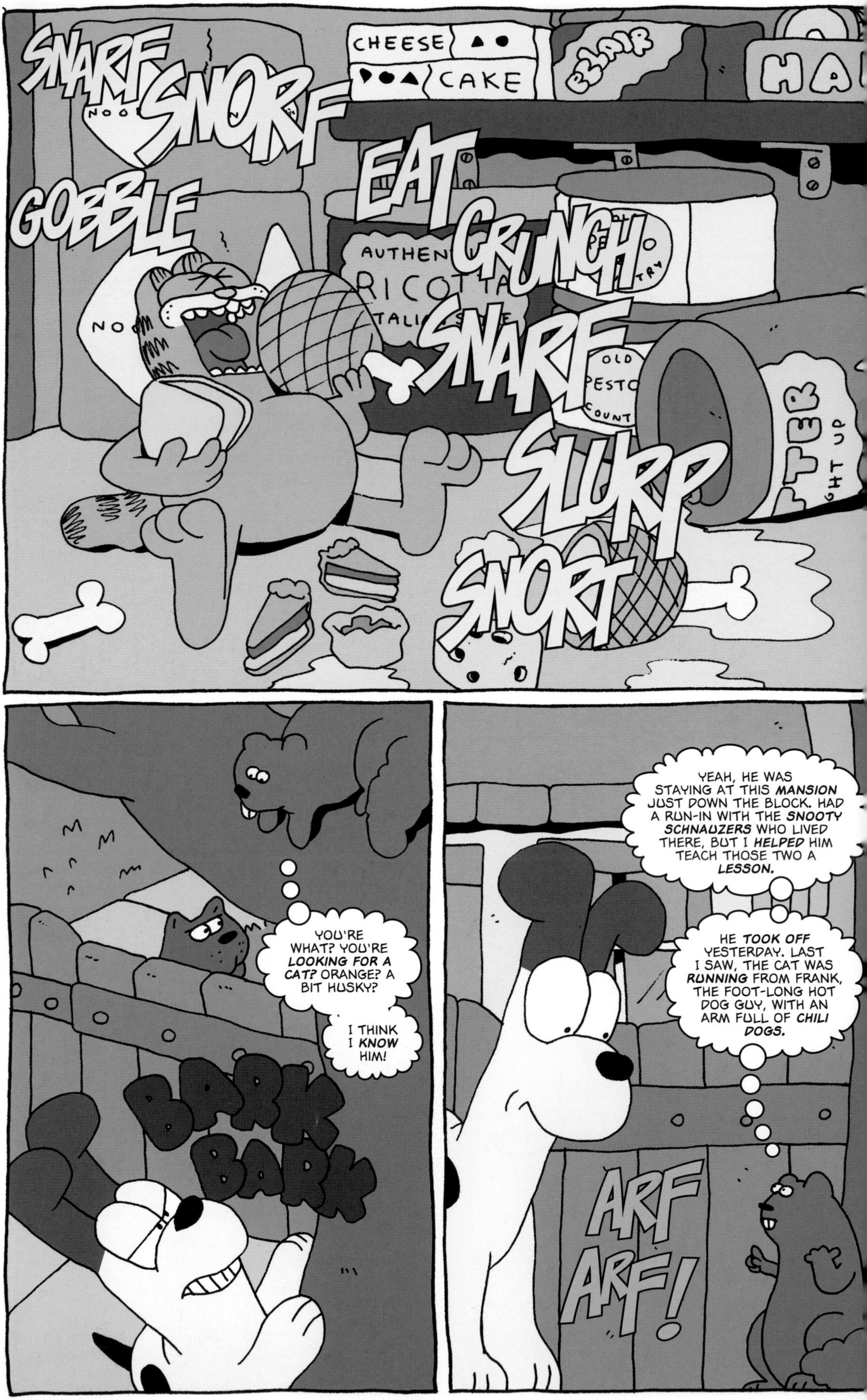
CHEESE
CAKE
SNARF
SNORF
GOBBLE
EAT
CRUNCH
SNARF
SLURP
SNORT
YOU'RE WHAT? YOU'RE **LOOKING FOR A CAT?** ORANGE? A BIT HUSKY?
I THINK I **KNOW** HIM!
BARK
BARK
YEAH, HE WAS STAYING AT THIS **MANSION** JUST DOWN THE BLOCK. HAD A RUN-IN WITH THE **SNOOTY SCHNAUZERS** WHO LIVED THERE, BUT I **HELPED** HIM TEACH THOSE TWO A **LESSON.**
HE **TOOK OFF** YESTERDAY. LAST I SAW, THE CAT WAS **RUNNING** FROM FRANK, THE FOOT-LONG HOT DOG GUY, WITH AN ARM FULL OF **CHILI DOGS.**
ARF
ARF!

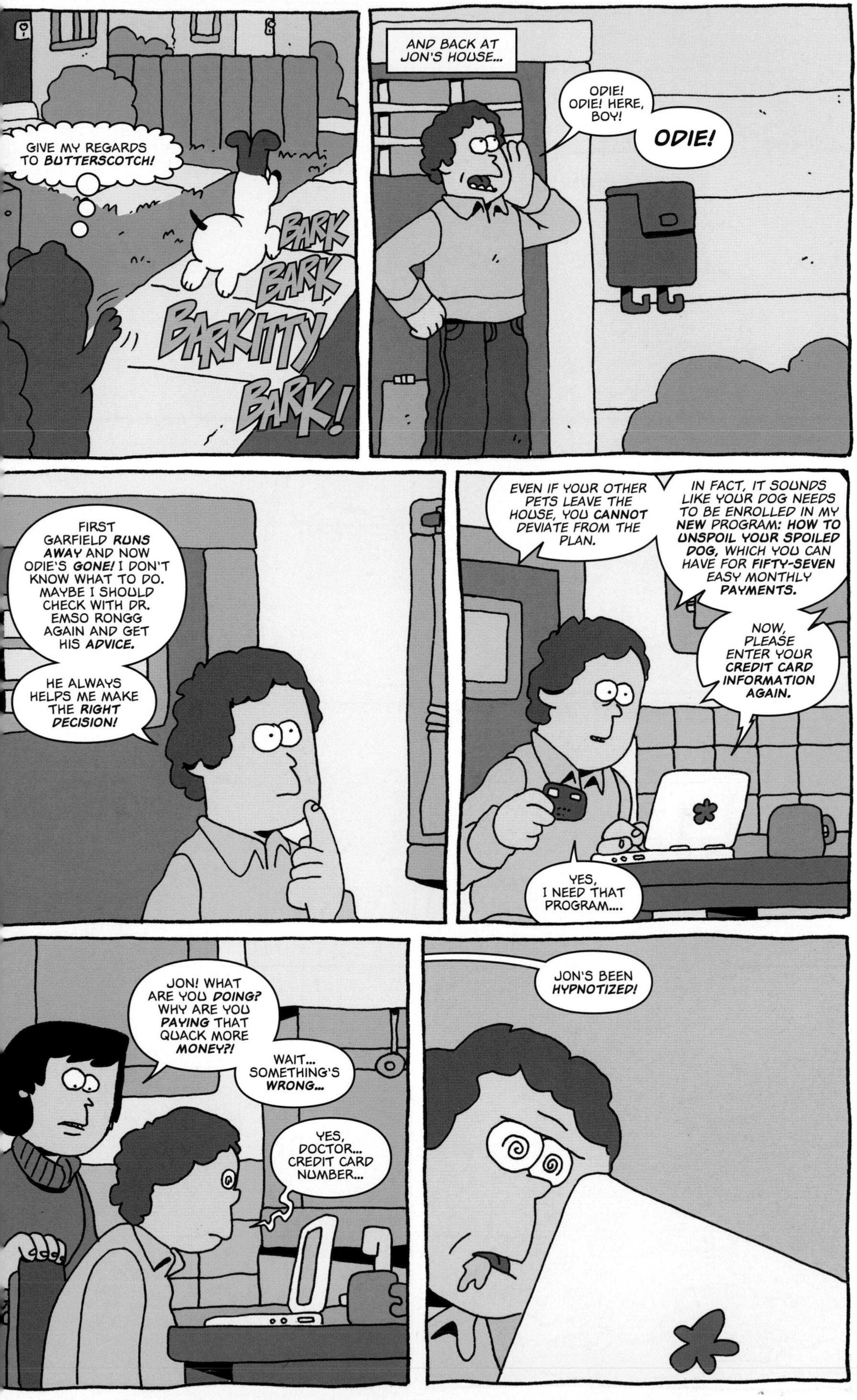
GIVE MY REGARDS TO BUTTERSCOTCH!
BARK BARK BARKITTY BARK!
AND BACK AT JON'S HOUSE...
ODIE! ODIE! HERE, BOY!
ODIE!
FIRST GARFIELD RUNS AWAY AND NOW ODIE'S GONE! I DON'T KNOW WHAT TO DO. MAYBE I SHOULD CHECK WITH DR. EMSO RONGG AGAIN AND GET HIS ADVICE.
HE ALWAYS HELPS ME MAKE THE RIGHT DECISION!
EVEN IF YOUR OTHER PETS LEAVE THE HOUSE, YOU CANNOT DEVIATE FROM THE PLAN.
IN FACT, IT SOUNDS LIKE YOUR DOG NEEDS TO BE ENROLLED IN MY NEW PROGRAM: HOW TO UNSPOIL YOUR SPOILED DOG, WHICH YOU CAN HAVE FOR FIFTY-SEVEN EASY MONTHLY PAYMENTS.
NOW, PLEASE ENTER YOUR CREDIT CARD INFORMATION AGAIN.
YES, I NEED THAT PROGRAM....
JON! WHAT ARE YOU DOING? WHY ARE YOU PAYING THAT QUACK MORE MONEY?!
WAIT... SOMETHING'S WRONG...
YES, DOCTOR... CREDIT CARD NUMBER...
JON'S BEEN HYPNOTIZED!

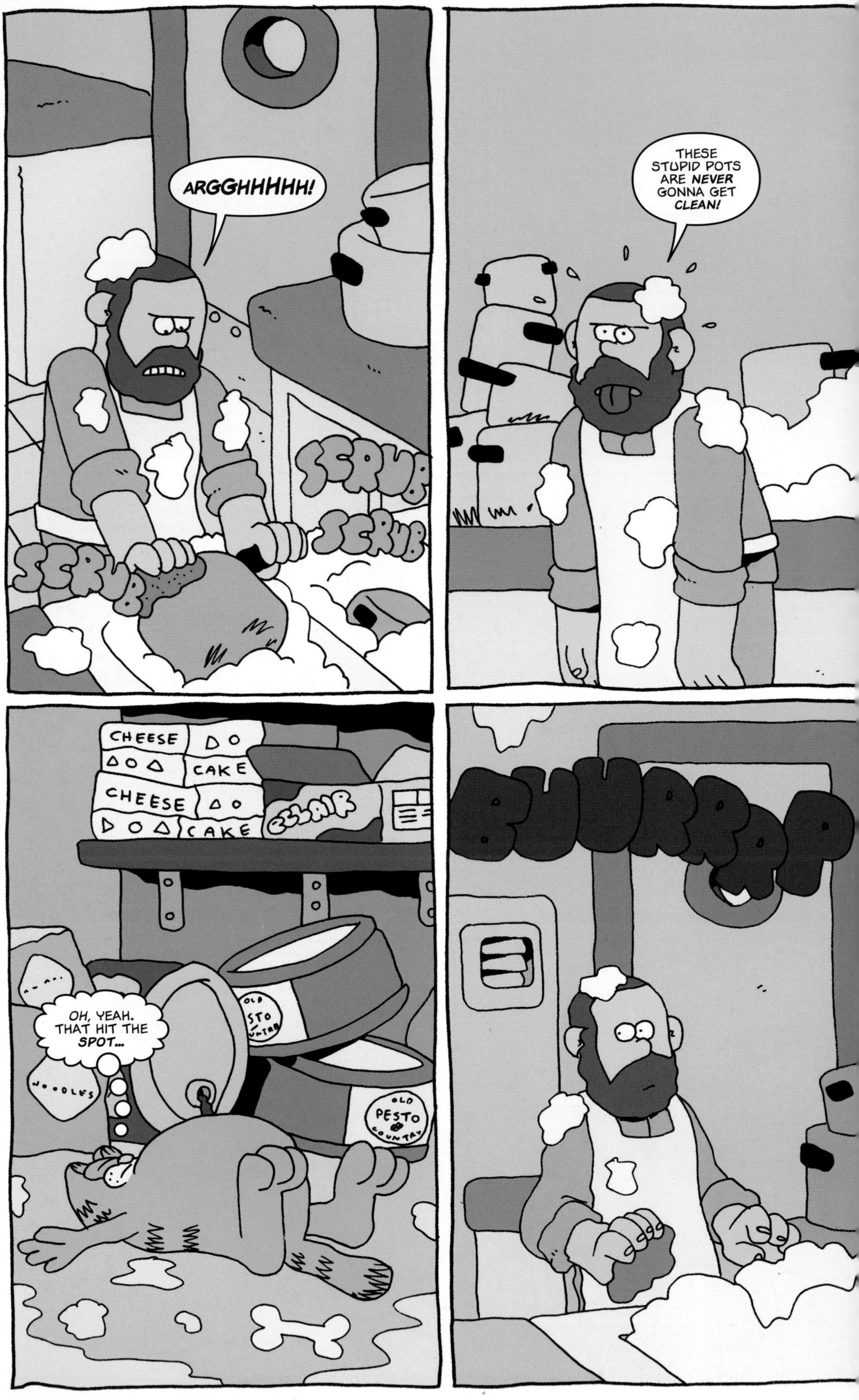
ARGGHHHHH!
SCRUB
SCRUB
SCRUB
THESE STUPID POTS ARE NEVER GONNA GET CLEAN!
CHEESE DOO CAKE
CHEESE DOO CAKE
NOODLES
OLD PESTO COUNTRY
OH, YEAH. THAT HIT THE SPOT...

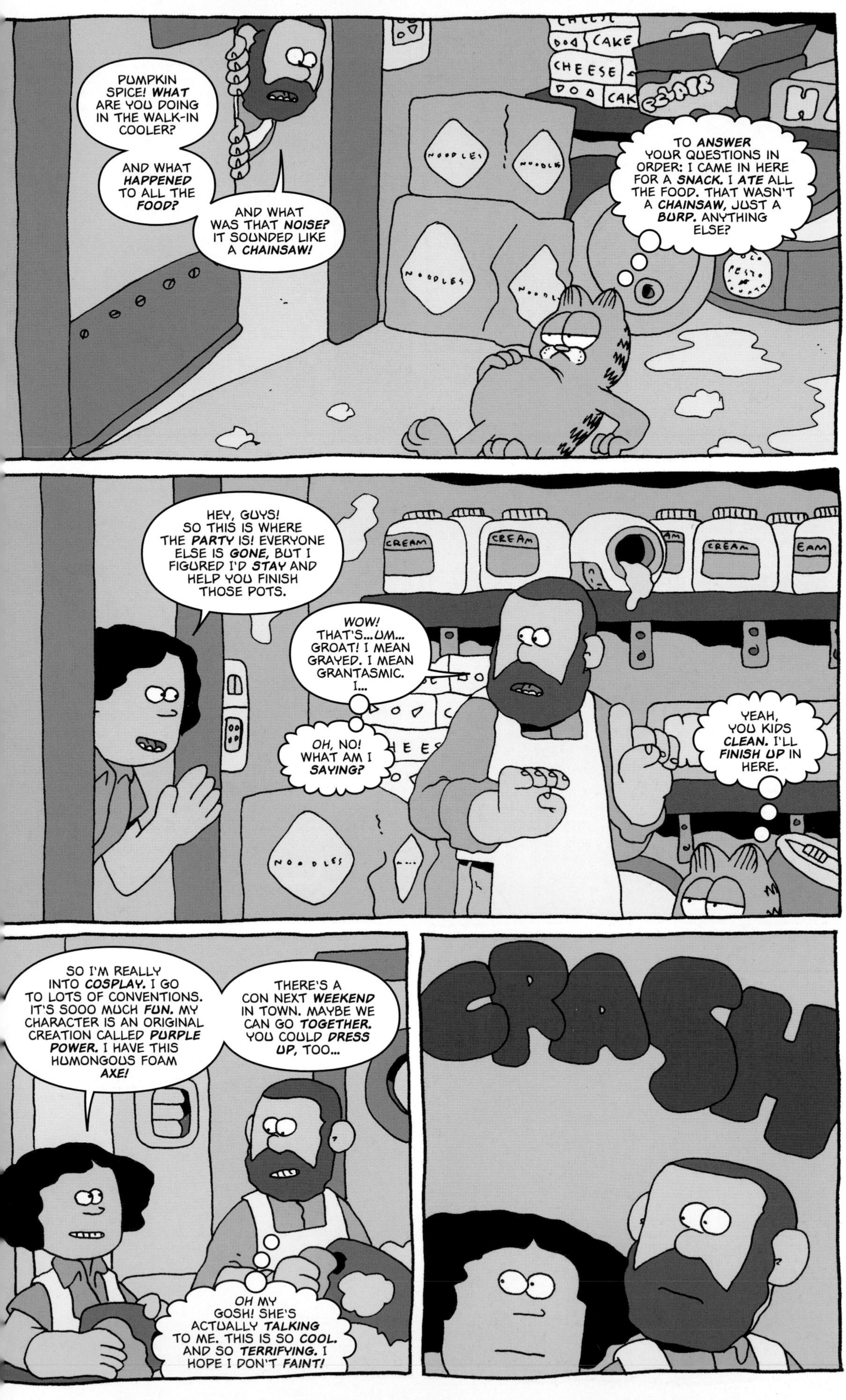
PUMPKIN SPICE! WHAT ARE YOU DOING IN THE WALK-IN COOLER?
AND WHAT HAPPENED TO ALL THE FOOD?
AND WHAT WAS THAT NOISE? IT SOUNDED LIKE A CHAINSAW!
TO ANSWER YOUR QUESTIONS IN ORDER: I CAME IN HERE FOR A SNACK. I ATE ALL THE FOOD. THAT WASN'T A CHAINSAW, JUST A BURP. ANYTHING ELSE?
HEY, GUYS! SO THIS IS WHERE THE PARTY IS! EVERYONE ELSE IS GONE, BUT I FIGURED I'D STAY AND HELP YOU FINISH THOSE POTS.
WOW! THAT'S...UM... GROAT! I MEAN GRAYED. I MEAN GRANTASMIC. I...
OH, NO! WHAT AM I SAYING?
YEAH, YOU KIDS CLEAN. I'LL FINISH UP IN HERE.
SO I'M REALLY INTO COSPLAY. I GO TO LOTS OF CONVENTIONS. IT'S SOOO MUCH FUN. MY CHARACTER IS AN ORIGINAL CREATION CALLED PURPLE POWER. I HAVE THIS HUMONGOUS FOAM AXE!
THERE'S A CON NEXT WEEKEND IN TOWN. MAYBE WE CAN GO TOGETHER. YOU COULD DRESS UP, TOO...
OH MY GOSH! SHE'S ACTUALLY TALKING TO ME. THIS IS SO COOL. AND SO TERRIFYING. I HOPE I DON'T FAINT!
CRASH

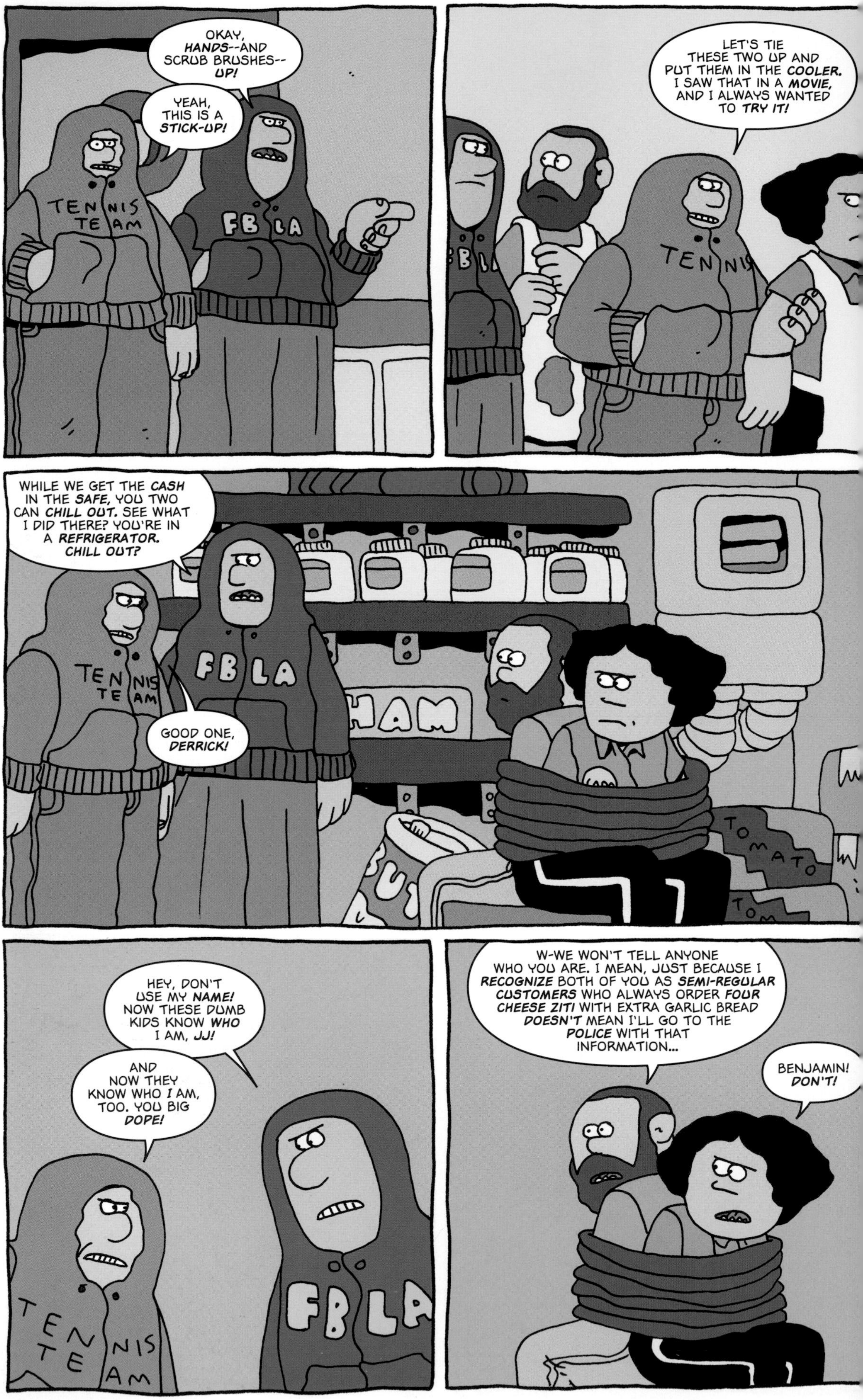
OKAY, HANDS--AND SCRUB BRUSHES--UP!
YEAH, THIS IS A STICK-UP!
LET'S TIE THESE TWO UP AND PUT THEM IN THE COOLER. I SAW THAT IN A MOVIE, AND I ALWAYS WANTED TO TRY IT!
WHILE WE GET THE CASH IN THE SAFE, YOU TWO CAN CHILL OUT. SEE WHAT I DID THERE? YOU'RE IN A REFRIGERATOR. CHILL OUT?
GOOD ONE, DERRICK!
HEY, DON'T USE MY NAME! NOW THESE DUMB KIDS KNOW WHO I AM, JJ!
AND NOW THEY KNOW WHO I AM, TOO. YOU BIG DOPE!
W-WE WON'T TELL ANYONE WHO YOU ARE. I MEAN, JUST BECAUSE I RECOGNIZE BOTH OF YOU AS SEMI-REGULAR CUSTOMERS WHO ALWAYS ORDER FOUR CHEESE ZITI WITH EXTRA GARLIC BREAD DOESN'T MEAN I'LL GO TO THE POLICE WITH THAT INFORMATION...
BENJAMIN! DON'T!

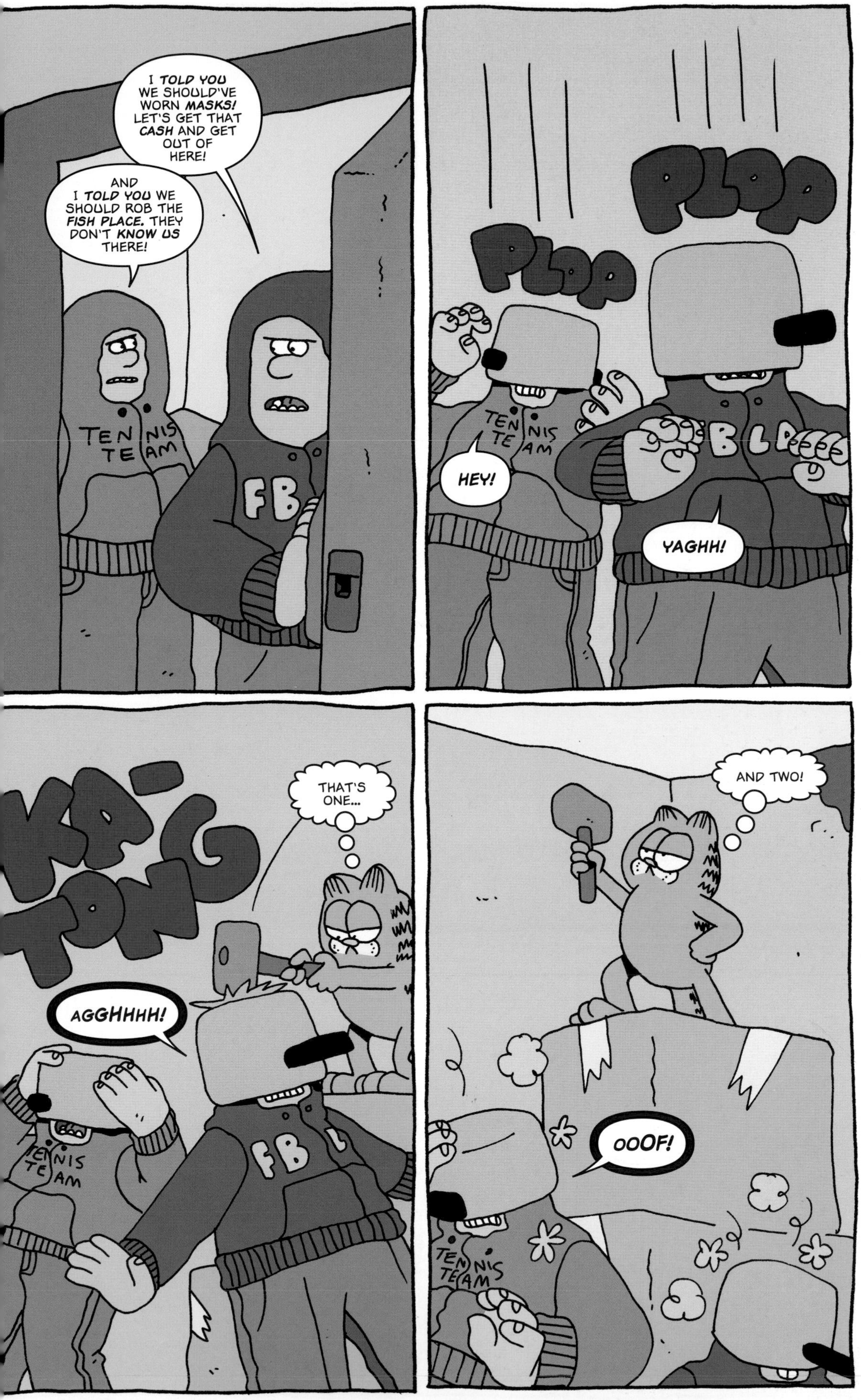
AND I TOLD YOU WE SHOULD ROB THE FISH PLACE. THEY DON'T KNOW US THERE!
I TOLD YOU WE SHOULD'VE WORN MASKS! LET'S GET THAT CASH AND GET OUT OF HERE!
TENNIS TEAM
FB
PLOP
PLOP
HEY!
YAGHH!
KA-TONG
THAT'S ONE...
AGGHHHH!
AND TWO!
OOOF!

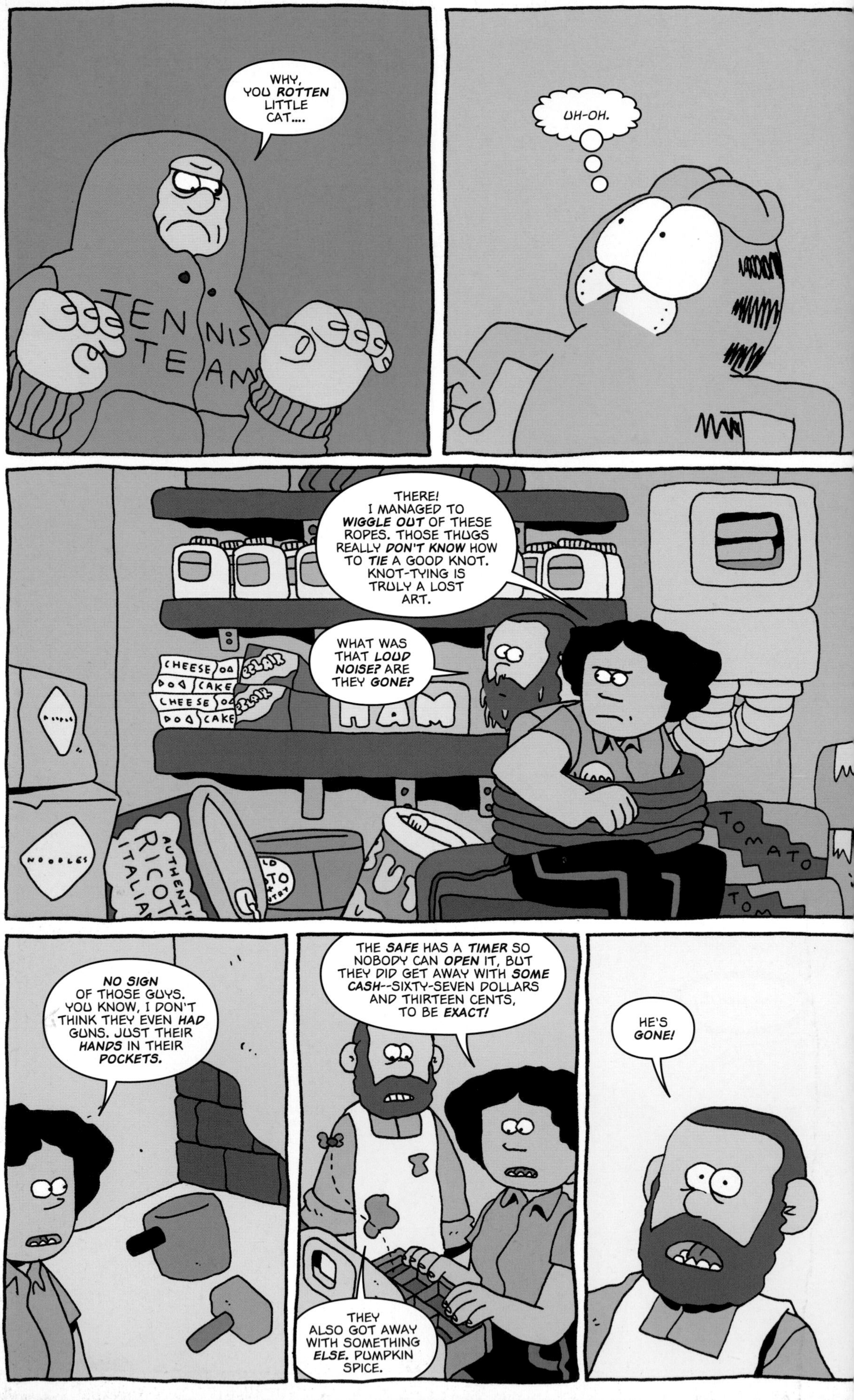
WHY, YOU ROTTEN LITTLE CAT....
UH-OH.
TENNIS TEAM
THERE! I MANAGED TO WIGGLE OUT OF THESE ROPES. THOSE THUGS REALLY DON'T KNOW HOW TO TIE A GOOD KNOT. KNOT-TYING IS TRULY A LOST ART.
WHAT WAS THAT LOUD NOISE? ARE THEY GONE?
CHEESE DOG CAKE
HAM
NOODLES
TOMATO
NO SIGN OF THOSE GUYS. YOU KNOW, I DON'T THINK THEY EVEN HAD GUNS. JUST THEIR HANDS IN THEIR POCKETS.
THE SAFE HAS A TIMER SO NOBODY CAN OPEN IT, BUT THEY DID GET AWAY WITH SOME CASH--SIXTY-SEVEN DOLLARS AND THIRTEEN CENTS, TO BE EXACT!
THEY ALSO GOT AWAY WITH SOMETHING ELSE. PUMPKIN SPICE.
HE'S GONE!

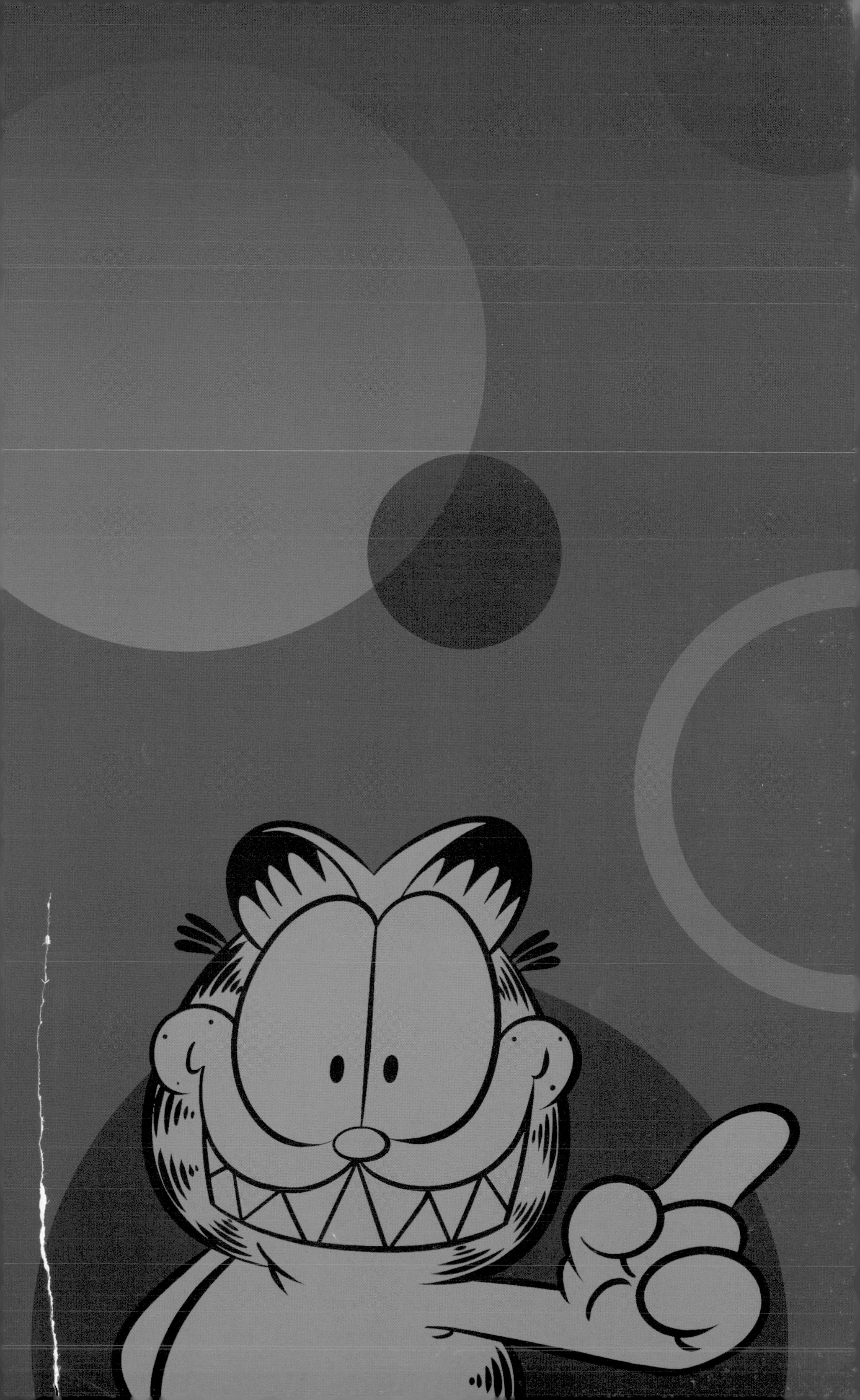

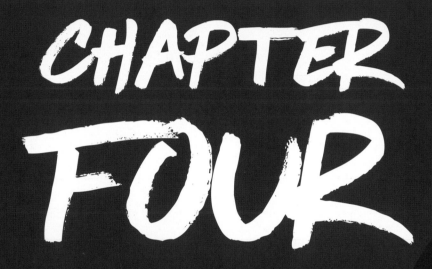

CHAPTER FOUR

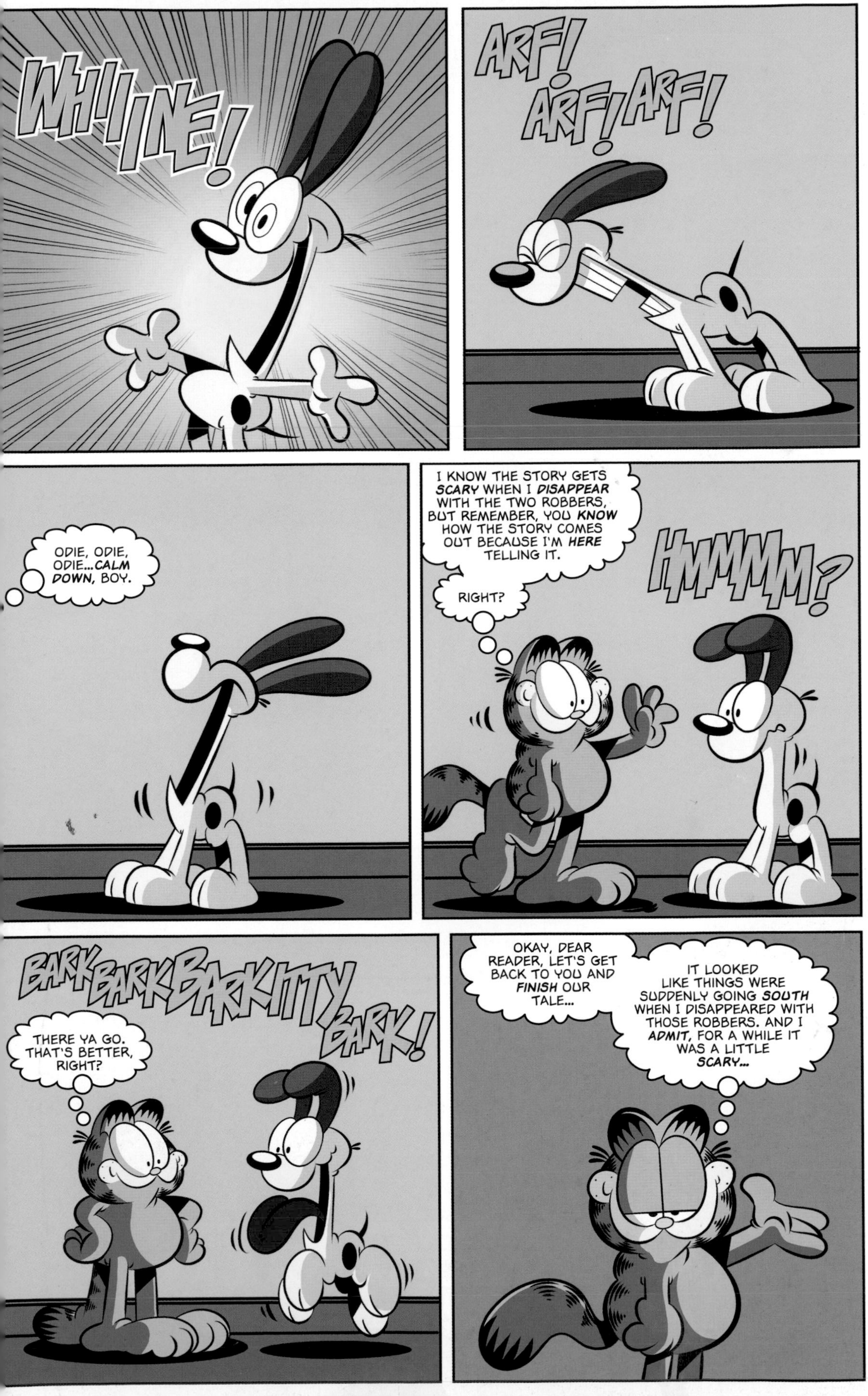
WHIIIINE!
ARF! ARF! ARF!
ODIE, ODIE, ODIE...CALM DOWN, BOY.
I KNOW THE STORY GETS SCARY WHEN I DISAPPEAR WITH THE TWO ROBBERS, BUT REMEMBER, YOU KNOW HOW THE STORY COMES OUT BECAUSE I'M HERE TELLING IT.
RIGHT?
HMMMM?
BARK BARK BARKITTY BARK!
THERE YA GO. THAT'S BETTER, RIGHT?
OKAY, DEAR READER, LET'S GET BACK TO YOU AND FINISH OUR TALE...
IT LOOKED LIKE THINGS WERE SUDDENLY GOING SOUTH WHEN I DISAPPEARED WITH THOSE ROBBERS. AND I ADMIT, FOR A WHILE IT WAS A LITTLE SCARY...

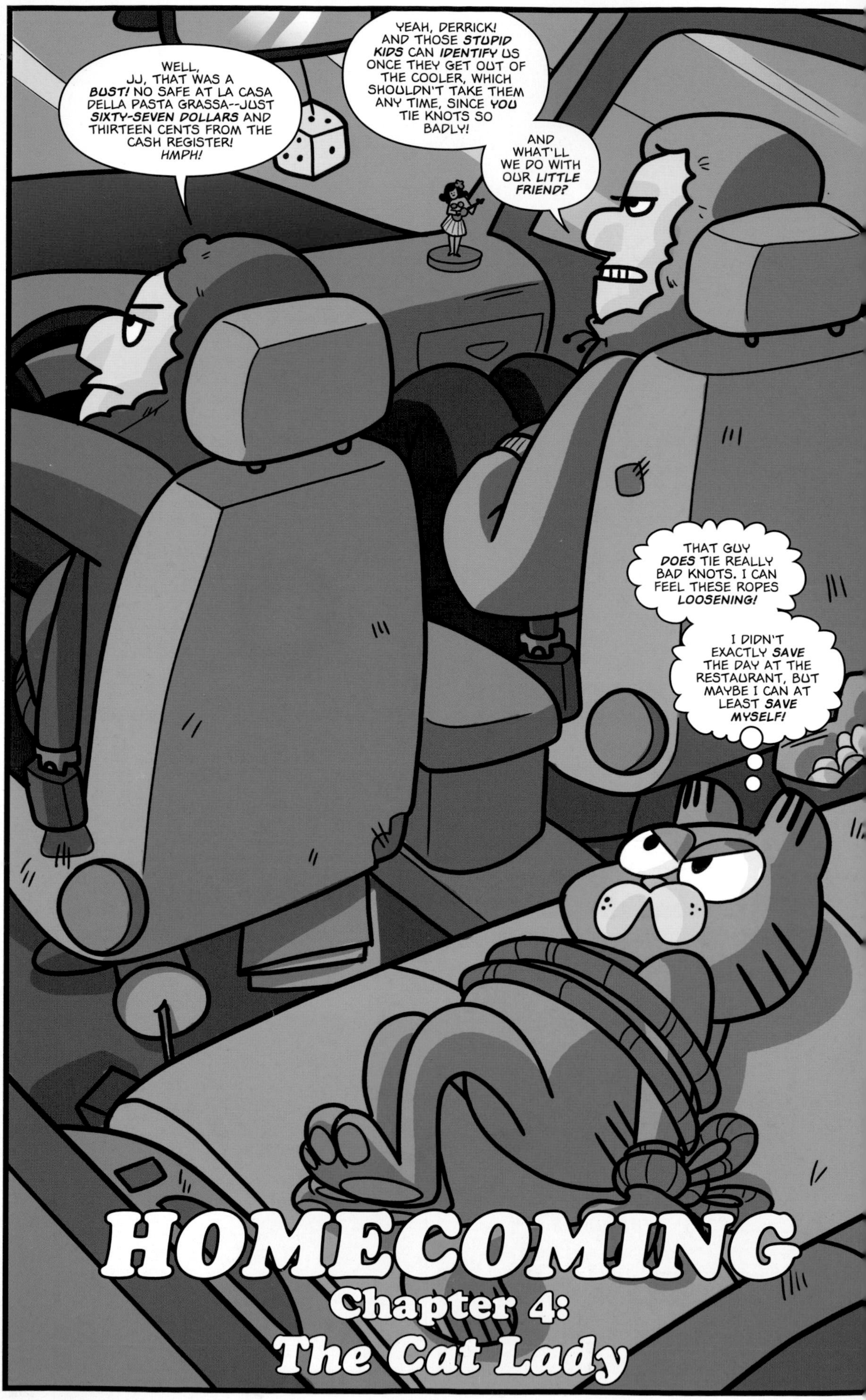

WELL, JJ, THAT WAS A BUST! NO SAFE AT LA CASA DELLA PASTA GRASSA--JUST SIXTY-SEVEN DOLLARS AND THIRTEEN CENTS FROM THE CASH REGISTER! HMPH!
YEAH, DERRICK! AND THOSE STUPID KIDS CAN IDENTIFY US ONCE THEY GET OUT OF THE COOLER, WHICH SHOULDN'T TAKE THEM ANY TIME, SINCE YOU TIE KNOTS SO BADLY!
AND WHAT'LL WE DO WITH OUR LITTLE FRIEND?
THAT GUY DOES TIE REALLY BAD KNOTS. I CAN FEEL THESE ROPES LOOSENING!
I DIDN'T EXACTLY SAVE THE DAY AT THE RESTAURANT, BUT MAYBE I CAN AT LEAST SAVE MYSELF!
HOMECOMING
Chapter 4:
The Cat Lady

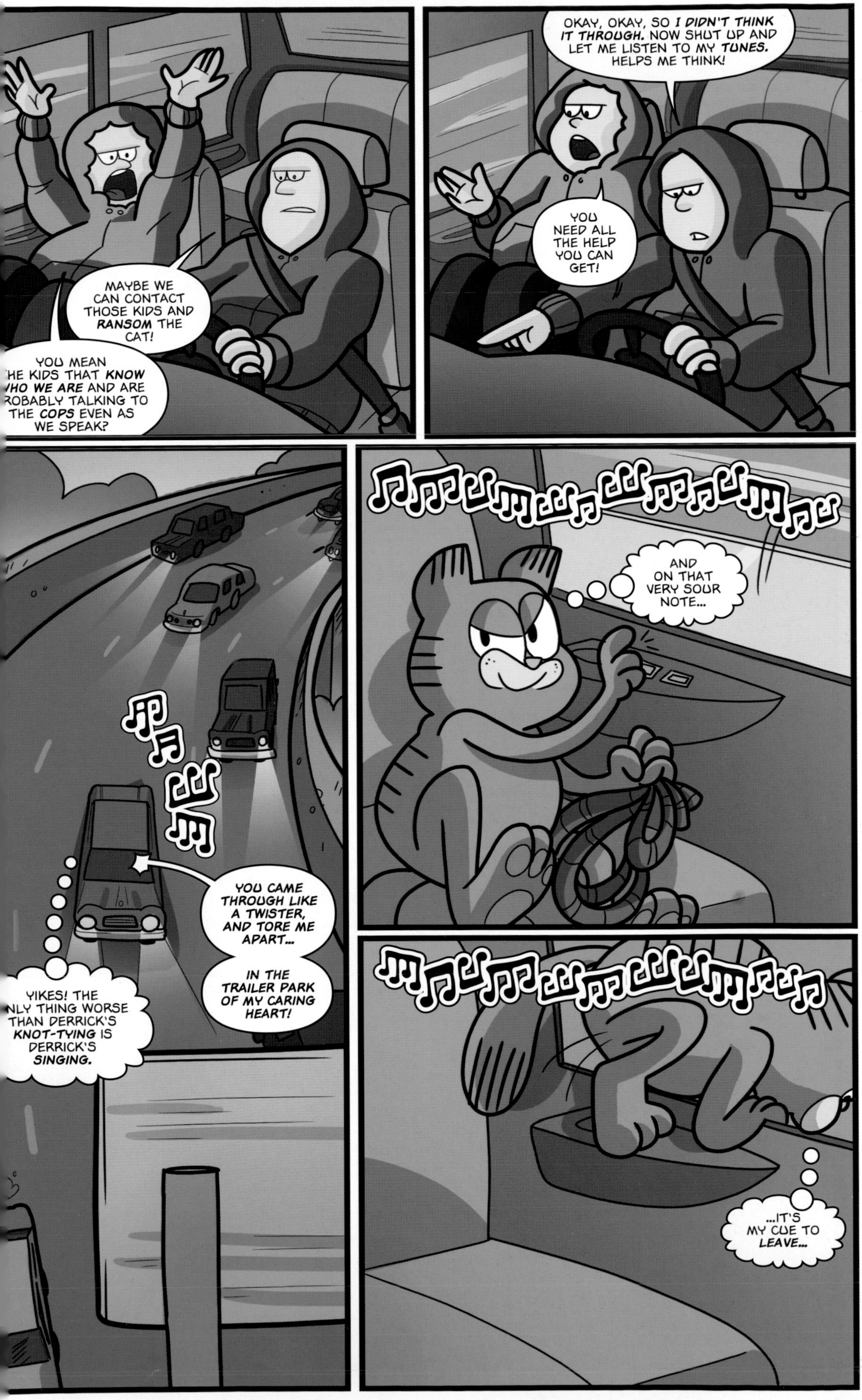
MAYBE WE CAN CONTACT THOSE KIDS AND **RANSOM** THE CAT!
YOU MEAN THE KIDS THAT **KNOW WHO WE ARE** AND ARE PROBABLY TALKING TO THE **COPS** EVEN AS WE SPEAK?
OKAY, OKAY, SO ***I DIDN'T THINK IT THROUGH.*** NOW SHUT UP AND LET ME LISTEN TO MY ***TUNES.*** HELPS ME THINK!
YOU NEED ALL THE HELP YOU CAN GET!
YOU CAME THROUGH LIKE A TWISTER, AND TORE ME APART...
IN THE TRAILER PARK OF MY CARING HEART!
YIKES! THE ONLY THING WORSE THAN DERRICK'S ***KNOT-TYING*** IS DERRICK'S ***SINGING.***
AND ON THAT VERY SOUR NOTE...
...IT'S MY CUE TO ***LEAVE...***

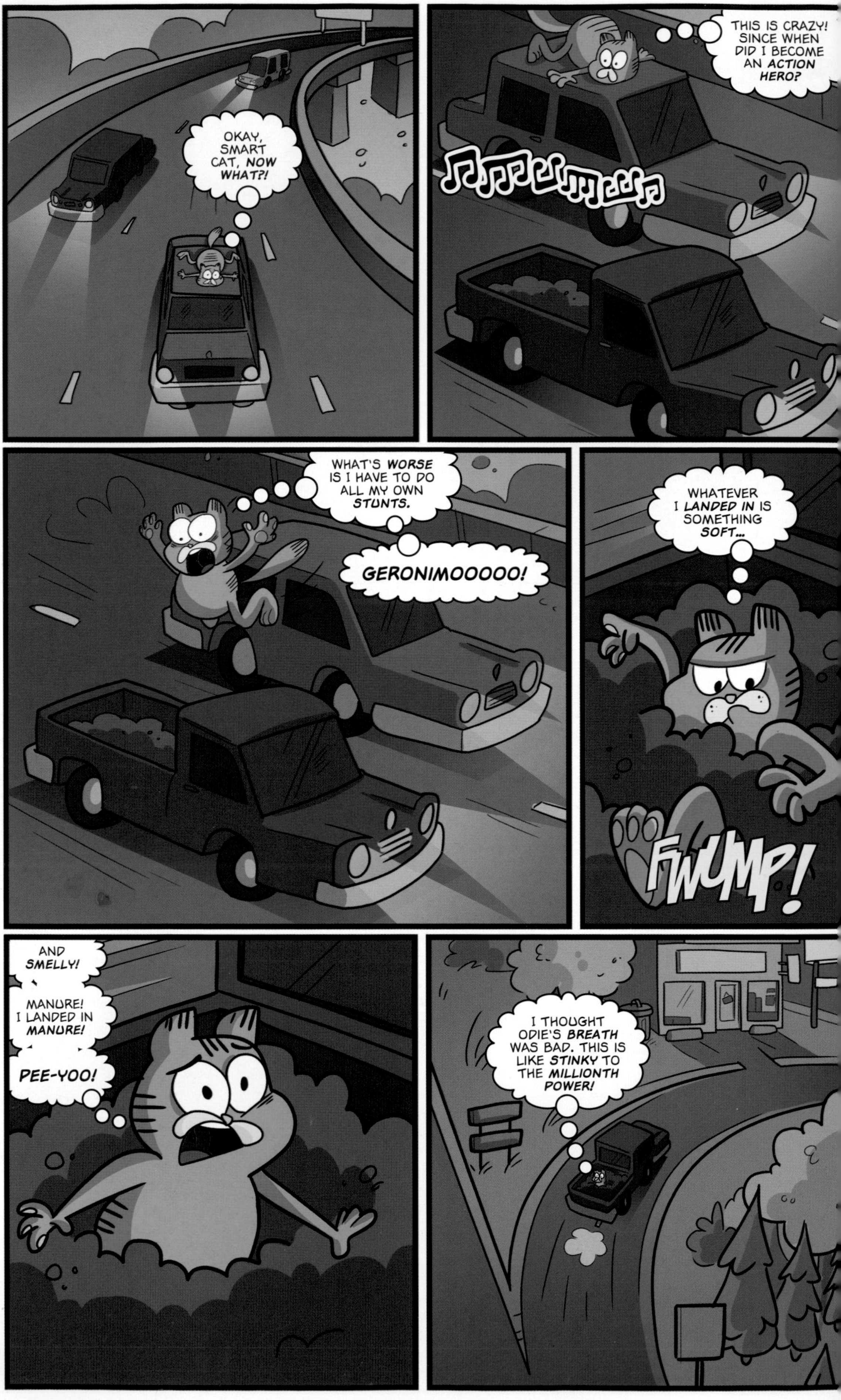
OKAY, SMART CAT, NOW WHAT?!
THIS IS CRAZY! SINCE WHEN DID I BECOME AN ACTION HERO?
WHAT'S WORSE IS I HAVE TO DO ALL MY OWN STUNTS.
GERONIMOOOOO!
WHATEVER I LANDED IN IS SOMETHING SOFT...
FWUMP!
AND SMELLY!
MANURE! I LANDED IN MANURE!
PEE-YOO!
I THOUGHT ODIE'S BREATH WAS BAD. THIS IS LIKE STINKY TO THE MILLIONTH POWER!

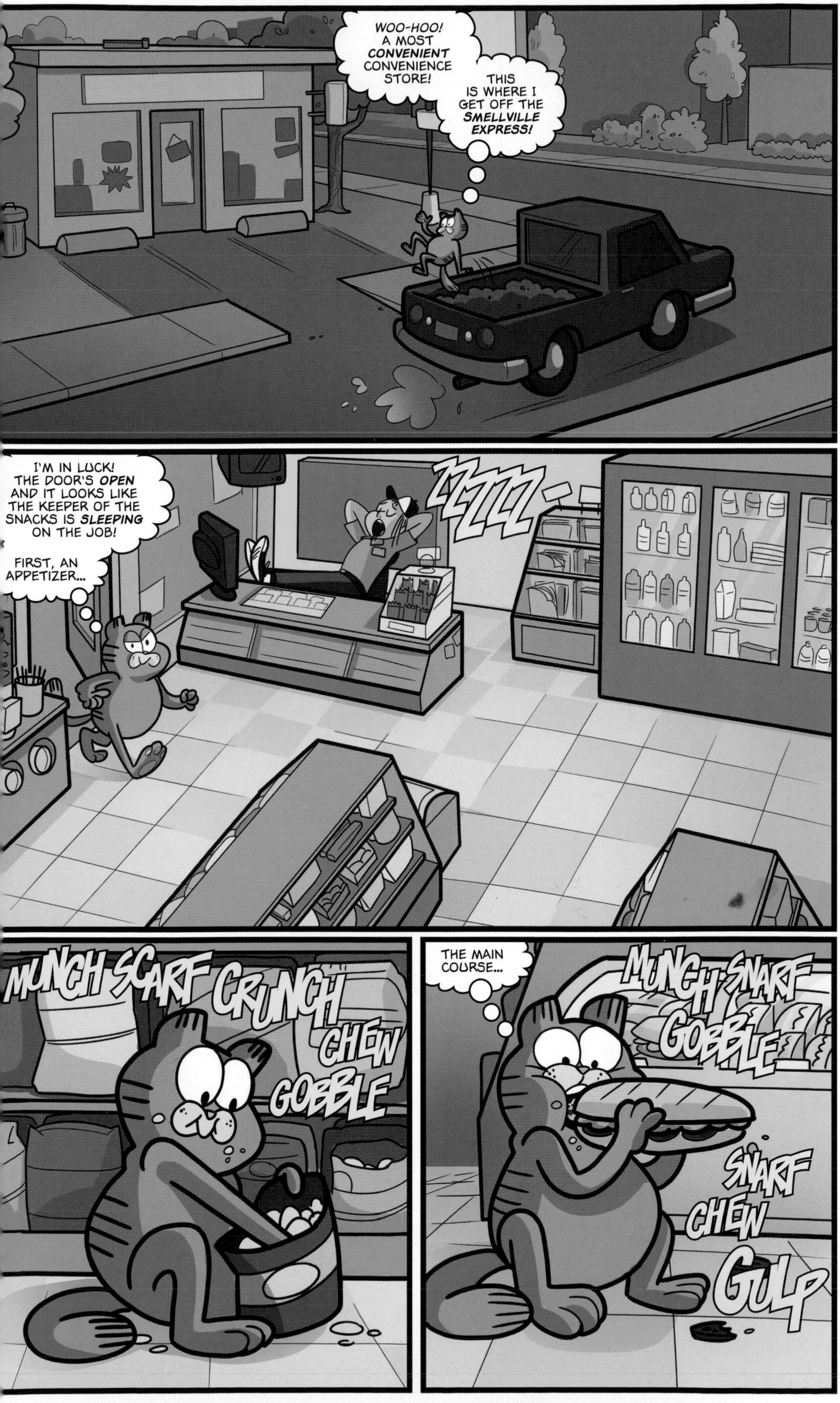
WOO-HOO! A MOST CONVENIENT CONVENIENCE STORE!
THIS IS WHERE I GET OFF THE SMELLVILLE EXPRESS!
I'M IN LUCK! THE DOOR'S OPEN AND IT LOOKS LIKE THE KEEPER OF THE SNACKS IS SLEEPING ON THE JOB!
FIRST, AN APPETIZER...
ZZZZZ
MUNCH SCARF CRUNCH
CHEW
GOBBLE
THE MAIN COURSE...
MUNCH SNARF
GOBBLE
SNARF
CHEW
GULP

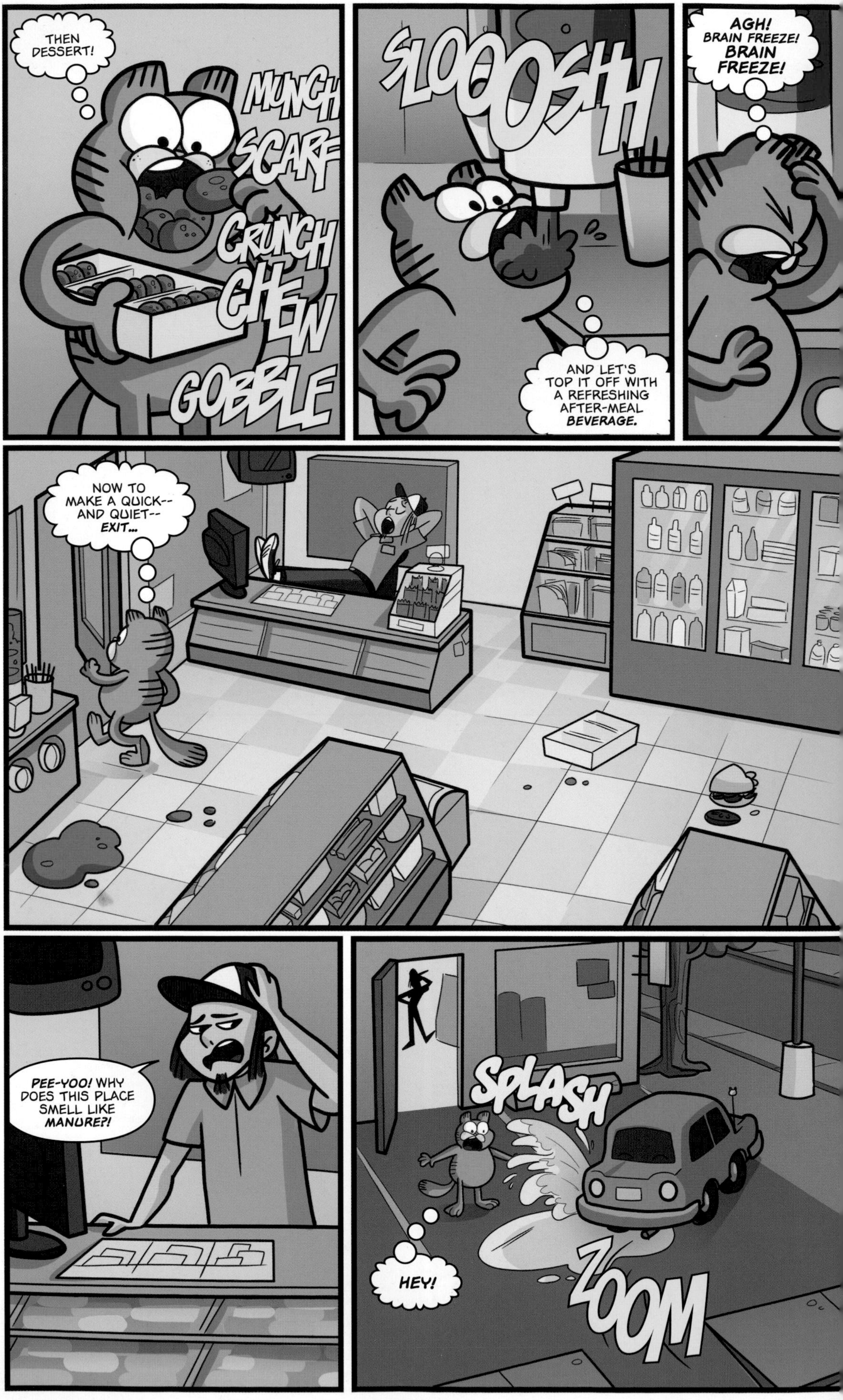
THEN DESSERT!
MUNCH
SCARF
CRUNCH
CHEW
GOBBLE
SLOOOSHH
AND LET'S TOP IT OFF WITH A REFRESHING AFTER-MEAL *BEVERAGE.*
AGH! BRAIN FREEZE! BRAIN FREEZE!
NOW TO MAKE A QUICK-- AND QUIET-- *EXIT...*
PEE-YOO! WHY DOES THIS PLACE SMELL LIKE *MANURE?!*
SPLASH
HEY!
ZOOM

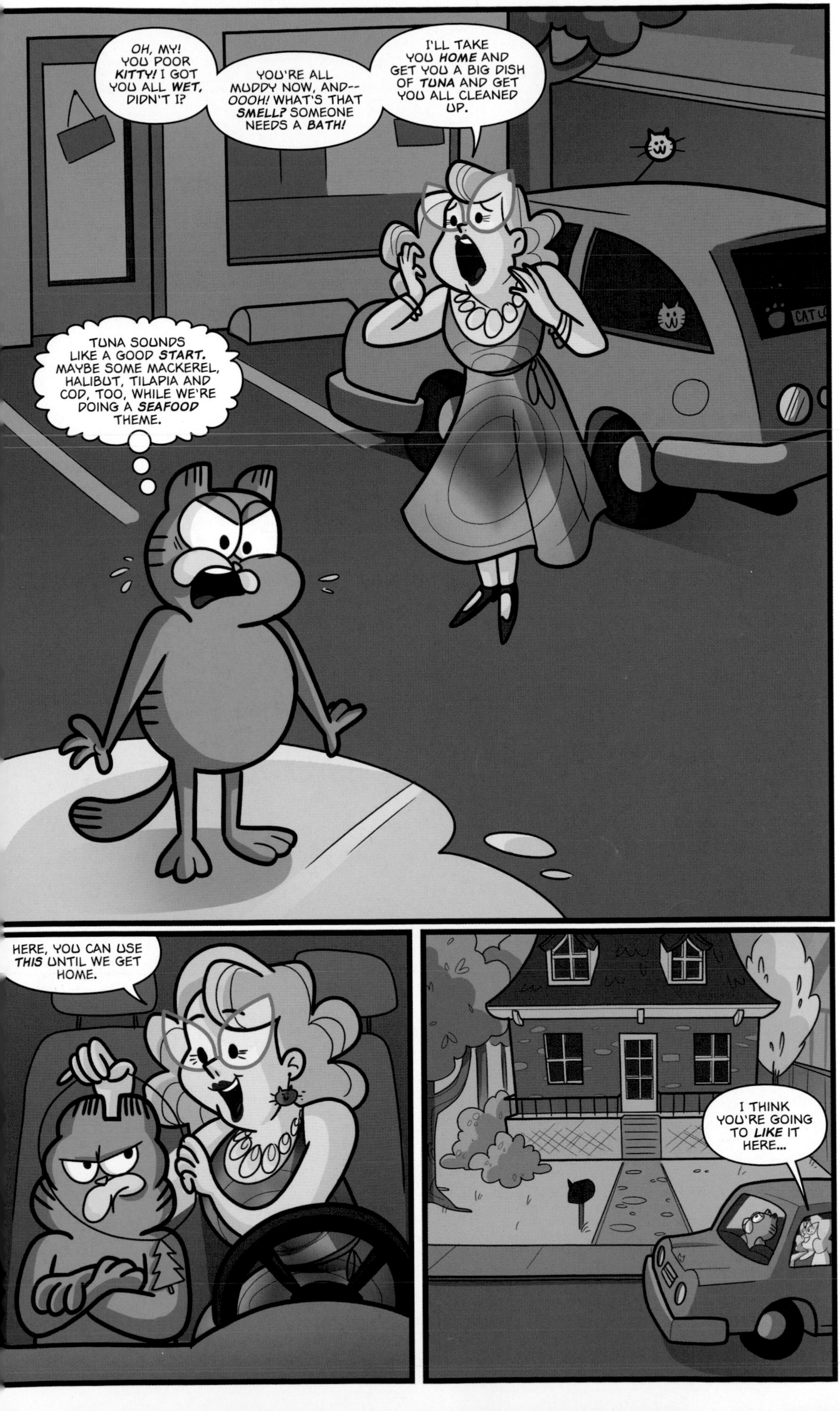
OH, MY! YOU POOR KITTY! I GOT YOU ALL WET, DIDN'T I?
YOU'RE ALL MUDDY NOW, AND-- OOOH! WHAT'S THAT SMELL? SOMEONE NEEDS A BATH!
I'LL TAKE YOU HOME AND GET YOU A BIG DISH OF TUNA AND GET YOU ALL CLEANED UP.
TUNA SOUNDS LIKE A GOOD START. MAYBE SOME MACKEREL, HALIBUT, TILAPIA AND COD, TOO, WHILE WE'RE DOING A SEAFOOD THEME.
HERE, YOU CAN USE THIS UNTIL WE GET HOME.
I THINK YOU'RE GOING TO LIKE IT HERE...

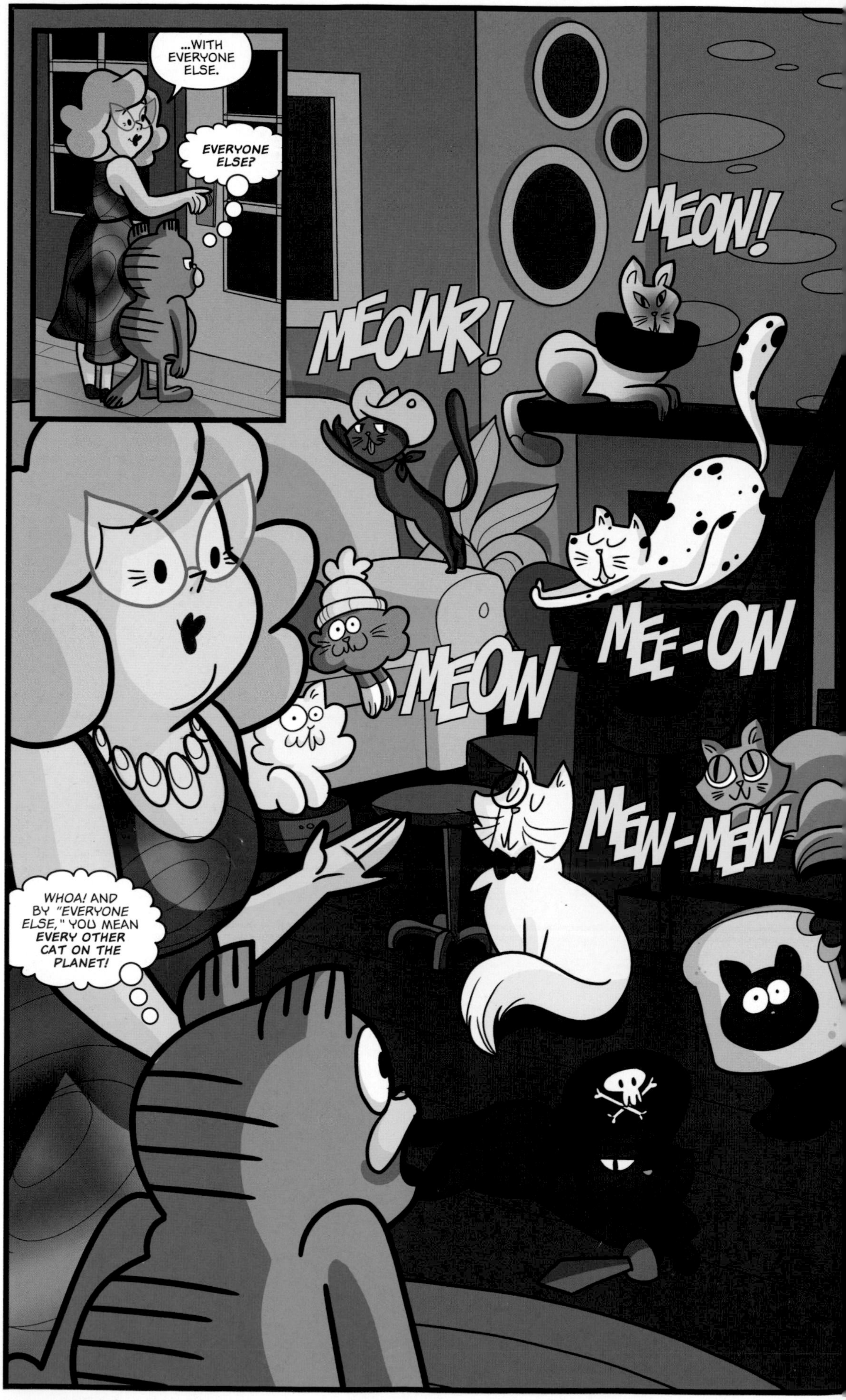
...WITH EVERYONE ELSE.
EVERYONE ELSE?
MEOW!
MEOWR!
MEOW
MEE-OW
MEW-MEW
WHOA! AND BY "EVERYONE ELSE," YOU MEAN EVERY OTHER CAT ON THE PLANET!

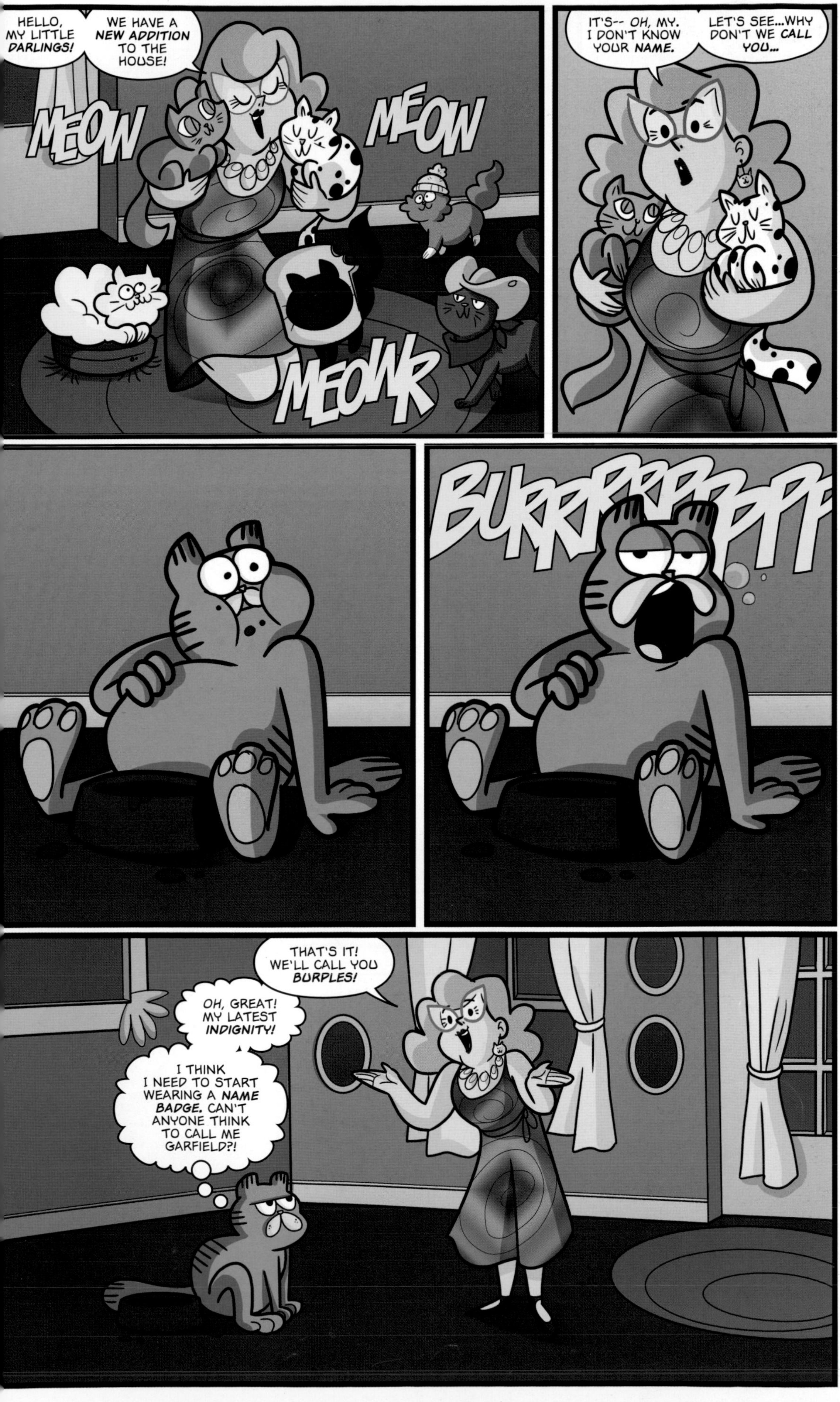

HELLO, MY LITTLE *DARLINGS!*
WE HAVE A *NEW ADDITION* TO THE HOUSE!
MEOW
MEOW
MEOWR
IT'S-- *OH, MY.* I DON'T KNOW YOUR *NAME.*
LET'S SEE...WHY DON'T WE *CALL YOU...*
BURRRRRPPP
THAT'S IT! WE'LL CALL YOU *BURPLES!*
OH, GREAT! MY LATEST *INDIGNITY!*
I THINK I NEED TO START WEARING A *NAME BADGE.* CAN'T ANYONE THINK TO CALL ME GARFIELD?!

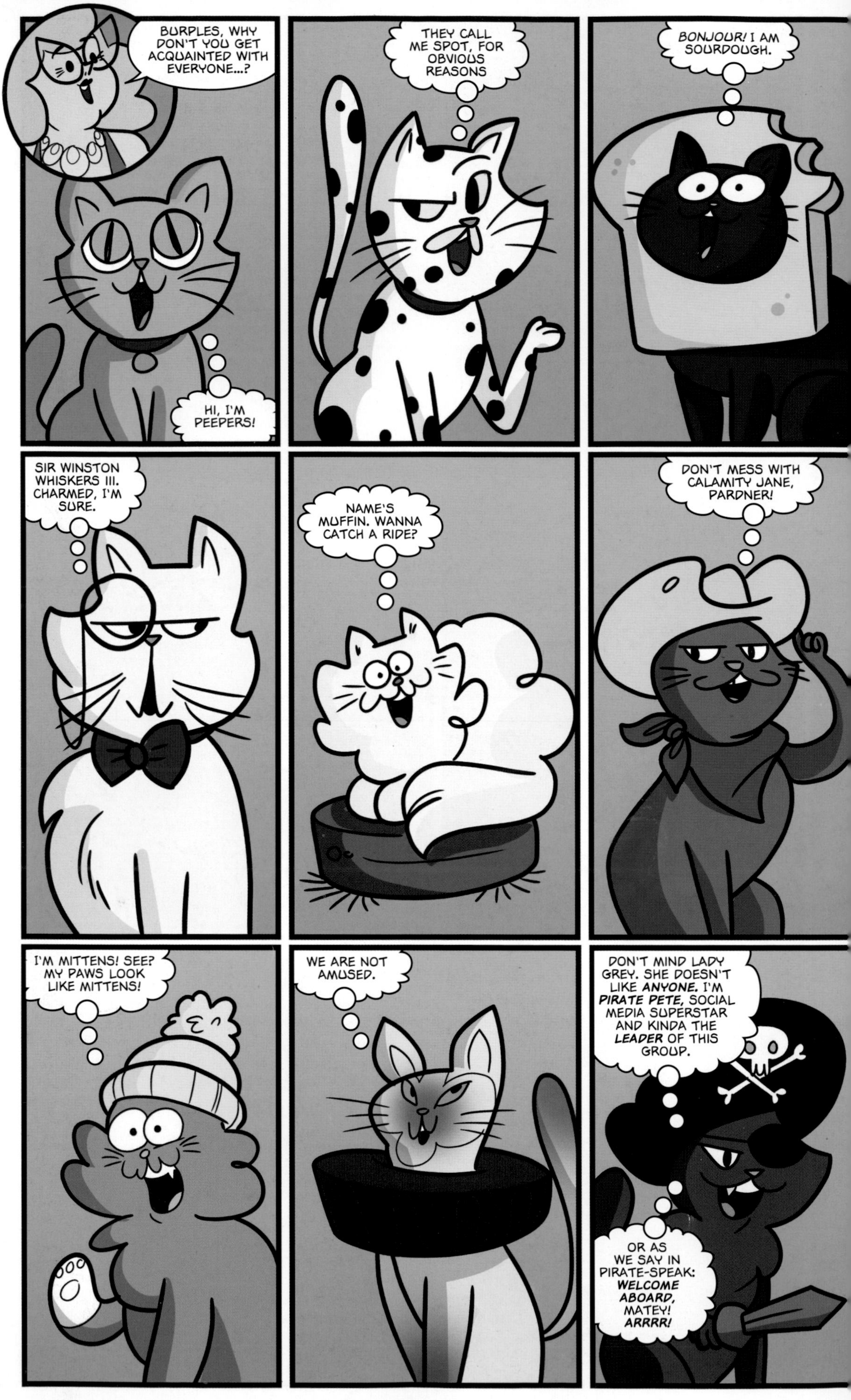
BURPLES, WHY DON'T YOU GET ACQUAINTED WITH EVERYONE...?
HI, I'M PEEPERS!
THEY CALL ME SPOT, FOR OBVIOUS REASONS
BONJOUR! I AM SOURDOUGH.
SIR WINSTON WHISKERS III. CHARMED, I'M SURE.
NAME'S MUFFIN. WANNA CATCH A RIDE?
DON'T MESS WITH CALAMITY JANE, PARDNER!
I'M MITTENS! SEE? MY PAWS LOOK LIKE MITTENS!
WE ARE NOT AMUSED.
DON'T MIND LADY GREY. SHE DOESN'T LIKE ANYONE. I'M PIRATE PETE, SOCIAL MEDIA SUPERSTAR AND KINDA THE LEADER OF THIS GROUP.
OR AS WE SAY IN PIRATE-SPEAK: WELCOME ABOARD, MATEY! ARRRR!

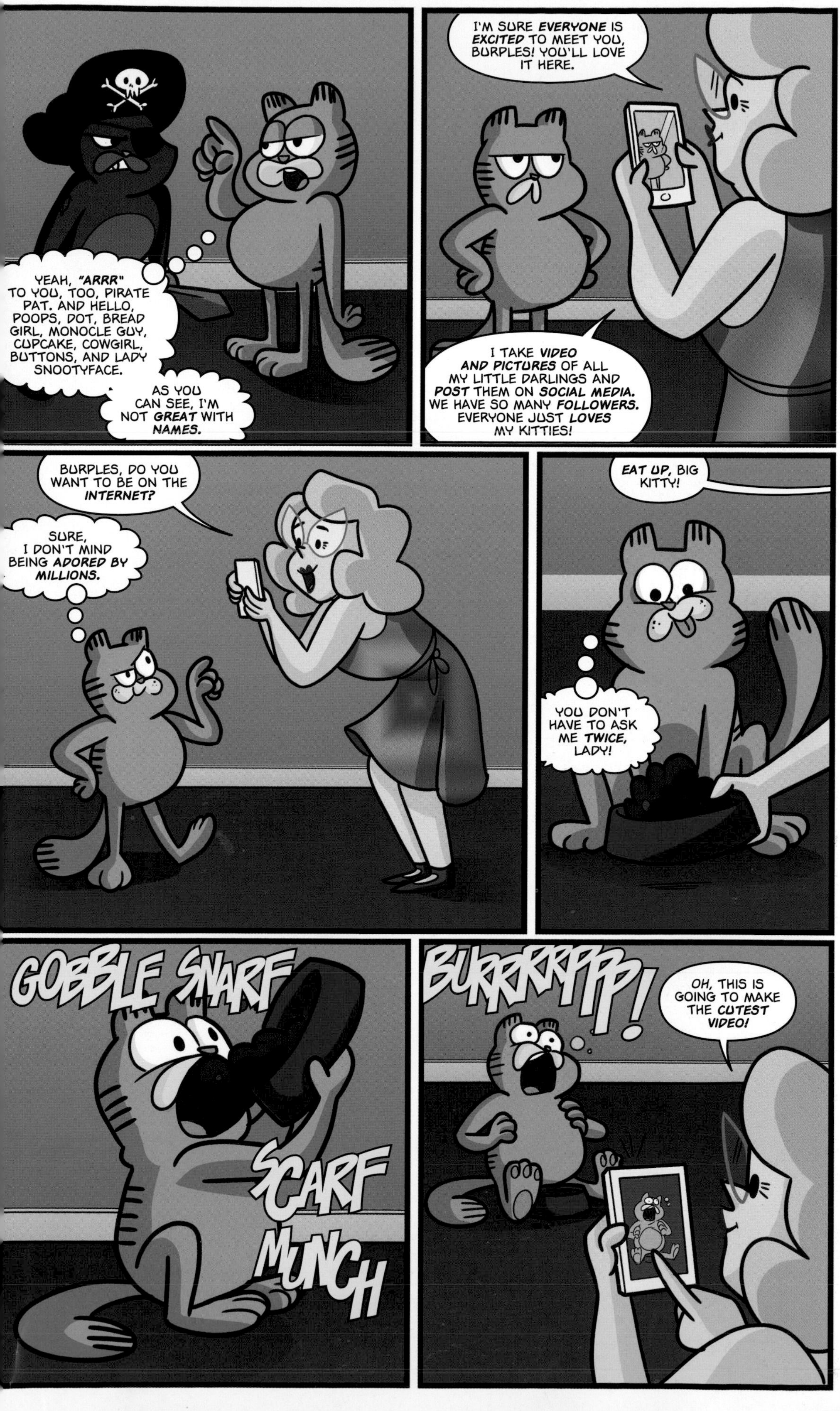
YEAH, "ARRR" TO YOU, TOO, PIRATE PAT. AND HELLO, POOPS, DOT, BREAD GIRL, MONOCLE GUY, CUPCAKE, COWGIRL, BUTTONS, AND LADY SNOOTYFACE.
AS YOU CAN SEE, I'M NOT GREAT WITH NAMES.
I'M SURE EVERYONE IS EXCITED TO MEET YOU, BURPLES! YOU'LL LOVE IT HERE.
I TAKE VIDEO AND PICTURES OF ALL MY LITTLE DARLINGS AND POST THEM ON SOCIAL MEDIA. WE HAVE SO MANY FOLLOWERS. EVERYONE JUST LOVES MY KITTIES!
BURPLES, DO YOU WANT TO BE ON THE INTERNET?
SURE, I DON'T MIND BEING ADORED BY MILLIONS.
EAT UP, BIG KITTY!
YOU DON'T HAVE TO ASK ME TWICE, LADY!
GOBBLE SNARF
SCARF
MUNCH
BURRRRPPP!
OH, THIS IS GOING TO MAKE THE CUTEST VIDEO!

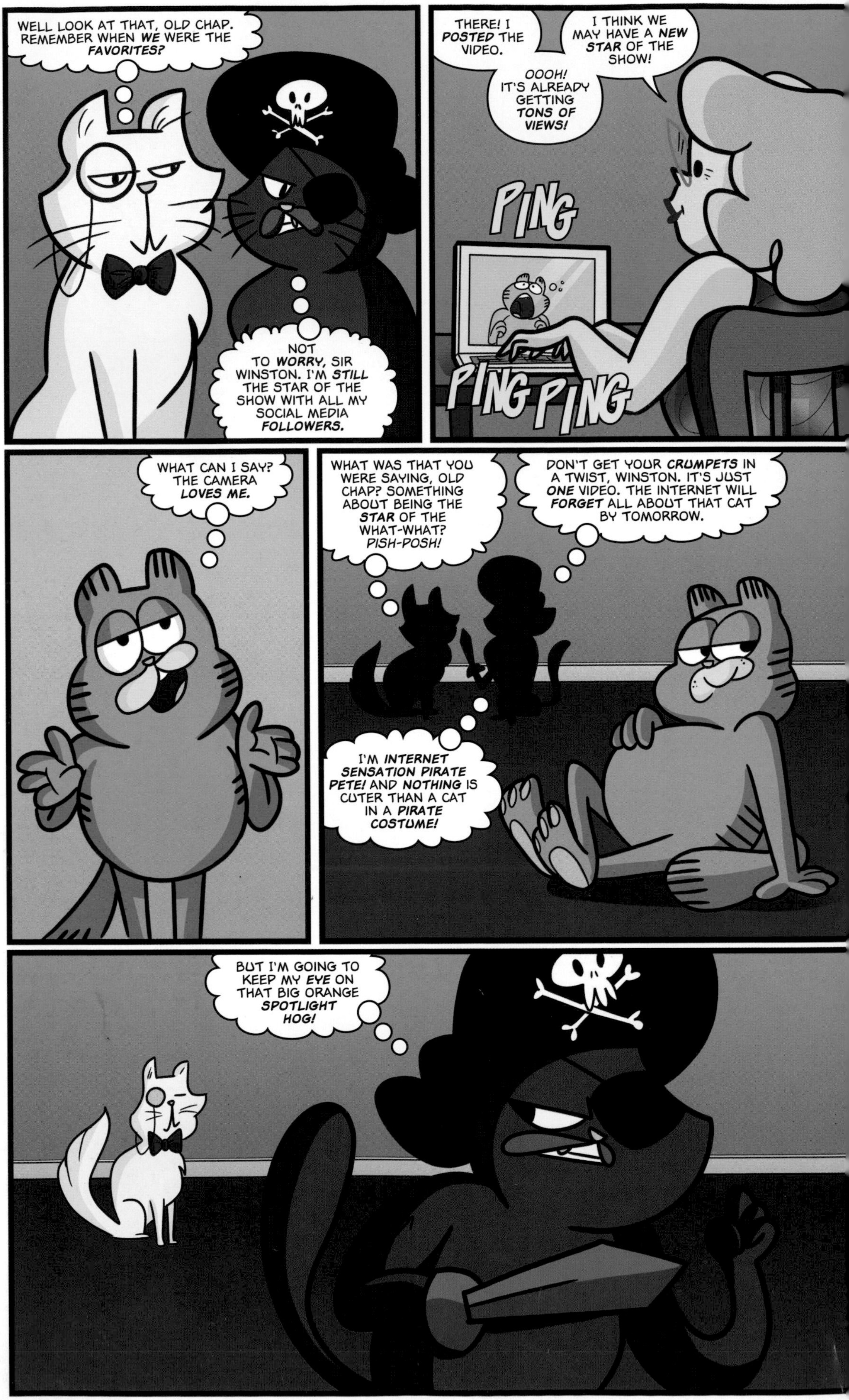
WELL LOOK AT THAT, OLD CHAP. REMEMBER WHEN WE WERE THE FAVORITES?
NOT TO WORRY, SIR WINSTON. I'M STILL THE STAR OF THE SHOW WITH ALL MY SOCIAL MEDIA FOLLOWERS.
THERE! I POSTED THE VIDEO.
I THINK WE MAY HAVE A NEW STAR OF THE SHOW!
OOOH! IT'S ALREADY GETTING TONS OF VIEWS!
PING
PING PING
WHAT CAN I SAY? THE CAMERA LOVES ME.
WHAT WAS THAT YOU WERE SAYING, OLD CHAP? SOMETHING ABOUT BEING THE STAR OF THE WHAT-WHAT? PISH-POSH!
DON'T GET YOUR CRUMPETS IN A TWIST, WINSTON. IT'S JUST ONE VIDEO. THE INTERNET WILL FORGET ALL ABOUT THAT CAT BY TOMORROW.
I'M INTERNET SENSATION PIRATE PETE! AND NOTHING IS CUTER THAN A CAT IN A PIRATE COSTUME!
BUT I'M GOING TO KEEP MY EYE ON THAT BIG ORANGE SPOTLIGHT HOG!

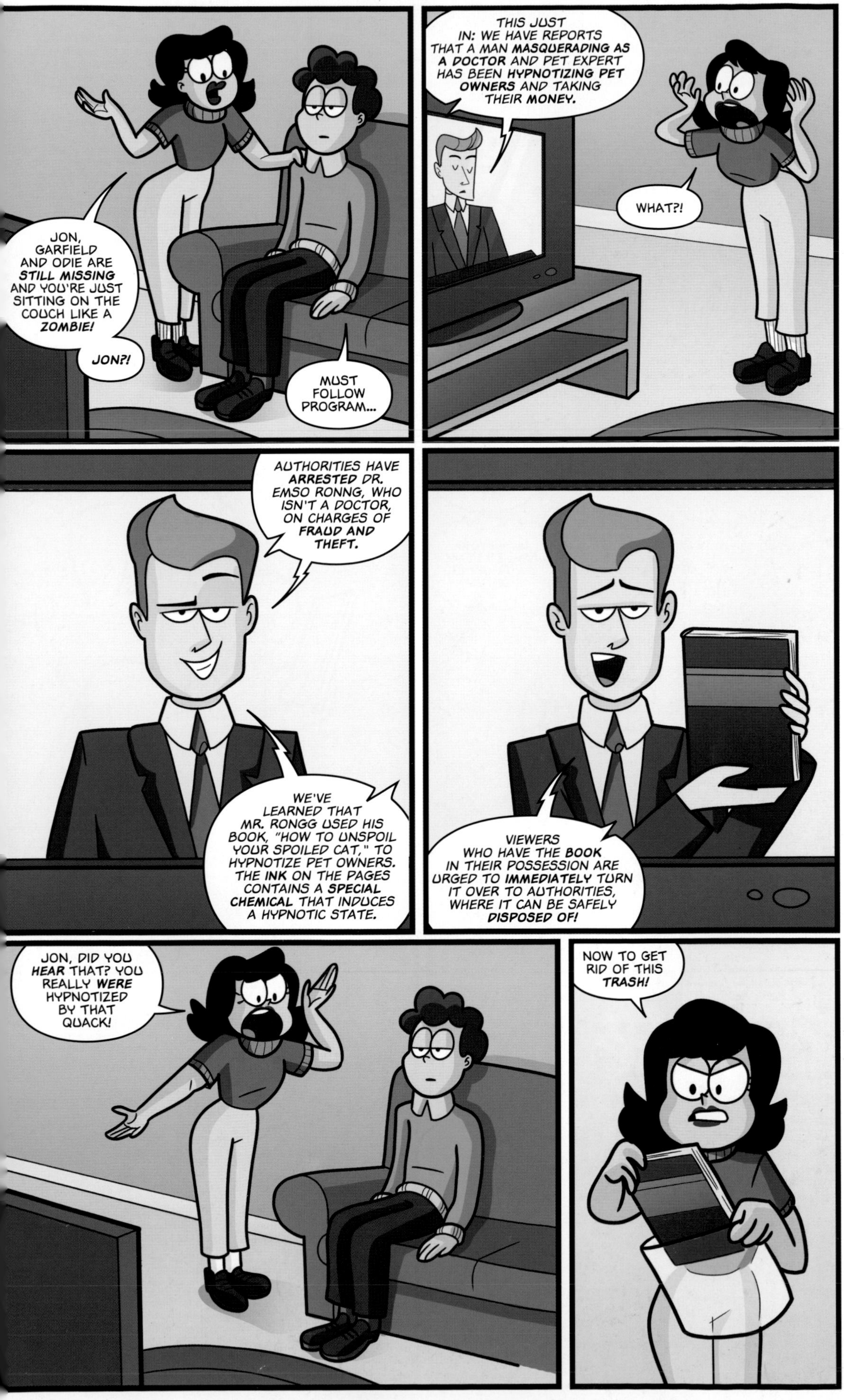
JON, GARFIELD AND ODIE ARE STILL MISSING AND YOU'RE JUST SITTING ON THE COUCH LIKE A ZOMBIE!
JON?!
MUST FOLLOW PROGRAM...
THIS JUST IN: WE HAVE REPORTS THAT A MAN MASQUERADING AS A DOCTOR AND PET EXPERT HAS BEEN HYPNOTIZING PET OWNERS AND TAKING THEIR MONEY.
WHAT?!
AUTHORITIES HAVE ARRESTED DR. EMSO RONNG, WHO ISN'T A DOCTOR, ON CHARGES OF FRAUD AND THEFT.
WE'VE LEARNED THAT MR. RONGG USED HIS BOOK, "HOW TO UNSPOIL YOUR SPOILED CAT," TO HYPNOTIZE PET OWNERS. THE INK ON THE PAGES CONTAINS A SPECIAL CHEMICAL THAT INDUCES A HYPNOTIC STATE.
VIEWERS WHO HAVE THE BOOK IN THEIR POSSESSION ARE URGED TO IMMEDIATELY TURN IT OVER TO AUTHORITIES, WHERE IT CAN BE SAFELY DISPOSED OF!
JON, DID YOU HEAR THAT? YOU REALLY WERE HYPNOTIZED BY THAT QUACK!
NOW TO GET RID OF THIS TRASH!

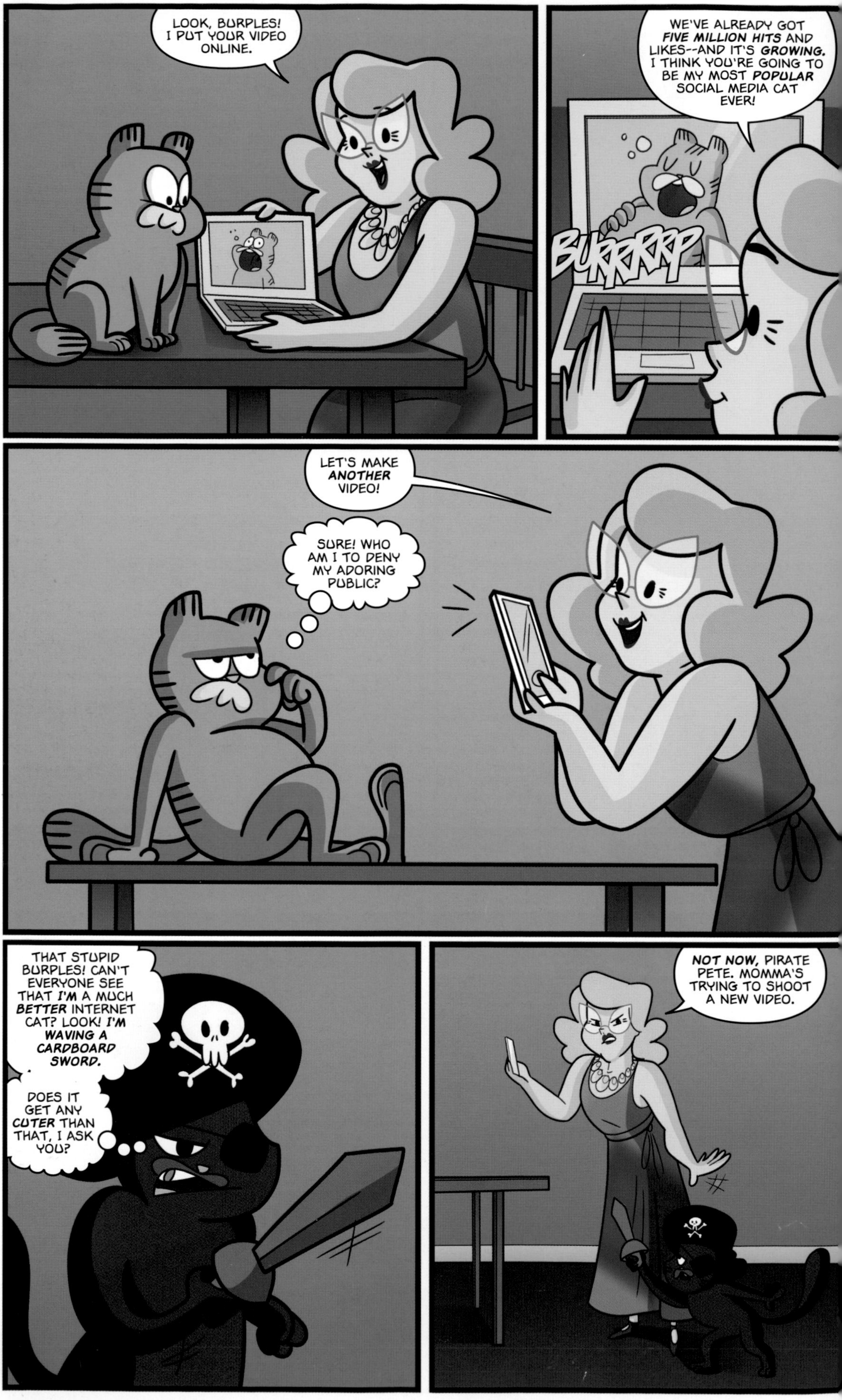
LOOK, BURPLES! I PUT YOUR VIDEO ONLINE.
WE'VE ALREADY GOT **FIVE MILLION HITS** AND LIKES--AND IT'S **GROWING.** I THINK YOU'RE GOING TO BE MY MOST **POPULAR** SOCIAL MEDIA CAT EVER!
BURRRRP
LET'S MAKE **ANOTHER** VIDEO!
SURE! WHO AM I TO DENY MY ADORING PUBLIC?
THAT STUPID BURPLES! CAN'T EVERYONE SEE THAT ***I'M*** A MUCH ***BETTER*** INTERNET CAT? LOOK! ***I'M WAVING A CARDBOARD SWORD.***
DOES IT GET ANY ***CUTER*** THAN THAT, I ASK YOU?
NOT NOW, PIRATE PETE. MOMMA'S TRYING TO SHOOT A NEW VIDEO.

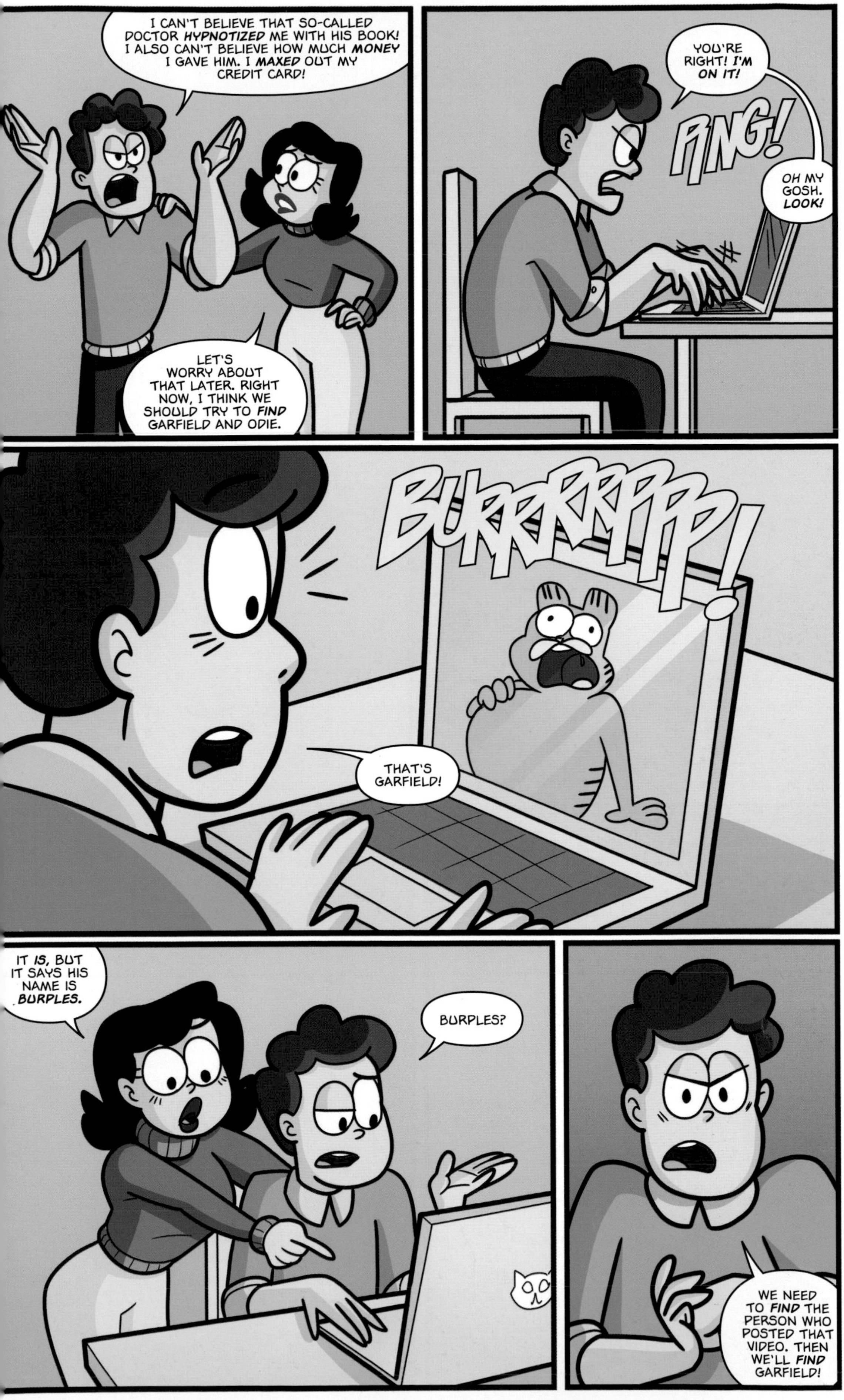
I CAN'T BELIEVE THAT SO-CALLED DOCTOR HYPNOTIZED ME WITH HIS BOOK! I ALSO CAN'T BELIEVE HOW MUCH MONEY I GAVE HIM. I MAXED OUT MY CREDIT CARD!
LET'S WORRY ABOUT THAT LATER. RIGHT NOW, I THINK WE SHOULD TRY TO FIND GARFIELD AND ODIE.
YOU'RE RIGHT! I'M ON IT!
RING!
OH MY GOSH. LOOK!
BURRRRPPP!
THAT'S GARFIELD!
IT IS, BUT IT SAYS HIS NAME IS BURPLES.
BURPLES?
WE NEED TO FIND THE PERSON WHO POSTED THAT VIDEO. THEN WE'LL FIND GARFIELD!

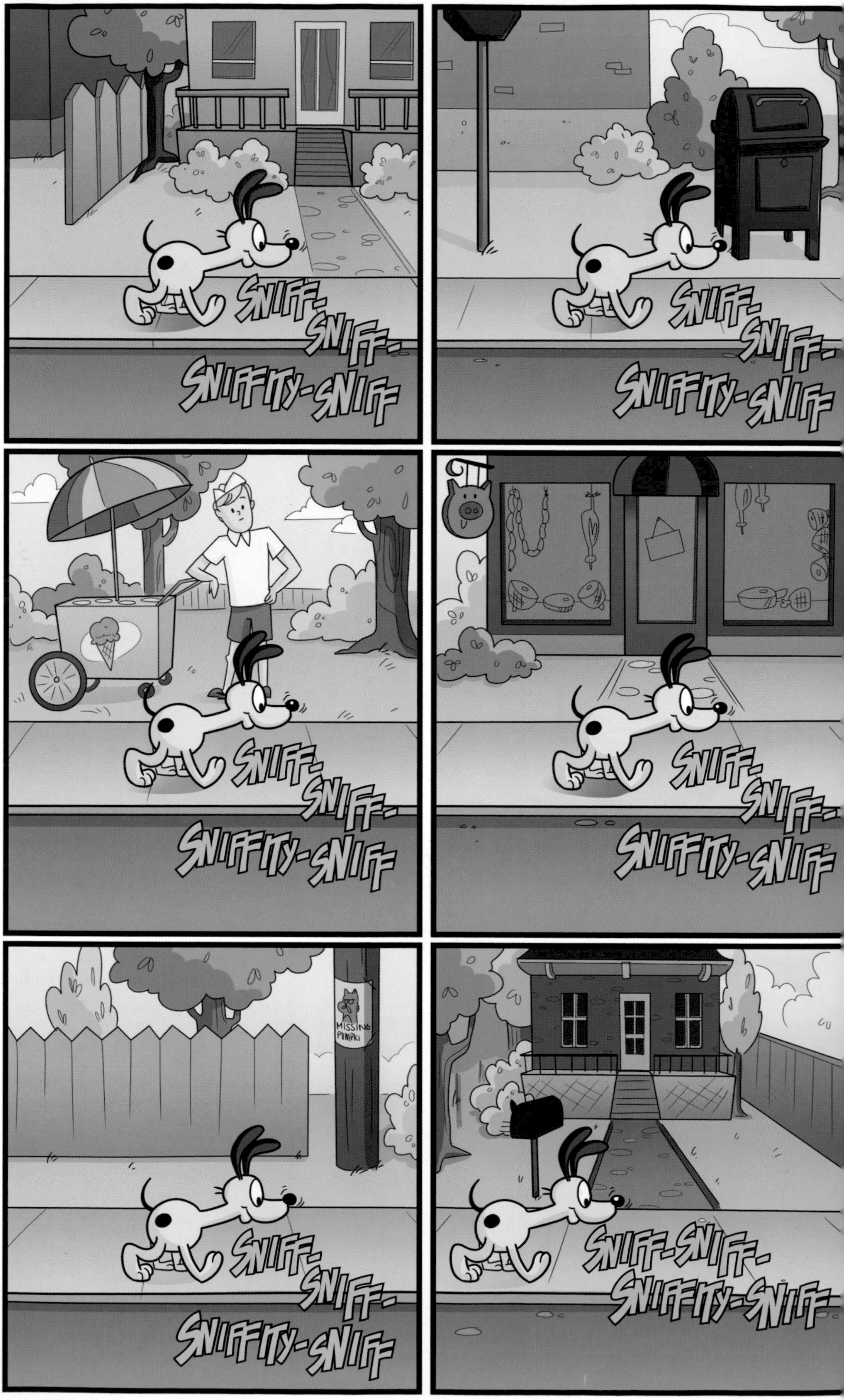
SNIFF-SNIFF-SNIFFITY-SNIFF
SNIFF-SNIFF-SNIFFITY-SNIFF
SNIFF-SNIFF-SNIFFITY-SNIFF
SNIFF-SNIFF-SNIFFITY-SNIFF
MISSING PUMPKI
SNIFF-SNIFF-SNIFFITY-SNIFF
SNIFF-SNIFF-SNIFFITY-SNIFF

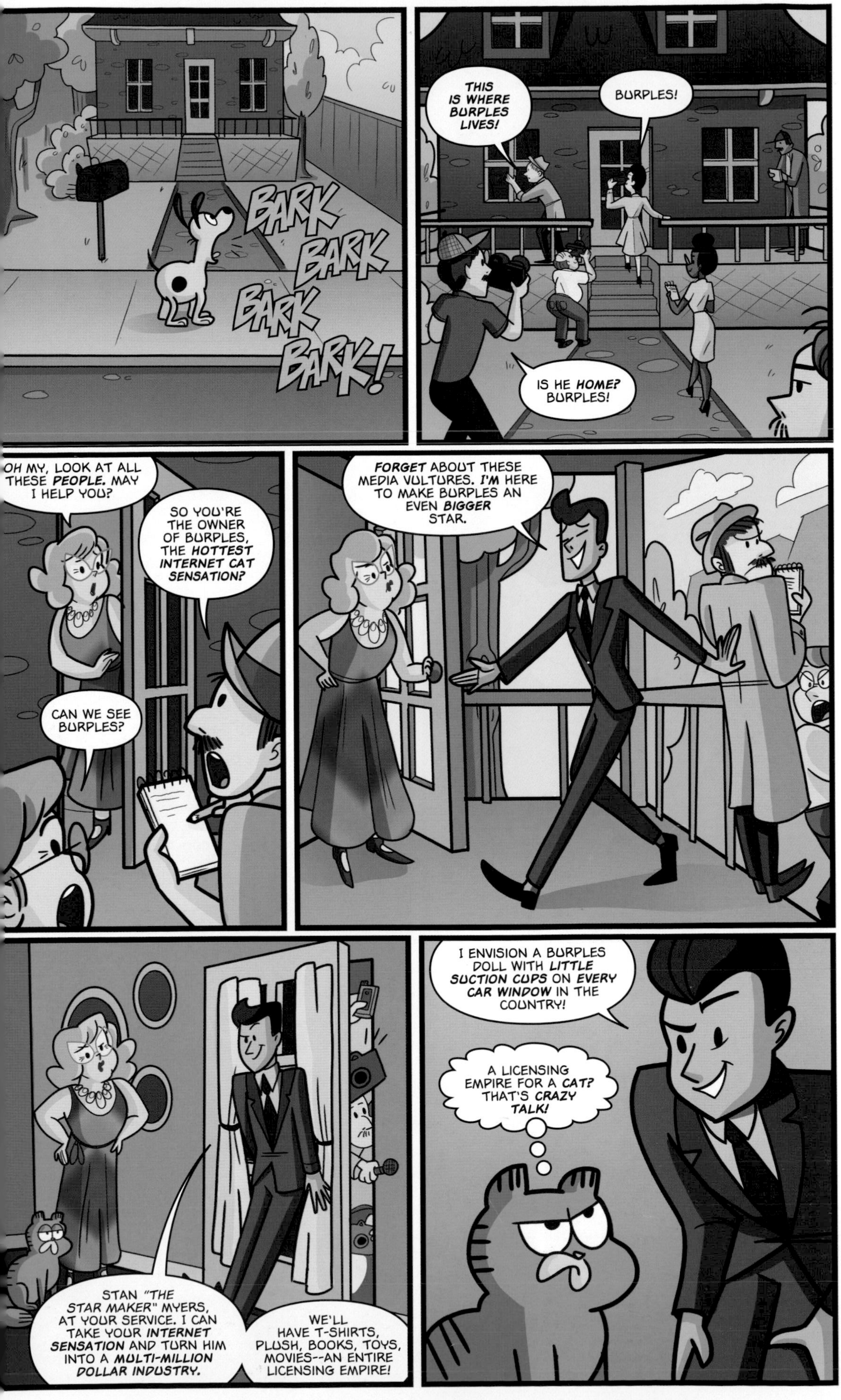
BARK BARK BARK BARK!
THIS IS WHERE BURPLES LIVES!
BURPLES!
IS HE HOME? BURPLES!
OH MY, LOOK AT ALL THESE PEOPLE. MAY I HELP YOU?
SO YOU'RE THE OWNER OF BURPLES, THE HOTTEST INTERNET CAT SENSATION?
CAN WE SEE BURPLES?
FORGET ABOUT THESE MEDIA VULTURES. I'M HERE TO MAKE BURPLES AN EVEN BIGGER STAR.
STAN "THE STAR MAKER" MYERS, AT YOUR SERVICE. I CAN TAKE YOUR INTERNET SENSATION AND TURN HIM INTO A MULTI-MILLION DOLLAR INDUSTRY.
WE'LL HAVE T-SHIRTS, PLUSH, BOOKS, TOYS, MOVIES--AN ENTIRE LICENSING EMPIRE!
I ENVISION A BURPLES DOLL WITH LITTLE SUCTION CUPS ON EVERY CAR WINDOW IN THE COUNTRY!
A LICENSING EMPIRE FOR A CAT? THAT'S CRAZY TALK!

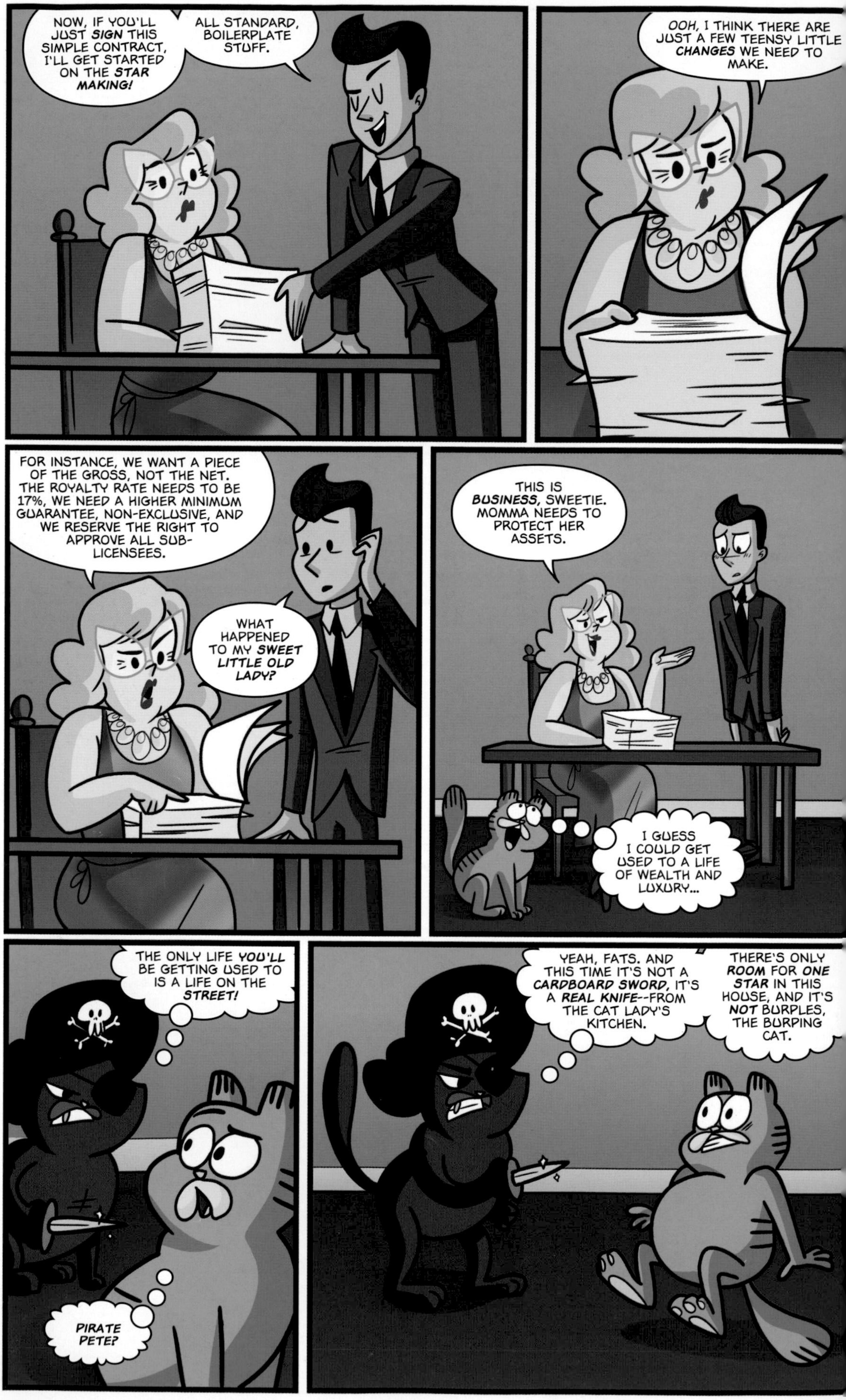
NOW, IF YOU'LL JUST SIGN THIS SIMPLE CONTRACT, I'LL GET STARTED ON THE STAR MAKING!
ALL STANDARD, BOILERPLATE STUFF.
OOH, I THINK THERE ARE JUST A FEW TEENSY LITTLE CHANGES WE NEED TO MAKE.
FOR INSTANCE, WE WANT A PIECE OF THE GROSS, NOT THE NET. THE ROYALTY RATE NEEDS TO BE 17%, WE NEED A HIGHER MINIMUM GUARANTEE, NON-EXCLUSIVE, AND WE RESERVE THE RIGHT TO APPROVE ALL SUB-LICENSEES.
WHAT HAPPENED TO MY SWEET LITTLE OLD LADY?
THIS IS BUSINESS, SWEETIE. MOMMA NEEDS TO PROTECT HER ASSETS.
I GUESS I COULD GET USED TO A LIFE OF WEALTH AND LUXURY...
THE ONLY LIFE YOU'LL BE GETTING USED TO IS A LIFE ON THE STREET!
PIRATE PETE?
YEAH, FATS. AND THIS TIME IT'S NOT A CARDBOARD SWORD, IT'S A REAL KNIFE--FROM THE CAT LADY'S KITCHEN.
THERE'S ONLY ROOM FOR ONE STAR IN THIS HOUSE, AND IT'S NOT BURPLES, THE BURPING CAT.

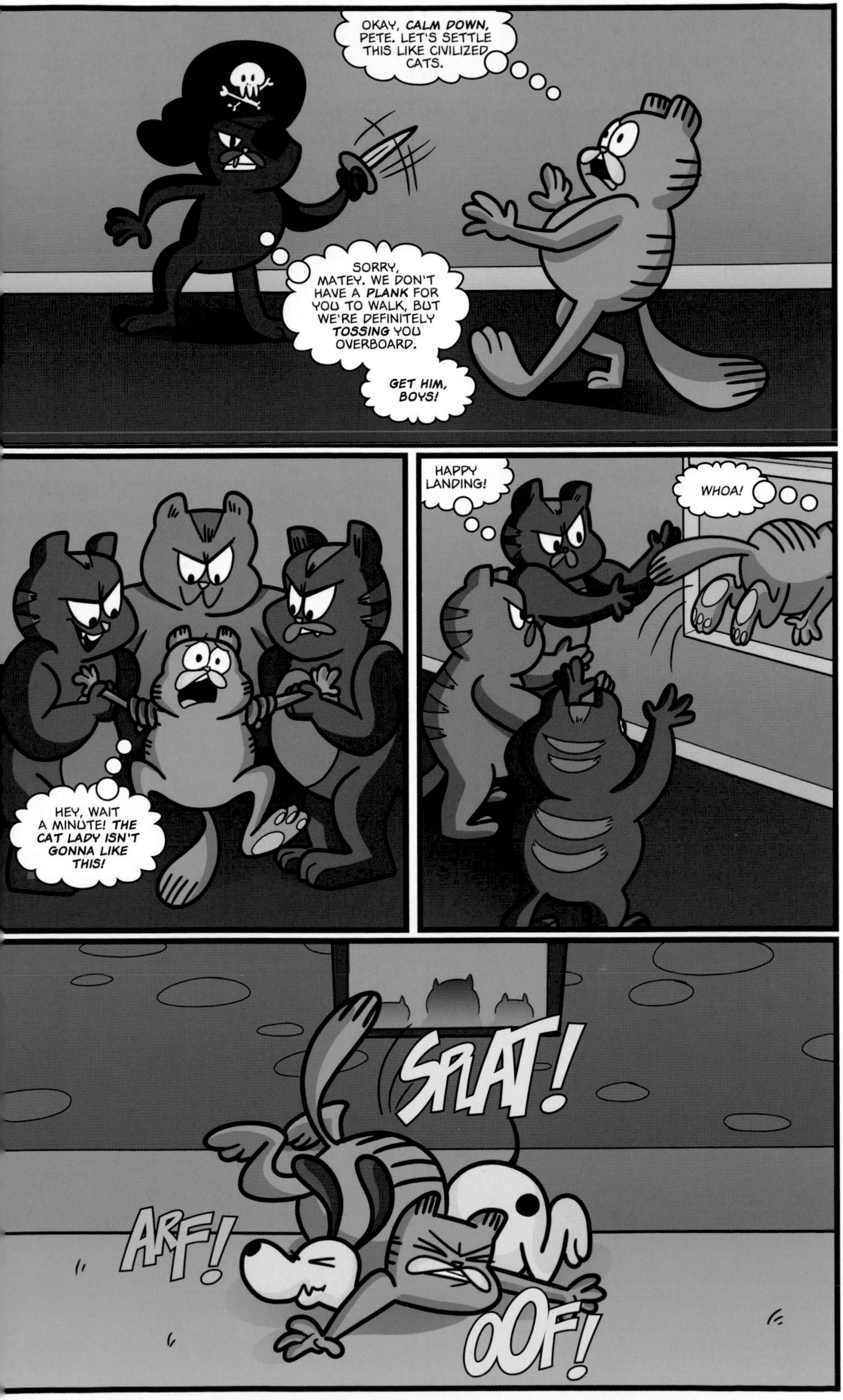

OKAY, CALM DOWN, PETE. LET'S SETTLE THIS LIKE CIVILIZED CATS.
SORRY, MATEY. WE DON'T HAVE A PLANK FOR YOU TO WALK, BUT WE'RE DEFINITELY TOSSING YOU OVERBOARD.
GET HIM, BOYS!
HEY, WAIT A MINUTE! THE CAT LADY ISN'T GONNA LIKE THIS!
HAPPY LANDING!
WHOA!
SPLAT!
ARF!
OOF!

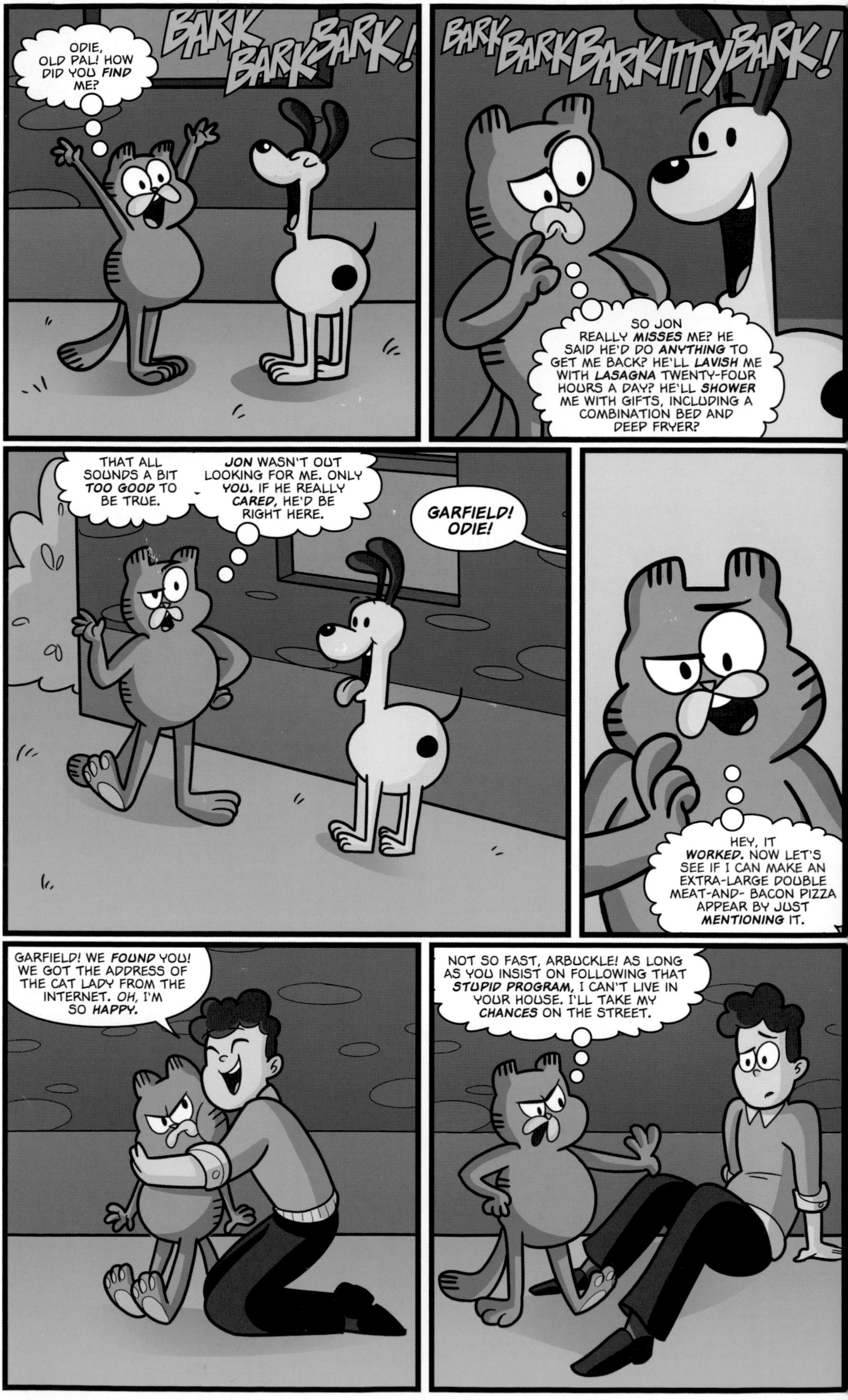

ODIE, OLD PAL! HOW DID YOU FIND ME?
BARK BARK BARK!
BARK BARK BARKITTYBARK!
SO JON REALLY MISSES ME? HE SAID HE'D DO ANYTHING TO GET ME BACK? HE'LL LAVISH ME WITH LASAGNA TWENTY-FOUR HOURS A DAY? HE'LL SHOWER ME WITH GIFTS, INCLUDING A COMBINATION BED AND DEEP FRYER?
THAT ALL SOUNDS A BIT TOO GOOD TO BE TRUE.
JON WASN'T OUT LOOKING FOR ME. ONLY YOU. IF HE REALLY CARED, HE'D BE RIGHT HERE.
GARFIELD! ODIE!
HEY, IT WORKED. NOW LET'S SEE IF I CAN MAKE AN EXTRA-LARGE DOUBLE MEAT-AND- BACON PIZZA APPEAR BY JUST MENTIONING IT.
GARFIELD! WE FOUND YOU! WE GOT THE ADDRESS OF THE CAT LADY FROM THE INTERNET. OH, I'M SO HAPPY.
NOT SO FAST, ARBUCKLE! AS LONG AS YOU INSIST ON FOLLOWING THAT STUPID PROGRAM, I CAN'T LIVE IN YOUR HOUSE. I'LL TAKE MY CHANCES ON THE STREET.

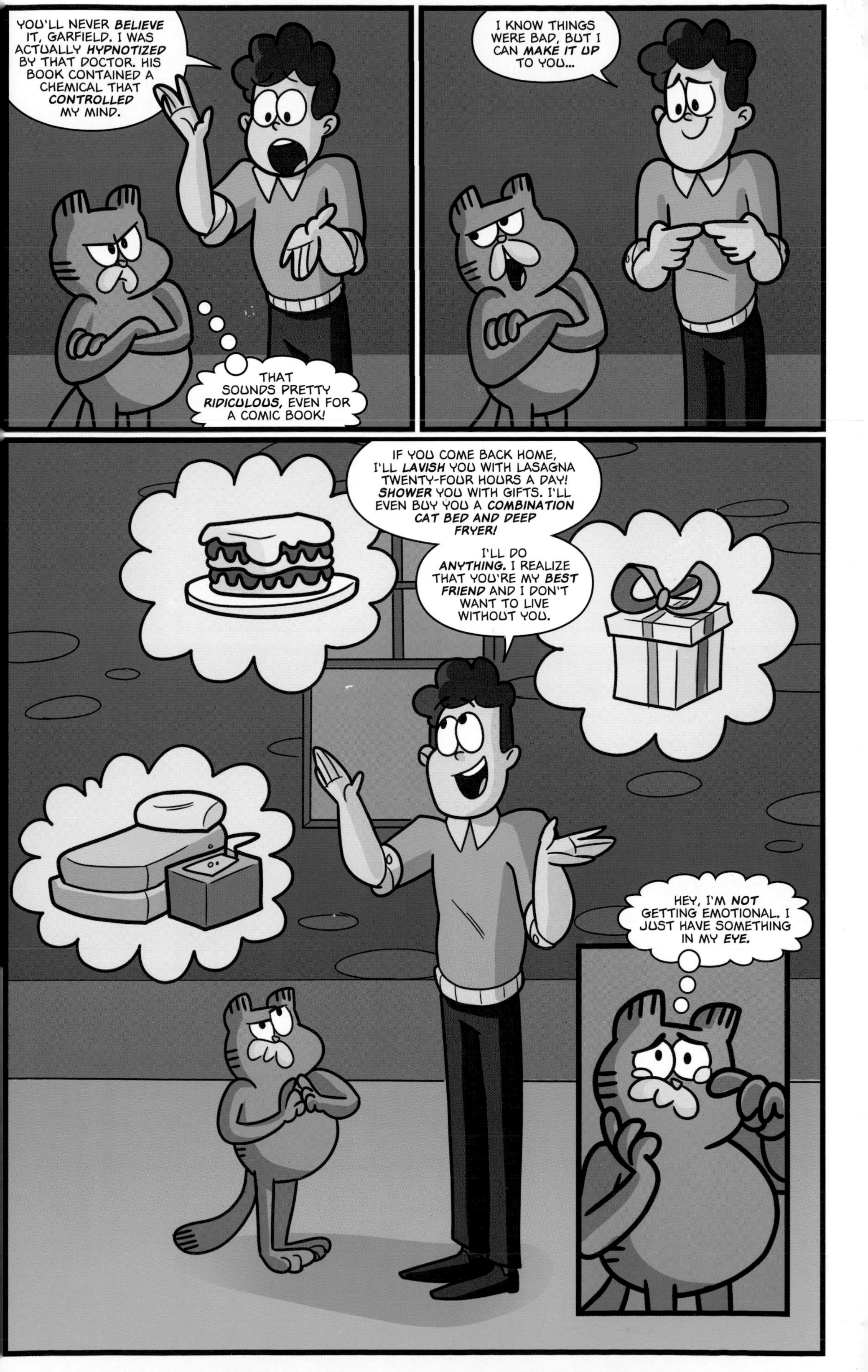
YOU'LL NEVER BELIEVE IT, GARFIELD. I WAS ACTUALLY HYPNOTIZED BY THAT DOCTOR. HIS BOOK CONTAINED A CHEMICAL THAT CONTROLLED MY MIND.
THAT SOUNDS PRETTY RIDICULOUS, EVEN FOR A COMIC BOOK!
I KNOW THINGS WERE BAD, BUT I CAN MAKE IT UP TO YOU...
IF YOU COME BACK HOME, I'LL LAVISH YOU WITH LASAGNA TWENTY-FOUR HOURS A DAY! SHOWER YOU WITH GIFTS. I'LL EVEN BUY YOU A COMBINATION CAT BED AND DEEP FRYER!
I'LL DO ANYTHING. I REALIZE THAT YOU'RE MY BEST FRIEND AND I DON'T WANT TO LIVE WITHOUT YOU.
HEY, I'M NOT GETTING EMOTIONAL. I JUST HAVE SOMETHING IN MY EYE.

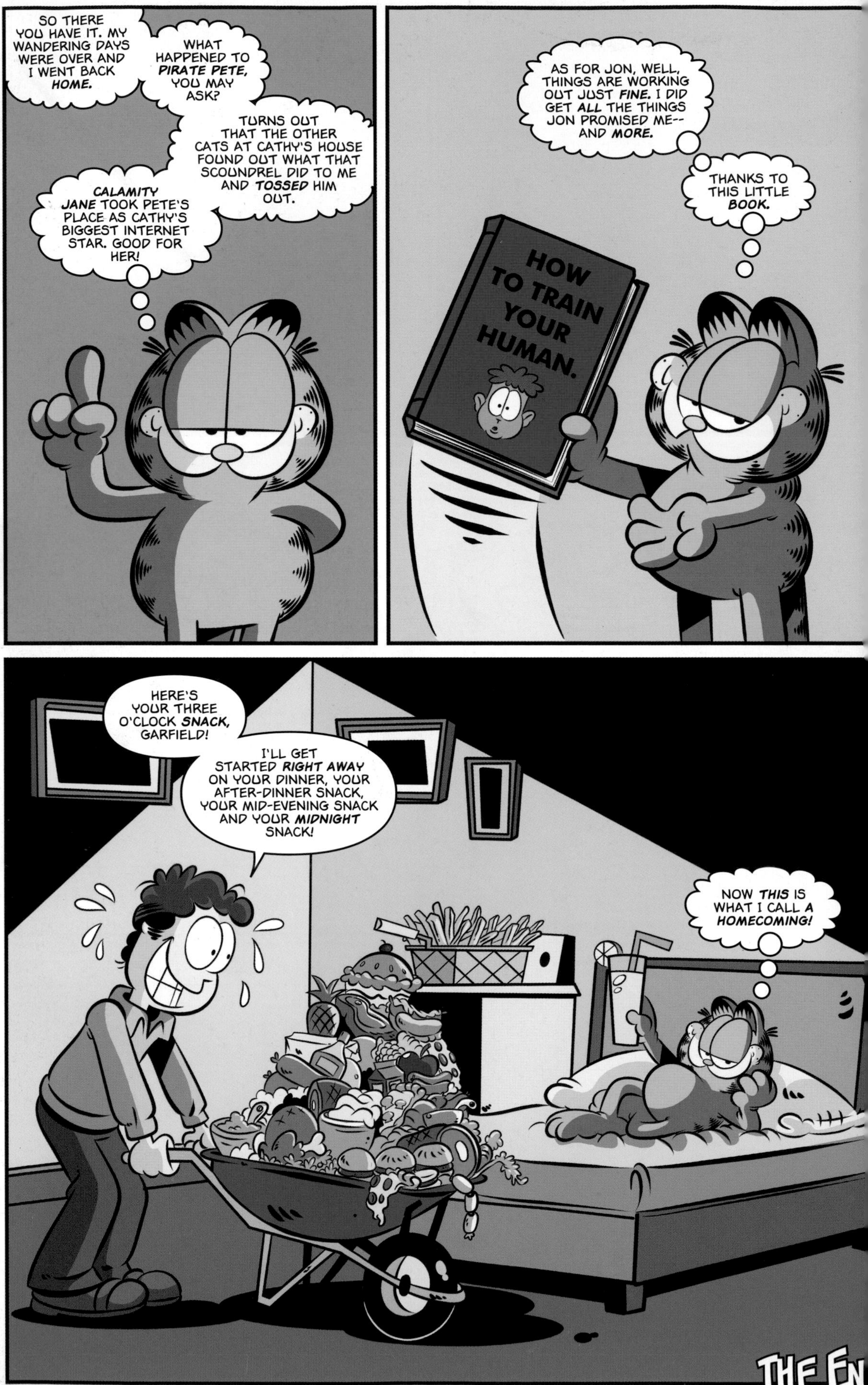
SO THERE YOU HAVE IT. MY WANDERING DAYS WERE OVER AND I WENT BACK HOME.
WHAT HAPPENED TO PIRATE PETE, YOU MAY ASK?
TURNS OUT THAT THE OTHER CATS AT CATHY'S HOUSE FOUND OUT WHAT THAT SCOUNDREL DID TO ME AND TOSSED HIM OUT.
CALAMITY JANE TOOK PETE'S PLACE AS CATHY'S BIGGEST INTERNET STAR. GOOD FOR HER!
AS FOR JON, WELL, THINGS ARE WORKING OUT JUST FINE. I DID GET ALL THE THINGS JON PROMISED ME-- AND MORE.
THANKS TO THIS LITTLE BOOK.
HOW TO TRAIN YOUR HUMAN.
HERE'S YOUR THREE O'CLOCK SNACK, GARFIELD!
I'LL GET STARTED RIGHT AWAY ON YOUR DINNER, YOUR AFTER-DINNER SNACK, YOUR MID-EVENING SNACK AND YOUR MIDNIGHT SNACK!
NOW THIS IS WHAT I CALL A HOMECOMING!
THE EN

COVER GALLERY

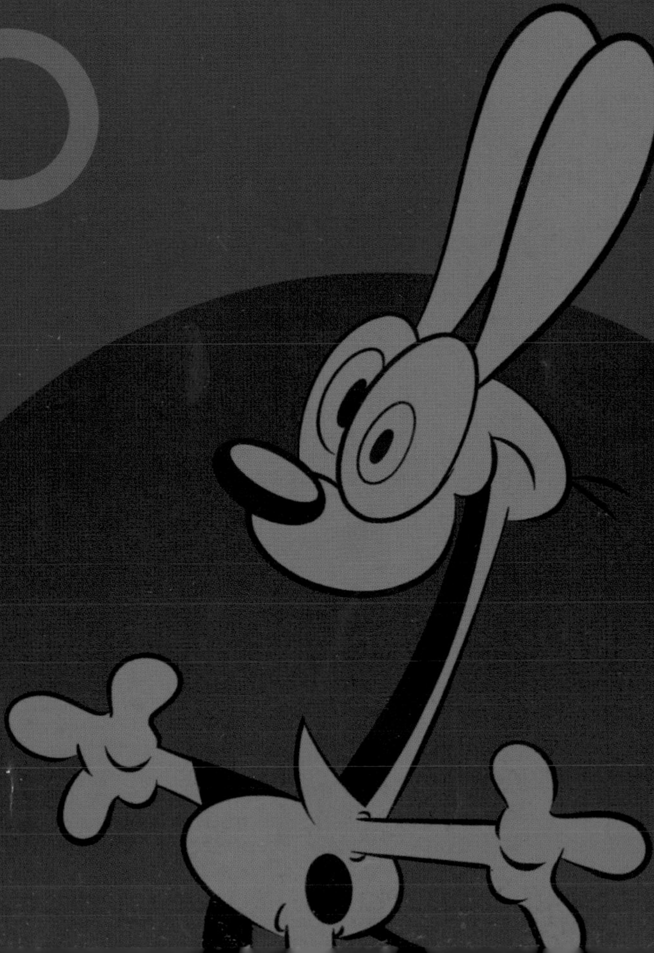

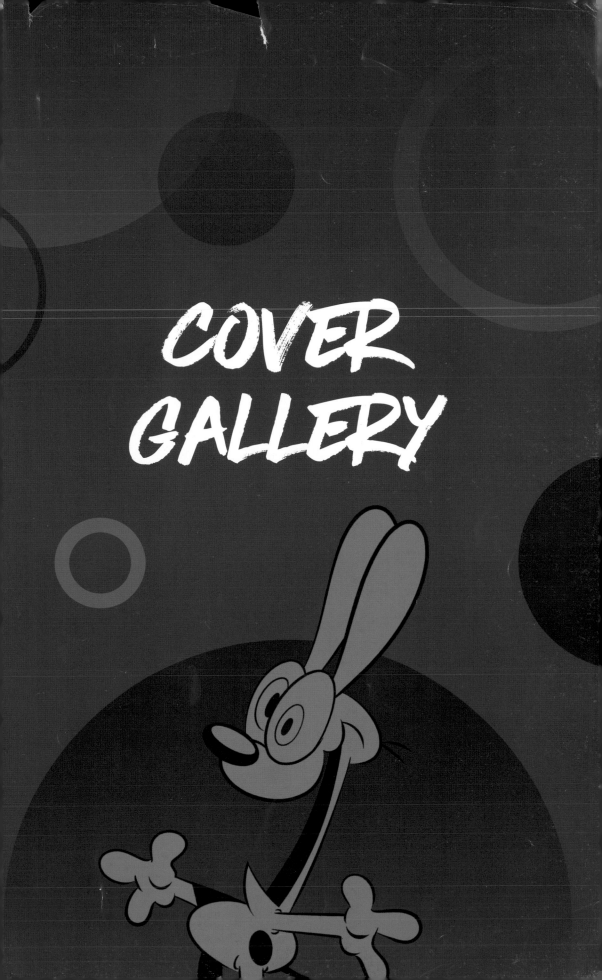

#1 COVER BY
ANDY HIRSCH
WITH SARA TALMADGE

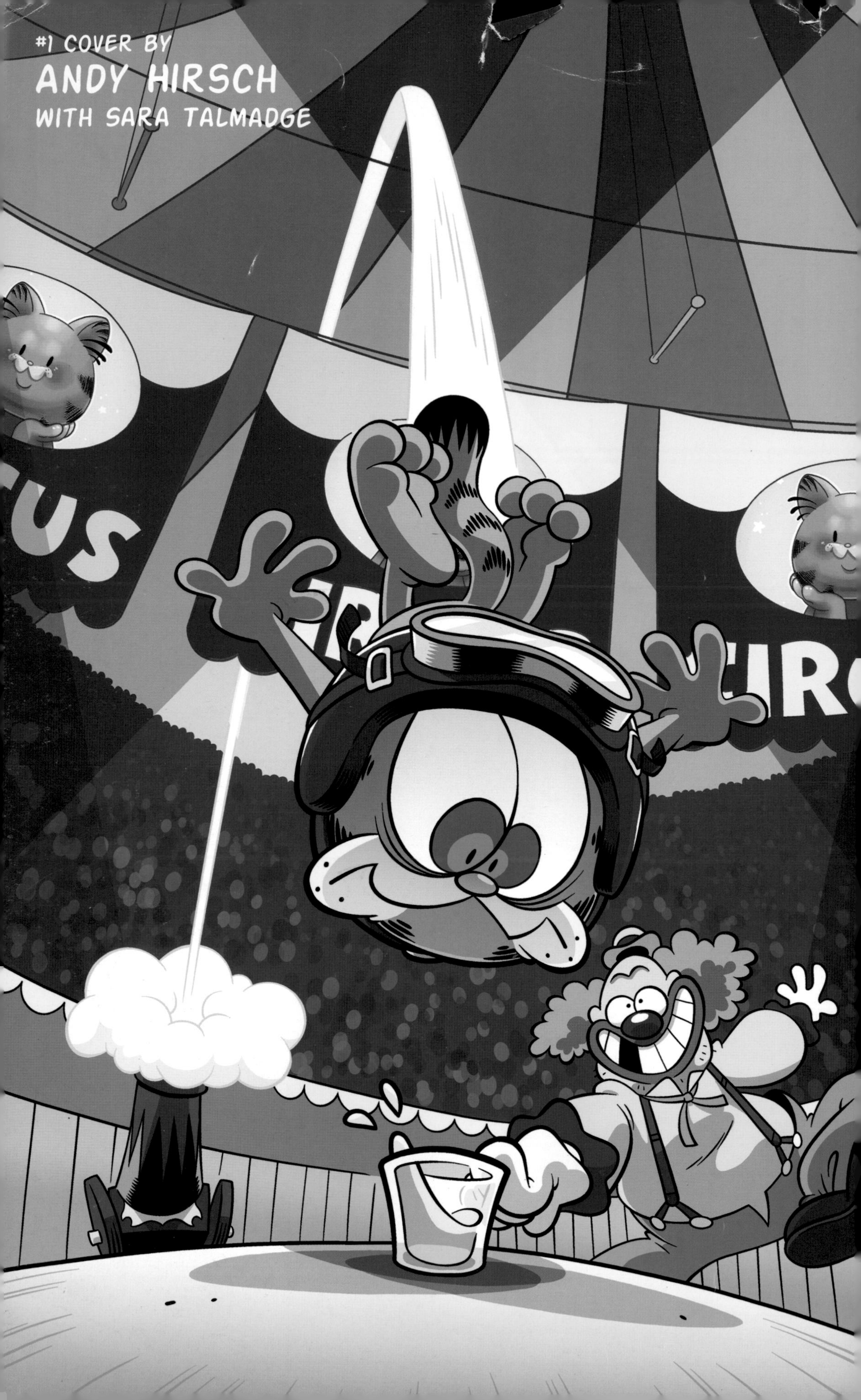

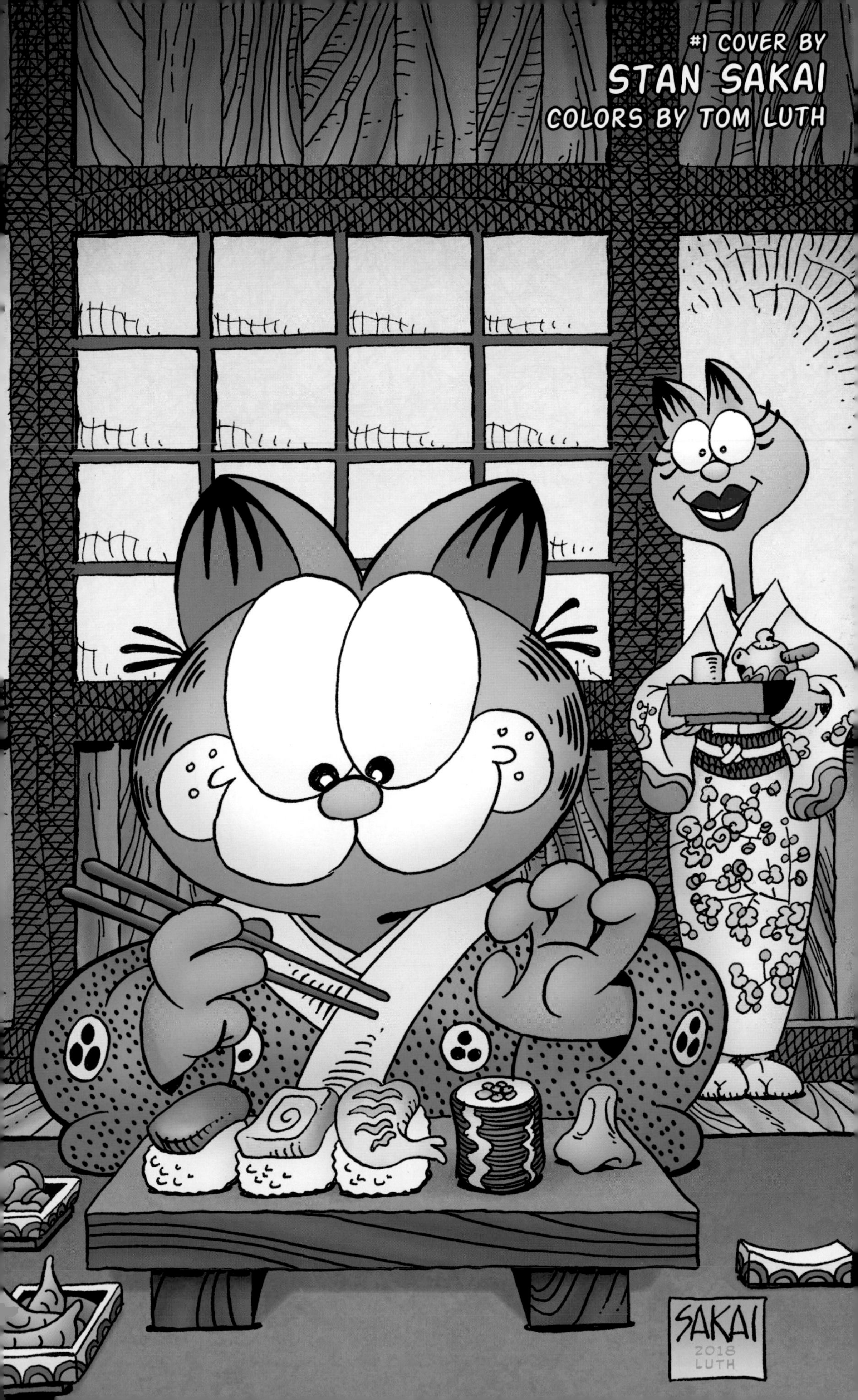
SAKAI
2018
LUTH

#1 COVER BY
STAN SAKAI
COLORS BY TOM LUTH

#2 COVER BY
ANDY HIRSCH
WITH SHELLI PAROLINE
& BRADEN LAMB

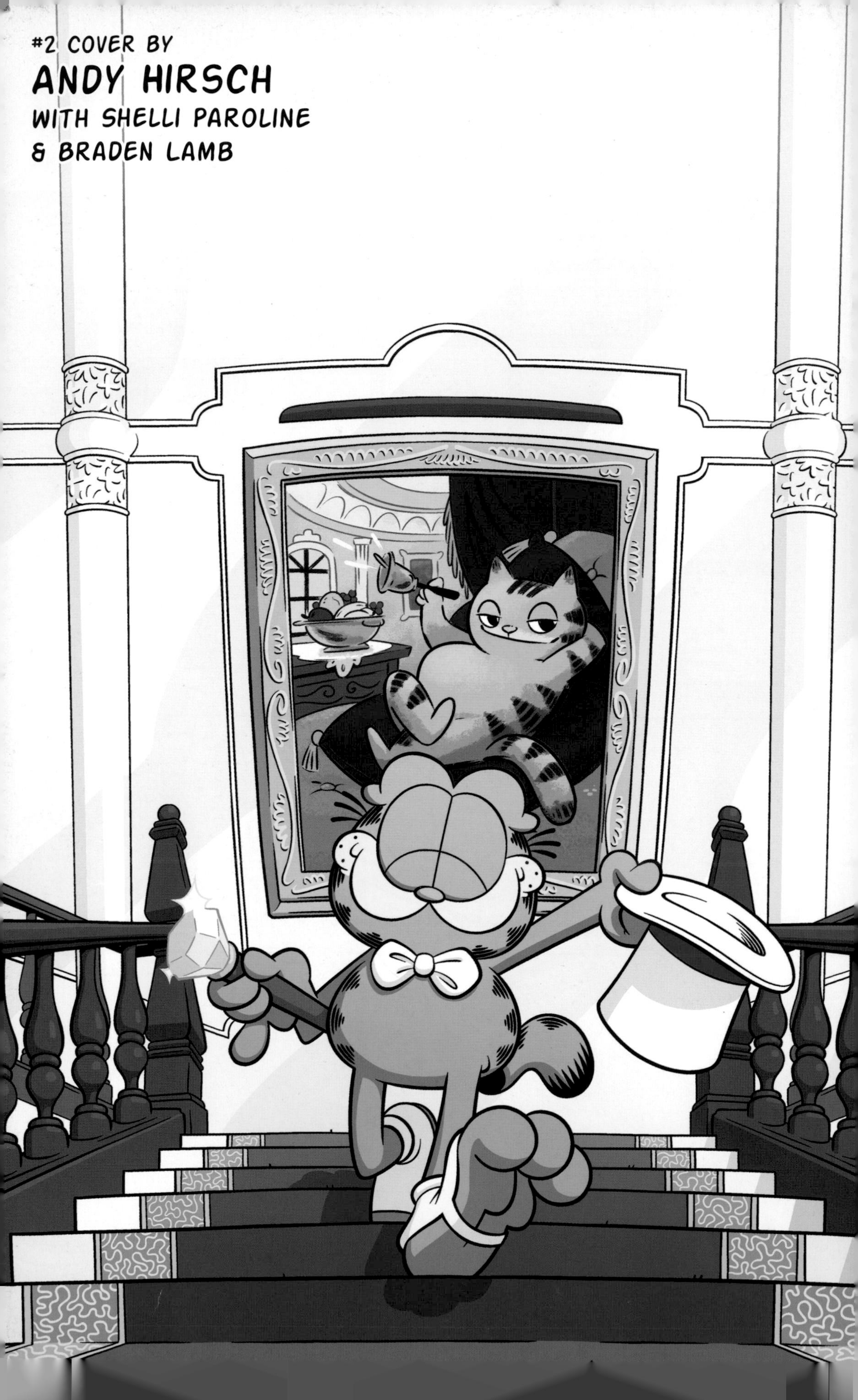

#3 COVER BY
ANDY HIRSCH
WITH BEN SEARS
SPOT ILLUSTRATION COLORS BY
LISA MOORE

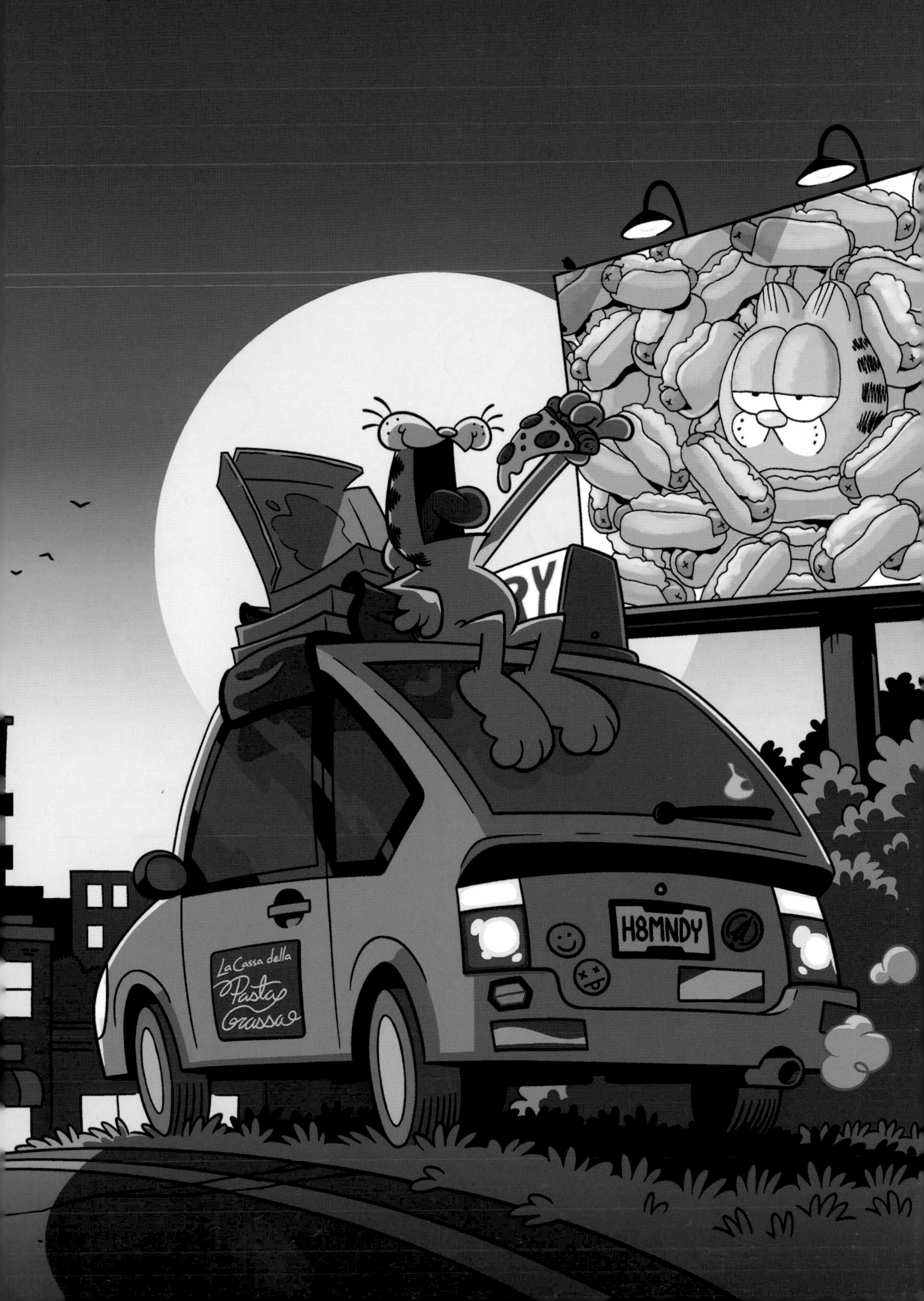

#4 COVER BY
ANDY HIRSCH
WITH GENEVIEVE FT

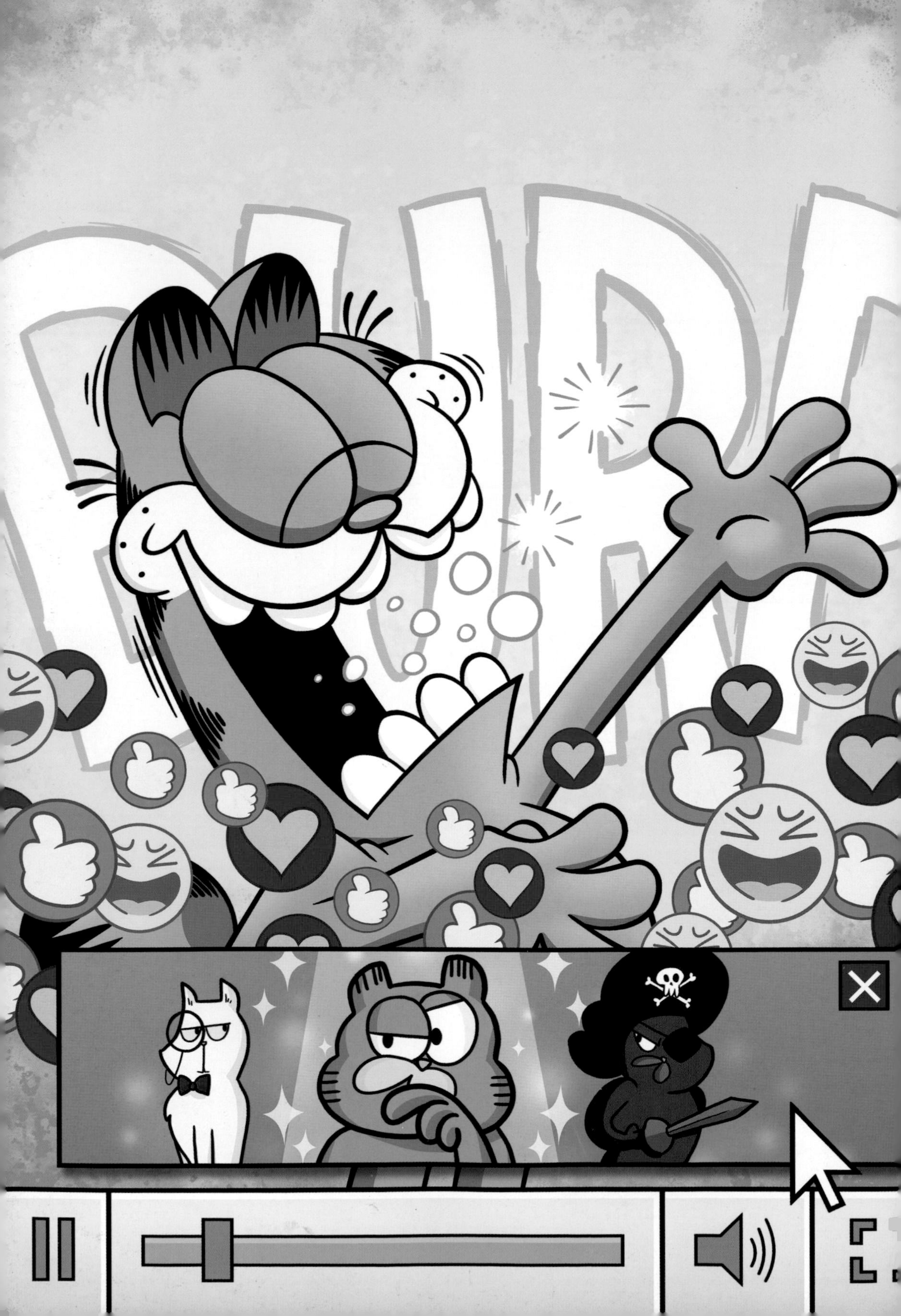

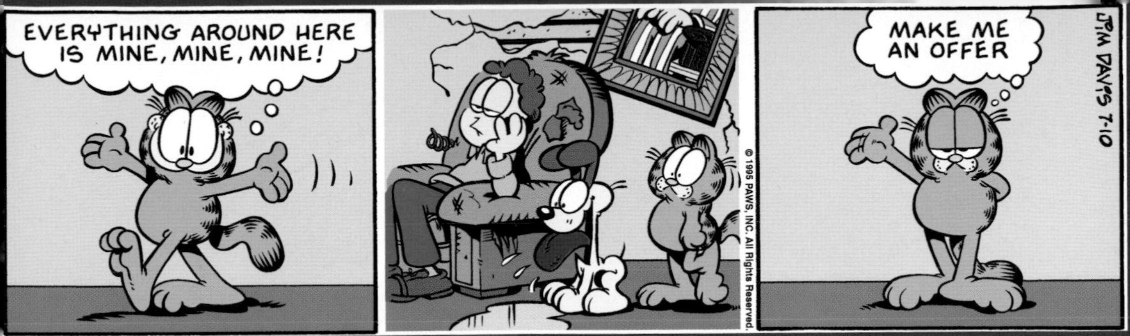
EVERYTHING AROUND HERE IS MINE, MINE, MINE!
MAKE ME AN OFFER
JIM DAVIS 7-10
© 1995 PAWS, INC. All Rights Reserved.

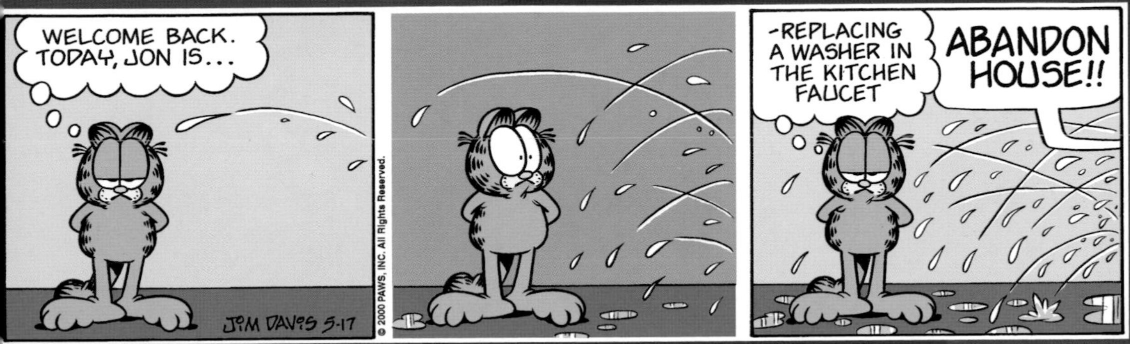
WELCOME BACK. TODAY, JON IS...
-REPLACING A WASHER IN THE KITCHEN FAUCET
ABANDON HOUSE!!
JIM DAVIS 5-17
© 2000 PAWS, INC. All Rights Reserved.

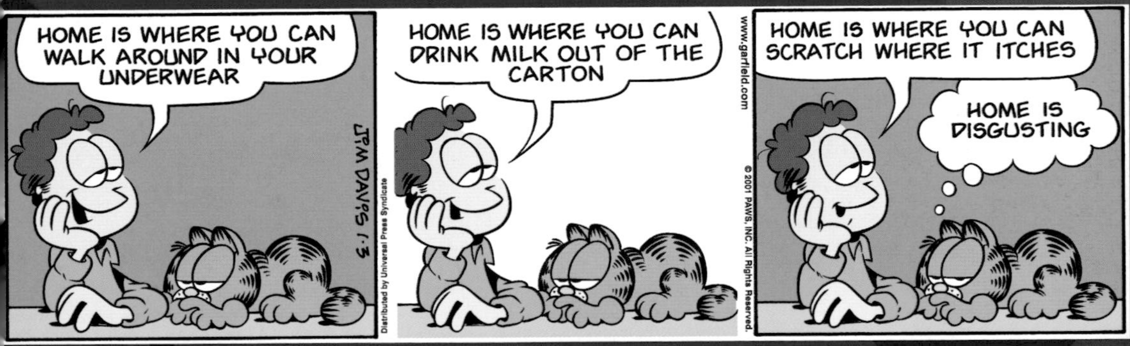
HOME IS WHERE YOU CAN WALK AROUND IN YOUR UNDERWEAR
HOME IS WHERE YOU CAN DRINK MILK OUT OF THE CARTON
HOME IS WHERE YOU CAN SCRATCH WHERE IT ITCHES
HOME IS DISGUSTING
JIM DAVIS 1-3
Distributed by Universal Press Syndicate
www.garfield.com
© 2001 PAWS, INC. All Rights Reserved.

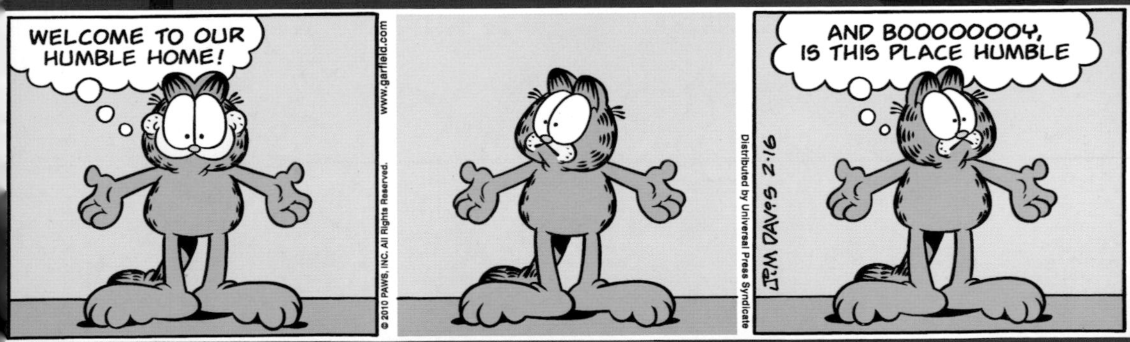
WELCOME TO OUR HUMBLE HOME!
AND BOOOOOOOY, IS THIS PLACE HUMBLE
www.garfield.com
© 2010 PAWS, INC. All Rights Reserved.
JIM DAVIS 2-16
Distributed by Universal Press Syndicate

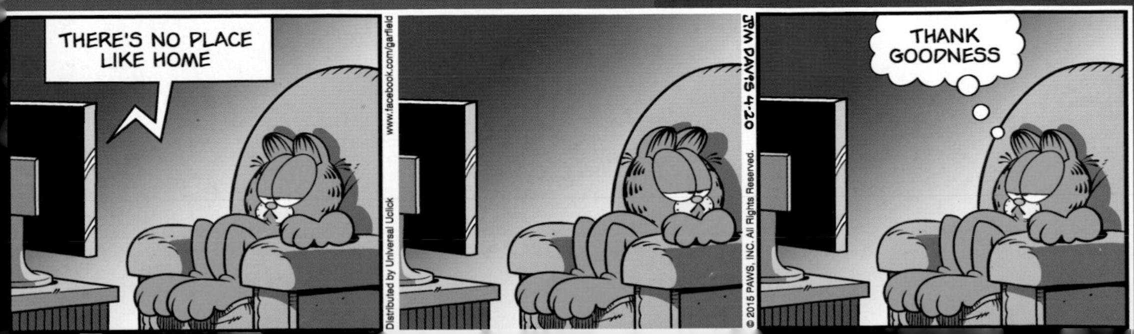
THERE'S NO PLACE LIKE HOME
THANK GOODNESS
www.facebook.com/garfield
Distributed by Universal Uclick
JIM DAVIS 4-20
© 2015 PAWS, INC. All Rights Reserved.

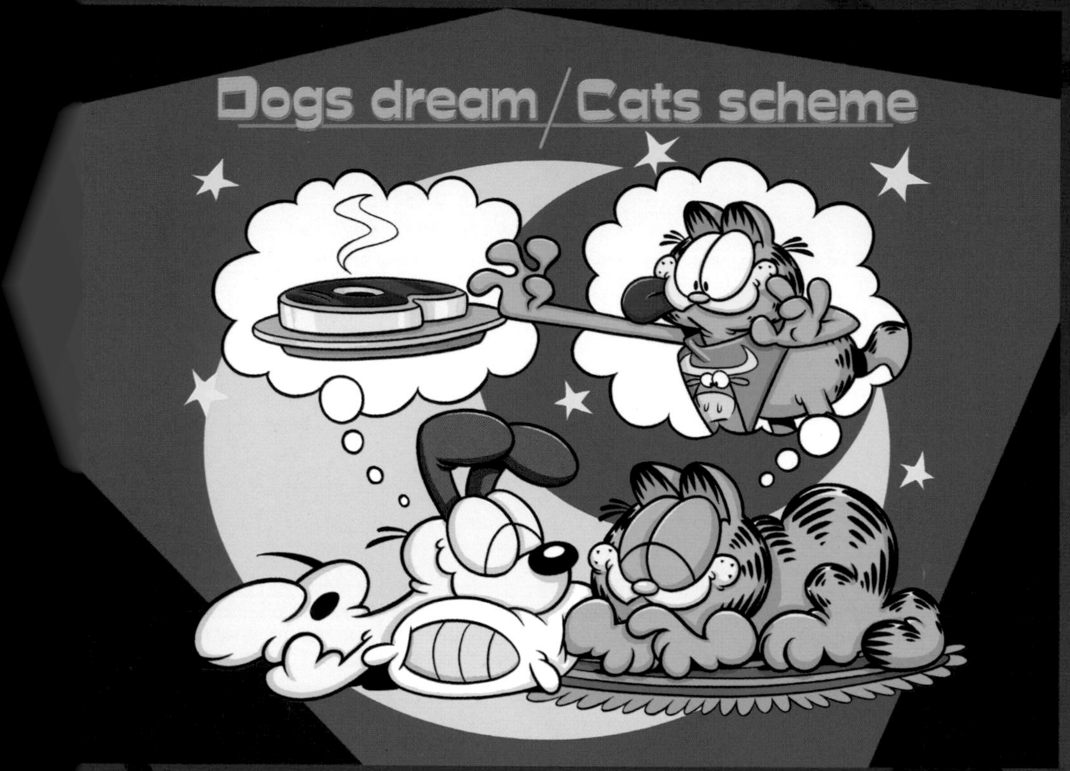
Dogs dream / Cats scheme

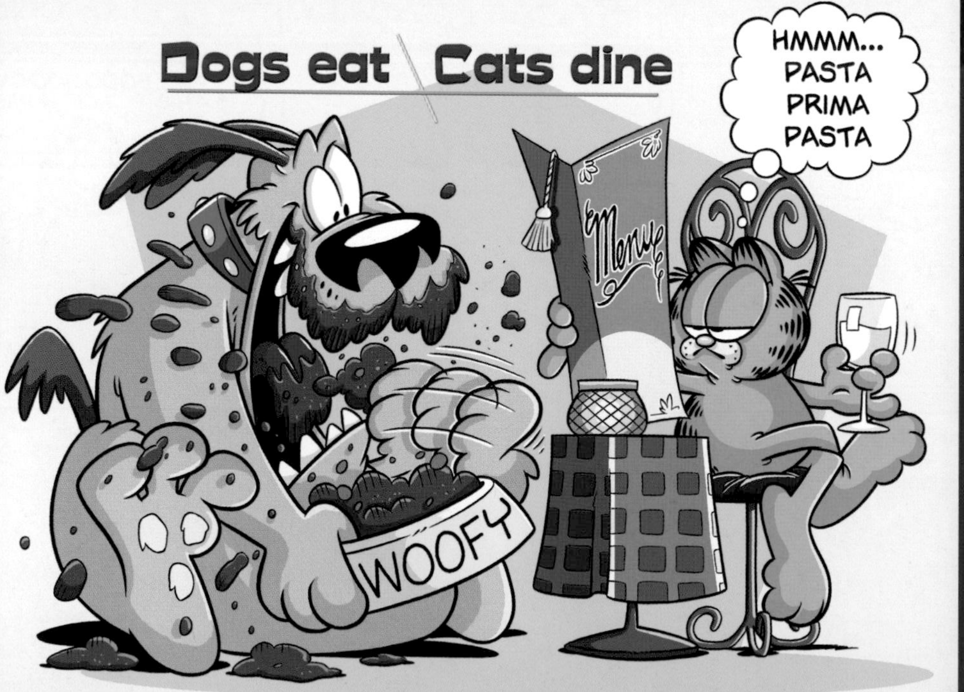
Dogs eat \ Cats dine
HMMM... PASTA PRIMA PASTA
Menu
WOOFY

Thoughts to Chew On

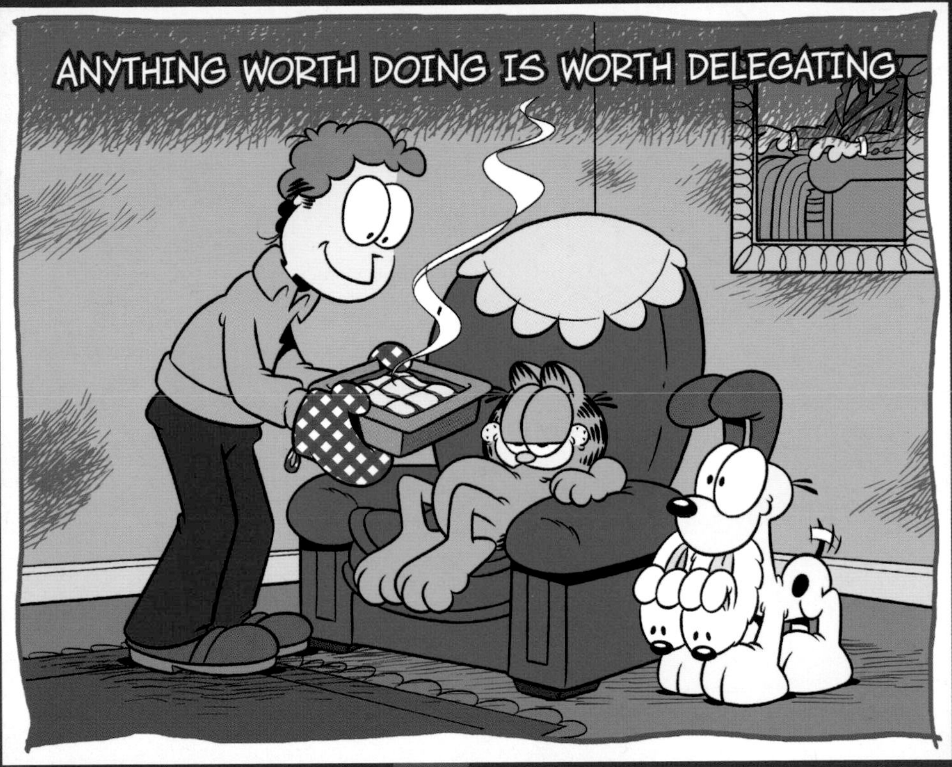
ANYTHING WORTH DOING IS WORTH DELEGATING

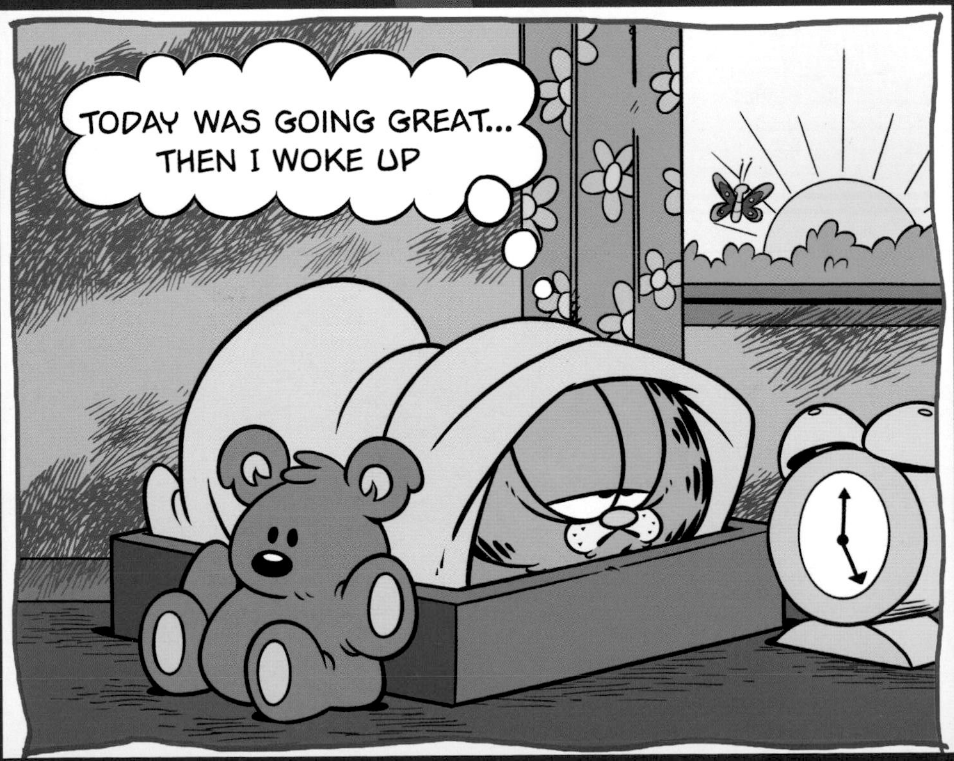
TODAY WAS GOING GREAT...
THEN I WOKE UP

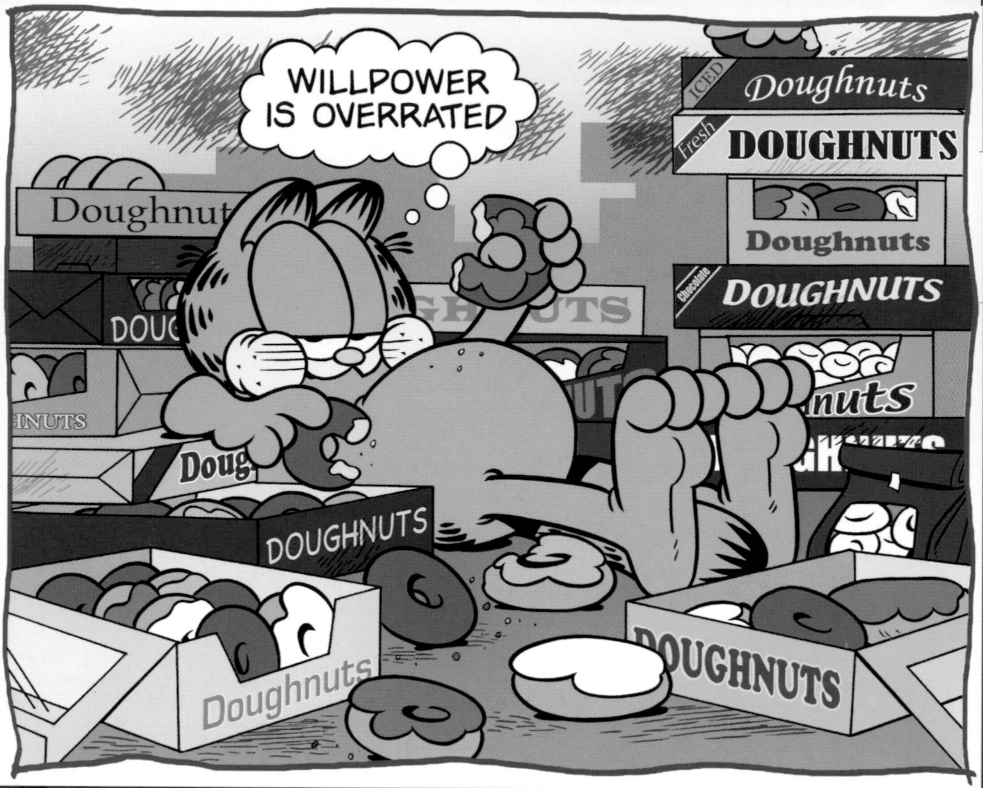
WILLPOWER IS OVERRATED
ICED Doughnuts
Fresh DOUGHNUTS
Doughnuts
Chocolate DOUGHNUTS
DOUGHNUTS
Doughnuts
DOUGHNUTS

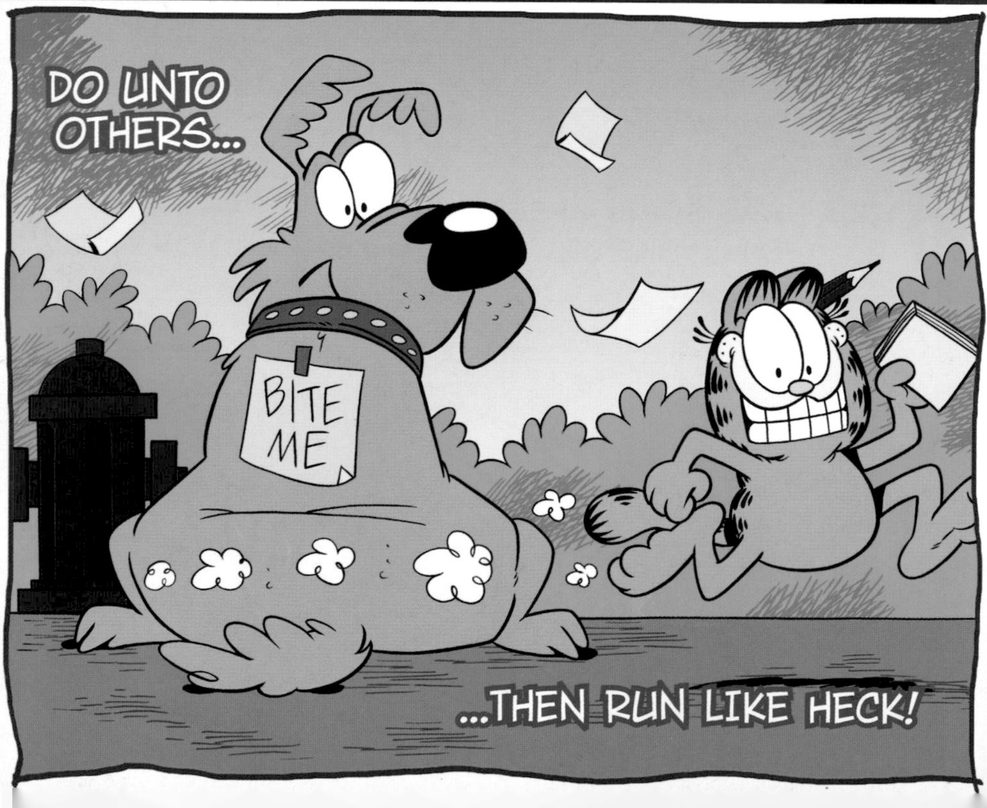
DO UNTO OTHERS...
BITE ME
...THEN RUN LIKE HECK!

Garfield Sunday Classics

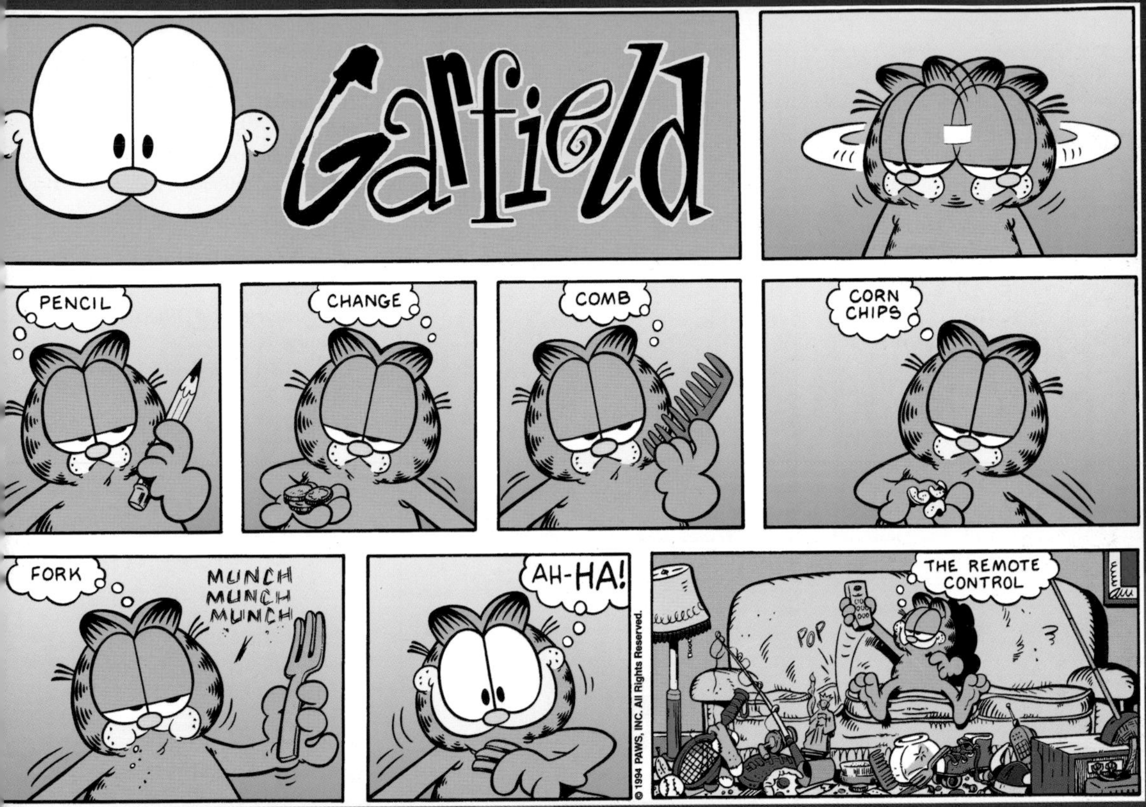
Garfield
PENCIL
CHANGE
COMB
CORN CHIPS
FORK
MUNCH MUNCH MUNCH
AH-HA!
© 1994 PAWS, INC. All Rights Reserved.
THE REMOTE CONTROL
POP

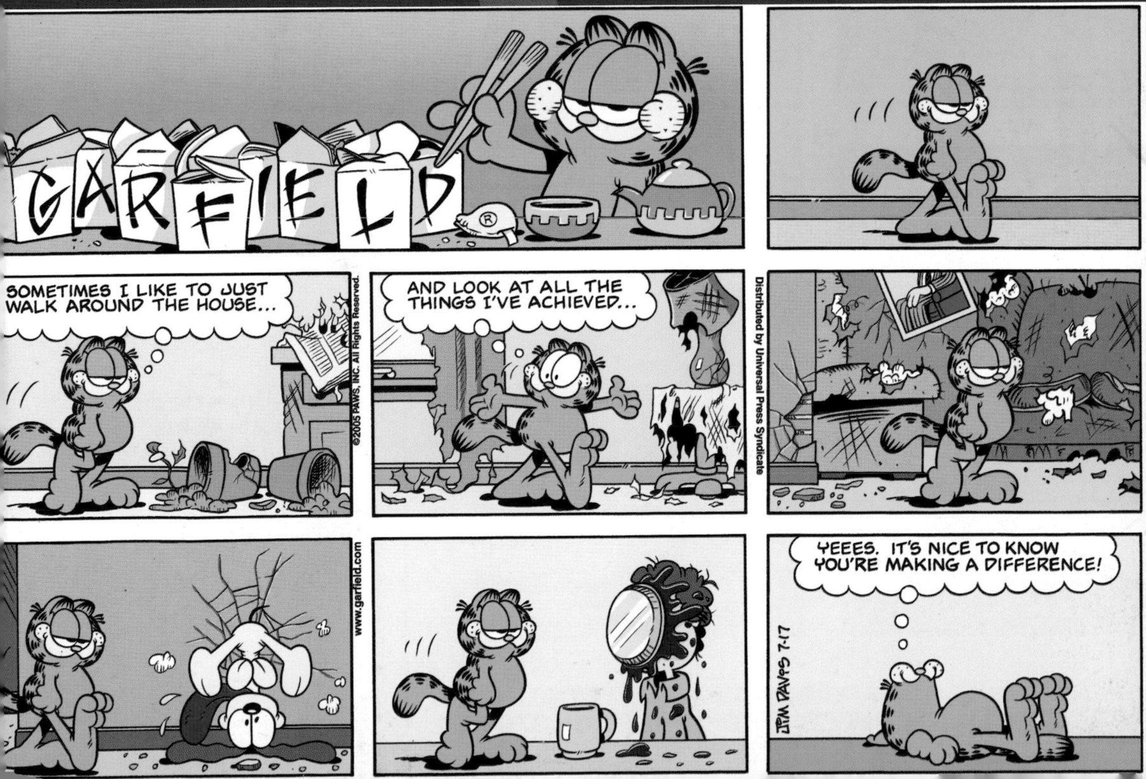
GARFIELD
SOMETIMES I LIKE TO JUST WALK AROUND THE HOUSE...
©2005 PAWS, INC. All Rights Reserved.
AND LOOK AT ALL THE THINGS I'VE ACHIEVED...
Distributed by Universal Press Syndicate
www.garfield.com
YEEES. IT'S NICE TO KNOW YOU'RE MAKING A DIFFERENCE!
JPM DAVIS 7-17